THE UNFAITHFUL

ALEX BLOODWORTH

WOLF PIRATE PUBLISHING
FORT LAUDERDALE, FL

This book is a work of fiction. Names, characters, places, and incidents are products of the author's imagination or are used fictitiously. Any resemblance to actual events or locales, or persons living or dead is entirely coincidental.

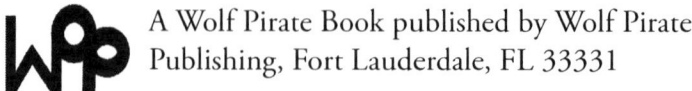 A Wolf Pirate Book published by Wolf Pirate Publishing, Fort Lauderdale, FL 33331

Copyright © 2008 by Alex Bloodworth

All rights reserved, including the right to reproduce this book or portions thereof, in any form whatsoever. For information, address Wolf Pirate Publishing, 4801 SW 164 Terrace, Fort Lauderdale, FL 33331

ISBN-13: 978-0-9798372-3-4
LCCN: 2007941747

First Wolf Pirate Publishing paperback printing June 2008

Cover design by C & S Designs

Manufactured in the United States

For information regarding special discounts for bulk purchases, please contact Wolf Pirate Publishing at 4801 SW 164 Terrace, Fort Lauderdale, FL 33331, or www.wolfpiratebooks.com.

This is to all those who have helped me along the way; the few, the deluded, and the much appreciated.

CHAPTER ONE

Late Spring

The last dream Adam Mogilvy had in his life was of bats. Whirling, spiraling, shrieking black bats circling overhead, high and dark in the sky, casting shadows on the ground that danced with eerie patches of flittering silhouettes. In the dream, Adam lifted his head and stared at them, curious and a little frightened, and a bit repulsed. The sound of their leathery wings slapping together and scrapping against one another made an ominous ruckus that created a sense of fear to grow in him. Piercing screeches of high sonar tones filled the night, growing louder as the colony spiraled down toward him.

Individual creatures darted out of the chaotic cyclone and dove at his head. Adam ducked the first one, his movements unusually quick for a dream, his head and shoulders twisting away but his legs planted firmly on the ground, his arms hanging rigidly at his sides. Despite his restricted mobility, he managed to avoid the initial attack, while another bat made a streak for his face, which he easily dodged, bobbing to the side with a quick and agile move. Springing back into position, he suddenly became concerned that these evil-seeming creatures thought he might be a threat to their colony, or that he was prey to be hunted, and were intent to do him harm first.

As the colony spiraled closer, Adam smelled the ammonia emanating from their putrescent bodies. The pungent odor made his nose crinkle and eyes water. Abruptly, another bat darted for his face, hissing and dripping saliva, wafting sour drafts ahead of it. Its convoluted face was wrinkled and insidious, and came entirely too close for comfort. Again, he ducked, narrowly avoiding the attack. Then a pair came at him from either side, a third, fourth, and then a fifth.

Adam tried to step back but found his legs were rooted too firmly in place. Running away was suddenly no longer an option, nor could he look down at his feet to see why they were planted so solidly where they were. Instead, he had to keep his eyes on the attacking creatures, lest they converge on him all at once. He sensed how dirty and diseased they were, with their nails filled with poison and their matted bodies smeared with excrement.

Two more creatures shot down like meteors falling from the sky. Adam crouched and avoided being hit, but one came in from the left and struck his arm.

Adam jolted at the touch, snapping awake. He stiffened with anxiousness, his eyes blinking until he managed to gain his bearings of where he really was. Gradually, his shoulders loosened. He wasn't on the ground being attacked by grotesque vermin, but 35,000 feet above the earth in a Boeing 747.

"Sir, you need to bring your seat forward and fasten your seat belt. We'll be landing shortly."

It was only the flight attendant who'd tapped him on the arm, not a creature of the night, and she smiled mechanically before moving on to the next passenger in violation of FAA rules.

Adam looked out the dark window and saw how brightly lit the city was beneath him. Obediently, he did as he was told and dry-washed his face with one hand, sighing with a relief he didn't quite understand. No matter how conscious he was that it had only been a dream, he couldn't quite shake the uneasy feeling its memory had left him with. Disturbing as it was, he soon discovered that he was even more anxious awake than asleep.

The plane gained clearance to land and began its gradual decent on schedule. The late night flight was hardly ever delayed, expected to arrive at 3:40 a.m. As far as Adam was concerned, the plane couldn't get on the ground fast enough. He'd taken a standby seat on the nearly empty flight immediately after the game and suffered the ride home alone. The whole trip had been a bust, what with the team's best center out with a groin injury and a slew of cracks crippling most of their spare sticks. He was just glad to be going home. Considering the pain in his body and the weariness of the exhausting night, he only wanted to slide into bed and sleep until noon the next morning.

Unfortunately, sleep wasn't what awaited him at home. Claire had called before the game to wish him luck and convey her love. It was her usual call, one that carried a lot of weight in a superstitious sport, and he relished her calls for more than the fortune they promised. In this case, though, her call had carried a grim pall of the ominous and he couldn't shake the feeling even after he'd hung up. Claire had added a little something when she'd offered her usual sentiments, something she hadn't meant to jinx the team with but nevertheless did. *By the way*, she'd added after wishing him luck, *Marie is sick. Nothing to worry about; just a little crankiness and fever.*

Three and a half hours later, with the game already recorded in the loss column, word had gotten back to him that Marie's blood sugar level had skyrocketed and Claire had given her insulin. Adam immediately called home and told Claire he was heading for the airport, to hell with the team's itinerary. Sounding relieved, she said she would wait for him before going to the hospital, if it was at all possible.

Now, with the plane having touched down, Adam stood and pulled his duffel bag from the overhead compartment. The flight attendant gave him a scornful look from the galley and made an infuriating gesture for him to sit down. Abashed, he turned aside and pretended not to notice, then slipped into his seat with his bag on his lap, ready to bolt for the door when it finally opened. Until then, he found himself growing more and more anxious as the minutes ticked by, with it being sheer torture to sit and wait for the plane to taxi up to the gate. For the life of him, he couldn't shake the uneasy feeling gripping him, tormenting him with thoughts and images of Marie being terribly sick. Such an ungodly hour as this always foretold of ill omens, and he sensed this wasn't going to be a happy homecoming at all.

Adam retrieved his car from the airport parking lot, paid the exorbitant fee for long-term parking, and left the city. Normally, the trip home would have taken him an hour to make, but in the dead of night, just before all the early day-shift laborers headed out for work, there was only a skeletal trade of traffic to contend with. He drove quickly, with one eye on the rearview mirror watching for state troopers and the other on the road ahead.

Before leaving the airport, he'd tried to reach Claire by phone, only to have the line ring incessantly in his ear, taunting him with the same funerary image he'd had after exiting the plane. He could only excuse the absence of an answer with the thought of Claire rushing Marie to the hospital, an explanation that didn't inspire relief from his worry.

Speeding down the expressway, Adam rubbed his temple in the hopes of stopping a headache from forming. His eyes were becoming painful with each pair of passing headlights facing his way. He couldn't erase the nagging feeling that he was heading in the wrong direction, and that Claire and Marie were no longer at home, but at the nearest hospital seeking medical attention.

Not long after marrying at a young age, he and Claire were unexpectedly faced with a baby in their lives. Invariably, they had known a baby would mean changes and concessions in their rather carefree lifestyle. More to concede to Claire's sudden anticipation for a child, Adam had made certain adjustments to his career, including agreeing to a contract that was less lucrative but more stable. It had been hard at first, but the rewards were worth it. Marie was more than either of them had expected, and in a short while, all the drawbacks that came with signing an incentive-laden contract were nothing he couldn't learn to deal with.

The introduction of a baby in their lives proved to be difficult but gratifying. Adam and Claire both agreed that even though they were too young to be raising a child of their own, it didn't seem so bad that they couldn't handle it. Unlike most babies, Marie proved to be an angel with the temperament of a saint, unburdened by colic or sleeplessness. For the first few months, life had been idyllic. Listening to the other players and their wives complain about their misfortune of having wailing insomniacs, Adam and Claire never regretted their luck in having Marie. What they hadn't expected—after half a year of the idyllic life—was the special attention and demands Marie would need with her sudden onset of juvenile diabetes. From then on, while most parents were able to coddle their babies and offer comfort for boo-boos, Adam and Claire were the ones who caused them, pricking Marie's tiny finger for a precious drop of blood, or injecting insulin into one of her fleshy limbs. Even after months of these ministrations, Adam still couldn't help but feel that he was an ogre for the pain he caused his daughter.

As Adam now struggled to keep the dismal thoughts from invading his mind, a siren suddenly blared beside him, sending him into an almost paralytic shock. A police car shrieked past him, startling him out of his musing. Surprised, he jerked the steering wheel to the right. The car went onto the shoulder of the road and spewed dirt and gravel from the tires until he was able to correct his course and regain the asphalt. Adam cursed and tried to soothe the nervousness growing in the pit of his stomach. Apparently, he wasn't the only one having a bad night.

He checked the rearview mirror and saw another police car approaching from behind, coming up at a rapid clip. Its red and blue lights were also rotating, its high beams flashing. Adam moved to the other lane and slowed to the legal speed limit until the car blazed past him in a flash. Its siren was only audible for a second, then distance silenced it.

As he took his exit off the expressway, the faint smell of smoke through the car's vents reached his nose. Evidently, it must be a fire that had the police in such a hurry.

Just as quickly as connecting a fire with the presence of racing police cars, Adam put them out of his mind and thought only of his own problems. If Claire had taken Marie to the hospital, she would have left a note on the refrigerator. If that was the case, he'd have to turn the car around and head back into the city, making this leg of the journey a complete waste of time.

Adam slowed at an intersection controlled by a flashing red light. A fire engine, tricked out in full emergency regalia, turned onto the street and went ahead of him. As it did, its air horn blared, insisting that he remain right where he was until the coast was clear. When it was, Adam went through the intersection and followed the truck, since it was headed in the same direction. He wasn't in the least bit curious about the tragedy it was headed to when his own might await him at home. He only wished he could pass the truck so he might get there sooner.

The smell of smoke was growing thicker and a grayish haze seemed to fill the sky, proof that a fire was raging somewhere. Probably one of the crack houses on the outskirts of the city, gone up in a blaze when someone knocked a candle onto a bed sheet. Not so unusual for this part of town; just an untimely distraction tonight.

A police car suddenly shot into the intersection Adam was going through and nearly collided with him. The errant officer quickly reacted to avoid the crash and whipped around him, then headed off in the same direction as the fire engine had. Adam fishtailed off the road and slammed on the brakes, his car coming to an abrupt halt, rocking him forward. With a release of all the tension gripping him at the moment, he fell back against the seat and sat in a state of stunned paralysis, unable to find the energy to even curse the officer for the close call he'd caused.

After forcing his nerves to settle, Adam threw the gear shift into drive and started home again. He drove toward the west end of town, where a patchwork of low-income projects comprised the area. Normally, even at this hour, the streets were rife with foot traffic and bicyclists—the drug dealers and prostitutes—and a constant flow of motorists who purchased their wares at all hours of the night. Tonight, however, there was no one roving the streets. The roads were empty and quiet, except for the emergency vehicles that had passed him already and a couple more he noticed coming up on him even then.

The fire, most likely. Crime scenes and tragedies gave people amusement for the night. Residents would gather around them for the excitement, delighting in the event, offering words of critical analysis, drinking beer or cheap wine out of a bag, some heckling and others just bitter. None would offer any help to save their fellow man and neighbor; rather, they would leave that to the civil servants paid to do just that.

Adam allowed two more police cars to pass him, then watched them turn left a few blocks ahead. He could smell the fire stronger then, with the smoke thick and choking.

In a short while, he passed an intersection glowing with the lights of police cars and fire trucks. Natural curiosity caused him to glance in their direction. The orange glow of a fire licked over the trees in the front yard of a house he couldn't see. Great plumes of smoke rose like a sacrifice to the gods. Adam forced himself to face forward and step on the accelerator, encouraging his car to pick up speed.

The area finally turned rural. Low-income housing gave way to cheap single-family residences, which gave way to small acreage homes, which finally gave way to farms and ranches. The smoke was still thick and acrid out here. Curiously, Adam noticed pockets of red and blue lights, and passed several police cars that had sped by him earlier. Other than those, he saw no other traffic. Grimly, he slowed his speed, his curiosity turning to fear, and he abruptly pulled over to the shoulder to stop the car. Tentatively, he got out and listened. Normally, sound traveled easily with the dew drop and the openness of the area in the early morning hours. Cows could be heard lowing in the barns, while roosters crowed long before the sun's first appearance. Now, instead, he heard shouts and screams from his fellow human beings.

And sirens.

As the smell of smoke caused his throat to swell closed until he began to cough.

"What the hell?"

He slowly turned and tried to decipher what he was hearing. Different sirens in varying levels of volume, approaching and retreating, all desperate to get where they were going. Shouted orders being given, cries for help, exclamations of disbelief. Cries of agony, pleas for relief, wails of what sounded to be the dying.

"Jesus . . ."

Adam slipped behind the wheel and pulled onto the road again. He sped home with a mounting concern for his own family, a different concern now. He passed several individual rescue efforts, pulled aside as paramedics raced by, and stared in disbelief when he saw how many fires raged in the area where he called home. Most went unchecked, buildings engulfed, yellow ash flying with gusts of wind shaking flames loose from raging conflagrations. He was barely aware that his hands were gripping the steering wheel in a death grip, his knuckles as white as bones bleached by a desert sun, his elbows shaking.

He passed an intersection that had been roped off with yellow crime scene tape. Police cars circled whatever lay within its perimeter. A fire was burning itself out in a house beyond the police line.

Adam shot his eyes toward his own home, suddenly realizing that a swath of destruction was heading westward, where his house lay.

"Shit."

He pressed his foot on the gas and sped forward, no longer yielding to the emergency vehicles. In his own mind, he had his own crisis to deal with. He now hoped Claire and Marie *were* actually at the hospital, away from this mess, whatever it was.

The closer he got to home the thicker the smoke grew. Houses and barns of distant neighbors burned out of control. No rescue attempts were being made to deal with the destruction. The first fully engulfed house caused him agony in passing it, seeing how the wooden clapboard Colonial collapsed under the weight of the blaze. The neighborly thing to do was to stop, call the fire department, and see if the residents were safe. But he couldn't even do that; not now, not when his own home lay ahead, his own family at risk, where stopping to help his neighbors might lead to his own wife and child dying.

CHAPTER TWO

Adam pulled into the driveway as the sun was only thinking of verging over the horizon. His muscles were tense and twitching, his body no longer hurting from the game. At first glance, the two-story house appeared unmolested in the predawn dark. He thanked God the fires hadn't reached his home yet, but the thick haze made his eyes sting and water, and he fell into a fit of coughing when he opened the car door.

Claire's car might or might not be in the garage, so he couldn't tell if she was home or not. He grabbed his duffel bag and hurried up the porch steps, his heart pounding from the anxiety of the night.

A loud explosion sounded a quarter of a mile up the street and a fireball lifted into the sky. Adam stepped off the porch and watched as the fireball rolled, expanded, and curled, burning black as it consumed itself.

"My God . . ."

Odam McArthur's silo, he thought. The old man kept tons of grain in there this time of year and the gases were highly volatile. Something must have set if off.

Adam mounted the steps to the porch and approached the door. It moved inward when his fingers touched the knob. Inside, there was only an eerie silence except for the ticking of an anniversary clock on the mantle. No sound came from Gabriel on his bed by the cold hearth, which was disturbing in itself. The black Labrador was ever vigilant over his territory and would never let anyone sneak up on him, not even the master of the house returning at such an ungodly hour. Now the dog's bed was empty and there was no sign of him.

"Claire?"

No one answered. Adam took a tentative step into the house, feeling an unruly sense of evil lurking in what had otherwise always been a haven to him.

A high-pitched screech startled him all of a sudden and a black shape flew from an overhead wagon-wheel chandelier. Adam ducked as the shape flew out the open door, leaving behind a whiff of sour ammonia as it passed. His head whipped around to follow its flight, a memory plucking at his subconsciousness.

A kick in his gut urged him forward.

"Claire!"

He ran for the stairs, grabbed the banister, and swung himself up the first few steps. Halfway up, his foot slipped in something wet. He looked down but couldn't make out anything in the dark. At first, he didn't think it was that important to waste time to investigate and hurried up the rest of the stairs, his knees pumping as he bounded up them two at a time. At the top, he stepped again in wetness, but this time he slid in it. With growing apprehension, his chest tightened and his stomach convulsed.

The acrid smell of smoke was in the house, despite how tightly shut the windows were. As Adam passed the window in the upstairs hall, he could see the fire from Odam's place over the tree line. Not only had the silo gone up, but the house and barn as well.

"Claire!"

Tears blinded his eyes and soot covered his cheeks and forehead. He tasted the grit and ash that filled the air and still smelled the sour odor of ammonia lingering in his nose. He rushed into the master bedroom at the end of the hall and saw it was empty, eerily deserted, the bed sheets tousled.

He paused a moment to breathe more easily, although the smoke kept him from breathing normally. He leaned against the door frame and clutched the wall for support, his mind racing with thoughts that might explain what was happening and where his family might be. In the best case scenario, Claire would be with Marie at the hospital.

He pushed away from the door jamb and hurried down the hall, went down the stairs and into the kitchen, where he planned to look for a note to see which hospital Claire had gone to. At the entrance to the kitchen, he suddenly froze, his eyes locked in horror on the shape slumped by the back door. By now, his eyes had adjusted to the dark and he could just make out silhouettes in the house.

"Claire . . . ?"

He was surprised to hear his voice cracking. He willed his legs forward but they felt numb and rubbery. The first step he took was a baby one, barely a step at all, but one that took him forward nonetheless. His knee buckled when he set his foot down, but he caught himself before he stumbled. All at once, he staggered to the shape on the floor and dropped to his knees, cracking them hard on the tile. He felt no pain as he reached for his wife lying face down on the floor, curled into a fetal position. He laid a hand on her shoulder and felt her warm, still alive.

"Claire, baby?"

He shook her lightly, afraid to move her in case she was terribly and irreparably hurt. When there was no response, he slid his hand down her back, hoping to inspire a reaction. Her shirt was wet and warm, and he jerked his hand back in horror of what that sticky wetness meant.

Adam felt as if a knife had been plunged into his chest, causing his limbs to tremble spastically. His head felt as if it had been removed from his body, plucked off his shoulders and set aside. He knew he had a soul then, because he felt the missing space in his heart where it must have been before it fled in anguish. Tears appeared in his eyes as he lurched forward and grabbed his dying wife, no longer gentle and cautious. He pulled her onto his lap and flung his head back so he faced heaven, where God was presumed to be. The Almighty God who had dominion over life and death. The guarantor of fate and fortune. The only force at this point that might be able to alter the tides on which Claire's life drifted.

Clutching her more tightly, more possessively, Adam felt her blood soak into his pants. The wetness impressed on him the futility of his prayers. "No. No. Aw, sweetheart, baby, no."

He hugged her tightly and felt the coldness enter her limbs, from the tips of her fingers, up to her shoulders, and into her body. So quickly it was amazing, as if the spirit that was the embodiment of his beloved wife slipped from his grasp and departed for good. The chill shivered up his arms and iced his heart, and he adjusted his embrace more tightly around her, tighter still, so he could keep her with him forever. Outside, another explosion rocked the coming dawn, this one closer, more powerful, shaking the foundation the house was built on.

When Adam finally pried his eyes open, he was surprised to see his daughter lying on the floor where his wife's body had covered her. A squeak escaped him as he lurched over Claire's body for the limp bundle of his baby girl. He lifted her into his arms and fell back on his heels, clutching her to his chest. Sobs wracked his shoulders as he squeezed his eyes shut and cuddled her.

Marie was burning hot in his arms, the temperature of her skin nearly scalding his icy flesh, which was strange, since Claire had been so cold. Adam suddenly recovered some of his composure and laid a hand over Marie's tiny chest, covering it completely. He barely felt the rapid, thready pulse beating within her breast, and a pathetic croak of excitement escaped him.

His daughter was still alive; burning up with fever, but still alive. Claire had said her blood sugar was irregular and she'd been trying to stabilize it. Maybe she'd been successful, maybe she hadn't, but Adam's first worry was what Marie's sugar level really was. Whatever it was, sugar would be a temporary reprieve, just until he could get her to a hospital.

He eased his legs out from under his wife's body and struggled to stand, shifting Marie in his arms. He staggered to the cabinet that held the Accu-Chek kit, only to come up short as he passed the window, his attention drawn to the flickering firelight outside. He walked closer to the window and drew the sheer curtain aside.

Adam gasped when he saw the barn was on fire. Flames shot from the hayloft as fire lapped under the eaves. The roof smoldered as the blaze burned beneath the ceiling, curling under the rafters and beams. Scorches of black charred the walls from the inside, bubbling the red paint into blister patches that crackled and popped, while the sound of timbers snapping and collapsing pervaded the rural silence that should have been predominantly peaceful otherwise.

"Oh God..."

Whatever was burning his neighbors' homes had finally reached his property. There was no doubt in his mind that the house and stables would be next, just as Odam McArthur's buildings had succumbed after his silo had ignited. He and Marie couldn't stay in the house; it simply wasn't safe anymore.

Adam remained where he was while he struggled with his conscience over what to do. He had to get Marie to a hospital, but he hated to leave his wife's body behind. The livestock in the barn would be trapped. Claire's beloved Jerseys and nanny goat, the Rhode Island reds and her pair of Hampshire sheep would all be trapped. If the stables went next, the horses would perish as well.

Resolutely, he pulled himself out of his uncertainty by focusing on his daughter in his arms. He retrieved the Accu-Chek kit, jammed it into his pants pocket, and slipped a sterile syringe into his back one. He hurried to the refrigerator and took out a vial of insulin and a bottle of sugared milk to be prepared for whatever her body might demand.

Again, he glanced out the window. He thought he saw a figure move within the large doorway of the burning barn, but he wasn't sure. Then a shadow moved again and he was sure. Someone was standing in the doorway of the barn. The light of the fire behind the figure framed it in a ghostly nimbus of yellow and ochre.

Adam raced from the kitchen without delay, into the foyer and to the hall closet, where he kept the shotgun his father had given him after moving his family to the outskirts of the city. Shaking with panic, Adam laid his daughter on the runner carpet and fumbled on the shelf for a box of shotgun shells he knew would be there. His hands were trembling to the point where they were almost useless. He moaned with misery until his fingers hit the box, knocking it a little farther out of reach. Desperately, he groped and drew it down.

His heart hammered in his chest. He knew how to handle the old Remington—had learned to skeet shoot with his father when he was just a boy—but his hands didn't want to work properly; they felt as if anything heavier than a feather would snap his wrists. His panic brought on a weakness he had never felt before and resented now.

"Damn it!" he cursed and tore apart the box of shells. He dropped four and caught one as it popped into the air.

Whimpering, he felt a gush of tears pushing to come out of his smoke-blighted eyes. Sucking it back, he jammed the one shell into the breech and racked the slide, then bent to gather the other shells rolling at his feet. One by one, he slid them into the feeder tube and prepared himself for whatever obstacle might try to stop him from leaving with his daughter.

He picked up Marie and juggled her in the crook of his elbow, carrying the shotgun in his other hand. He kicked open the front door and stepped onto the porch, wary of who might be coming from the barn to set the house ablaze. Deftly raising the shotgun to pan around the front yard, he waited for whoever had been in the barn to make an appearance.

No one appeared. To the east, a grayish horizon announced the coming of dawn. A glimmer of hope came with that view. Adam thought if he could only make it to sunrise, this whole nightmare might be over. With that in mind, he ran down the porch steps and toward the car in the driveway. At the passenger door, he laid the shotgun against the quarter panel and hefted Marie into his other arm so he could open the car. With practiced dexterity, he strapped her into the baby seat and shut the door, all in record time.

As he reached for the shotgun, a black shape hurtled from the sky and was reflected in the car's window. Adam spun around, fearful of what might have been thrown his way, thinking it might be a Molotov cocktail. However, what lay at his feet was something larger than any incendiary device he could imagine. Instead, it was an unidentifiable lump curled into a fetal shape, looking more hulking than mechanical. Adam stepped back, but his body met the car and he was suddenly trapped by the very route meant to be his means of escape. He fumbled in his pocket for the keys so he would have them in his hand when he slid into the driver's seat.

A sudden burst of movement brought the thing on the ground to its full height, exposing a humanoid figure that towered over Adam by a whole head, making the figure gigantic. Its exact features were lost in the smoky haze of the dark morning, but Adam sensed something was hideously wrong with the person.

A claw-like hand shot out and grabbed his shoulder, pinning him in a pincher grip and trapping him against the car with a sudden and unexpected violence. The thing's rigid fingers clamped down on the nerves in the pocket of his shoulder and sent a shocking pain down his arm, making his limb go numb. As he winced in pain, the keys slid from his slack fingers and fell to the dirt.

A growl issued from the figure's throat just before it lunged toward Adam's face, its mouth gaping wide. Adam wasn't sure what his eyes registered from the brief glimpse of the thing's face, but it was enough to make him react instinctively. He brought the shotgun up between their bodies and pulled the trigger. Suddenly, the figure stood headless before him, with only a bloody stalk of a neck at eye level pumping black ichor into the air, spattering him with the foul stuff. Whatever hideous features the thing once had were no longer in evidence to support the image still etched in Adam's mind.

Repulsed by his actions and the consequence they caused, Adam screamed. He jerked away as the body toppled to the ground before him, crumpling in a gory heap of flailing limbs. The black fluid now flowed from the ravaged stalk of the thing's neck. Adam's stomach convulsed at the sight and a bout of vomit nearly came up against his control. Grossly sickened, he kicked away from the body and ran around the car to get to the driver's side.

The police were swarming down the street; he knew that much from passing them on his way home. When he reached them, he'd let them know that he'd killed one of the crackheads who were burning the farms, may have even killed his wife. They could take him into custody for questioning if only they would end this madness and help him get his daughter to a hospital.

Another black object swooped down from the sky and landed behind him, while yet another crossed over his left shoulder. Adam spun back and forth to see what they were, only to stagger back when he saw two heaps on the ground like the one that had unfolded into the figure he'd just killed. They both sprouted into pillars of humanoid shapes, shrieking at him as they lunged with claw-like limbs and hideously contorted faces.

"No!"

The attacking creatures froze at once, and Adam spun around to face the voice that commanded them. He watched in mesmerized fascination as a man strode confidently from the area near the burning barn, the structure now fully engulfed in flames, its once rich timbers crumbling like dry kindling. The man was tall and dark, with the hem of a coat unfurling gloriously behind him. He walked out of the smoky haze like a phoenix rising, his stride the gait of a warrior. In his hand, he held what appeared to be a sword, its blade curved and glinting in the orange fire framing his body like an aurora.

"Don't touch him!"

The grotesque figures took an obedient step back. Adam quickly took one of his own away from them. As much as he wanted to scramble even farther from the things, he kept near the car, protecting his daughter with his body and the shotgun still in his possession.

"*You*," the approaching stranger said, his voice deep and commanding, "are not supposed to be here."

Adam opened his mouth to speak but found that only his jaw worked; his vocal chords seemed frozen and useless and issued no sound at first. When he tried a second time, he sputtered, "Did . . . did you do this?"

The stranger approached no farther. He cocked his head as if to question what Adam meant, then looked over his shoulder to survey his handiwork. When he turned back, he was smirking. "It's almost daylight." He tilted his head provocatively, luxuriating in a breeze that blew a swirl of smoke across his face. "It's been a good night, I'd say."

"Did you do this?" Adam bellowed, taking another step forward. His grip on the shotgun was tight and deliberate.

The stranger lifted his head high, sniffing down his nose. "They call you Slash, don't they? In the game you play. A rather inglorious title for a man of your stature, but one you've earned, eh, Adam? You're a sportsman, and I'll wager a deal with you. If you can kill me, I'll let you live."

Adam froze, refraining from taking any additional steps toward the man. "How do you know my name?"

"A trifle bit of information," the man replied matter-of-factly. Then, with some enthusiasm, he said, "Will you accept my terms? Answer me now; time's running out."

Adam's mouth worked soundlessly around his tongue. He glanced over his shoulder and noticed the man's henchmen were watching him from a few paces away, motionless. Adam whipped his head back to the stranger. "Did you kill my wife?"

The man brought his sword up to rest the blade on the palm of his hand. He stroked its length as he admired its craftsmanship. "Claire? I severed her spine in the same way I'll cleave that head of yours from your body." He returned his attention to Adam, his feral eyes hooded under the ledge of a deep brow. "Would you kill me to save your life? If you're not man enough to avenge your wife, that is."

Adam felt the sweat drench his back and forehead. His headache had reached a level equal to that of a spike being driven into his temple. He begged for this to only be a nightmare, an extension of the dream he'd been jarred from on the plane. But he felt the bruises that had surfaced on his ribs during the game and the headache that persisted, and knew it was no dream.

"Would you kill me to save the life of your only child?"

Adam's back suddenly stiffened as he watched the figure take a menacing step toward him. He drew the shotgun up and wedged the stock into the pocket of his shoulder, pointing the barrel against the stranger's approach. The stranger stopped and spread his arms, his sword held aloft, his gesture one of acceptance.

Adam hesitated. He tasted bile as it rose into his throat and lay bitterly on his tongue. His vision blurred around the edges so he was focusing only on the threat before him.

"Are you a coward outside the arena?"

Adam's finger lay tensely against the trigger, ready for the weight of his decision. He found it beyond his ability to fire the weapon—to commit murder—even when the victim was a murderer himself. He felt tears slip through his betraying eyes when he realized he might not be able to protect himself or his daughter.

"You'd rather see your child sliced in half?" the stranger asked, his eyes narrow and shadowy, his voice sultry and dangerous. Very slowly, he raised a foot to take another step.

Adam squeezed the trigger as easily as that, firing off a round of buckshot. The wad struck the stranger at center mass, the spray of pellets tight across his torso. He staggered backward with the force of the impact and nearly lost his balance, but as Adam recovered from the recoil, he watched in dismay as the man simply laughed.

CHAPTER THREE

Adam racked another shell into the chamber and prepared himself for a second shot at the stranger, who still stood despite the first slug striking him dead center in the chest. *A bulletproof vest*, Adam thought. The next shot he took would be to the man's head.

"Stay where you are," Adam ordered, gaining mettle from taking the first shot. If the stranger wanted to force him into deals slighted in his favor by wearing body armor, then Adam was going to make his own rules as well. "I don't want to hurt you."

"Ah, but you didn't," the stranger stated, taking a step forward as he spread his arms, displaying his formidableness. "And now, Adam, it's my turn."

The stranger approached with long quick strides, his weapon held aloft over his shoulder. Adam stumbled backward and was about to fire the shotgun when he was hit from behind by one of the man's henchmen. The sharp blow to his lower back numbed his legs and buckled him to his knees. The shotgun was wrenched from his possession with a vicious twist that nearly disjointed his fingers, while a claw-like grip clamped his shoulder and held him down, forcing him to kneel before his approaching executioner.

Before he knew it, the stranger towered over him, his sword about to swing in an arc to lop off his head. With a second thought, the man hesitated. His black eyes locked with Adam's, who icy blue ones glared balefully back at him, petrified. The stranger's eyes narrowed and became slits of which only a black slice of a pupil remained, goatish and wicked.

Adam winced when the stranger snickered.

Abruptly, one of the henchmen snaked an arm around his neck and pulled him off balance. Unwittingly, Adam fell backward. His right arm was stretched out to full length and laid flat on the ground, palm splayed upward. The stranger came forward and stomped on his wrist, while one of the creatures behind him uncurled his fingers. Adam desperately clawed at the choking hold around his throat but he could gain no release. He was only vaguely aware of the pain emanating from his crushed wrist as he struggled with the vice around his neck.

"We'll meet again, my friend," the stranger said, somehow sounding congenial and ominous at the same time. Then, with unmistakable malice, he added, "Once you get to the other side, that is." He knelt down and took a wickedly ornate dagger from his belt. With it, he made five practiced slashes on Adam's outstretched palm, delivering them with a rapidness that defied imagination.

Adam screamed with the searing stroke of the first and subsequent slices, jerking in pain, bucking to dislodge his captors. Despite how strong and desperate he was, he was unable to free himself. He thrashed in an effort to heave them off but he was held by too many arms that seemed to be corded with steel. His other hand was suddenly caught and laid flat on the ground, under the same boot that had stomped on his first one. Again, the stranger made five skillful cuts in the same order and configuration as the marks he'd made on Adam's other palm. Again, Adam screamed. He kicked with his legs and twisted his whole body, but he couldn't defend himself with his hands flayed and burning, and one still pinned by the stranger's boot.

Then the man straightened and moved away, disregarding any further torment on his hapless victim. He casually wiped the blade on his thigh. "You belong to me now, Adam; now that you bear my mark."

"Fuck you!" Adam cursed hoarsely. Tears brimmed in his eyes as he cradled his hands against his chest.

The arm around his neck mercifully slid away. Adam bounded over and tried to push himself to his feet. He cried out when his shredded palms pressed into the dirt and gravel, proving just how useless they were in their current state. Instead, he tried to pull his feet up under him, using only his balance to stagger upright. From years of perfecting skills on the ice, he had excellent equilibrium to do it.

He was just about to stand when a thick rope suddenly looped around his neck and jerked him off his feet, dropping him onto his backside again. He gurgled against the choking hold and tried to grab it. His fingers just managed to slip under the noose to provide some relief before it became too tight around his windpipe. At the same time, he found himself being hauled backward, through the dirt, his legs kicking wildly.

They pulled him relentlessly through the front yard, around the house, and into the back yard. From there, he was dragged through the dewy grass, toward the stables, over gravel and hard-packed earth. The pungent odor of fire made breathing difficult, yet the rope around his neck made that problem almost moot. His body twisted along the way as he tried to slip free of the noose.

He was dragged into the stables, which had yet to be set ablaze. The horses in their stalls were already panicked by the acrid smell coming from the burning barn. They stomped and kicked the walls, tossed their heads and snorted. Their eyes flashed wild and terrified, matching Adam's own. They snorted when the three strangers hauled Adam inside. One stallion reared and came down hard, its backside colliding with the wall and cracking a wooden plank. A gelding in the next stall whinnied and pranced unsurely.

Adam's backward movement finally came to a stop. He quickly tried to stand on his own, but as soon as he regained his feet, his legs were yanked out from under him. Yet not exactly, because he felt no ground under them as he was hoisted into the air by the rope around his neck. His legs kicked uselessly, scissoring back and forth, his body twisting as the rope adjusted to the rafter it was hoisted over. He watched the ground recede as his body rose, until he was just out of arm's reach of the wooden beam he hung from. The stalls spun beneath him as he rotated on the rope, his legs still trying to gain a purchase they would never get.

A distant tap on his foot stopped him from spinning. Adam's eyes strained hard to see what stood before him. The stranger used his sword to stabilize him, and he stepped back for Adam to get a better view of him.

Adam jerked when he saw what the man held. He would have cried out if he had the breath to make the effort, but he didn't. Marie lay limp in the crook of one of the stranger's arms, passive and unresponsive.

"I won't kill her," the stranger promised, cuddling the child as if she were his own. He cooed to her for a moment, moving a curl of hair from her forehead and stroking her cheek with a thumb. Afterward, he stepped back in order to lay her on the ground, so Adam could see her, then moved away to show that he wouldn't harm her.

Adam tried to tell the man that his daughter needed medical attention but only unintelligible guttural croaks came out. He felt the presence of the vial of insulin in his pocket and fought to speak coherently. The rope had been tied around his neck and he'd only been able to wedge his fingers beneath it for a bit of circulation. But even with that his head began to swell with the accumulation of blood in his brain. Desperately, he fought to stay conscious in the hopes of saving his daughter, since he was her only hope of making it out of this night alive. With that in mind, he focused wholly on Marie and managed to keep his eyes open.

"Daylight's coming," the stranger said ponderously.

Adam blinked, only to discover a sheen of tears misting his vision, blurring his view of Marie.

"I've marked you, Adam. When you reach the other side, I'll find you. And then you will be mine to do with as I please."

The creak of the rope on the rafter filled the uneasy silence following the stranger's promise. The horses snorted but remained motionless, fearfully awaiting what would happen next. The acrid smell of fires burning nearby terrified them, but the presence of their master gave them some small comfort.

Adam gathered his strength and tried to haul himself up, using the rope around his neck for leverage. His legs beat in midair but he couldn't lift himself any higher. He considered releasing the noose in an effort to reach above his head for the beam, but he knew if he did, the noose would only tighten around his neck.

"Just remember that I didn't kill your child," the stranger reminded him. Then he strode from the stables, disappearing into the thick smoke clogging the yard outside. Behind him, two dark shapes flitted away on long black wings, jittering in their course.

Adam's struggles slowly dwindled. He swung back and forth at the end of the rope. He gurgled with saliva as it filled his throat. His head began to fog with the blood swelling in his brain. He blinked back tears only to shed more. His fingers grew numb with the pressure of the noose cutting the circulation from their tips. He felt the rough strands of the rope chaff against his neck, creating a stinging necklace of raw flesh, abrading his skin. On the floor, his eyes were riveted on Marie, her body curled limply, laying passive and quiet.

All of a sudden, Adam began to sob.

The piercing shriek of a predatory creature abruptly drew his thoughts away from his misery. A dark form streaked into the stables, headed on a straight course past him. Adam's body swung back and forth, slowly settling. His languid motion caused a monotonous creak against the rafter. Another shrill cry pierced the otherwise tainted silence that filled the stables.

A new flow of tears coursed down Adam's cheeks. He couldn't imagine what had caused the shriek—could care even less what it was—but it still bothered him on a more primal level. Consciously, he only wanted to find peace for himself and have no one around to witness his despair. But subconsciously, he sensed there was something tantamount to the cry he heard.

A streak of brown flashed before his eyes, coming from behind, arcing gracefully in silhouette to the brightening sky, then losing definition once it was out of range of the morning sun. Soon, though, Adam could make out what it was, a large predatory bird swooping in front of him and landing on another rafter that was even with his face.

Adam blinked away the stinging tears and saw a red-tail hawk perched on the wooden beam, its head turning fluidly to regard him. Dark, knowing eyes blinked with an infernal slowness, taking in all that was happening. Its head twitched as it turned its focus on Marie, then twitched again to regard Adam. Its hooked beak opened to issue its shrill cry again.

With a momentary sense of déjà vu, Adam stifled his sobs and returned the hawk's obsidian stare. A distant memory came to mind as he remembered Claire crying out when a similar bird had swooped down on a hatchling in the barnyard. The chick had peeped as it was carried away in the bird's talons. Claire had called for him to do something to save the chick, but Adam only told her it was nature's way; everything had a right to survive in the wild, even though he felt a certain sadness for the gross unfairness that plagued the course of life. Now he feared this hawk would swoop down on his daughter and feed on her before his very eyes, and he convulsed at the idea that he'd have to watch. He'd truly lose touch with sanity if that happened and he would enter the ever-after as a raving madman.

Please, don't, Adam tried to voice, hearing his thoughts clearly in his mind. But he barely had the breath to fill his lungs, much less vocalize the words, to get the message across. Instead, his mouth worked on silent pleas, hoping to convey his message through some ridiculously telepathic link all lower species must surely have with human beings. Thinking about the possibility of that link—actually hoping for the possibility of it—Adam knew he was just one step closer to insanity than he thought he could be.

The hawk crouched low just before leaving its perch. It flew toward him, then arced upward and out of sight, landing on the rafter Adam hung from, making its presence known by a quick ruffle of its feathers. After a brief moment of preening, it attacked the rope thrown over the rafter with its hooked beak.

Adam couldn't see the bird or what it was doing, and his concern for it soon slipped away. He blinked wearily, losing his perseverance to keep conscious. With each closing of his eyelids, he found it even more difficult to reopen them. A distant numbness seemed to envelope him like a soft blanket, which he fought off so he could remain vigilant over his daughter yet. He had no concept of time slipping by, no idea if minutes or hours passed, only empty time. He heard nothing but the creaking of the rope as he lazily hung from the rafter. His fingers had long since lost their sensitivity and his head throbbed painfully.

Daylight filtered through the open stable doors, creeping along the hay-strewn ground like a pale tide. Swirls of smoke danced in the rays of sunlight.

He watched the advent of the day, finding it comforting in its brightness, but sad nonetheless. As his eyes shifted to envision the light, he saw something approach. His heart soared with hope. The prospect of help coming gave him enough strength to suck in more oxygen than he normally drew. He opened his mouth to beckon the newcomer forward but only managed a pathetic croak. Instead, he kicked out in an effort to make some noise and only caused the rope to creak more often.

A gossamer figure came into the doorway without causing a blot on the light from outside. The day's brilliance created a nimbus around the figure that prevented Adam from seeing its true features. Then the figure moved out of the light and the silhouette took on a more discernible outline. With disbelief, Adam saw it was

Claire, and she walked into the stables with a stride so graceful he almost believed in angels.

Hanging from the beam, Adam looked down on his wife with a longing so painful he found himself wanting to sob again. He was shamefully aware that he'd left her behind when he'd only meant to take Marie to the hospital. Now he wanted to take her in his arms and explain how sorry he was, but he could only open and close his mouth on voiceless words. When she smiled up at him, his heart tore in half, because he knew he wasn't looking at his wife, but at an angel; one so beautiful her presence was enough to bring him comfort he didn't deserve. Tears welled up in his eyes, and he blinked to shed them, if only to continue watching this vision of beauty a little longer. But keeping her in view for any length of time was painful, like looking too long at the sun, and he had to give his eyes a reprieve before they burned themselves blind.

When he finally reopened his eyes, hoping to get another glimpse of her, Adam moaned and allowed his head to fall loosely against the taut rope. Now, in Claire's arms was their daughter, the same angelic apparition as Claire appeared to be. Marie sat perched in the crook of Claire's elbow, a tiny arm thrown casually over her neck, the other hand plucking at her mother's hair. Her head turned curiously to regard her father, and her clear blue eyes were confused and a little frightened. Claire stroked her cheek and uttered hushed words to soothe her, and Marie grew less anxious. Then Claire turned her attention to Adam.

She looked up at him with an expression of pure anguish. Her free hand left Marie's cheek and went to cover her own heart, conveying an unspoken expression of love she otherwise couldn't speak out loud. Tears were in her eyes that only made her face seem more beautiful.

An incredible ache shattered Adam's courage. He simply wanted to fall at her feet, alive or dead, just to pay homage to her. She was no less than an angel, a miraculous vision of righteousness and decency, and she deserved to be worshipped. But he could no sooner do that than get himself down from the rafter.

Claire pulled her hand away from her breast. When she opened her fingers, a white dove flew away, its wings fluttering rapidly as it took flight. It flew straight up, away from her and toward Adam, so close he could feel the breeze of its flapping wings. A comforting sense of peace filled his mind despite his anguish.

You don't have to be afraid anymore.

Tears of surrender washed away the previous tears of frustration. Adam saw only one way out, only one way to salvation. With the last of his strength, he peeled his dead fingers out from under the rope and let his arms drop weakly to his sides, letting the noose tighten completely around his neck.

At the same time his windpipe pressed into the edge of the noose, the hawk picked apart the last remaining strands of rope. The weight of Adam's body snapped the final cords and the bird screeched as he fell. He hit like a sack of concrete, dropping onto the hard-packed earth, his feet touching down and his legs buckling at the ankles and knees, his body toppling over to his side.

In a short while, his eyes opened, even though he'd rather they not. He wanted to keep the vision of his wife and daughter in sight, because such an image gave him more ease in his dying than any balm possibly could.

He raised his head weakly and turned in the direction of the stable doors. There he stared into the bright sunlight of the aging morning, where he wasn't able to see Claire and Marie any longer. Instead, a pillar of white light rose from the ground where they had once stood, and it abruptly burst apart with an impression of hope and promise. A dozen white doves flew away, their wings fluttering as they flocked on a straight course toward him, their gleaming feathers leaving contrails of scintillating light behind them. Adam blinked as they neared, disbelieving what he was seeing. These weren't like any normal doves he had ever seen before, but figments of his imagination fashioned out of a radiant light glowing blindingly bright in his eyes. As they neared, he winced at the increasing brilliance of their approach. He was forced to squeeze his eyes shut, lest his eyeballs melt right out of their sockets, and he twisted his head in a meager effort to avoid their fluttering. But what he thought might be a brief touch of feathery wings stroking him was something more violent and gut-wrenching than that, and he found enough of his voice to scream in shock and pain as the invention of his imagination passed through him in the many layers he existed as—flesh, muscle, bone, organ, and soul—flensing each and every one until he felt like he was nothing but a skeletal husk of emptiness without even the essence of the man he used to be.

For that, he welcomed death.

CHAPTER FOUR

Early Spring

The clock on the wall reluctantly ticked off the final seconds of the workday—and the workweek—as Grace Fitzpatrick looked out the window of the high-rise office she worked at. She stared forlornly at the drizzle misting the glass and laid her fingers against the cold pane, relishing the sensory perception of the rain through the window. The sunless afternoon made her sad somewhat, and she allowed herself a little chuckle in spite of herself.

Hormones, she reasoned, turning away from the dismal afternoon just as the clock's minute hand made a thunking noise by striking the hour. In the utter silence of the office, the sound was loud and officious, and she took it as a parent's word of permission to leave. She was the only one left at the office; no one would have known any differently if she had left already. All the others had done just that to beat the traffic. Which didn't make sense, since all the other employees of the other offices in the building—and in all the other buildings in the city—were thinking of doing just the same thing. As for her coworkers, they always left her for a head start on the weekend, offering the gratuitous invitation to join them at Rush Street for an after-hours drink, knowing full well she would decline.

Despite the time, Grace didn't hurry to leave. Instead, she lingered at her desk and contemplated what lay ahead for the weekend. She slid a hand across her midsection and looked down. A huff of appreciation escaped her as the corners of her lips curled upward. A warm sensation filled her gut with hopeful thoughts and dreams, even though she was somewhat anxious. Anxious and nervous, that is, with butterflies fluttering in her stomach.

She checked her watch against the clock and noticed it was three minutes slow. She bowed to the authority of the larger timepiece and reset the one on her wrist.

The phone on the desk rang and she snatched it up, realizing that she hadn't moved too far from it in her wandering. She'd been waiting for a call.

"Hello?"

"Grace?"

"Christopher, you're so precise," she said gleefully. "Five o'clock on the dot."

"I could hardly wait. Will you be ready?"

"Of course. I'm the only one left in the office."

"Hmm," he mused naughtily.

Grace laughed and looked out the window, her mouth pursing at the idea of the rainy night. "It's wet outside."

"A little," he observed. "Do you have a raincoat?"

It had been raining steadily since morning, so she'd worn a raincoat to work. But something about a raincoat was so unromantic. It spoiled her image of what the weekend would entail. She would much rather walk in the rain and allow herself to get drenched than bundle herself up in a bulky vinyl slicker. Unfortunately, Christopher was too proper for such flights of fancy and would frown at the idea. *His* wardrobe wouldn't stand up against such harsh elements.

Besides, she thought petulantly, men looked so attractive in trench coats. So very chic.

"Don't worry," Christopher said, taking her silence to mean that she had no foul weather wear. "I have reservations for us at the Rialto. I'll send a car over."

"Oh, you're so scandalous. When can I expect you?" She threaded some errant strands of hair behind an ear.

"Fifteen minutes?"

"Fine. Til then, I love you."

She listened as he said goodbye, a little perturbed that he didn't reciprocate her sentiment. She was accustomed to his aloofness and had grown used to it, although she wasn't generally happy about it. He had apologized for it enough times in the past to where it became an accepted habit, even though she would have preferred something more earnest and intimate instead of apologies.

Grace hung up and hurried around the desk to fish out her bag from the bottom drawer. In it were a white lace negligee and a change of clothes. She went to the coat rack in the office foyer and took down her slicker. She didn't put it on as she left the office and took the elevator down, but kept it slung over her arm.

The lobby was occupied only by a single security guard behind the information desk, and he nodded politely as she strolled over to the front window. There she slipped into her coat, planning to be ready when Christopher's car drove up.

"Wet out there tonight," the guard observed, his voice echoing in the hollow lobby.

She turned to him with a smile. She didn't know his name but they often exchanged brief pleasantries in passing. "It would certainly be nice to see the sun sometime soon."

"They say it's going to stay like this for the next couple of days."

She glanced out the window, not wanting to miss her ride. She checked her watch again and saw that there were five minutes left in the fifteen-minute promise.

"I guess it'll be a weekend to stay inside," the guard remarked.

Grace laughed to herself and felt a thrill shiver through her stomach. She touched her midsection to quell her impatience, imagining the events of the evening. Dinner and romantic passions throughout the night, whispered inconsequentials, sentimental promises, preparations for the future . . . The idyllic weekend.

When a two-tone Mercedes pulled up to the burgundy awning of the building's front door, Grace pulled herself out of her reverie and bid the guard a nice weekend, then skipped out into the damp evening. The Mercedes' driver met her under the awning with an umbrella to shelter her until she slipped into the car's back seat.

No words were exchanged during their encounter, but there usually never were. Christopher's driver had no personality, which was only a minor flaw that rubbed Grace the wrong way. Deeper down, there was a hardness in him that frightened her, but Christopher assured her there was nothing seedy about the man. Of course, with Christopher's vote of confidence, Grace accepted the man at face value, although she could never make herself warm up to him.

Nevertheless, she sat in the back seat with a cheery smile, clutching her oversized bag on her lap as if to protect the sanctity of what was hidden within it. She glanced at the back of the driver's head and wondered briefly what he thought about these trysts he helped facilitate.

Although it didn't bother her what Christopher's chauffeur thought of her, it did grate against her at times that Christopher was married. Despite his estranged relationship with his wife and his assurances that a divorce was only a circumstance of timeliness, she suffered bouts of conscience when she considered the ramifications of their love. Yet her heart always overruled rationale, and she assured herself the love they shared couldn't possibly be wrong, a sentiment that allowed the affair to go on.

The Rialto was only a fifteen-minute drive through Friday's rush hour traffic. If it had been a dry evening, she would have asked Christopher to walk her over from the office. But the drizzle made the sidewalks wet and slick, and the pungent smell of sewage from the gutters might have dampened the mood she was hoping to create for the evening. Perhaps, if she wanted to stretch her legs during the weekend and it was still dismal outside, they could take a carriage ride through the streets, the rain be damned.

Grace closed her eyes and leaned her head against the seat, enjoying the quiet thrum of the car's tires across the cracks in the street's asphalt. In a few minutes, she slipped into a doze that was as close to pure bliss as she was ever going to get. Far too soon, she was jostled awake by the chauffeur, who ventured only so far as to touch her elbow.

"Ma'am."

He said nothing else to her. The car under the vast overhang in front of the

Rialto told her that they'd arrived. She slipped out of the back seat and went into the lobby, where the glorious richness of the décor staggered her. This wasn't her first time at the Rialto, but walking through the huge brass and glass revolving door, into the marble and alabaster reception center, always made her feel small and insignificant. Especially when she walked alone, among all the coupled self-important people.

A hand slid along the small of her back, and Grace turned to face a handsome man more than a decade her age.

"Grace," Christopher whispered and gave her an innocent peck on the cheek, where the corner of her lip angled up in a welcoming smile.

She longed to throw her arms around him and give him a proper reception, but his eyes shifted back and forth as he suspiciously surveyed the people who were watching. Grace backed away to put a respectable distance between them, adequate for old friends just meeting by chance.

He slipped a room key into her hand as his fingers slid down her arm. "Go up to the room and make yourself comfortable. I'll be up shortly, after I make a phone call. Business, you know."

She nodded and walked away, glancing at the room number on the key. She took the elevator up to the thirtieth floor and got out, heading for the last door along the corridor to her left. No one noticed her as she let herself into the room. A large suite with a sitting room, a separate bath, and a bedroom. Victorian décor, muted golds and embossed prints. The smell of roses from a bouquet set in a Lalique vase on the coffee table. Floor-length lace drapes pulled shut to mask the dismal night, but which could be opened to expose a spectacular view of the city skyline on a clear night.

Grace smiled and slipped the key into her coat pocket. She walked into the suite and dumped her bag on the floor of the entryway closet, feeling giddy as she experienced a thrill of anticipation. Going through the door to the bedroom, she noticed an ice bucket on the bedside table with a bottle of champagne turned into the ice. She picked it up and admired the vintage, once again complimenting Christopher on his ability to make everything seem so perfect.

As she was marveling at the view from the bedroom window, she heard Christopher call out to her from the front room. She let the drapes fall back into place and hurried out to meet him, throwing her arms around his neck and laying a lingering kiss on his lips. After a moment, they separated, and Christopher smiled that winsome smile of his, evoking one of her own as well.

"I've got wonderful news," he said, taking her hand and drawing her toward the couch.

"Yes?" she said, feeling a wonderful heat emanate from the back of her neck. She allowed herself to sit next to him, their knees touching. He still held her hands in his lap.

"Crenshaw's decided to step down from office and the city council asked me to run in the next election. They guarantee the endorsements of the police and fire unions and the station networks, as well as the local judiciary branch. The only other candidate who has any chance in the running is Susan Blasek, and she's rumored to be under investigation by the Feds for mortgage fraud."

Grace's mouth worked soundlessly on what to say. She understood that congratulations were in order but she couldn't help but worry about her own relationship with him. His enthusiasm seemed to be more a distraction than sincere. Still, Christopher expected her to share in his jubilation, so she said, "Well . . . that's . . . that's wonderful."

"Do you think?" Christopher asked, not questioning her support but wishing she was as excited as he was.

"Yes, of course," Grace said, falling into character. "This is what you've been working so hard for. You're the perfect candidate, and there's no reason the people of this city shouldn't elect you as their next mayor."

He leaned back and pulled her next to him, cuddling her by throwing his arm over her shoulder. She said nothing as she allowed herself to feel appreciated. She refused to spoil this moment by the sheer selfishness of her own needs. This was what Christopher had been working for his whole life. He was a born politician and a charismatic lobbyist. His success in the District Attorney's office only paved his way to being the city council's favorite golden child. She wasn't going to be the one to rain on his parade. She would enjoy his glory with him and spend the weekend in the arms of the man who was sure to be the next mayor.

Not much later, as they enjoyed a whirlpool bath together, Grace sat nestled between Christopher's legs. His arms were wrapped around her waist as his hands played with the underside of her breasts. She lolled her head against his shoulder, her eyes closed and her mind drifting far away, falling into a world of mystery and sensuality. Christopher's fingers on her nipples triggered scenes of color and piercing electricity, and she allowed low moans of gratification to slip past her lips.

"I must have been blessed in life," he whispered, his breath blowing playfully in her ear.

"Hmm?"

"Everything seems to be falling right into place."

Grace craned her head back to glance at him, her eyes curious as to where she might fit into all this. His eyes were distant, not meeting hers, and she let her cheek fall against his shoulder.

"This is the perfect opportunity for me. I'm young yet, and the endorsements are coming in at the most advantageous time. The city is in a state of stability now, and there's nothing pending at the D.A.'s office to rally displeasure with the constituents. I've even removed myself from being anywhere near Susan's fiasco so I don't look like I'm mud slinging. The stars seem to be in perfect alignment."

Grace felt herself pulled back to reality. Despite the circling motion he continued around her nipples, it no longer felt erotic. Coupled with his talking, it was becoming an irritant. She considered saying something but she didn't want to mislead him. She wondered if shifting in his lap would bring his dreamy attention to other matters.

His hands suddenly cupped the whole of her breasts and hefted them. "And the good Lord must have honored me with these glorious melons. Are they getting bigger?"

She did shift then, abruptly, nearly slipping in the water when she pushed off the side of the tub. She turned around and sat at the opposite end of the whirlpool, facing him.

Christopher looked strangely at her, his hands still poised in midair where they'd been playing with her breasts. A devilish grin twisted the corners of his mouth. "What?"

She tried to look directly at him but demurred instead. At twenty-seven, she felt childlike in his presence. He was a decade older and wiser by generations. He had seen worlds collide when she had only tried to forget the juvenile years of high school. Looking at him stripped of all his clothes, with the heat of the water causing beads of perspiration to form on his forehead, his hair plastered with wisps curling along his temple, she thought he might be less intimidating. But what she had to say, what she'd been hoping to find the best time to tell him, made her only look at him as if he was a stranger.

"I'm pregnant, Christopher," she said mildly.

His smile remained robotically in place, but the clouding of his eyes gave his expression a look of tragedy. His face became white as the blood drained from his cheeks and forehead, and even his eyes glazed with obvious horror. His reaction caused her to panic, and she clutched at her midsection as it convulsed and heaved with anxiety.

"What . . . ?"

"I'm going to have a baby," she clarified slowly, one word at a time, suddenly feeling the full impact of the meaning herself. "Your baby."

He shook his head, closing his eyes and straightening in the tub, the act placing inches more between them. "How . . . ? We were . . ."

"Careful," she helped. Yes, she had been on the pill, daily, religiously, without fail. And Christopher had used condoms, because, he said, it was fail-safe to pharmacological error. She'd thought his remark was hilarious back then, but now she realized it was probably just because he'd never really trusted her. The look he gave her now was one of betrayal. An accusatory look.

"Listen, that doesn't matter," he said with a dismissive wave of his hand. He shook his head. "This is bad, very bad."

"What?" she nearly screeched. Her own face turned white, even though anger flushed her cheeks a rosy hue. "What do you mean this is bad?"

He checked his direction and held out a placating hand. "The timing, sweetheart. The timing is bad. I'm still married, remember."

She closed her mouth with that. Somewhere in her heart, in the swell of that muscle that pumped blood to every vital organ in her body, to the child she carried, some place where she imagined an unidentifiable tissue controlled the function of love and passion and tenderness, she had thought this unexpected miracle of life would be the catalyst by which Christopher would end his estranged marriage.

"But . . . I thought . . . you and Anne . . ."

"Honey, Anne and I have to play this game a little longer. For the sake of the election. The constituents frown on scandal, even the simple scandal of an affair. But a baby . . ."

A tear slipped out of the corner of her eye. She had never thought her child would be considered a scandal. In her mind, she envisioned this child to be nothing less than a miracle.

Christopher detected her dismay and tried to reason with her. "Listen, Grace, this is a bad time. A child would be a wonderful thing . . . at a later date. Once the election is over . . ."

She swiped her hand at an errant tear and looked away, shutting him out.

". . . once I get settled in office, Anne and I can end this farce of a marriage. You and I can be together, out in the open, in public. You'd like that, wouldn't you? To stop all this skulking around."

She sniffled.

"Only another six months," he promised. "Eight, at the most."

She put a hand to her eyes and pressed lightly into them, forbidding any more tears.

"Right now," he muttered, "we'll just have to take care of this slight setback."

She hiccupped on a sob, feeling her eyes burn behind her eyelids.

"I'll get you an appointment with a doctor—"

Grace burst up from the bath like a geyser as her eyes let a deluge of tears out. She got out of the tub, snapped a towel from the rack, and fastened it around her body. She tripped from the bathroom, blubbering incoherently.

Christopher cursed and rose as well. He looked around for another towel but there was only a hand towel and a wash cloth. Annoyed, he ignored those and followed Grace into the bedroom, sighing and rolling his eyes in exasperation. She had dropped onto the bed and was crying uncontrollably.

"Oh, come on, sweetheart," he said gently, laying a hand on her shoulder.

She twisted her body to throw him off. "Leave me alone."

"Grace, you have to see how this is just bad timing for us."

"It's our child."

"It's just an embryo right now. You can't be that far along. You're not even showing yet."

"It's our child!"

"Hush!" he said. "The people next door will think we're fighting."

"We are."

"It's none of their business."

"Exactly. It's your business." She glared up at him. Her eyes were red and glistening, her cheeks pink with the flushing of anger. "How can you just stand there so smug and talk about killing your own child?"

He heaved another sigh, this one obvious. When he spoke, he did so slowly, as if he was speaking to a petulant child. "Sweetheart, you can't possibly have this baby."

"Give me one good reason why *I* can't have this baby."

His jaw clenched. "You'd ruin my chances of getting elected."

"That was never my intention, but if it happens, so be it."

"Now you're just being selfish."

"*I'm* being selfish?" she demanded, bolting up from the bed. She walked around in a huff, her arms gesticulating wildly. "I'm being selfish when I'm the one who's willing to give life to this child? I'm the one who's had to put up with all the sneaking around and adjusting schedules, the jilted dates and forgotten phone calls. I'm the one who's had to keep secrets and come up with lies. I'm the one who's had to live with my conscience and make excuses. I'm the one who's given up opportunities to have a meaningful and honest relationship with someone else. I'm selfish? I'm selfish!"

She walked out of the bedroom and headed for the door. "You're a horrible man, Christopher, and you have no right to be the father of this child."

"Grace, where do you think you're going?" he asked as she strode for the door. At any other time he would have thought it comical to see her stalk toward the door in nothing but the hotel's oversized bath towel. But now, with the disturbing prospect of an unwanted child in his future, he saw nothing funny about it.

"I have no intention of staying with you this weekend. You've got a lot of thinking to do and I think you need to do it in private."

"Grace, you can't leave like this."

She snapped down her raincoat and slipped her arms through the sleeves. Her intention was to be strong in walking out, but she felt the tears battling to come and her heart trembling. If she didn't leave the suite soon she was going to make a fool of herself.

"You're being silly," Christopher added.

When Grace showed no sign of stopping—having opened the door and crossed the threshold—Christopher ran back into the bedroom to grab his pants. He jabbed a foot into one leg and danced as he tried to pull them up. The wetness of his skin caused the fabric to stick to him. He threw himself on the bed and struggled into them, bucking as he pulled them up past his hips. The door slammed in the outer suite, and he cursed. Quickly, he closed the snap and zipped up. He bolted off the bed and ran to the door, fumbling with the knob, slipping at first and then grabbing it tight. When he stepped into the hallway, he saw Grace had already entered the elevator and was gone.

CHAPTER FIVE

It wasn't until Grace stepped off the elevator that she realized she wasn't wearing anything under her raincoat but a bath towel. She glanced up to where she'd just come from, at the four walls encircling the lobby, and knew she couldn't go back. She had to make a point of walking out on Christopher. If she returned, he would only use his silver tongue to persuade her to his way of thinking. She now saw that he'd used his wiles to convince her that his feelings for her were more than just the pathetic overtures of lust they really were. Now she saw the truth. No man who loved a woman would ever ask her to kill a child they'd created together.

She wrapped her raincoat more tightly about her body as she strode for the entrance of the hotel. She got no more than twenty feet from it when it struck her that she'd left her purse in the room upstairs. Her money, keys, and a change of clothes were up there in enemy territory, sitting on the floor of the entryway closet, exactly where she'd dropped them.

She reached into her pocket, pulled out the room key, and studied it as if it were an oracle. If she went back up to the room, she'd only be bending to Christopher's will, heeding to his argument and spreading her legs to a doctor who would dice up her baby as if it was a malignant tumor. On the other hand, she could toss the key from her possession, and with it, Christopher, like an old carton of milk, sour and empty and useless.

With a sniff of fortitude, she chucked the key over her shoulder and strode toward the entrance of the lobby, her shoulders pulled back, her spine stiff, and her head held high. Her mouth pursed in resolve as she walked away, finding her grit a singular reward for this first triumphant victory in her new life.

Yet, despite her bravado, no sooner had she reached the revolving doors, did she discover that the one thing she wanted to do most in life was to find a bathroom where she could throw up.

As the key took its short midair flight over Grace's shoulder, rising in an almost slow-motion arc, a tall dark-haired man watched in fascination as it flipped end over end until it landed with a solid clink at his feet on the marble tiles. His eyes shifted to the woman walking away, and he chuckled to himself, wondering again how things always fell so perfectly into place.

Christopher waited for more than an hour for Grace to return. He noticed that she'd forgotten her purse and convinced himself that she'd be back for it once she tried to hail a cab and discovered she had no money to pay the fare. She lived in the city, but on the other side of town, a far cry from the Rialto, through neighborhoods best left untraveled after dark. He was certain she'd return for her clothes and money, so he waited, sitting in numb reflection of what she'd revealed to him.

Pregnant.

A foreign, obscene word in the context that she'd used it.

I'm pregnant.

In any other sentence it would have been an innocent term, nothing more than a statement of fact. But when Grace had said it, Christopher's idyllic world had shattered.

He and Anne had never had a mutually loving relationship, but they'd experienced a courtship of passion at the beginning, followed by a union of convenience. They had never pursued children because they both knew their marriage was a tenuous one and could end at any time. More than that, children would only complicate the casual sense of the marriage, alluding to everyone involved that there was something there that really wasn't. It wasn't for any noble reason of not wanting to harm an innocent child by creating one from a lackluster union, but for his own reasons—and Anne's, for that matter—why they didn't have any. Neither of them had wanted any more responsibility than they already had.

Christopher knew a divorce would cost him dearly if Anne ever pressed the issue. Since his home life wasn't unbearable, and in fact was comfortable at times, he'd only needed to go elsewhere for the passion that was missing. In his reasoning, he couldn't be blamed for his adulterous lifestyle, not after Anne had lost her sexual appetite for him. He knew she suspected his philandering and accepted it, as long as neither of them brought it up or flaunted it, and it was an arrangement both of them could live with. But this new twist in his life was just the thing he could do without. Anne would take it like a slap in the face and return with one of her own, which would leave him reeling.

Christopher blinked away his perplexity. He pulled himself up from the couch and headed into the bedroom, where he finished dressing with a growing depression hounding him. He fumbled in his pocket for his wallet and checked the contents. He had cash and a good idea where to spend it.

Without much regret for the wasted weekend, he left the suite with all he'd come with and headed down to the hotel lounge. He would leave Grace's purse and clothes right where they were in the off-chance she did return for them. The room was paid for through the weekend and she had the key, so she wouldn't have any trouble getting back in. As for himself, he wouldn't stay another minute in the suffocating suite where all he could think of were the words Grace had left him with: *I'm pregnant.*

An hour later, sitting on a park bench under a dripping maple tree, Grace cried as she dwelled on her miserable situation. Here she was, sitting on the only seat that was well-lit by a street lamp, wallowing in her misery. She felt cold, despondent, and abandoned. Her bare feet trembled in the chilly night. The towel had long since worked itself loose and slipped from under the raincoat, bringing on a bout of sobs that caused a young man passing to stare strangely at her. She had sniffled and sneezed then, her hair flopping into her eyes and briefly obscuring her vision. The nausea that had plagued her during the morning now gripped her stomach with the anxiety she felt. Home was a place far, far away, past low-income housing and multi-ethnic hoodlums who terrified her on a good day, much less on a dark night.

As the night progressed into the more ominous hours, she realized she would have to move from the park soon. It was getting late and her chances of becoming a victim of a violent crime became increasingly more probable. She laughed when she imagined what someone might take from her when all she had was her ridiculous rain slicker; and then cried when she thought about being violated. Once again, the hiccups tormented her.

At least the rain had stopped. But that didn't mean she'd had a chance to dry out. The trees piddled on her as she passed under them, always at the right moment when a breeze blew, their limbs sprinkling water on her until she'd finally given up trying to avoid it and accepted a seat beneath the maple. If anything, the droplets hid the fact that she was crying. No one would suspect anything if they saw her, as long as they didn't see how red and puffy her eyes were, or notice the hiccups wracking her shoulders every so often, or hear how she made pathetic mewling sounds as she sobbed.

She sighed and hiccupped as she weighed her options. She felt comfortable with only one. She would go back to the Rialto and ask the concierge to accompany her up to the room to retrieve her belongings. The concierge would understand the delicateness of the situation. He would act as a shield if Christopher tried to keep her there. Once she had her purse and clothes, she could take a taxi home and put the miserable night behind her.

An unusual sound came from over her shoulder, and she looked up, seeing that the noise came from a bird of some sort. She tried to make out the creature in the tree but could only see the shadows of the boughs concealing everything hiding in the interlacing limbs and dappling leaves, anything from birds and squirrels to peeping toms and muggers—or even psychotic killers. Grace abruptly got up, afraid with her luck—if it was only a bird in the tree and not one of the latter prospects—that it would surely drop its dirty business right on her.

The leaves chattered as the bird flew from its perch. It passed her, swooping low, and landed on the path winding through the park. Its head twitched as it regarded her. Then it cawed, its long black beak opening and closing like a snapping bear trap.

"I don't have anything for you," Grace said dismally, showing her empty hands and despairing over the fact that what she said was the absolute and honest truth. "I don't have anything but this stupid, ugly raincoat."

The bird cawed again, then flew off, apparently disappointed with her. The bird's dismissal only heightened her sense of abandonment, and she hiccupped again.

It was a long walk back to the hotel and she only wanted to be at home in bed, nestled in her thick comforter with a cup of hot chocolate to warm her chilled insides. Sullenly, she wrapped her arms around her chest and took the first few steps back the way she'd come.

Christopher motioned for the bartender to refill his glass. He'd taken a seat at the bar to get prompt service and had already had several shots of whiskey to dull the ache of stupidity he felt.

He watched with fascination as the liquor splashed into his glass and juggled up to the top. A few drops jumped out and he considered licking them off the scarred counter. Because he was bent so close to the bar, he saw how vast the puddle on the counter appeared. It seemed a perfect shame to waste all that good liquor. After all, there was courage in that alcohol, and he needed as much as he could get.

The bartender swiped the spill with a rag and moved off to cater to another drunk at the end of the bar. Christopher tried to lift his head to look around but it felt too heavy to raise.

"Is this seat taken?"

Christopher angled his eyes up to watch a man indicate the stool next to him. With a hand, he waved permission for the newcomer to take the seat. The man perched himself on the stool and motioned for the bartender to come over. When he did, he asked for a Chardonnay. The bartender complied without a word, and the stranger sipped his drink when the glass arrived.

Christopher peeked slyly at the newcomer, appraising him as he did everyone. The man was of an indeterminate age, with dark, brooding looks and a strong profile. His exact features were indefinable, but Christopher suspected it had a lot to do with the blur that came with intoxication.

The stranger sensed Christopher's scrutiny and turned to regard him. Abruptly, he twisted on his stool and held out his hand. "My name is Malachi Drudge. My friends call me Mike."

Christopher stared at the proffered hand, wondering what it was for a moment. He frowned, his eyes narrowing with suspicion. "I'm not gay."

Drudge pulled his hand away and laughed, returning to his drink. In a moment, he looked back at Christopher. "I'm sorry, but you seem familiar somehow. I was just curious."

"They say curiosity killed the cat."

"Cats have nine lives. Surely they should learn from their mistakes and lose only a few."

Christopher burst out laughing, finding it hilarious to be discussing cats with a complete stranger. He imagined a big tomcat playing with a brown grocery bag, like Anne's cat did after she came home from shopping. In his fantasy, the cat put its head into the bag and *BOOM*, a shotgun at the bottom of the bag blasted poor kitty's head off. He slapped the bar as he laughed.

"Yes, that is comical," Drudge said, grinning. "But really, Christopher, curiosity isn't the only thing that killed the cat."

Christopher silenced his laughter and narrowed his eyes. "Who told you my name?"

"You did."

"Oh."

"I can help you."

"Oh?"

"You have a problem."

"Oh . . . yes."

Christopher's arms reached out over the bar, his forehead falling on the counter in a gesture of dejection. His mind reluctantly found itself wondering about his dilemma and his mood turned morose.

"Will you trust me to take care of your problem?"

"Hmm?" Christopher murmured.

"Let's just say you'll owe me one."

CHAPTER SIX

Drudge bought Christopher another round of drinks as their conversation led nowhere fast. They talked about nothing in particular but found hilarity with each passing topic. When Christopher nearly fell off the stool during one of his uproarious renditions of a councilman arguing one lame issue or another, it was Drudge who grabbed him by the arm and held him steady, saving him from a nasty and embarrassing spill. Christopher laughed at his clumsiness and Drudge smiled to encourage him to pick up his mockery where he'd left off, and all was well. Suddenly there was another drink in Christopher's hand, which he considered with puzzled appreciation but accepted without complaint. When he finished the shot in short order, Drudge patted him on the back and eased him off the stool.

"Hey," Christopher slurred, putting a palm against Drudge's shoulder. "I . . . tol'ju . . . I'm . . . not . . . gay."

"Yes, so you've said already. I only think it's time you head on home." No slur marred Drudge's words despite the number of drinks he'd indulged in.

Christopher abruptly recovered some of his composure and leaned against the bulk of his companion. He clutched at Drudge's coat lapels and wondered untimely why the man had never taken it off. It was terribly hot in the bar and the drinking only made it all the hotter. He himself had already stripped out of his suit jacket, loosened his tie, and unbuttoned the first two buttons of his shirt. For some inexplicable reason—other than the liquor distorting his perception—this tickled him to no end; and he chuckled while he rubbed the material of Drudge's coat between his fingers, fascinated by the faintly iridescent shimmer to it.

"Aye . . . I . . . ain't . . . got . . . no . . . 'ome."

"Yes, you do." Drudge gently pried Christopher's hands from his chest and turned him around to guide him out of the lounge.

As Christopher leaned against Drudge, his need for support almost tender and intimate, Drudge half carried, half dragged him between the clutter of tables and chairs in the way, then through the door leading out to the main street in front of the Rialto. They stood on the sidewalk immersed in the gleaming light from a street lamp, the wet pavement glistening with a golden hue from several sodium vapor lamps. Drudge looked east toward a queue of cabs parked along the curb, waiting for fares from the bar or hotel. He snapped his fingers and the first one rumbled up to them. Drudge maneuvered Christopher to the back door and slid him into the back seat.

"Take him to this address," Drudge told the driver, handing him a business card with an address embossed on it.

When Drudge tried to retract his arm, Christopher grabbed it. His watery eyes looked beseechingly up at him with an expression of a lost little boy. "Yer a . . . good . . . friend . . . Mike."

"Just sleep it off," Drudge said, peeling Christopher's fingers off his sleeve. "In the morning, all your problems will be solved."

Drudge slammed the door and stepped back from the curb. The hem of his coat swirled around his legs in a sudden brisk wind blowing out of nowhere, sending a scatter of leaflets from a theater engagement dancing down the street, while the awning of a bistro across the way flapped noisily. Drudge watched the cab disappear into the stream of traffic. Once the cab was far from the hotel's vicinity, Drudge held up his hand and dangled the suite key from its fob.

Off in the distance, in the direction where the cab was headed, a sixty-story building jutted up from the skyline. It appeared to be nothing but a black obelisk among other skyscrapers around it. No lights shone from the windows, and there were nothing but slits in the concrete to act as windows on the uppermost levels. Only four red beacons for air traffic safety showed where the top of the building was in the blackness of the night, and those blinked steadily to a rhythm of a rotating bulb at each corner of the tower.

From one of the slits near the top, unseen by the naked eye, perhaps not even picked up by a voyeur with a telescope sweeping across the buildings in search of something of interest, a black shape flitted out on leathery wings, its course uncertain, sweeping around and around as it circled toward the street several hundred feet below.

In a pigeon coop on the rooftop of a building not far from the tower, a mottled gray pigeon flew from an aerial antenna, down to one of several flag poles jutting from the side of that building. Its feet gripped the metal staff, its balance sure and rigid in the stiff breeze. The downy feathers of its body ruffled. Its soft round eyes blinked knowingly, its head turning smoothly as it fixed its gaze on a black shape ungainly descending between the buildings.

In a cathedral devoted to the Blessed Virgin Mother, in one of the back pews, a young man lifted his head from his reflection and glanced eastward.

Grace trudged through glistening black puddles on the sidewalk as she headed back toward the Rialto, her arms folded over her stomach because it hurt so badly. The tears she'd shed and the side splints from walking so much caused her stomach to tighten and cramp. She worried about the baby, but something told her that it didn't live in her stomach and wouldn't be affected by her exertion this early in its gestation. It lived lower than that, closer to where it had been conceived, and there was no pain there. Yet she was soaked to the bone, having suffered through sporadic drizzles and brief deluges, and her body shivered from the cold. Her makeup ran down her cheeks and made her look garish; and her hair was curled and plastered to her face to the point it had become annoying.

She wandered the streets, pondering which route to take, almost certain she was lost. She kept up her forward course, certain she could trust her sense of direction to find her way back to the hotel. She could either take the main streets and suffer the pandering and panhandling of hookers and bums, or she could make hasty shortcuts through alleys and risk becoming just another statistic on a police report.

Once again she looked at her wrist, only to remember that she'd left her watch on the bathroom counter. She wondered briefly if Christopher would still be there after all this time and considered whether the concierge would give her the opportunity to bathe before retrieving her belongings if he was gone. She didn't think it was such an unreasonable request to make of management. After all, the room had been paid for through the weekend.

But she would only take that luxury if Christopher was no longer there.

After a brief debate between id and ego, she decided to keep to the main streets and optimize her safety. The traffic rolling steadily and noisily by—if not a bit malodorously—offered the comfort of human company. The bums who lolled in the darkened doorways took notice of her as just another homeless tramp and let her be. The hookers never presumed her to be a real threat and only harassed her with insults as she passed.

She made it to the corner of Fifteenth Street and Chestnut when she was held up by the street light and traffic. A caw sounded off to her right, and she looked up at the street sign identifying the intersection. A black crow stood on the bar holding the placard for the street name, its black stick legs set wide apart for balance. The bird looked curiously at her, angling its head to one side, its movement more like a ratcheting twitch than a smooth pivot. Abruptly, its neck swiveled so its eyes could look skyward, and it let out another cry, this one sounding different somehow.

Grace gave the bird no more than a second's attention, then stepped off the curb when the pedestrian light gave her permission to do so. She dodged around the front end of a car jutting too far into the intersection and made it safely across the street before the light changed again. The bird took off from the sign and flew ahead of her, disappearing among the black shadows and glittering lights of the main street.

Drudge stepped off the elevator on the penthouse level of the Rialto. He could already hear the steady beat of a nightclub around the corner. A gold sign with florescent backing emblazoned the wall ahead, proclaiming the nightclub's name with an expensive and elaborate metal script. Drudge walked with a swagger into the club, flipping a twenty dollar bill at the bouncer guarding the door, never looking back to see if he took offense or gestured any appreciation for the gratuity.

The music was a techno-punk variety, with electronic synthesizers battling percussion instruments in an excruciatingly loud tempo that seemed impossible to dance to, yet dozens of people tried. The overhead area was foggy and luminescent, and a cloud of blue-gray smoke swirled above the patrons. That fog was pierced by a variety of colors from stroboscopic laser lights spearing the upper strata of the room.

Taking no interest in the special effects, Drudge wended his way through the people without bumping into anyone, his shoulders twisting this way and that to cut a path toward the booths against the far glass wall. The area he was interested in was raised to a higher level and cordoned off from the dance floor with a brass rail. In those booths, people enhanced their problems and pleasures in drinks and narcotics. Dreary lives fulfilled brutal fantasies as an unobtrusive needle prinked an arm or the underside of a knee; or powder flew to a nostril like fairy dust; a few pills to the back of a throat on the wave of a cordial; or a tongue flicked off the bitter stain on a swatch of paper. Consciousness swirled in varying levels of stupor, and Drudge passed through their faded dreams like a wraith through a graveyard, his presence sensed but not wholly noticed.

His fingers trailed along the shoulders of a woman whose face turned up longingly at his touch. A man suckling at the throat of his consort, who tapped white lines on the enamel of a table, barely acknowledged the stroke of his own neck as Drudge passed. And still Drudge continued, studying the menagerie with a diffidence only he understood, until his eyes alighted on a man so out of place he appeared to have been frightened into a corner. This uncomfortable, overweight, middle-age man nursed a drink in a large glass, his sips coming too quickly to show that the alcohol was putting him at ease. His tongue nervously licked his lips as his eyes shifted back and forth, wary of those who seemed more and more like creatures of the underworld.

Drudge slid into the booth next to the man, his move fluid and sensuous, folding the excess of his coat over his lap. The man regarded him as Drudge slid in close, infringing on his personal space, his leg touching the man's thigh. Drudge cocked his head and watched him, his face only inches away. The man's lower lip began to quiver as he tried to maintain Drudge's gaze. Drudge moved his face slightly closer, so his lips were only an inch from the man's ear.

"Poor . . . poor . . . Charlie," Drudge whispered, his breath sending a bolt of electricity through the man's body.

Charles Driskell let out a mousy whimper as his eyes strained to look beside him, his head frozen where it was, his neck rigid.

Drudge's hand found Charlie's elbow, his fingers moving slowly down its length, alighting on his wrist, then sliding into his hand, clasping it. He gave one squeeze and let go. When he pulled his hand away, Charlie held the hotel room key.

Grace looked across the street and breathed a sigh of relief. She was three blocks from the Rialto, and in her eyes, the night was almost over. She started to step off the curb but jumped back when a car roared past in the nearest lane, honking briefly, its front tire splashing a plume of dirty water from the gutter, then the rear tire causing another to spew up. Twice she was doused with filthy runoff and twice she cursed, too startled by the near miss to step away. Gray water beaded on her legs and ran in rivulets around her ankles. She glanced down at herself and swallowed back another stream of tears.

"Great."

She checked the traffic on the street before attempting to cross again. For good measure, she trotted across it, hugging the raincoat tightly against her body so she didn't expose too much of her legs in her haste. With her goal getting close, she rounded the corner . . .

. . . and ran smack dab into an old bum dressed in tattered rags, his face wrapped thinly in old gauze from jaw to crown. Blisters crusted with dried pus and oozing watery excretions through the old wrappings, emitting a fetid odor, populated his cheeks and forehead; while his hair stuck out like a wiry nimbus of straggly gray tendrils.

Grace barely touched him before she jumped back with a shriek. Her fright was compounded by her revulsion that she might have touched him. Her heart fluttered sporadically, giving her some concern that she might faint at his feet.

"Well, 'scuse me, yer highness," the bum sputtered with thick lips smacking his words. He made a hasty, contemptuous curtsy and an obscene gesture with his hand.

"Sorry," she muttered, quickly putting distance between herself and him. "I didn't see you there."

"No one ever does," he snapped, patting his thick midsection, his tongue jutting in and out of his mouth between words. He abruptly stepped aside and flourished an arm for her to pass unmolested.

Grace apologized again and averted her eyes to the sidewalk, ashamed for having been so open in her disgust. Tonight, people had looked at her and misunderstood her situation, suspecting her to be a bit touched in the head because of her physical state and emotional distress. No one had offered her help or solace because she was just another one of the world's desperate little people. She felt if this night didn't end soon, she might actually lose touch with who she really was and never find her way home again.

With her eyes cast down in embarrassment, she didn't see an elegantly dressed couple strolling up the sidewalk, gazing into each other's eyes as they clutched one another. When Grace bumped into them, she was suddenly overwhelmed by their coats and contempt. She recoiled from their anger and burst into another fit of tears, stumbling backward until her body hit the unforgiving wall of a huge office complex.

"Watch where you're going, tramp," the man said caustically, retaking his lady friend's arm and helping to compose her. The woman gave Grace a haughty look and made no pretense of brushing off any elemental trace that might have transferred during their contact.

"Sorry," Grace mumbled, terrified that the man might be so angry as to strike her. She bit down on her lip and tried to bring her tears under control.

A black shape flitted overhead and disappeared into the alley. The noise of its passing made her watch its quirky dance until it was out of sight. Deeper in the alley was an orange light flickering off the walls and wet pavement. A fire burned inside a fifty-five-gallon drum set up on two blocks of wood. Scattered skirmishes of embers and ash were caught in a draft coming from the opposite end of the passage—a hobo's version of central heating.

The orange light from the fire glinted off the tears on Grace's cheeks. This must be where the bum lived. Her heart felt the slap of accusation again. Her home lay far across town, a warm apartment with four walls and electricity and running water. She didn't have to live in the open with a drum of dangerous flames to keep her warm, nor the broken-down cardboard of discarded boxes to shelter her from the rain. Nor did she have to walk the streets to beg for money and food just to live.

She decided she would make one stop before heading home once she retrieved her belongings from the hotel. She had some money in her purse she could give the bum before she hopped in a cab to go home.

"What'cha got in that coat, bitch?" a voice snarled from the shadows of the alley.

Grace's gut kicked as a wave of heat swept over her. Her eyes tried to pierce the dark but she couldn't see anything. The entrance to the alley was darker than its illuminated deeper recesses. She tried to scream for help—the couple shouldn't be too far away and might still hear her—but her voice was only a squeak. Perhaps all the crying she'd done during the night had rendered her mute.

She caught a movement in the alley and felt her arm jerked toward the mouth of it. Her feet scrambled to maintain her balance, but she still fell against her assailant. A knife pressed against her throat.

"Please, don't hurt me," she cried in whispers, respecting the rules of the crime. She knew she was to keep quiet and do whatever he said. She would also have to give him all her valuables, which she didn't have, and that might be a problem. Once he discovered that she had no money or jewelry . . .

"Gimme whatcha got," the voice said in her ear, the breath foul and warm against her cheek.

"I don't have anything," she explained. "I . . . only . . . have . . ."

She closed her mouth on what she was about to say, realizing that she was wearing nothing beneath her coat. Her mind reeled with what this person would do if he knew that.

The man cursed and grabbed her from behind. He lifted her slightly off the pavement and dragged her farther into the alley. The point of the blade pricked her throat, causing a small cut that seeped blood. Grace squeezed her eyes shut and sobbed, surrendering to the mercy of her assailant. The arm around her midsection was rough and tight, and she bumped against his hip as he propelled her forward.

"What's this?" the stranger queried curiously, depositing her against the wall.

Grace felt her knees buckle as she pressed her back against the wet wall, sliding down to her haunches, whimpering. "Please, please . . ."

Her attacker grabbed the lapels of her raincoat and brought her to stand up straight. He gave her a shake hard enough to crack the back of her head against the wall, bringing on a new rush of tears. Abruptly, he wrenched her coat open and exposed her nakedness.

"Well, Lordy-Lordy, it must be my lucky day. Looky what lady luck brought me."

His dirty, calloused hands didn't hesitate in groping her breasts. Grace bit her bottom lip until a new ache clouded her brain. Regardless of her effort to distract herself from the molestation, she felt his foulness smearing greasy filth over her body. She refused to open her eyes to see the man who fondled her, realizing how even the physical sensations she got from his handling were not enough to pry her mind from believing this was just a horrible nightmare.

The man stepped closer and pressed his waist against her abdomen, his hands roving down between their bodies, his hips grinding repulsively against hers.

"You like that," he breathed into her face, which she turned aside to avoid the foul stench of his breath. "You like that, bitch."

"Let her go."

Grace's eyes shot open when she heard the words spoken not too far behind her attacker. Her head whipped around to see a shape in the dark very near the man whose hands froze on her hips. She couldn't make out his features and only knew it was a man because his voice was deep. He seemed tall, and that was all she knew because he was hidden in the shadows her attacker made with his own body.

The thug who pawed her tensed, coiling his muscles to spring into action against the newcomer. Grace worked her mouth in order to warn her savior about the man's weapon, but nothing but a pitiful gasp escaped her. Tears of hope filled her eyes, but she also sobbed because she knew her attacker had a knife. She felt one hand leave her waist and slide down between their bodies. She wept harder, squeezing her eyes shut and thinking the worst would happen. But then she felt herself suddenly pushed aside, out of the way. Her attacker whipped his blade around in a nasty swipe to hack at the stranger's face.

Darkness enveloped the newcomer as he nimbly stepped back from the lighter shadows, into deeper ones. He lifted his arm to block the attack and caught the thug's wrist in his other hand. With a wrench that barely moved him from where he stood, he flipped the felon head over heels into a pile of garbage. A *whoomph* sounded as the air trapped inside the plastic bags escaped. The stranger dropped low over the rapist and easily removed the knife from his hand, much like a mother would when taking scissors from a child.

Grace slid away from the two men, her back pressed against the wall, her hands guiding her as she kept her eyes riveted to the outcome of the encounter. The mouth of the alley was blocked but she was sure there would be another exit at the other end. She sucked in her sobs and hoped the two men would forget she was even there.

Overhead, out of sight, a black shape dropped from its perch on a window sill several stories above the commotion. It swooped down into the alley, alighting on the cobblestones.

The newcomer flipped the knife over in his hand, deftly catching its handle. He pressed the point of the blade into the throat of the would-be rapist and said, "Walk away from this." His command was low and insistent, and he added, "I didn't come here for you."

When he moved aside, the thug rolled off the garbage bags, scrambled to his feet, and tripped out of the alley, looking fearfully over his shoulder to make sure no knife was thrown at his back.

The man watched him leave, then whipped his head around to stare murderously in Grace's direction. His eyes caught the flickering light of the fire only a few feet away. With the knife, he pointed. "But I did come for you."

CHAPTER SEVEN

On the thirtieth floor of the Rialto, in a suite at the end of the corridor, Charles Driskell waited breathlessly for someone to knock on the door. He paced nervously, impatiently, feeling the excitement of seduction course through his body like an electric current. He jerked abruptly at the knot on his tie, wrenching it off his throat. It hung loosely from his neck, allowing him to unfasten the top button at his collar. Better, much better.

He walked over to the floor-length windows and looked out on the small ornamental terrace jutting from the building. Self-consciously, he closed the drapes and barred the world from peering in on his tryst. Telescopes on terraces far outnumbered patio furniture in the city, and voyeurism was considered more of a hobby than an aberration.

Charlie wiped the sweat from his upper lip. The temperature in the room was comfortable, but anxiety plagued him. Pleasant spasms rippled through his body as he wandered through the suite.

A light knock sounded at the door, and Charlie stopped in his tracks. He swiped down his hair and hefted the waistband of his pants, sucking in his gut and hoping the extra bulk would rise up around his chest. The effort was too much to withstand for very long and he had to let it go. With a sigh, he went to the door and opened it.

The man who'd slid into his booth in the nightclub stood like a brooding Adonis in the doorway. His hooded eyes looked out from sockets that shadowed their black irises. His face was chiseled from granite so strong it made his features sharp and statuesque. His jet black hair fell from a central part on his scalp and framed his cheeks like a satin sheet. Thin, bloodless lips met in a flat line beneath a long aquiline nose.

Charlie stood in the doorway, blocking the entrance, wondering how such a god-like figure could have chosen him among all the more cosmopolitan people in the club to gambol with.

The man made a slight inclination with his head. Its very tilt caused Charlie to swallow nervously and step back so the man could enter. As he did, Charlie marveled at the smooth sanguine stride of his seductor. One of his delicate hands trailed along items he passed. He was tall—unbelievably tall—and lithe, like a Cirque du Soleil dancer, but wearing a dark overcoat reaching mid-calf, unbuttoned and swirling in a provocative manner. Beneath that were a black shirt and dark slacks, each designer made and expertly tailored to accentuate the firm physique of his body.

Charlie eased the door home, not wanting the noise to break the intoxicating tension filling the room. His excitement mounted, and he only wanted to ease his trembling as he shuffled after the man.

"I found the champagne," he said, his voice sounding strange in his own ears.

Drudge's head turned slightly to indicate that he'd heard something, his profile exposed in stunning relief against the silk wallpaper of the suite. Then he blinked and turned fully to face Charlie, his lips lifting at one corner to create a smirk. The gesture eased Charlie, who smiled in return.

"Do you like it?" Drudge asked.

"Yes," Charlie answered, moving off to the bedroom to retrieve the bottle. He came back with it, wiping off the water from the ice with a white cloth he found lying beside it. A corkscrew had been on the cloth, next to two champagne glasses. Charlie struggled with the corkscrew, his face twisting with the effort. When he looked up, he saw that Drudge had moved to stand in front of him.

Drudge gingerly took the bottle and corkscrew from him and easily popped the cork with his fingers. He held the bottle up in triumph as white foam erupted and spewed onto the carpet. Charlie laughed and ran to snatch up the glasses.

After Charlie's glass was filled, Drudge swung the bottle to his lips and drank, his Adam's apple bobbing prominently in his throat. When he'd had his fill, he pulled the bottle from his mouth and flung it across the room. It hit the wall with a thud and rebounded to the carpet, rolling a few feet, foam gurgling from the spout. A heady aroma of alcohol filled the room.

Charlie gaped at this display of recklessness. But the room hadn't been reserved in his name, so he joined Drudge in his amusement, laughing merrily. He drank his champagne, then threw the glass against the wall, shattering it.

Drudge suddenly stepped up to Charlie and caught the back of his head in one of his hands. Without warning, he kissed him hard, his teeth biting Charlie's lips, his tongue thrusting into his mouth. Charlie tasted the alcohol on his breath and felt the probing tickle of Drudge's tongue on his palate. The pain in the back of his head slipped away with a heat that washed over him like a warm blanket, clinging to him as Drudge conformed his body against his. Charlie staggered backward with the weight of Drudge pressing into him, maneuvering him into the bedroom. His feet found better balance then, and he shuffled backward to accommodate his lover.

Drudge's free hand fell between their bodies and groped for Charlie's abdomen. He slid his long fingers beneath the waistband of Charlie's pants and deep into the curly hair of his pelvis. Charlie cried out against Drudge's harsh kiss, his lips peeling apart. He walked more urgently backward, nearly tripping in his fevered attempt to get into the bedroom. His legs felt weak and rubbery, and he thought he would fall to his knees. But his back bumped into the door frame before that could happen, and he slid around it into the bedroom, moaning as Drudge worked him into a sexual frenzy.

Drudge released Charlie's hair and pulled his hand from his pants. He stepped back and locked eyes with him. The depth of his black pupils was like onyx. Drudge's fingers worked dexterously over Charlie's tie and shirt buttons, sliding the shirt from his shoulders and off his back. Then Drudge's fingers worked down to the snap and zipper of his pants, slipping into its yielding waistband and against Charlie's buttocks, his wrists nudging the pants from his hips.

Drudge stepped back. He trailed his long index finger up Charlie's hips, around his thick waist, across his rounded belly, and up between his conical breasts. The sharp nail left a white phantom trail across his flesh. Charlie's breath came quickly and deeply, his heart racing, the warmth of Drudge's hand palpable across his spasming muscles. He felt wondrous, filled with electric excitement, about to burst but forced to wait. His mind fogged with the course of blood moving downward, filling him to the point of aching.

Smiling, Drudge took another step back, a single step, as his hands left Charlie's body and went to the seams of his overcoat. He grasped the lapels and pulled them apart, as wide as they would go, exposing the chattering, savage faces of dozens of creatures hidden within its folds, hanging upside down, their clawed feet hooked into the material of the coat's inner lining. The grotesqueries awoke with a hideous screech, fangs bared while saliva pulled in strings between their vicious jaws.

Charlie opened his mouth to scream but croaked instead. He stumbled backward and threw up his arms as the little beasts broke free from their roosting and flew at him.

Grace watched as her would-be savior turned in her direction. The flickering firelight cast him in shadowy images and played harrowing silhouettes of his size against the wall. She remained frozen, her eyes round saucers of fright. She'd thought he had come to be her rescuer, to save her from the thug who'd only wanted to rip away the one remaining thing in her possession. She had rejoiced at his arrival, thrilled to his first words of redemption, but now she trembled at the words he'd spoken.

But I did come for you.

A cold shiver ran up her spine and branched out on the tendrils of her nerves, touching the farthest reaches of her body. She felt frozen by the chill, immobilized by the terror coursing through her. The man remained as rigid as she but she could tell he wasn't afraid. He was in complete control. She could see him now, as the fire in the drum flared with a draft that swept through the alley, sending a whirlwind of orange embers up like a dervish.

With him highlighted by the firelight she could see that he was somewhat tall, as she'd first suspected. His black hair was long and loose, twitching in the same draft that brought up the fire. He wore a white cloth tied around his forehead, concealing his eyes in the depths of its multiple folds. A red scarf was wrapped around his neck and buried his chin and mouth, something someone might wear out on a frozen tundra, but not here, where it was chilly but not frightfully cold. But even with that she could tell he wasn't old. Not even as old as her, either. He was just a kid really, barely a man at all. A dark overcoat concealed the physical features of his body and only shifted slightly in the wind; but she got a sense he was fit, since the way he moved showed an ease of body and sinew that only came with practice. Both his hands were swaddled in white rags, wrapped at the wrists with knots. He wore old high top sneakers with their laces tied loosely, and that seemed incongruously out of place. But more disturbingly, in one hand, he still held the knife her attacker had previously wielded.

Grace took this all in and gathered enough courage to bolt. She clasped the edges of her raincoat and fled deeper into the alley, getting only a few steps away before a black shape burst up from the ground and towered over her. It opened its arms and enveloped her as she barreled into its thick, hairy body. She recoiled instinctively, but uselessly, screaming with terror, her eyes registering its features before she became a part of its hideous embrace.

Leathery wings enveloped her, wrapping a blanket of darkness around her that should have given her peace if it had only been the comforter from her bed. But she was stricken with terror, the foul, bitter smell of ammonia and musk filling her nose with odors making her gag. She beat against the leathery shroud around her, but her arms only punched uselessly at the membranous wings.

The creature's head reared up. Its fang-filled mouth opened wide to let out a screech, barely acknowledging the frantic struggling within its embrace. Across from it, the stranger barely moved, except for a twitch at the corner of his eye. He listened to the screech, then cocked his head as a more settling sound reached his ears. A hawk let loose a piercing cry from where it was perched on an iron fire escape near the rear of the alley, behind the creature and its prey.

The young man took a few menacing steps forward, his footsteps nothing more than hushed scrapes against the trash in the alley.

"Let her go."

The creature's head snapped from its baleful ululation to eye the approaching stranger. Its hideous face twisted into an expression of confusion as it cocked its head inquisitively.

The young man took two more steps before he snapped his arm forward and flung the knife in a pinioning spiral toward the creature. Glints of orange shone off the blade as it sped forward and buried itself in the fleshy extension of one of the creature's wings. The thing howled as it twisted and jerked its injured appendage. With the bony digits of its clawed hand, it gripped the haft of the blade and tried to pry the knife loose. As it fumbled with it, Grace crumpled to the ground, her body unconsciously coiling into a fetal shape.

The stranger sprinted forward, quickly broaching the distance separating him from the creature. He brought one of his steps down on the end of a broken piece of wood and popped the other side up. He snatched it in a two-handed grip. Completing the rest of the distance, he brandished the length of wood like a baseball bat. He didn't break stride as he swung the weapon at the creature's face. The flat of the club connected with a devastating smack against the thing's head, affording a rewarding sound that promised a broken skull at least.

The momentum of the attack threw the creature several feet, where it crashed into the wall at the side of the alley. The wood then met the beast's face over and over, turning it into bloody pulp. The stranger swung his cudgel in alternating arcs, striking blows to either side of the black head, turning it into a meaty lump, crushing the bone beneath, mashing the brains into a gelatinous mess.

The young man allowed his rage to fill him, his body nothing but a machine working in accordance to muscle contractions. His movements around his victim were graceful, bracing, his body twisting with the momentum of his swings. He barely made a sound himself, his breath regulated through teeth clenched tight. When the creature finally began to swipe blindly at him, he rammed the sharp edge of the wood directly into its thick chest, crunching bone and vital organs, bringing an inevitable end to its miserable existence. Blood and gore gushed in spurts as the young man jumped aside, giving the demon room to stagger and clutch at its grievous wound, screeching, and dropping to its knees, crumpling face down on the wet pavement.

Breathless and shaking with rage, the stranger released his hold on the piece of wood and backed away. He reached out behind him to make sure he didn't stumble into anything, realizing in a distant part of his brain that the woman was slumped somewhere in the alley.

The creature trembled and shrank, becoming nothing but a small crushed bat with its wings bent and folded in obscure angles. Its tiny, vicious mouth lay slack, its razor-sharp teeth no less threatening in the rictus of death.

A shriek came from the hawk overhead, which had watched the beating with stoical interest. At length, it launched itself from the fire escape, its long mottled wings catching a draft and riding it until it was close to where the man stood, then veered sharply to snatch the bat in its talons. With singular purpose, the bird carried the corpse out of the alley and into the night.

The stranger turned to Grace, a little concerned for how she lay motionless on the ground, crumpled like a broken doll, her yellow slicker hiked up to show a length of bare leg. He crouched next to her, laying a hesitant hand on her arm, growing even more fearful when he felt how cold her skin was. He laid a finger on her throat and felt the distant thump of a weak pulse.

He hastily slid his hands under her body and lifted her into his arms. Her body settled against his chest in a profoundly disturbing way. With a continuous prayer, he left the alley.

Drudge suddenly stopped what he was doing and raised his head, his back stiffening with gristle. He cocked his head to one side as his jaw set firm. It quivered slightly as he clenched his teeth. After a minute, his mouth pursed in commiseration. Eventually, he took a deep breath and let it out with a loud exhale, his chest heaving.

"Well . . ." he mused, his voice attracting no attention to himself. His eyes arched and he gave his head a little shake. "That's one that won't be coming back."

The wide automatic doors opened when a sensor beam was activated, a hiss of air announcing the arrival of the young man bearing a burden in his arms. The stranger from the alley shifted Grace's weight against his chest and wended his way through a multitude of sick and impatient people on his way to the reception desk.

The hospital emergency room was chaotic and in disarray, exuding an angry atmosphere reflecting the actual pain of the injuries and diseases filling the beds and gurneys. Patients who had waited for hours rallied against anyone taken out of turn, while nurses and orderlies skirted their angry protests, dislodging complaints with an indifferent wave of their hand. The possibility of a fist fight was only a nudge away.

Unconcerned with the madness, the young man bore Grace's burden as if she weighed nothing at all. As his eyes roamed over the administering staff, he searched for one doctor in particular, always only catching glimpses of white coats ducking in and out of rooms, from behind curtains, popping up from counters, spinning like whirlwind dervishes from one task to another. Triaging one patient, scribbling on the chart of the next, checking the dressings applied by a nurse. No one paid him any attention, a strangely dressed man with a haggard-looking woman in his arms, her head lolling against his shoulder in obvious unconsciousness.

In the white florescent light he didn't appear as dangerous as he had in the shadows of the alley, and Grace wouldn't have been so frightened if she'd awakened to see him then. His scarf was pulled away from his face, where it hung loosely around his throat, exposing a strong chin and wide mouth with thin red lips. Shadows no longer made his eyes appear hooded and harsh, but soft and pleading, his face pale and sullen. His mouth was curled into a questioning hook, giving his expression one of uncertainty and anxiety, while a white scar ran the entire length of one side of his jaw, more on the throat side than near his cheek.

Then he spotted her, the doctor with gentle hands, tender eyes, and few words. She looked tired and worn, but her movements were precise. A lock of hair had worked itself free from her ponytail and hung over her ear, which her hand unconsciously swiped at every so often.

He moved forward quickly, his burden becoming suddenly heavy. Without preamble, the doctor turned to face him as he came up on her.

"What . . . ?" she said, startled by his sudden appearance.

"Will you take a look at her?" He glanced over his shoulder at the crowd ruffling at his impertinence. "Please."

Noticing the brimming anger in the crowd, the doctor tossed a chart aside and beckoned him to follow. She swiped a misplaced bedpan off a gurney and indicated that he should lay Grace down, which he did, gently. When he pulled his arms away, he made sure the raincoat remained modestly in place. Then he took a step back, his eyes moving slowly up from Grace's face.

The doctor immediately checked Grace's eyes and made note of their pupil dilation. She slid her hands expertly around the back of her head, and then reset it to rest more comfortably on a thin pillow. She lifted a limp hand and palpitated the wrist for a pulse. When the man took several steps away, she looked up and frowned. "What happened to her?"

"I . . . found her . . ."

"How? Like this?" The doctor's eyes became suspicious. She started to straighten up.

He stammered and turned his head away, mostly in an effort to hide his face so it wouldn't be recognized. "Yes."

"So you don't know what happened to her?" Her words were demanding, distrustful. Her back stiffened even more to give her a strong and determined bearing. "Who are you? You look familiar."

He gestured to her patient. "Shouldn't you be more concerned with who she is?"

The doctor returned her attention to the woman, reluctantly admitting that he was right. Her hands went hesitantly to the raincoat and pulled it away. Abruptly, she looked up, ready to shout for security, or at least curse the young man for the anger she felt surging to the surface. But before she could, she found that he'd disappeared.

CHAPTER EIGHT

Christopher moaned and rolled over. He wasn't fully awake yet but he was in the process of pulling himself out of a drunken stupor that might have resembled sleep except for his stomach roiling and the world behind his eyelids spinning off-kilter. His mouth felt thick and dry, like paste with crusty edges, and his tongue was swollen and hairy. His limbs were distant and uncooperative, and his head seemed as if it had been tacked on with wooden pegs on either side of his neck. Irrationally, he wondered if it had been removed during the night and set back on; and he experimentally touched beneath his ears to make sure no fasteners were there. His fingers against his throat felt heavy as they thumped the veins beneath his skin, and each tap sent a series of shockwaves through his bloodstream, into his very brain. He became aware of a headache the likes of which he never had before, and again moaned in earnest.

He opened his eyes slowly and winced when the dim light struck them. Throwing an arm over his forehead, careful not to let it touch his temples, he opened his eyes to mere slits and looked toward the ceiling.

Something about where he was felt wrong, as if he was in a place he didn't recognize. Instead of sitting up to glance around, he wracked his brain for a memory of where he might be. Thinking only created a more rhythmic thumping in his brain, and he cursed his lack of self-control.

Grace.

He remembered Grace and smiled, then frowned when he recalled her fateful words.

I'm pregnant.

He groaned, and the sound made his head hammer harder. "Owww."

He let his head roll slowly to either side so he could take note of his surroundings. Curiously, he stared with fascination at the room around him. It was nothing like the hotel suite he'd reserved for the weekend—if his memory served him correctly—and he slowly braced his elbows on the mattress to push himself up.

The room was lit by a dozen braziers set in niches. The burning torches gave off a yellow light to illuminate the walls. Except the walls were actually only one wall, which was a continuous stone construction without corners encircling him. There was only one wooden door opposite the bed and no windows to speak of. The bed he lay on was the only furniture in the room, a huge mattress on a platform, filled with black pillows and satin coverlets. The luxurious texture of the linen should have evoked provocative urges and images, but the pounding in his head and the confusion of what had happened during the night dissolved any erotic sense from his mind.

Christopher looked down at his body and noticed alarmingly that he was naked. He struggled with his memory to recall what had happened during the night to bring him to such a state and dreaded the worst of what his imagination had to taunt him with.

He remembered he had plans to spend the weekend with Grace but she'd fled the hotel in nothing but a raincoat. He even remembered that he'd waited for her to return, and when she hadn't, he'd gone down to the lounge to drown his sorrows in whatever alcoholic beverage was set before him. Things had gotten a little hazy after that, but he remembered a man pouring liquid into his shot glass from a bottle the bartender had left them.

Somewhere between that and where he found himself now there must have been a woman. Surely he must have met a woman during the night to find himself naked and in a strange bed. He tried to smile, relishing the idea of a tawdry one-night stand, but the idea of a night of nasty sex wasn't as pleasant as the actual memory of having it. Instead, he began worrying, thinking that if he'd gotten so drunk he'd forgotten those last few hours of his life, it might not have been worth remembering anyway.

"Oh Jesus," he moaned dismally. Had he gone home with the man who'd shared his company at the lounge? He couldn't remember, nor could he recall what the man even looked like.

If there had even been a man.

There was a light rap on the door and it opened almost at once. A pale, gaunt man with a head incredibly long and narrow glided into the room carrying a tray. On the tray were a crystal glass and a decanter of orange liquid.

"Good morning, Mr. Purcell," the man greeted, his voice deep and atonal. "How are you this morning?"

"Puzzled," Christopher replied, his voice sounding alien and harsh. His tongue stuck to the roof of his mouth and wouldn't fall back into place. He pried it loose and worked his mouth to develop enough saliva for lubrication. "Where am I?"

"You're at the Spatial Tower, on Nineteenth and—"

"I know where it is," Christopher said softly. If he only kept his voice low, so would the other man. "The question is more why I'm here?"

"Mr. Drudge thought you were in no condition to drive last night, so he made sure you had a safe place to sleep off your . . ." The man respectfully hesitated. He bent to place the tray on the floor and poured some liquid into the glass, which he handed to Christopher. "Orange juice."

Christopher grimaced and held out a restraining hand, declining the drink. He knew his stomach wouldn't be able handle the acidity in the juice, but that was only a minor concern at this point. He still worried about the extent of his liaison with the man the servant had mentioned, this Mr. Drudge. A glimmer of a memory came into focus.

Embarrassed by the idea that he might have engaged in some sexual liaison with a man from the bar, Christopher didn't broach the subject any further with the servant. Instead, he wracked his tortured brain for any memory of what had happened after things had gotten foggy during the night. Unfortunately, he still came up with nothing. It was blank, which bothered him, because he was normally a meticulous and self-possessed person. Without the affects of alcohol in his system, he could honestly say he didn't have it in him to have sex with another man. Even though he wasn't homophobic, he still preferred heterosexual relations. There was no way he could have crossed that line. Not even if the man had been as handsome as that man had been. What was his name, Christopher mused, trying to jog his memory, only to find it lying very close to the surface, since the servant had mentioned it only seconds ago. Drudge.

Malachi Drudge.

Oh, yes, he remembered the name. He knew the name.

"There's a remedy in the juice to counteract your overindulgence," the servant advised. He pressed the glass into Christopher's hand. "It will cure whatever ails you."

"Boy, you have no idea what ails me now," Christopher bemoaned.

"Mr. Drudge would like you to stay until you've recovered some of your senses. He asked me to tell you that he has to discuss certain points that occurred during the night before you leave."

Christopher began to sweat, the heat of his embarrassment flushing his cheeks. "What . . . um . . . points?"

"I'm just the butler, Mr. Purcell. I'm not privy to what Mr. Drudge's personal affairs entail."

Weakly, Christopher took the glass and watched as the butler departed. When the door closed, he realized he'd forgotten to ask where his clothes were. His nakedness felt entirely too public, even in the concealed bedroom of the peculiar Spatial Tower.

He wondered briefly about that, knowing only how the dark, pencil-thin skyscraper seemed gloomy among several other buildings in the area that were constructed of glass and metal. The lights illuminating the skyline with seasonal trim made the tower nothing but a blacked-out section on the horizon. He knew where the Tower was—everyone knew *where* the Tower was—but he didn't know anything about Spatial Industries. Nothing had ever passed through his office to attract his attention to the obscure corporation, so he had no reason to delve into its history or dealings. But he did know the Drudge name, only because the man was one of the wealthiest financiers in the city and owned the Tower. Christopher's gut twisted with an anxiety that came from realizing that he might have had sexual relations with a man who could financially destroy people like him.

Distractedly, he sipped the juice, ruminating over the consequences of the worst case scenario and wincing from more than just the citric taste of the drink. He detected a bit of an underlying almond flavor and waited to see how his stomach would accept the first few drops. Then he drank more ardently, finding himself thirstier than he'd initially thought. His stomach didn't retch, but it did remind him that it was the center of a violent turmoil waiting to erupt and he should proceed carefully with taking anything by mouth. His headache did seem minimally appeased by the drink, and he wondered if it was the vitamin C that was the panacea the butler had been referring to.

Drinking steadily, Christopher's mind dwelled more deeply on his problems. He'd have to talk to this Drudge fellow to find out what had happened during the night, deal with it accordingly, and then worry about Grace.

While he considered those points, he slipped back into a supine position. His empty glass dropped from his limp hand. He looked dully at his errant fingers and wondered if the juice would stain the floor, then blinked and slowly slid into unconsciousness.

A uniformed officer stepped aside as a plainclothes detective slipped under a string of crime scene tape tied across the door of a hotel suite. Inside, there was a flurry of activity. Pops of flash bulbs went off sporadically as a photographer moved around the bedroom. Two uniformed officers talked between themselves in the sitting room. Another crime lab technician sketched the layout of the scene, while two plainclothes detectives bent over the body of a naked man on the bed in the bedroom.

The corpse lay on the rumpled covers with its arms splayed wide and legs slightly apart. Its face was a mask of horrific disbelief and its eyes were half lidded.

THE UNFAITHFUL

The only mark on the body was a small wound over its left breast, puckered and with very little blood dried around it. The flesh had a grayish cast to it, with purple contusions along the underside of the body reflecting lividity.

"Whatcha got?" the newcomer asked as he slipped on a pair of latex gloves from the pocket of his coat.

The two detectives examining the body looked up. One was old, overweight, and bald. He wore a dress shirt without a jacket, and his tie was pulled loose from his throat. The other was younger and wore the full compliment of his suit. His physique didn't suffer from the same activity of movement that hindered his partner.

"Mr. Charles Driskell, deader'n-a-doorknob," the larger one said. He came around the bed and tossed a brown wallet at the arriving detective, who caught it in mid-air and flipped it open. He checked the identification and the number of bills still there, then glanced at the body and noticed that it still wore a watch and wedding ring.

"Robbery's ruled out?"

"My guess is a crime of passion," the slim detective said, turning his back on the body. "One puncture wound to the heart, right on target. The coroner's on the way. Should be here in a few minutes."

"Sergeant Markey."

The detective who'd just arrived turned to look at one of the lab technicians. The tech brought a woman's large purse into the bedroom, which he held delicately with one gloved hand. He carried it over to an empty dresser bureau.

"We found this in the closet at the front door. I don't think it's the victim's. Unless he was into women's fashion."

"Doesn't match what he was wearing last night," the obese detective remarked, indicating the man's clothes strewn across the floor beside the bed. "I would think a man who appreciates women's fashion would also know how to accessorize."

"It belongs to someone else," the technician stated without a hint of humor. He dumped the contents on the dresser bureau. Women's lingerie, a white negligee, a peach-colored pants suit, makeup, wallet, hairbrush, and a travel toothbrush. When Markey picked through the clothing, he noticed the sizes were all petit. He snatched the wallet and pulled out a driver's license.

"Grace Fitzpatrick," he read off the card. "Lives on the south side. I think I'll leave you two to Mr. Driskell and go talk to Ms. Fitzpatrick."

"Hey, Sarge," the heavy detective beckoned, coming up to his superior. "Shouldn't one of us go with you?"

Markey handed the license to the detective. "Would you take another man with you to visit a woman like that?"

Peter Lumas glanced at the picture on the license and pursed his lips in appreciation. Even for a driver's license photo, the woman was beautiful. Young and attractive. Not many killers in the city were such a sight for sore eyes. He smiled cunningly at Markey as he handed the license back.

"We haven't found the murder weapon yet. She could be dangerous."

"I'll keep that in mind." Markey tossed the wallet back on the clothes, where they would be collected and packaged by the lab technician as evidence. "What name is the room registered under?"

The slim detective glanced unnecessarily at his notebook. "A Mr. and Mrs. Smith."

Markey gave him an unpleasant look. He shook his head. "Find Mrs. Driskell and break the news to her. Try to be a little more diplomatic than you usually are. The woman's going to find out her husband was having an affair when he was killed. Talk about adding insult to injury."

Lumas made a gesture with his hand to simulate firing a gun and winked. Markey left the suite and headed for his car parked outside the Rialto.

Grace awoke from a nightmare. The backs of her legs were sore from having dreamed of running. She became aware of other aches plaguing her body and winced when she tried to move. Her head hurt, especially at the back where it had connected with the wall in the alley, and she suddenly remembered everything from the night before. She jerked up to make sure nothing threatening existed in her immediate vicinity and saw that she now lay on a twin-sized bed with guardrails. A plain white curtain was pulled around it, offering her privacy. She looked behind her and saw a call button on the wall, within easy reach, along with receptacles for hook-ups to various plugs.

A hospital. With relief, she allowed herself to relax. Breathing easier, she pulled the sheets up to her chin and sank deeper into the folds of their comfort.

Remembering bits and pieces of the traumatic night, Grace noticed she was no longer naked. Instead, she wore an unflattering hospital gown that wasn't much better than the raincoat she'd worn the night before. At least it wasn't cumbersome. Her hair was dry but gritty, yet the rest of her body felt relatively clean.

Taking stock of herself, she suddenly grew frightened for the unborn baby inside her. Her hand scrambled for the nurse's call button with tears brimming in her eyes. The nurse came quickly, pushing open the door after a light rap of warning.

"Where am I?" Grace asked, her voice tremulous and on the verge of sobbing.

The nurse came forward and spoke in hushed tones, her words soothing. "You're at St. Jude's Memorial. You're safe here."

"But . . ." Grace stammered, "how . . .?"

The nurse looked quizzically at her, showing that she didn't understand. She watched as Grace's lower lip trembled and said in sudden understanding, "How did you get here?"

Grace nodded.

"I wasn't on duty when you came in, but I believe you were brought in through the emergency room. Doctor Perez was the admitting physician, but she's off right now. She'll be back tonight to do her rounds. You can talk to her then."

Tears finally let loose from Grace's eyes, and she buried her face under her arm, weeping. The nurse came to her side and patted her other hand where it lay on her waist. "Would you like to talk to someone?"

Grace sniffed and brought her arm slowly down from her face. She clutched at the nurse's hand. "Is . . . is . . . my baby . . .?"

"Oh, sweetheart, don't fret. Everything seems to be all right with the baby."

Relief washed over Grace. She didn't understand this bond she felt with a child that was only eight or nine weeks in her womb, but it existed nonetheless. She also felt incredibly disconnected from her previous life, in which she'd simply been living for herself. Now she had someone who was depending on her, an innocent baby she carried in her gut, which she didn't know but had a tremendous urge to hold and love.

She also didn't feel comfortable where she was, in an unknown bed with clothes that weren't her own and around people she didn't recognize. She wanted more than anything to go home, put on her robe and slippers, and curl up on the couch with a hot drink. She didn't like the smell of this place, the medicinal and antiseptic odors. Her apartment smelled of vanilla walnut potpourri, a soothing scent she was familiar with and longed for now.

"I want to go home," she murmured.

"You'll be going home soon," the nurse said. "Doctor Perez wanted to keep you for a twenty-four-hour observation. What's your name, honey? We've got you listed as Jane Doe on your chart."

Grace sniffed and wiped a tear from her cheek. "Grace," she stammered. "Grace Fitzpatrick."

"Well, isn't that wonderful. A pretty name. Can I get you anything while I'm here? Something to eat? The cafeteria's still open. We had roast beef tonight."

She shook her head. "I'm not hungry."

"Nonsense," the nurse scolded. "That baby you're carrying needs her nourishment. I'll bring you up something light. Doctor Perez should be on duty around ten. I'm sure she'll be by sometime after that."

Grace relaxed against the pillows and allowed herself to settle into the comfort and security of the bed. She thought she could probably muster up enough energy to eat if it was for the sake of the baby.

"I'll be back in a bit. If you need anything, just push the call button."

And the nurse, who had yet to introduce herself, moved off on a mission that was mostly unbidden.

Sergeant Markey made it to the station just shy of sunset. He'd ripped off his tie and discarded his coat, which had since become damp with the incessant rain falling all day. Funny how sunsets always seemed to bring an end to the constant drizzle. He was just thankful to see a little break in the dreary clouds.

Peter Lumas was the only member of his squad still in the office when Markey walked in, and he was busy with a coffee in one hand and a sandwich in the other. He absently sipped and bit from either while he studied the paperwork in front of him.

Despite his uncouth behavior and lack of social graces, Markey liked Lumas. The overweight, upbeat detective was a workaholic, if he was anything. He applied himself fastidiously to his cases until he finally got his man and dabbled in unsolved homicides going back thirty years or more. He was a hobbyist and murder was his hobby.

Markey threw a plastic bag keeping some loose papers dry onto his desk. "How's it going?"

"You find our black widow?"

Markey shook his head and dropped wearily into a chair near Lumas. Allowing himself a show of casual airs, he kicked up his feet and propped them on the desk. Frowning, he studied his shoes and noticed they were shot. The leather showed the water marks of all the puddles he'd tromped through during the day.

"Speaking of widows, did you make the notification to Mrs. Driskell?"

"Yeah, and I can see why the man went to another woman for compassion." Pete looked sullen. "The woman was a bitch. Didn't have a kind word to say about her dearly departed husband. She seemed quite surprised, though, that Mr. Driskell had been with a woman for the evening, if you get my drift."

"Asexual or bisexual?" Markey snickered. "Or maybe dysfunctional?"

"Driskell had anything but a satisfying sexual orientation, according to his wife. I'd say we put her down as a suspect."

"Why don't we?"

"Because she was at a bible retreat until three a.m. The coroner marks the time of death around midnight."

"What type of bible retreat goes on until three a.m.?"

"The kind that would drive a wife batty and a husband to bisexuality, I guess. But we checked it out and it holds water."

Lumas looked at his sandwich and then his coffee, and tried to remember which one he'd indulged in last. His lips twitched until he finally took a bite of his sandwich. "What about Ms. Fitzpatrick? She wasn't home?"

"Nope, and none of her neighbors seem to know much about her. I'm inclined to think she may have gone on the lam. I've got a uniformed guy sitting on the apartment until I can get a warrant in the morning."

"If she's running scared, you don't think she'd go home before taking off, do you?"

Markey shrugged, interlacing his fingers behind his head. "Tomorrow's Sunday and I think the on-call assistant D.A. is Prescott. He's pretty cooperative."

"If you don't mind, I'd like to be there when you open 'er up."

"No problem. We're talking about a pretty small item. We'll need to cover a lot of area, so I could use all the hands I can get."

Markey brought his hands to his lap as his legs fell down from the desktop with a thud. He thought he heard the leather soles squish. "I'm going home. Don't stay up too late. The city can't afford all that overtime."

"See ya, Sarge."

CHAPTER NINE

Christopher woke a second time with a splitting headache, his eyes barely able to open without causing slivers of his brain to catch fire. He moaned and rolled over, his hands clutching his temples. God, if he ever drank so much again, he'd just keep on drinking until he drowned in his own vomit.

The sleep he'd indulged in had been plagued by alternating nightmares and sensuous dreams, fluctuating so rapidly that he couldn't keep up with which pleasure or horror his mind dabbled in. Dreams of power and riches and glamour and seduction were intermittently interrupted by nightmares of madness and mayhem and having sold his soul to the devil.

"Do you think you even have a soul to sell?"

Christopher jerked his eyes open, his gut pierced by the sultry nuance of the words just spoken. He let out a squawk when the light of a menorah pierced his eyes, sending pain flaring through his brain again. He could make out nothing but the shimmering phantoms of the candlelight flickering wherever he tried to focus, until after a few seconds of struggling with his concentration he was finally able to discern vague shapes. Eventually, after blinking several times, he noticed the man who'd called himself Malachi Drudge last night now standing at the foot of the bed, holding a lighted candelabrum.

"What?" Christopher asked, shielding his eyes from the brightness of the flame.

"I asked if you thought you'd survive your spell?"

"Oh," Christopher said unevenly, rubbing his eyes. He struggled to sit up, managing to press his back against the cold, hard wall of the circular room.

"You had a nasty one," Drudge said. He began to walk around the bed, his stride fluid and graceful, the light from the menorah creating a shimmering nimbus around him. "I thought I might have to call a doctor."

"Um . . . ?" Christopher mumbled. He had no idea what had happened, only that he now suffered a nasty headache and amnesia of the night before. "How long have I been out?"

"It's Saturday night," Drudge said, turning and walking to the other side of the bed, pacing around it so Christopher's eyes were never allowed to rest on any one spot. "You had a nasty reaction to all the alcohol you drank. I think they call that alcohol poisoning."

Christopher wanted to tell him to stop moving, that his pacing was causing him to become nauseous, but his tongue felt thick and dry, and talking wasn't a skill he seemed to have mastered yet.

"You had a bad night," Drudge soothed, his voice a mixture of sweet honey and liquid gold. "But it's all behind you now."

Christopher dry-washed his face with one hand, his other still propping himself up in an unsteady position on the spinning bed. "Thank God."

"By now, Grace Fitzpatrick is being sought for the murder of a petty little man found in your hotel room last night."

Christopher's hand froze in mid-swipe, uncertain if he'd heard correctly. Peering out from behind his fingers, which had separated for him to see his host, he croaked, "Pardon me?"

"When the police find her, she'll tell them that she was with you last night and that she left you in your hotel room."

Christopher used both hands to push himself farther up in bed, his back pressing against the unforgiving stone wall. He stared with blazing forthrightness at the man. All the while, the candelabrum created a strange St. Elmo's fire marking Drudge's path and then fading.

"What are you talking about?"

"When the police come to you, you'll tell them that you don't know this woman, that she must have been given the wrong name by her lover. You were away for the weekend in an attempt to raise campaign funds. I have three associates who will testify that you were with them this weekend. Even your driver will corroborate your story."

"Whoa, whoa, whoa, hold up a minute," Christopher interjected, slapping the air with his hand. "What are you talking about? A man murdered?"

Drudge stopped pacing and turned on him. His eyes were marked with red embers, and Christopher wondered if it was only the reflection of the candlelight that caused such an effect. He kept his mouth shut, realizing he'd rather not know. He saw in his host a very dangerous and calculating man, and any plan he set in action wasn't something to be taken lightly.

"Listen well, my friend, because your entire career and life depends on what I have to say," Drudge continued. "Grace Fitzpatrick will be blamed for the murder of this man. Her alibi will have his own alibi that contradicts hers. You don't want to be caught up in this scandal, nor do you want your affair to become public knowledge. By playing out these simple lines, you'll never hear your name mentioned in public. If you fail to comply with these plans, not only will your chances as the next mayor be snuffed, but so will your career as the district attorney."

Drudge came to the side of the bed and pulled out a corkscrew, which he held within the circle of candlelight. "This simple object can easily find its way to the police, who will find your fingerprints on it and accuse you of the murder of this pathetic man. Is he worth your career and freedom?"

"I don't even know who you're talking about," Christopher yelled, then dropped his head in his hands for speaking so loudly.

"Listen to me," Drudge whispered, his voice just a silky breath against Christopher's ear, startling him.

Christopher jerked his head up and pulled away, his eyes mere inches from Drudge's own. Fear paralyzed him when he saw how feral they appeared. There was a glint of evil in them, and it became clear that Christopher might have unwittingly aligned himself with something twisted and demented.

Drudge's slender fingers came up to stroke Christopher's cheek, like a loving caress meant to soothe but didn't. "There's one problem that requires some seeing to."

Christopher became caught up in the cadence of Drudge's singsong voice. His own voice croaked like a bullfrog's. "What . . . ?"

"That infernal baby growing inside Grace's gut," Drudge said with the strained air of contempt. His jaw grew rigid as his teeth clenched tight, and ugly veins stood out on his temple. The breath he spoke with suddenly grew hotter and noticeably staler. The visage with which he faced Christopher was frightening.

"My . . . ?" he struggled to say.

"The fetus lying curled in her womb. If the pregnancy is left to continue, certain tests can prove you are the child's father and all our work will be undone. That child validates you as Grace's alibi."

Drudge pulled back, moving away from the bed until he stood a good distance away. That was when Christopher saw he'd been holding the candelabrum the whole time and the backlight of his face was devilish.

"I . . ."

Drudge held up his hand to hush him, his fingers impossibly long and delicate, but not in a feminine way. More like they'd been sculpted from marble and had the same durability of granite. It wouldn't take much to imagine those fingers squeezing blood from a stone. "I'll take care of it. You wanted the child gone anyway. I'll see that it is."

A chill went up Christopher's spine, his body going cold. Last night, when he'd talked about aborting the baby, it had seemed clinical and safe, an acceptable medical procedure done a thousand times a day. The way Drudge spoke of destroying this child now was anything but. It was evil and murderous, bloody and unnatural.

But what other choice did he have.

His eyes dropped to his lap where the sheets had fallen in folds. Beneath them was nothing but the flesh and bone of his body, so vulnerably exposed to this man that he might be torn apart by the slashing of his fingernails. Christopher's headache grew as he considered his predicament. He worried about Grace for a brief moment, then looked up to follow Drudge's pacing, which he'd begun again. "Why . . .?"

"I want to own this city," Drudge said simply.

A bolt of electricity ran up Christopher's spine and brought a piercing pain to the back of his head. "What makes you think I'll go along with this?"

"I can give you great wealth and power, more than you can ever imagine." Drudge's voice was back to the melodic cadence that had quelled Christopher's fears last night. "Or I can destroy you without leaving a stain on my name. I can put another figurehead in the position I offer you now and give him everything you could have had. It's your choice."

Again, Christopher thought of Grace. He suddenly heard Drudge let out a chilling laugh. When he looked at him, Drudge had thrown his head back to do so. His jaw stretched to enjoy some bit of hilarity Christopher couldn't appreciate. Then he stopped, snapping his attention back to Christopher. His eyes were narrow and hooded, but they also burned with a gleam of evil.

"You coward," Drudge cursed bitterly. "I offer you the world and you quibble over how you'll kill an unborn fetus. You're a pathetic hypocrite. I should kill you now where you lay and dispose of my plans while I have the chance. Anyone would jump at the opportunity to enjoy unlimited success and fortune. But while you spoke of aborting your child only last night, you balk when I say I'll have it done for you now."

"I just don't want to see Grace get hurt," Christopher stammered, tears developing in his eyes. Strangely, they were not for Grace, but for himself, because he was afraid he might have upset his unlikely benefactor.

Drudge tilted his head quizzically. "Love, Christopher?"

"No," he said as he quickly shook his head. "No, I don't love her, but I do care about her. It's hard not to care about someone you've been fucking for the past year."

Drudge grinned at Christopher's vehemence. "And with that in mind, I believe I can bring you around. There's only one thing you have to do."

Christopher's eyes narrowed suspiciously. "What?"

"Just enjoy the remainder of your stay here until the weekend is over."

A bat flew from the Tower in jerky, sweeping movements, its rotund body bloated from feeding on the juices of canine carcasses found in an alley. From another slit in the Tower, another bat burst free, and then another, and another, until six of them flew around each other in a swirl. One by one, as if they'd elected a sequence to proceed by, they left the area of the Tower and headed westward.

And for every bat that flew from the Tower, a peregrine falcon left the building across the way.

The young man wearing a white cloth around his forehead and a red scarf around his throat heaved a heavy sigh as he rose from one of the pews. He almost cursed out loud but quickly curtailed his tongue in respect for the sanctity of God's house. He even tamed the vile thought from his mind until later, when he left the cathedral, finding that it had no business in the peace he sought there. He genuflected to a large crucifix behind the tabernacle before he turned to leave.

A shadow crossed his path as he walked down the main aisle to the double doors leading outside. He drew up with coiled reflexes, then relaxed when he saw who it was.

"Might I interest you in the Sacrament of the Eucharist tonight, my son?"

The question came from an elderly priest dressed in a black cassock with purple piping. In his hands he held a platen of unleavened bread and a chalice of deep purple wine.

The young man turned his eyes from the holy offering and kept his head bowed out of respect. "No thank you. I . . . haven't given penance lately."

"I can give you absolution, if you wish."

The priest seemed ready to set aside his possessions and do just that, but the young man shifted uneasily, his eyes avoiding the priest. "No, thank you, Father. I . . ." He shook his head. "I've sinned, for sure, but I feel no remorse yet to ask for forgiveness."

The monsignor stood before the brooding man, considering him with a deep concern steeped in curiosity and worry. The young man was dressed in dark clothes and swathed in strips of cloth that covered his forehead and hands, and a scarf around his throat. His coat was wrapped about him as if to ward off a chill, even though the cathedral was warm and dry. His eyes were the color of ice floes—a feature vain men would bargain dearly for—but he kept them cast down most of the time, seemingly ashamed.

"Father, I beg your pardon, but I have to be somewhere else right now." Uneasily, the young man edged around the priest and made a slight genuflection in the direction of the cross, before he pushed the door open and departed.

After leaving the cathedral, he sped through the streets with a sure and silent stride, his shadow moving ahead, then behind him, as he passed streetlights spilling glistening pools over the wet pavement. He kept mainly to the alleys and side streets, disdaining the main roads populated with pedestrian traffic. He skirted vagrants and pushed aside hands reaching out to beg of him. Normally, he wasn't so brusque, but the need to get to the west side of the city was urgent.

He paused at a corner, catching himself on the cornice of a building to glance at the sky glowing a murky gray. The dark cloud cover was heavy with rain that hadn't fallen yet, although the moisture in the air indicated it was only a matter of time. He pressed his eyes shut and grimaced. Peregrines. They were out already and that was good. He would need every last one of them.

A shriek sounded ahead of him. He opened his eyes to the welcoming sight of the red-tail hawk that was never far off. As the predatory bird swooped in front of him, he pushed off the side of the building and continued to run, following his guide with a fleet-footed agility he'd only recently acquired.

CHAPTER TEN

Grace dreamed fitfully, her eyelids twitching as her eyeballs darted back and forth while she viewed the horrors of her nightmare. Regardless, she understood that she was safe from the harm created by her mind and nothing physical could cross the boundaries of her subconscious. She felt the distant recognition of the dream state she was in and knew there would be an end. Only the mental anguish of her own fabricating forced her to suffer the anxiety that chased off a blissful night of sleep.

She dreamed of demons with gleaming red eyes and razor-sharp claws and teeth, the former dripping of poison and the latter glistening with saliva. She knew they'd been sent to kill her, and they chased her through thick woods choked with early morning mist. The moisture in the air was cloying and clung to her clothes, which also snagged on brambles and twigs, twisting her about in her flight until she was lost. Eventually, the undergrowth became so thick it clogged the path she ran along, making it almost impossible to wend her way through. She glanced over her shoulder and saw the demons gaining on her, their eyes bleeding in the dark. She turned back to the path and pushed her way through, making it a few steps before she became caught on the grasping fingers of a thicket. With desperation, she struggled forward, tearing her clothes and cutting her legs, until she could finally go no farther. She was held immobile in the unforgiving thorns of a patch of dead rose bushes.

She looked over her shoulder as tears formed in her eyes. She couldn't see the demons anymore. Instead, only the darkness peered back at her through the interstices of the dry sticks of the thicket she was caught in. She listened to the stillness of the woods, wary of predators around her, and felt a fear build in her that had the potential to become all controlling. There was nothing but the sound of the wind through the trees and a chattering of leaves as gusts swirled, but it was enough to exacerbate her panic. The sound should be soothing, but it only instilled more fear, forcing her to realize how truly alone she was.

Chattering leaves and a coolness of the breeze against her damp body.

Chattering . . .

Grace opened her eyes and saw that she was safe in the hospital, a warm blanket drawn up and tucked in at her sides, defying the feeling of being wet and cold. She found herself clutching her midsection, suddenly afraid of what terrible procedures were being discussed about her baby that she would have nothing to do with.

Chattering leaves.

She turned to the window, realizing the noise was coming from that direction. When she saw the black shape at the pane, she thought at first it was only a shadow from a cloud—until it danced in front of the window without passing. Then, as her eyes adjusted to the dark and she was able to discern the body behind the shadow, she saw it was a bat.

Startled, she clawed the sheet to hide from the beady eyes of the flying rodent. It was repulsive, its face wicked, looking like a creature straight out of Hell. Its ears rose high and pointed from the side of its head, and its wings twittered behind it. Its clawing legs scratched at the window, making the noises she'd dreamed were the wind through the trees.

Then it was gone and in its place was a creature she'd seen once before. She'd been trapped within its leathery wings before feinting away, smelled its rancid stench before gagging on her rising gorge, and felt its prickly flesh. Now its claws caught on the frame of the window as its wings swept languidly behind it, holding itself aloft, its eyes staring hungrily at her, burning a blood-red hue more unnerving than any other demonic aspect of its body.

Grace opened her mouth to scream but felt no breath enter her lungs. Instead, only gasps and wheezes came out. She clawed her way upright, while her legs scrambled to push her body higher against the headboard, her mind terrified and not functioning properly.

The creature suddenly brought its head back and smashed its crinkled brow against the window. The pane broke and buckled in, but the window remained intact by a thin mesh of wires tempered into the glass. Grace screamed, her mouth opening wide and uttering the highest pitch she could evoke, shocking the respectful silence of the hospital.

The young man skidded to a stop as he rounded one last corner and glanced up at the side of the hospital. The building was surrounded by bats, but the peregrines were there also. The birds circled higher, warily watching as their prey unwittingly stalked something beneath them.

The red-tail hawk suddenly shrieked. The young man looked up at a window on the fifth floor. A dark form clung to the window, its sweeping wings spanning over eight feet in width, its body blotting out the window and whatever lay beyond.

The flock of peregrines dove as a single organized force at the bats. The hawk flew on an updraft of wind, folding its wings against its body as it speared toward the creature clinging to the window, zeroing in on its head and uttering a shrieking war cry. As the bird reached the creature, it unfurled its wings, extending them to their fullest, which wasn't even half that of the suspended creature's wingspan. Regardless, the hawk put forth its talons in an effort to tear at the demon's head, slashing at it to rip the leathery flesh from its face. The hawk screeched as it attacked, tearing at the eyes of the demon with its hooked beak, gouging, blinding, rending.

Enraged, the demon flailed at the bird to fight it off. As the hawk flew away, the demon fell from the side of the building. It clutched at its wounds and found its eyes had been plucked out, leaving hollowed, bloody sockets. Blinded, it had to emit high sonar screeches to orient itself as it plummeted, confused. The piercing shrieks it issued echoed off the sides of the building with ear-splitting intensity. Before it could transform back into a bat and wing away to safety, the ground met it with such force that every bone in its body snapped like a twig.

The young man on the ground watched as the peregrines engaged the enemy. He knew the bats would eventually turn into their demon counterparts when they discovered they couldn't fend off the birds in their current state. When that happened, the creatures would have to land. It would be up to him then to contend with them.

He puzzled over why the bats would single out this one hospital among all the other buildings in the area. Then, realizing it was the same hospital where he'd delivered the woman the night before, he wondered why they would be so desperate to seek her out. The creature from the other night hadn't been scavenging for food among the city's homeless populace. It had been on a specific mission to find this one woman who'd managed to escape its clutches only with his help, now to have a slew of other demons sent after her. A realization that she was in danger for a reason he couldn't quite comprehend spurred him into action. The only thing he knew for certain was that if she was in danger from the demons, he wanted to know why.

He ran to the side of the building where a fire escape zigzagged up to the roof. That was where they would make their entry into the building. There was a door leading from the rooftop helipad into the hospital and it was a point of vulnerability. Uncontested and unseen, the demons could slip into the hospital and wreak havoc, slaughtering anyone daring to cross their path. A bloodbath would mark their way to the woman.

He leapt up and grasped the metal rung of the ladder, where he hauled himself up until he was able to put his feet on the rungs and climb up to the fire escape. Level by level, he climbed, pulling himself along as he turned on each landing. He kept a wary vigilance of the battle raging overhead and urged his legs to pump more urgently. At one point, he saw a black shape overwhelm one of the peregrines and sail over the parapet, disappearing onto the rooftop, one step closer to its goal.

Incensed, he climbed the rest of the staircase up to the roof with an unflagging endurance. As he reached the parapet and gripped the final rungs, he vaulted over the edge and landed solidly on his feet. His hands reached into the folds of his overcoat and pulled out two long daggers.

The demon turned on him with a hiss and fly of spittle, its leathery wings unfurling as one of its arms tried to swipe a razor claw at his throat. The young man feinted to his right. He held the weapon against his body in his left hand and displayed the other where the demon could see it.

The creature drew up and shrieked. It took alternating swipes as it advanced on him. The young man drew the demon in, rolling the dagger in his hand in a taunting gesture of a challenge. Enraged, the creature made a running charge, its eyes focused on the obvious weapon out in the open, its fangs dripping viscous poison.

As the demon closed in, the hidden blade swept up from the dark coat and severed the creature's neck all the way to the spine. Its head tipped backward and hung from a sliver of cartilage as its spasming body toppled.

With instinct ruling at the sense of a shadow approaching, the young man spun around and confronted a figure rising before him. He slashed with both daggers in a cross cut, missing with one but gouging the chest of another demon with the second weapon. He followed through with the attack and kicked the creature hard in the midsection. Stunned, it fell backward. He dropped on it, crushing its wings under his pinning weight. Moving quickly, he ran a cutting line across the creature's throat and jumped aside as a black ichor erupted.

The young man immediately regained his feet and twisted around, looking for other opponents, desperate to find them. He'd already killed two and the hawk had dispatched one, which meant three were left, presumably for the peregrines to deal with.

He saw the hawk wing over the parapet and fly past his shoulder, where it alighted on a rail of the helipad. The bird made no noise as it swiveled its head from side to side, looking about curiously, taking in the spoils of the short battle. It finally blinked its round black eyes and considered the man, who finally allowed himself to relax.

The young man walked to the edge of the rooftop, leaned over, and saw that the window outside the fifth floor was no longer bothered.

Deep in the bowels of the Tower, Drudge screwed up his face and said, "I'll be damned."

Grace screamed and screamed until she thought she could scream no more, and then she screamed again. The door to her room had been partially open but now it slammed against the wall as two people ran in to see what was wrong. They pawed at her as she flailed her arms, trying to get a grip on her wrists, to pull them down and settle her hysterics, but she fought them off. They called her name but her eyes were riveted to the damaged window and the horror of what had showed itself beyond the blackness.

"Grace!" the nurse shouted as she caught one wrist. She struggled to bring it under control as Doctor Perez snatched the other. "Grace, settle down!"

Slowly, as Grace saw that she was in the company of hospital staff, she began to quiet down. Her screams turned into hyperventilations. The doctor eased her forward so her head was between her knees, while the nurse rubbed her back. Doctor Perez ordered her to breathe slowly, steadily. In a few minutes, she did, and her head began to throb. Tears burst from her eyes as she buried her face in her hands.

"That's all right," Doctor Perez soothed. "If it helps to cry, by all means, cry." She motioned for the nurse to get a glass of water. "Whatever happened is just a bad memory now. Nothing will hurt you here. You're safe."

Grace sniffed and dragged her face from her hands. She blinked stupidly as she shook her head. "It was trying to get me."

Doctor Perez frowned. "What was trying to get you?"

"The monster."

"Honey, you just had a nightmare."

"Yes, I was having a nightmare." Grace fell into a strange calm now that the crisis was over. Only it wasn't a rational calm, since there were hysterics lurking just beneath it, like a shark under the crystal surface of the ocean, languidly swimming back and forth, its dorsal fin skimming the surf. She spoke slowly, tentatively at first, then raised her voice and rushed her words together. "But I woke up from the nightmare and saw that thing at the window."

The doctor shook her head and shushed her. "I wish I could give you something to help you sleep, but it wouldn't be good for the baby. I might be able to find you some warm milk, though."

"I'm not kidding," Grace nearly shouted. She pointed at the window. "See!"

Doctor Perez blithely looked in the direction Grace indicated. Then, with a double take, she turned to consider the window in earnest. She wandered over to the sill and laid a hand on the glass, where she felt how it bowed inward. Spider-web cracks snaked through the window pane, but the shards didn't fall out, not with the wire mesh holding it in place. Curiously, she pursed her lips together.

"That monster tried to break through to get me," Grace insisted.

Doctor Perez turned away from the damaged glass. "A bird, maybe, but not a monster. Birds sometimes crash into windows. The poor thing probably broke its neck on impact."

"It wasn't a bird," Grace cried. "I saw it. It was a repulsive thing with a black face and fangs and pointed ears and red eyes. It smashed its head into the window on purpose, to break the glass to get in. I watched it."

Doctor Perez returned to the bed and grasped Grace's hand, stroking it soothingly. She pulled the sheet up to cover Grace's body as much as possible, prompting her to slide down on the mattress. "You've had a traumatic experience and I think you need to talk about it."

"Yes," Grace nodded, grateful that someone would be willing to listen.

The nurse returned with a pitcher of ice water. Doctor Perez took it and poured a glass. She motioned for the nurse to be on her way, and Grace and the doctor were left alone.

"What happened last night?" Doctor Perez began. "Do you feel like you can talk about it?"

Grace nodded vigorously, desperate to talk about the incident. She felt that if she didn't get a chance to talk about what she'd seen—experienced—it would only exist in her mind, and that would mean she was crazy, since it would soon become just of a figment of her imagination.

"Okay," Doctor Perez said, pulling up a chair and taking a seat, assuming the posture of an attentive listener.

Grace hesitated as she considered just how much she should tell the doctor. She didn't know the woman, but Doctor Perez seemed genuinely concerned. However, there were aspects of everyone's life that should remain private. As Grace thought about the previous night's events, she began to realize there wasn't much she could tell her—or anyone, for that matter—that wouldn't make her seem despicable or altogether crazy. Eventually, she dropped her head and said, "I don't really remember much."

Doctor Perez studied her for a minute before resigning herself to Grace's reluctance to talk about it after all. "That's all right. Parts of the night, or all of it, may come back to you. A gentle reminder, a significant time, a face or word, anything may help refresh your memory." She leaned forward and patted her on the wrist.

Grace looked up beseechingly. How could she tell the doctor that the face in the window had brought the entire night back into focus? She wouldn't need any gentle reminder, significant time, or word to refresh her memory. The face in the window had done everything to accomplish that. Personally, she would have preferred never to remember anything of the incident.

"Do you remember the person who brought you here?" Doctor Perez asked, feeding out a line to see how much she did remember.

Grace pondered the question. She'd lost consciousness when she'd run into the monster in the alley and then had awakened in the hospital. The only person she remembered was the young man who'd pulled her would-be rapist off her.

"A young man," Doctor Perez hinted. "Probably one of the homeless, bundled up like it was winter."

"With a red scarf?" Grace inquired.

"Yes."

She shrugged. "I remember him but I don't know him. He . . . I thought he was trying to help, but then I thought . . ." Her lower lip quivered as she remembered the creature as it rose up before her and how its wingspan enveloped her in its stinking embrace. "I don't remember what happened, to tell the truth."

Doctor Perez heaved a sigh and patted her hand. "That's all right. We'll talk some more a little later. I've got to finish my rounds and tend to the ER, but I'll stop by before I go off duty in the morning. Get some sleep."

CHAPTER ELEVEN

Grace found it mildly curious the next morning to see two police cars parked on the curb outside her apartment complex when the hospitality shuttle dropped her off. Doctor Perez had been kind enough to arrange her transportation home and saw that she had hospital scrubs to wear instead of the raggedly raincoat she'd arrived in.

In the lobby, she tried to check her mail, but she didn't have her key. Instead, she went directly upstairs to her apartment on the seventh floor. She wondered briefly if she should have gone back to the Rialto to fetch her purse and clothes, but she imagined Christopher would eventually bring them by. If and when he did, she would tell him through the heavily barricaded door that he could leave her property right there on the hall floor and skedaddle. After what she'd been through, she never wanted to see him again.

When she got off the elevator, she noticed activity by an open door, which turned out to be the door to her own apartment. Putting more urgency into her stride, she soon found herself running toward the uniformed officer who guarded it. Beyond the open door, she could see people milling around in her living room, going through her things, judging her by what they saw, as if they had any right to. Her first instinct was to barge through the doorway, kicking the officer in the shin on her way, and demanding to know what the hell they were doing in *her* apartment.

"Whoa there, Miss," the officer said, holding out his arm to prevent her from entering. He stood massive and brooding before her, a gargantuan specimen of the city's police force, with an emphasis on the word force.

Grace looked over his shoulder and saw plainclothes officers pulling out drawers in her kitchen, tossing the cushions on her couch, swiping their hands under tables, along the seams of the upholstery, and examining her knickknacks. Their movements were callous and quick, unconcerned about putting anything back in its proper place, leaving her home a mess.

"This is my apartment," she informed the officer. "What's going on here?"

"You live here?" the officer asked. When she nodded, he took her by the arm and brought her into the apartment, nearly lifting her up on her toes as he marched her inside, his grip painful.

"What's going on?" she demanded, wincing at the pincher grip on her elbow. "I want to know what's going on here. This is my place."

"Sergeant Markey," the officer called, propelling Grace into the presence of a detective wearing a gold shield around his neck. "This lady here claims to be the resident."

The sergeant in question straightened from his search, which was presently concentrated on a hutch in the dining area. He immediately came forward, pulling out a folded packet of papers and handing it to her.

"Grace Fitzpatrick, we have a warrant to search your apartment."

"What . . . ?" she uttered, hesitantly taking the proffered papers without knowing what to do with them. She looked back at the sergeant, who was watching her reaction with great interest. "I don't understand. Did I do something wrong?"

"Housecleaning at the Rialto found your boyfriend dead when they went in to clean the room," Markey replied curtly. "You were at the Rialto Friday night, weren't you?"

. . . *your boyfriend dead* . . . was all she heard before the outer fringes of her vision began to blur, becoming gray, then black, leaving only a pinprick of vision directly in front of her. She suddenly felt faint as her knees threatened to buckle. When her legs went rubbery, she felt the detective reach out to steady her, his hands on her arm not as distressing as the uniformed officer's had been. She still felt far away and disconnected from her corporeal self, more like a disembodied spirit watching from outside her body.

". . . don't you sit down."

She allowed herself to be guided to the couch, which had to be put back in order before she could drop onto it. She sensed more than heard the detective tell someone to get her a glass of water, and she was vaguely aware of movement in the kitchen.

"You look pale . . ."

Christopher dead. Only minutes ago, she'd sworn she would never be able to care for a man who would promote aborting his own child. Friday night, in the thick of her misery, she might even have wished him dead. But after a night in the relative safety of the hospital, she'd become more lucid and civil. Death wasn't in her character to wish on anyone. No, she would rather Christopher grow old by himself, without the comfort and company of a loving wife and family. Yes, that was exactly what she would have hoped for him, had he not . . . died.

She suddenly experienced a one hundred eighty degree change of heart.

Poor Christopher. Dead. Her baby's father gone before the child was even born. Grace was sure he would have come around to love it, given time. He had none of his own, so he could hardly dismiss the one she was carrying. Once the baby had been given life and Christopher no longer saw it as a threat, he would surely have taken it to heart.

But not any longer. Christopher was dead.

"Miss Fitzpatrick, we'll need you to come down to the station to give a statement."

She looked up to see the detective passing a glass of water to her. "I can't believe this."

Markey handed her the glass. "You were at the Rialto Friday night?"

"Yes," she said, feeling her eyes begin to water and her nose start to drip. She sniffled.

"You were the last person to see your boyfriend alive. We need you to come down to the station. One of the uniformed officers will take you."

Her eyes shifted around the room, seeing the mess they'd made of her home. A thought struck her as to why they were there. "You think I killed him?"

"Someone did," Markey responded, beckoning a uniformed officer over, a different one than the hulking monstrosity who'd escorted her into the apartment. "Take Miss Fitzpatrick to the Homicide office and stay with her until I get there."

The officer nodded and stood expectantly to the side. Grace's eyes shot back and forth between the two policemen. When the detective first mentioned that Christopher was dead, she'd thought it was of natural causes. A heart attack, stoke, embolism, or some other sudden affliction. It hadn't occurred to her that they were searching her apartment because they believed she might have murdered him.

"How did he die?"

"Miss Fitzpatrick," Markey said impatiently, "please, just go with the officer."

Shakily, she stood, the glass of water gripped weakly in her hand. Tears again threatened to flood her eyes, but she swore she wouldn't crumble. "Can I change first?"

Markey studied her peculiar attire and called a female officer to accompany her to the bedroom. Grace stepped tentatively around the clutter and went into her room, where she did cry. The mere sight of her bed torn apart and the linens stripped from the mattress gave her such a gut-wrenching kick that she began to sob. The female officer stood in the doorway while she slowly opened drawers for fresh undergarments and went into the closet for a denim sundress. Between the intermittent straightening of a toppled figurine and the closing of an open drawer, Grace dressed, then followed the officer out.

The assigned officer took control of her from that point on. She meekly allowed him to lead her out of the apartment, just thankful he wasn't putting her in handcuffs. In a daze, she went down to the sidewalk in front of her apartment building and slid into the back of a police car, feeling herself removed from reality. She made no conversation nor asked any questions to set herself at ease, nor did the officer make any attempt to comfort her. He was only the back of a head above the driver's seat, turning to look either right or left as he navigated his way through traffic. Grace spent the drive to the police station in a stupor, her thoughts on the man she'd once loved.

She had no idea how long it took the officer to drive her to the station, but it seemed as if she'd only gotten in the car when he pulled into a fenced lot with other police cruisers. He stoically let her out of the back seat and made her walk in front of him as he gave her directions which way to go. To the back door, wait while he punched in a code, down the hall, turn left, toward the elevator, up, take a left, three doors down to a door with a frosted glass top half that said in big bold letters: HOMICIDE.

Grace swallowed bile at the ominous word printed at eye level, until it swung inward as the officer opened it. A nudge on her back convinced her to move forward, and she stepped into a world as alien and terrifying as the night before had been. There were people at various jobs, tasks she performed every day at work: typing, filing, pouring coffee, and making phone calls. But these people were typing the final touches on a person's life, filing away autopsy reports, sifting through mounds of evidence, making phone calls to loved ones. The gravity of their work was overwhelming, and it affected the lives of others in such a profound way. Miserably, she was now a part of their work.

The uniformed officer made inquiries as to where he should put her until Sergeant Markey arrived. A heavyset detective glanced up from picking at a collection of grapes in a Tupperware container. His cheeks bulged like a chipmunk's, and his mouth worked quickly to pop the grapes one by one down his throat.

"That the femme fatale?" Peter Lumas asked when he stopped chewing.

The officer moved closer to the detective and explained that Markey had told him to sit with Miss Fitzpatrick until he returned. Lumas got up and swaggered over to a row of doors along the far wall. He opened one and motioned for Grace to go in and have a seat.

"Please," Grace started, terrified by the prospect of being shut in a room with nothing but a flat table and a couple of chairs. "I really don't understand why I'm here."

"Listen, Miss, Sergeant Markey'll be here in a bit and he'll tell you all about what happened. Then, at that point, you can answer whatever questions he has."

"Will I be able to go home?" she asked hesitantly.

"We'll see."

She jumped when the door closed behind her, sounding like a resounding drum being hit with a baseball bat. She turned to face a room adorned in filth. The flat carpet was frayed and stained, the walls were marked and flaking, and the table was scarred and scratched. It left her with a feeling of depression and self-deprecation.

How had she come to this point in her life all of a sudden? Why had falling in love with Christopher left her with such a sense of whorish disgust that she felt foul and unscrupulous, when she had only thought it would be such a wonderful thing to be in love?

She pulled out a chair and sank into it with a sense of abandonment. Only the few people she'd met at the hospital had offered her any compassion during her horrible weekend ordeal.

Thinking such miserable thoughts, Grace dropped her face into her hands and cried. She felt no sense of comfort from the bawling, no soul cleansing from the effort, no uplifting of her spirits. She only wanted a chance to repeat the last few weeks of her life so she never would have agreed to Christopher's proposal for the weekend. She wished she had stayed home and read a good mystery instead of becoming part of one. Right now she wanted nothing more than to see the outside of this room just one more time, so she didn't feel like it was her prison. Yet only time ticked by as she waited stiffly in one of the hard chairs positioned at the table.

She wasn't aware how long it was before the door opened again, nor how many tears she'd shed, nor how many inconsequential thoughts swirled through her head. Eventually, the door did open and her head whipped up from hanging low, her eyes puffy and hot.

Three men walked into the room. The door closed again, leaving Grace feeling as if the lions had just entered the den. One of the men was Sergeant Markey, the other was the overweight officer who'd put her in the room, and another was a man she didn't recognize but who was dressed in a snappy brown business suit. He looked rather dapper for an officer, and she believed in her heart that he wasn't.

Sergeant Markey took one of the chairs in front of her, the other seat being taken by the unknown gentleman. Markey laid a legal pad in front of him and took out a pen. He scribbled a few notes on the top of the first sheet, which Grace strained from the other side of the table to read upside down. It only hurt her eyes to try to decipher his illegible scrawl from where she sat, so she gave up. When she saw Markey look up and catch her spying, she quickly glanced away, embarrassed. Markey pulled a sheet of paper from within his pad and turned it for her to read.

"Miss Fitzpatrick," he said rather dryly, "you have the right to remain silent and do not have to talk to me. You do not have to answer any of my questions. Do you understand?"

The context of those words overwhelmed her, and she felt like she was going to cry again. But she suffered through it and bit on her lip to redirect her misery. Slowly, she nodded.

The detective handed her the pen. "Would you please initial on the line that you understand."

Her hand reached out and weakly took the pen. It was weighty and cold in her fingers. Gingerly, she scribbled her initials and tried to hand the pen back. He indicated the next line.

"Should you talk to me, anything you say may be introduced into evidence in court against you. Do you understand that right?"

She nodded again and scribbled her initials. Markey proceeded through the rights waiver form until she had initialed each of the subsections, then signed the bottom. She chose to speak with him without an attorney, mainly because she had no attorney, nor could she afford one on her pittance of a secretary's salary. She wouldn't know the first thing about finding one, even if it was a court-appointed attorney. Finally, she returned the pen to him.

"Miss Fitzpatrick, I'm Detective Roy Markey, and this," he indicated over his shoulder to the overweight plainclothes officer, "is Detective Peter Lumas. Beside me is Assistant District Attorney Robert Prescott. We're here to take your statement of what happened on Friday night, when you were at the Rialto, in room 3004. Just so we don't have any misunderstanding as to the crime in question, we're investigating the murder of Mr. Charles Driskell, of 375—"

"What?" Grace interrupted, drawing herself up from her terrible depression. She heard only monotone blather, but she suddenly picked up on two words that didn't sound right. "What name did you just say?"

Markey hesitated, then glanced at Prescott. "Charles Driskell."

Grace thought her face might have cracked into a smile but it didn't, although she did feel her heart kick appreciatively at the name the detective spoke. "Charles Driskell? I don't know any Charles Driskell. I didn't have any plans to spend the weekend with anyone by that name."

Markey again hesitated. He tapped his pen on the pad. "That's the name of the man who was murdered in room 3004. You did spend Friday evening in room 3004, didn't you?"

"That's the room I was supposed to be in, yes."

"Were you there at all on Friday?" Markey asked.

"Yes, but I didn't stay all night."

Markey flipped the pen to a more functional position. "Why don't we start from the beginning. What happened on Friday, say, in the morning?"

Grace felt more in control, her spirits buoyed by the fact that she didn't know the man who'd been murdered. "I went to work at Demars, Braxton, and Hilfinger. It's an architectural firm. I work as a secretary for Mauricio Hilfinger—"

"That's fine," Markey interjected, showing a bit of impatience. "You were at work all day?"

"Except for lunch."

"And what time did you leave? For the evening, that is."

"I get off at five, but I didn't leave the office until five fifteen."

"Where did you go?"

"I was picked up downstairs by a driver and taken to the Rialto. I was supposed to spend the weekend there with my boyfriend."

"And who *is* your boyfriend?" Lumas asked from his place against the wall.

Markey glanced over his shoulder at Lumas, as did the assistant D.A. and Grace. Despite the interruption, Markey picked up on the question. "If it wasn't Charles Driskell you were with, who was supposed to be in that room with you?"

Grace hesitated before replying. She glanced at the assistant district attorney and winced when she considered the answer. Christopher was already upset with her for getting pregnant, primarily because of what it would do to his campaign chances, but she suspected he would be absolutely furious if he was pulled into a murder investigation.

"I would prefer to keep his name out of this."

"Miss Fitzpatrick," Markey said, pursuing the line of questioning Lumas had started. "Your indiscretions are not this Department's concern. However, the reason why your identification and personal effects were found at the scene of a homicide is."

"Then I'll tell you why my things were there," she answered as graciously as she could, hoping not to irritate them with her hedging.

"Miss Fitzpatrick," the assistant district attorney interjected. "How well you answer these questions will determine whether or not you go home this afternoon. Do I make myself clear?"

She swallowed thickly and nodded slowly.

"How about this, Miss Fitzpatrick," Markey cut in. "Did your boyfriend ever show up at the hotel?"

"Yes," she answered, her lip quivering. She was beginning to see that she might have to mention Christopher's name to pull herself out of the fire and put herself back into the frying pan.

"What time did you and your boyfriend reach the room?"

"Just before six. I went up to the room alone but he joined me shortly thereafter."

"And he can corroborate that he was with you?"

"Yes," she murmured.

"Then you would want to tell us his name," Markey pointed out.

The corner of her lip tugged unwillingly. She washed her face with her hands and sighed. Again, she looked at the assistant district attorney. "He's a married man."

"So was Mr. Driskell."

"He's a well-known married man," Grace clarified.

"Your choice, Miss Fitzpatrick," Markey advised.

Again, she sighed. "It's Christopher Purcell."

"Ho boy," Lumas said.

Markey pulled back until he sat ramrod straight in his chair. Prescott blinked, and blinked again.

"The district attorney?" Markey finally inquired.

She nodded.

Markey turned fully on Prescott. He flourished a hand at Grace. "Do you want to take over?"

Prescott shook his head to throw off a muddle of confusion. He looked at Markey, registered his words, looked at Grace, then gestured to Markey. "You're doing just fine."

Markey sighed. "Well, um, let's see, uh, your boyfriend—the D.A.—um, was in room 3004 at around six o'clock, Friday night."

Their confidence had been shattered by the name she'd dropped. Grace found it thrilling and frightening at the same time. "Yes, I'd say it was around then."

"And it was just the two of you?"

"Yes."

"You, the two of you, did . . . were . . . um . . ."

"We were alone the entire time I was there," Grace helped out. "But I didn't stay. We had a fight. I'm not going to say about what. That's a personal matter and it has nothing to do with why I was there or why a man was murdered. Suffice it to say, I got upset and ran out on him."

Markey regained some of his composure when she spoke with angst again. "What time was that?"

"I'm not sure, but it couldn't have been too late. Probably eight. I was so upset I left all my things there."

"Where did you go?"

"I just wandered around. I'd realized that I'd left my purse and money behind and I couldn't take a cab home. But I didn't want to walk home in the dark, either. I thought about going back to the hotel and even headed there."

"Did you make it back?"

"No," she said softly, remembering the horror of that night, the grimy feel of her attacker's hands on her flesh, then, worse, the stench of the creature she'd been embraced by. An involuntary shiver ran up her spine. "I was attacked."

"Did you report this to the police?" Markey asked, one brow upraised.

"No. I . . . I was knocked unconscious."

"Really?" Markey said. "For the entire weekend?"

She snapped out of her dismal reflection to glare at him. "No, not for the entire weekend. I was taken to the hospital."

"Which hospital?"

"St. Jude's. I was there until this morning. That's why I was wearing those hospital scrubs."

"I suppose we can check that out. Who was the attending physician when you came in?"

"Doctor Monica Perez," Grace answered, relieved that her alibi could be checked out. She felt inadequate explaining that she'd been wandering the city when they believed she was in a room with a murdered man. The hospital records would show the time she had to account for.

Or would they? She thought about asking what time the man had been murdered, but such a question might lead to suspicions about her interest in the specifics of the crime. She calculated that she could have been wandering the streets between eight and ten, during which time she'd been attacked.

What time had she arrived at the hospital? Had the young man who'd come to her rescue dawdled in her delivery to the emergency room? Had he taken her by car or walked her in?

How long had it taken him to get her to the hospital, and more importantly, what time had Charles Driskell been killed?

Grace began to chew on the inside of her cheek. She glanced down at her hands and noticed how they fiddled restlessly on the table. Discreetly, she pulled them off the table and hid them in her lap, aware that they were betraying her discomfort.

Markey leaned back in his chair and beckoned Lumas forward. He whispered to him from behind a cupped hand and Lumas left. Markey shared some secret words with Prescott, who pushed his chair back to follow Lumas out of the room.

Grace stared suspiciously at Markey, blinking nervously and finding the room suddenly very hot. Her eyes drifted to other parts of the room in an effort to avoid Markey's stare. However, her eyes wouldn't remain still and, instead, gave her the illusion of guilt.

Finally, she couldn't stand the persistent silence any longer. "Where did they go?"

"To check out a few details."

"Oh."

Again, the silence continued. Grace shifted. She pushed aside a lock of hair that fell across her face, then sat on her hands to prevent them from shaking.

"Nervous?" Markey asked.

She jerked at his question. "Wouldn't you be?"

He made a casual gesture of dismissal with his hand. "Not if I hadn't done anything wrong."

"I may be guilty of adultery, Detective, but I'm not guilty of hurting anyone. Maybe I just don't feel comfortable talking about my sins."

"Maybe you need a priest."

She pretended to laugh at his sarcasm, then looked away. Markey leaned back in his chair, taking on an air of leisure that was infuriating to her. Finally, the door opened and the assistant district attorney returned, closing the door and retaking his seat. Markey straightened up.

"I got a hold of his wife," Prescott began. "She said he's been out of town for the weekend on a campaign rally. He won't be back until later tonight."

"Christopher? Are you talking about Christopher?"

Both Markey and Prescott looked at Grace with annoyance. Markey ignored her question and turned back to Prescott. "If Purcell and Miss Fitzpatrick were supposed to spend the weekend at the Rialto, where did Purcell spend the rest of it after Friday night?"

Prescott leaned back and said nothing.

CHAPTER TWELVE

Three hours after being released from police custody, Grace found herself wandering the same streets she had Friday night. She'd been told not to plan any weekend trips with Mr. Purcell—or anyone else for that matter—to which she assured them that she had no plans. The police had grilled her for another hour before finally deciding her story was consistent, but there were points they needed to check out before they'd be in touch.

The sergeant and his colleagues had been condescending, at best. They'd exuded contempt for her from the beginning and obviously suspected she was the murderer, or at least the mistress of a man she'd never actually met.

Which led her to wonder why a stranger had ended up in Christopher's suite anyway. What liaisons had Christopher arranged after she'd fled the room? Was Mr. Driskell one of Christopher's campaign contributors? Was he a benefactor or an enemy? And why had he been murdered? Had Christopher committed the crime, or was he merely an unsuspecting pawn?

She shivered in the chill of the afternoon. The sky was overcast but it hadn't let loose its deluge just yet. Striations in the clouds made it appear as if a cold front was moving in. She wished she'd brought a sweater to cover her sleeveless shoulders, but she'd never made it home after leaving the police station. Instead, she found herself walking the same course she'd taken Friday night, before she'd been attacked.

In the time since she was taken into police custody, Grace had come to the conclusion that she just might be used as the ultimate scapegoat. The more she thought about Christopher being brought in for questioning the more she became aware that he was Sergeant Markey and the assistant district attorney's puppet master. There was no way Christopher would allow himself to become wrapped up in a murder investigation when he was campaigning to be the next mayor. He wouldn't even allow his name to be connected with an extramarital affair and love child. Whatever had happened in that hotel room, it was likely to fall entirely upon her shoulders. Her only alibi was the kid she'd met in the alley two nights ago, a stranger wrapped in all dark clothing and masked in shadows, who'd provided her no name or calling card.

Which was why she now found herself wandering the same streets where she'd encountered him Friday night.

She'd begun her search by tapping people on the shoulders and asking them if they knew of a young man who fit the description of her rescuer. Most people looked at her as if she had no right to address them, much less touch them, and turned away without giving her the benefit of an answer. Some merely shook their heads and went on their way. Regardless, none gave her an answer she could pursue. She spent hours walking in circles, asking everyone she met the same question, only to receive a cold reception for her troubles.

The afternoon grew old as the evening approached. She considered the coming dusk and was quite sure she didn't want to be there when darkness came. She'd already seen how mean the streets could get at night and didn't want to risk another encounter with whatever had attacked her in the alley, both human and inhuman.

"Ya ain't never gonner find who yer lookin' fer durin' the daylight."

Grace spun around and jumped when she saw the same old bum she'd collided with the night she was attacked. He was dressed in the same filthy, tattered clothes and still reeked an odor that was foul and rancid. He smelled of liquor beyond the stench of bodily excretions, and crumbs littered the beard at his chin. His mouth smacked fitfully as he chewed on something that only showed as stringy crud when he opened his mouth, and pieces of food were caught between his brown teeth. His dull blue eyes were rheumy and rimmed with jaundiced corneas.

Grace involuntarily recoiled from him. "Pardon me?"

He continued to stare at her, his jaw chomping on something indescribable, his cracked lips coated in a crusty film. Grace wondered if he had spoken to her at all, for the empty way he looked at her, not responding to her question. She remembered what Doctor Perez had said about the kid who'd brought her to the hospital—how he might have been one of the homeless living on the streets himself—and wondered if it was possible this old man might know him.

"There was a kid Friday night," she began, no longer focusing on the bum's grotesque features, but now seeing him as a source of invaluable information. "He was in this area and he saved me from being . . ." She held herself back from giving away any intimate details to a horribly embarrassing experience. "He was dressed in dark clothes, with a long overcoat and sneakers. He wore white rags around his hands and a red scarf around his neck. I couldn't see much of his face—"

"Aye," the old bum said, chewing.

"You know who I'm talking about." She took a hopeful step forward, then hesitated getting any closer when she got a whiff of him.

The bum laughed, showing her the residue trapped in his mouth. He scratched his stomach and patted his girth. "Everyone on the streets knows Slash."

"Slash?" she said, working the name on her tongue. It made no significant tug on her memory, and she shook her head. "No one's admitted knowing him but you."

"That's 'cause ain't no one knows where to look fer an angel."

She screwed up her face and offered him a crooked smile. "He's an angel, then?" she asked sardonically.

He leaned forward and brought his hands up in front of his face, which he used to stress what he was saying. "You don't go lookin' fer an angel, deary. He'll find you when you need his help."

"I need his help now," she said petulantly.

He looked at her with distinction and shrugged. "Ain't no one gonna find him in the daylight."

She watched helplessly as the old bum turned and strolled away, dismissing her as easily as that. Desperately, she ran after him. "Please tell me where I can find him. I need to speak to him. I'm in deep trouble, and he's the only person who can help me out of it."

The old bum continued to shuffle away, his head scrunched down between his shoulders, humming to himself. When he gave no response, she stomped her foot like a child.

"Please, I have no one else to turn to."

The bum turned slowly to face her. He peered at her out of the corner of his eye. "You can try Our Lady of the Blessed Virgin Mother. There's plenty of help there for wayward souls."

She tossed her head. "Come on, please. I need to find him."

The old bum turned his back on her and shuffled along, stooped with age. "'ware the darkness, little lady. There's evil out at night."

Grace looked west and saw that the sun was setting. She knew dusk would suddenly take over and night would follow. She shivered when she thought of being caught in the darkness, until she remembered that she had money for a cab.

She turned back to ask the man another question but he'd already disappeared, slipping into the shadows of the buildings. Feeling nothing but the hopelessness of the weekend weighing upon her, she ran her hands through her hair and headed in the direction of the main street, where she could hail a cab home.

* * * * * *

"Night's coming."

A man dressed in a second-hand army jacket and a baseball cap leaned out the window of a van parked at the curb and made a show of his prediction. When he pulled back inside, his forehead was wrinkled. "I don't want to be anywhere near that broad when those fucking bats show up."

The van's driver had been watching Grace as she meandered through the streets, his interest piqued as to what she might be doing.

John Murdock and his business associate had been following Grace Fitzpatrick at a crawl, keeping well out of sight. The woman seemed to be looking for someone or something, and she was growing more frustrated as time went by. Murdock looked at his watch. G.W. was right. They only had another half hour before the sunlight was entirely gone.

Murdock heaved a sigh of exasperation. "I don't give a fuck about the bats. I just don't want to lose the cash. A simple fucking job and the bitch is gonna get snatched by the bats instead. Why doesn't she just go home?"

G.W. leaned forward and watched Grace. "She's on the move again."

Murdock glanced out the window and sneered. "Let's hope she's finally calling it a day." He grasped the gear shift and slipped the van into drive.

"Why don't we just snatch her now?"

Murdock looked sideways at his partner, his eyes narrow and dangerous. He opened his mouth to say something but then glanced back at the woman, who was digging in her purse. The pedestrian traffic was light on this block. Sunday evening didn't hold much interest for strollers and commuters on a street of drab tenements and closed shops. Just a few homeless bums who were settling in for the night in the doorways, their beds nothing but the flattened sides of cardboard boxes. Grace Fitzpatrick stood out like a lost soul, her vulnerability blazing around her like a halo.

"Let's not let that bonus go to the birds," Murdock decided.

"Spare some change, buddy?"

Murdock jerked on the steering wheel when a bum popped up at the open window. The old coot's breath stank of liquor and halitosis, and Murdock pulled back to get away from its almost palpable stench. He went for the window crank to roll up the glass but the old man's hands were on the open frame.

"Get the fuck away from me, old man," Murdock snapped. He groped between the two seats and snatched up a block of wood, which he used to smack down on the bum's fingers.

The old man cursed and cradled his hands against his chest. He backed away from the window and stepped onto the curb as the van shot away like a cannon. Its ugly bulk rocked on its skinny tires when it made a hasty, uncontested U-turn and headed back in the opposite direction. It continued down the street at an exceedingly slow rate of speed.

Murdock stopped the van about fifty feet behind Grace as she walked unsuspectingly toward the corner. G.W. jumped out and slammed the door, then walked after her at a brisk pace. Murdock sped forward, passed Grace, and pulled over to an empty space on the curb. He watched from the side mirror as his partner skip-walked up on the woman, pacing out his stride so he reached her just short of where the van was stopped. Murdock clambered between the captain's chairs to get into the cargo area. He grasped the handle and slid the side door open at the same time G.W. was confronting Grace Fitzpatrick.

Grace looked up in surprise when the man in the army jacket pressed the barrel of a gun into the side of her ribs. He was whispering something to her, to stay calm and make no sound. If she screamed or cried for help he would pull the trigger and leave her with a gaping hole in her side. She gawked at him, her mouth opening and closing without making any sound.

Murdock made an impatient motion for them to hurry. G.W. grabbed Grace by the elbow and propelled her toward the open door. She hesitated, but the gun drilled more painfully into her side. Murdock heard her plead for her life with a voice stricken with terror.

Good God, why did he have to listen to this?

He moved aside as his partner pushed the woman into the van, now growing more irritated with her tears and unwillingness to cooperate. G.W. looked up and down the sidewalk. He raised the gun to strike her, but Murdock caught his wrist in the downward stroke and stared hard at him.

"No marks," Murdock warned.

G.W. sneered viciously at him, then jumped into the van and slammed the side door. He scrambled over the woman and Murdock in order to get into the driver's seat.

"Please, please, please," Grace whimpered, clawing her way to the corner of the van, away from the man who told her other attacker to leave no marks. She brought her legs together and her knees up to her chest, hugging them with her arms. "Please, just leave me alone. I was just going home. Take my purse. Anything you want in there is yours; just leave me alone."

"Lady, shut the fuck up," Murdock snapped as he put a hand to his temple. He checked his watch to note the time. When he'd opened the door, he'd seen the sunlight fading fast. They'd have to bring Grace to the Tower before it was completely dark. Either that or the fucking bats would be after them, too.

Grace stripped her purse from her shoulder, the gesture abrupt and angry. With venom, she threw it at him. "Take the goddamn thing. It's yours, you fucking queer."

Her hand flew to her mouth to cover its unexpected outburst. "I didn't mean that. Just take the purse and let me go. Please, I don't need this. I can't take it anymore."

Murdock batted the purse aside, the strap tangling up in his hand. "Drive," he ordered G.W.

When the van jolted away from the curb, Grace squealed and toppled forward. Murdock threw his hands out for balance, pressing his back against the wall and shimmying up. He glanced out the front windshield and saw that they were heading west, into the only remaining light of day, pursued by the night like an ominous ghost ship on the waves of a black sea. A shiver ran up his spine. He clung to the back of the passenger seat and braced himself as G.W. turned sharply to avoid going the wrong way down a one-way street. He didn't need to tell his partner that they were running out of time; G.W.'s frantic driving was evidence that he already knew.

"Please don't hurt me," Grace wept. She spoke meekly. "I don't have much, but you can have whatever's there. Just let me be."

"Lady, shut up!" Murdock barked, his hand going to his temple to massage it. He looked over at his partner. "Can't you drive any faster?"

"I'm not the dickhead who waited till the last minute to grab her," G.W. said, his hands repositioning themselves on the steering wheel. He leaned forward to look through the windshield.

Murdock opened his mouth to curse his partner but closed it when a loud thud sounded against the roof of the van. He looked up, squinting his eyes in an attempt to see through the ceiling. Although he couldn't see what was on the roof, he could just make out an indentation where whatever had made the noise remained. He reached into his jacket and pulled out his own pistol, pointing it at the roof of the van, the barrel trembling.

The thing on the roof began to move, making hollow thunking noises as it moved forward, until it was finally over the cab.

"What the fuck?" G.W. cursed, hunching his head down between his shoulders. The van rocked back and forth as his hands jostled the steering wheel.

"Just drive!" Murdock commanded.

"It's the bats!" G.W. shrieked. "They're already here!"

"It's not time yet," Murdock shouted, seeing yet a glimmer of daylight ahead of them, above the skyline. Drudge had promised them the bats wouldn't leave the Tower until full dark. They couldn't.

Still, he didn't trust Drudge any farther than he could throw the wily bastard.

"Fuck it, shoot it!" G.W. shrieked. "Shoot it!"

Murdock pulled the trigger. A deafening boom echoed within the van, filling the compartment with the smell of gunpowder. A gaping hole puckered the roof where the depression had been. Grace screamed and covered her head.

Murdock seemed to gain confidence with the shot. He pointed the gun and fired again, letting out a rallying cry as he did. Gray smoke puffed around the barrel and dissipated in a blue swirl. Grace cried out again, while G.W. barked maniacally from the driver's seat.

A blunt object smashed into the windshield, creating a shattered—but still intact—depression in the safety glass. The immense spider web spread across the entire window. G.W. screamed and jerked the wheel to the side. The vehicle lurched up on two wheels, hit the curb and rebounded. G.W. slammed on the brakes and the van fishtailed, throwing Murdock to the floor.

Grace braced herself in the back corner. She watched in horror as the driver's body was flung over the steering wheel and Murdock became tangled among his own arms and legs. In the confusion, she looked at the back door and reached for the handle. Slowly, but decisively, she yanked on it and found it unlocked. With a lurch of desperation, she flung herself at the doors and barreled out the back, tumbling to the hard asphalt with an unforgiving thump. Her shoulder took the brunt of the impact but her terror blinded her to any pain delivered by the fall.

G.W.'s breath was forced from his lungs when his chest made contact with the steering wheel. He quickly recovered, remembering the bats must be about, and looked through the damaged windshield to see if he could spot them in the sky. Instead, through the few inches of undamaged glass, he saw a dark figure standing in front of the van, its form silhouette against the darkness of the alley, barely discernible.

In the back, Murdock clawed after the gun he'd lost, then pulled his legs under him and gripped the back of the captain's chair to upright himself. He, too, looked through a small area of undamaged windshield and saw the figure in front of the van. He pointed the gun at the shape, his hand shaking tremulously. Under his breath, he cursed his fear.

The figure moved out of the darkness and into the perimeter of the headlights. A dark coat obscured whatever else he was wearing, but both Murdock and his partner could tell it was the same bum from earlier.

"You got no business with the lady," the old vagrant said, moving closer still.

CHAPTER THIRTEEN

Drudge looked at his watch and frowned. He'd hoped his original plan would have worked, but without the woman at the Tower by now, he'd have to send his minions to get the job done right.

Poor Grace, he commiserated, fate didn't shine too brightly for that young woman. A pity. Oh well, he'd get over it.

Christopher wasn't home more than a half hour—having uncharacteristically kissed his wife on the lips and acted as if nothing had happened over the weekend—before he received a phone call demanding his attention behind closed doors. He made sure Anne was busy preparing supper before he settled behind his desk in his home office and reconnected the line he'd put on hold in the living room.

"All right, I can talk now," he said.

"Mr. Purcell, I hate to bother you, but . . ."

Christopher knew what was coming. A kick in his gut warned him that the homicide case Drudge had told him about had finally made it to the District Attorney's office. He worried how deeply he'd been implicated.

"What is it, Robert?"

"Well," Prescott started, clearing his throat with a cough. "Well, um, there's been a murder."

"Yes?"

"At the Rialto."

"Yes?"

"A woman's identification was found in the room."

"Yes?" Christopher found it fascinating how calmly he spoke.

"We spoke with her."

"And?"

"She, um, she mentioned she was with a man the night of the murder."

"The murdered man, I suppose," Christopher said.

"No, sir."

"Who, then?"

"You."

"Really?"

"Yes."

"Well," Christopher said in a contemplative voice, "was she pretty?"

"Beautiful."

"Well, then, I'm sorry I wasn't there."

Prescott chuckled. He seemed relieved that his boss was taking this so well and making light of it. However, that didn't conclude their conversation. "Mr. Purcell?"

"Yes?"

"May I ask you a question?"

"Yes."

"Where were you Friday night?"

"Mr. Prescott?" Christopher asked, using Robert's surname for effect.

"Yes?" Prescott squeaked.

"I think the appropriate procedure would be for you to read me my rights."

"Well, um, sir, uh—"

"Robert," Christopher chuckled softly, "I'm toying with you. Let's see, Friday night I was in Lancaster with a Mr. Ford Brandon from the Chesterfield-Flaxton Foundation. We had dinner at eight and cocktails afterward. I stayed at his estate, in the guest bedroom. Do you need to know how I spent my Saturday? My Sunday?"

"No, sir," Prescott answered nervously. "Sir, I'll have to . . ."

"Yes, I understand. But, please, Robert, don't mention the details of your inquiry to Mr. Brandon. He's going to endorse me for mayor, and I wouldn't want my name to be slandered by association."

"Yes, of course."

"Now, may I ask *you* a question?" Christopher asked.

"Of course, Mr. Purcell."

"Who was this lady who claims she was with me Friday night?"

"A Grace Fitzpatrick. Do you know her?"

"Blonde hair, blue eyes, killer body?"

"Yes, sir," Prescott responded, sounding slightly miffed that the District Attorney might know the woman who claimed him as her alibi.

"Curious, Robert?"

"Slightly."

"About two years ago, when I was an assistant D.A., I was working a fraud case against a land developer. Grace Fitzpatrick worked for Demars, Braxton, and Hilfinger, I believe it was, a surveying/architectural firm that helped put the case together. She was a secretary for one of the firm's partners, and she and I passed a lot of information back and forth. We shared a few late night dinners, had a brief affair, and then we broke it off. I'd say it lasted no longer than a couple of months. I haven't heard her name in ages."

"She remembers you," Prescott said.

Christopher drummed up a smile. "I'll take that as a compliment."

"This is very serious, sir."

"Yes, Robert, I understand that," he said somberly. "But I trust you'll keep my past indiscretions out of the public eye. What happened two years ago shouldn't have any bearing on what happened Friday night just because this young lady remembers my name."

"I understand. Mr. Purcell, in your opinion, is Ms. Fitzpatrick capable of murder?"

"I don't remember her as being violent, but I suppose we all have our limits. Robert, I'm not going to pursue this investigation with you. If I'm a suspect, then I trust you'll do a thorough and professional investigation without my interference. I'll be more than willing to cooperate, but the only thing I ask is that this doesn't become a matter of public interest."

"Yes, sir. I appreciate your candor."

Christopher hung up and leaned back in his chair, wiping the sweat from his brow. He was amazed at how easy it was to answer Prescott's reluctant questions. He only hoped that he'd be able to maintain his composure in a face-to-face interrogation. He felt strangely disassociated from Grace now, as if the last time he'd had any social interaction with her had actually been two years ago.

Going over their relationship, Christopher realized that he'd never given Grace a card or letter of affection with a signature of any kind. Nor had he been photographed with her or had anything inscribed as a gift given to her. Grace's only evidence of their relationship should be a timeless entry of his name and phone number in her address book. That is, other than the baby she was carrying.

Dry-washing his face with his hands, he only hoped Drudge could pull off what he promised without it becoming a problem.

It was nearing seven in the evening when Sergeant Markey walked into the emergency room of St. Jude's Memorial Hospital. He strode in with an air of superiority, his gold shield hanging from a beaded chain around his neck, ready to demand answers without a subpoena. When the first three staff members ignored him after asking where he might find Doctor Perez, he found himself shuffled to the back of their priorities. Instead, they tended to the sick and injured and paid his presence no mind.

Getting nowhere, Markey made his way to a horseshoe desk where the hub of activity surrounded. Staff walked in and out from behind the desk, trading files, documenting vital signs, denoting changes in conditions, and altering prognoses. Markey gave them wide berth while he watched their fluid movements, eyeing the chaos for a lull in the activity in order to attract someone's attention. There seemed to be an unending stream of patients and tasks for the medical staff to tend to, and they didn't have time for him. Eventually, he grew bored with watching their antics and finally blustered among them, hoping his sideline patience might have racked up a few points in his favor.

"Excuse me," he said to a nurse who'd taken a seat behind the horseshoe counter, presumably becoming sedentary for the moment. He showed her his identification and prayed she hadn't been ticketed recently for a traffic infraction. An unfortunate run-in with a cop usually made his job more difficult.

The nurse dragged her eyes up with boredom barely masking her irritation. "Yeesss?"

"Is Doctor Perez working?"

"She doesn't come in until ten."

Markey looked at his watch and dreaded waiting another couple of hours. "Maybe you can help me."

"Maybe," she intoned, glaring at him as if she doubted any such thing.

"Friday night, a woman was treated here in the emergency room. The patient's name was Grace Fitzpatrick. Can you tell me when she was admitted?"

The nurse stared at him with a mute expression adorning her flaccid face, her lack of interest making Markey realize he was dealing with one officious bitch.

"Please," he added with a strained sense of politeness.

She huffed with exasperation. "I believe that could fall under the scope of doctor/patient privilege. I might have to contact our legal department, and they won't be back until eight in the morning."

"Lady," Markey started with his own frustration beginning to show, "you can answer one simple question and send me on my merry way, thereby preventing an innocent woman from spending the night in a dirty, stinking jail cell. Or you can maintain your sense of self-righteousness and force me to march right over to Ms. Fitzpatrick's apartment and take her into custody for a crime she may or may not have committed. Your choice."

The nurse pursed her lips in such a way as to make her upper lip crinkle unattractively. Markey almost said something to that affect but maintained his opinion in silence. Finally, she broke her level, challenging stare and pushed away from the desk. The chair she sat in rolled a distance to a filing cabinet. She pulled out a drawer and flicked through the files until she found one matching the name Markey inquired about. Again, she thrust off the cabinet and sent her chair rolling, bringing her back to the desk where she consulted the file, holding the cover so it concealed the contents from Markey's view.

"She was brought in at 11:54 p.m.," the nurse said, slamming the cover in a conclusive fashion.

"How was she brought in?"

The nurse glared back at him. He gave her a demanding look, and she grudgingly returned to consult the file. "It doesn't say."

"Would it normally say such a thing?" He asked this with his voice toning down from its sternness.

She seemed to soften her own mask of hardness in response. "If she was brought in by any means requiring payment through insurance, it would. An ambulance or rescue unit."

"So she wasn't brought in by either one of them?"

"It would have been indicated on the report."

"And you don't remember her coming in?"

"My shift ends at ten. I wasn't here when she came in."

Markey hoped the nurse might be more receptive to answering more of his questions now that they were being halfway civil to each other. "Does it say why Ms. Fitzpatrick needed medical attention?"

The nurse slammed the file shut, her face becoming angry. "You said one question would keep her out of jail and I believe I answered that question. Get your subpoena for the rest of her medical report."

Markey showed his hands to ease the anger fuming in her. "I suppose I can always check back with Doctor Perez when she comes in. Thank you for your help."

He turned quickly from the nurse's station and consulted his watch. 8:03. Two more hours before Doctor Perez came in. He felt his stomach growling and decided it could stand a bit of attention. With some reluctance, he moved off to the exit in search of a place to get a bite to eat.

CHAPTER FOURTEEN

Murdock saw Grace's legs scissor as she fell to the street. He cursed out loud and flung himself after her, scrambling to get to the back doors from where she'd made her escape. Mindlessly, he grappled with the gun as he used his other hand to propel himself along the inside of the van. He saw her look over her shoulder with an expression of desperation. A sneering grin came up on his face as he readied himself to jump out. But just as he made what he thought was going to be a graceful vault from the van, the door swung unexpectedly back into his face. It hit him with such force that the edge cut a two-inch gash across his temple. He never knew his smooth move was cut short by an attack he'd never seen coming, and he toppled backward, cracking his head on the bare metal floor of the van.

As for Grace, she watched in awe as the door suddenly smashed into her abductor and caught him squarely on the forehead, dropping him where he stood. Then a shadow fell over her. She pulled her eyes away from Murdock to look at the figure who came out of the shadows cast by the van. Startled, she scrambled away from him, thinking he was just another thug dressed in all dark clothing. But then the young man stepped closer, into the dim light of the street lamp, and she saw who it was. He wore the same dark overcoat and sneakers, and the same red scarf wound around his neck, as when she'd first seen him on Friday night. When he reached out to help her to her feet, she saw there were strips of leather this time wrapping his hands up to his wrists.

Despite all her efforts to find him in the afternoon, his sudden and unexpected appearance gave her the impression that something unnatural was at work. And because she was uncertain what serendipity that might be, she shied away from his offer of help.

"I can help you," he said, his voice deep and soothing, carrying with it a quality of reassurance that was insistent yet impatient.

"Please," she said, though her tone was all but pleading. She had a fleeting concern that all the bumps and jostles she'd taken couldn't be good for her condition, and she began to worry about the baby. Absent-mindedly, she pressed a hand against her midsection and scorned his offer.

He looked up, studying the sky a moment, then glanced inside the van where

Murdock was moaning and rolling around on the floor, clutching his forehead and uttering foul obscenities.

In the driver's seat, G.W. was shaking his head to knock the confusion from his brain. He was the first to gain some semblance of reorganization and struggled from the driver's seat, stumbling between the two chairs and catching himself as his knees buckled. His eyes fell on Murdock, then shot up to see the woman and her rescuer getting ready to make their escape.

Grace's would-be hero and alibi for Friday night suddenly grabbed her by the elbow and hauled her to her feet, his gesture rough but insistent. Grace balked and sobbed at his forcefulness, feeling a clinch in the pit of her stomach that made her worry it might be the dislodging of her unborn child.

"No, don't," she cried, while actually struggling to help herself up. "You don't understand."

"No, *you* don't understand," he said. "The minions are coming, and I'll be damned if I'll let them have you."

He settled her on her feet and immediately tugged her along, chancing a glance at the pair of kidnappers in the van. G.W. was helping Murdock up, being none the less rough than he'd been with Grace, while G.W. blathered about how the woman was getting away and the bats were coming.

"This can't be happening," Grace sobbed, tears coming to her eyes. The kid's presence offered a sense of hope, but his words carried a terrifying meaning to them.

"We need to get to a safe place," he said, dragging her across the street, toward an alley that opened like the maw of a leviathan. "He's released the bats by now."

"What . . .?" she uttered.

"Hey! Stop!"

Grace snapped her head around. All of a sudden, she shrieked, jerking on her arm when she saw a gun extended her way.

At her side, the young man sensed a change in her resistance and looked in the direction her petrified eyes were riveted. At the sight of Murdock brandishing the gun, he spun Grace behind him and faced the gunman himself. He kept one hand on her elbow and brought his other one up as if to hold Murdock from firing the weapon.

"You don't want to be around her right now," he warned cautiously.

G.W. allowed a look of fear to cross his face, his hand clutching Murdock's shoulder in an effort to emphasize his vote to quit their campaign for the woman Drudge wanted. Murdock, on the other hand, shook his partner's hand off and used the door to leverage himself out of the van. He stepped down clumsily, his gun maintaining the advantage over Grace and her would-be rescuer. Carefully, he ambled a few feet away.

"Kid, I don't know who the fuck you are or what you think you're doing interfering in this exercise of free enterprise, but I do know that you just bought yourself a whole shitload of trouble." Murdock took another venturing step away from the support of the van and his foot took an unimpressive step. Blood leaked into his eyes, which he blinked angrily at it, slapping it away with a swipe of his hand.

Grace shrank behind her savior and tried to make herself as small a target as possible. She clutched his coat tightly so she could move with him; but hearing the words of her kidnapper, she began to wonder if this mysterious stranger might suddenly realize his mistake in coming to her aid and move aside, leaving her for the taking.

But the young man stood tall and imposing, even taking a step back as he threw his arm around her to move her with him. "In a few minutes, the minions will be here. Then they'll tear all of us apart just to get to her."

G.W. warily searched the darkening sky for any approaching shapes. "He's right, Murdock. They'll rip us to shreds."

"Shut the fuck up," Murdock snapped over his shoulder. He took another step in the direction of Grace and her companion and waved the gun at them. "Just step aside, sport, and we'll take what we came for. Ain't no reason for anyone to get hurt."

The young man protecting Grace took another step back, pushing her even farther behind him. He looked skyward and saw nothing. He turned his eyes on the gunman, narrowing his gaze and tainting his voice with every ounce of threat he hoped for. "You can't have her; and just to be clear, I'll do whatever it takes to keep you away from her."

Murdock laughed out loud, then quickly stifled it, his face becoming stern and rigid all of a sudden. A slight tilt to his head demanded to know if this kid was more of a fool than he originally judged him to be. "Step away from the lady, bub."

"I can't do that."

"Murdock," G.W. whined, clawing at Murdock's shoulder. "He's right. We can't stay here. Leave the bitch to him. It ain't worth our lives."

"You don't understand," Murdock sneered viciously back at G.W. "She's worth more than ten thousand bucks. If we don't bring her in, Drudge'll think we ain't worth shit and knock us off the payroll. Why do you think those fucking bats are going to tear us apart? Because we're dispensable."

G.W. snatched his hand away. He looked around uneasily, becoming unusually jittery, his arms waving uselessly. "Man, we gotta get out of here. We gotta get out of here!"

"Calm down," Murdock snapped, turning to kick ineffectually at him, trying to bring G.W. back under control, which worked somewhat. However, when he turned back to Grace and her savior, he saw only the barreling ridges of a leather-wrapped fist pistoning toward his face. His extended gun hand was slapped aside, nearly spinning him off balance as the fist slammed into his chin and rocked his head back. His last thought before he lost all sense of consciousness was that his neck must surely have been snapped by the blow.

The young man the old bum had called Slash snatched the gun from Murdock's slack fingers. He spun around and leveled the weapon at G.W., who stared with wild-eyed terror into the barrel of his bleak fate. G.W. whimpered as his hands came up in supplication.

"Please," he whined, "we weren't going to hurt her. We were only going to take her to the Tower." Sobbing pathetically, G.W. dropped to his knees and clasped his hands in prayer, his eyes blinking beseechingly upward. "That's all, I swear. I swear on my momma's grave, that's all."

The young man stepped away from Murdock and his partner and groped for the woman who'd huddled behind him. Only he couldn't feel her near him, and when he looked over his shoulder to see where she might have gone, he saw her running away, stumbling and sobbing as she ran down the street. Once she got to an intersection, she started screaming at the top of her lungs, and he cursed her stupidity as he bolted after her.

Grace staggered forward and nearly tripped to her knees. Tears streamed down her face as the only car in sight blew its horn and squealed around her. The driver ignored her pleas for help and continued on his way. She uttered a foul oath at his paternity and turned back to the intersection in the hopes that she would see more traffic. The only other car in sight was going down the avenue, away from her, unaware of the incident taking place up the street.

She caught movement out of the corner of her eye and turned around, seeing at once that her erstwhile rescuer was charging after her. Fearfully, she shrieked and ran up the street, going in the direction where she saw the last car come from. She continued to scream for help, unaware that no one was in the business district this late on a Sunday evening to hear her, just the two men who'd tried to kidnap her and the man who'd interfered with their plans.

It was him, the one who'd come to her rescue, who overtook her, and he did so easily. He caught her arm and jerked her to a halt, spinning her into his body as he jammed the barrel of the gun into his waistband. With his other hand, he covered her mouth, muffling her screams.

"Shut up! You don't know what you're doing."

Her eyes widened with doe-like fear, her mouth working in vain to cry out. She thrashed within his arms but his hold was much too powerful for her flagging strength to break. Desperately, she kicked his leg. At the same time, she heard the echoing explosion of a gunshot.

Her rescuer-cum-captor held on despite the obvious pain. It emanated from his shin and arm, where Grace had kicked one and a bullet had seared through the other. The pain in his leg dissipated quickly enough that he was able to maintain his balance as he turned in the direction of the gunshot.

G.W. was sobbing and laughing at the same time. He held the weapon extended in a two-handed grip, his knobby legs splayed wide apart so that he looked ridiculous. His finger contracted again and another deafening explosion sounded, its reverberating echo warbling down the street.

The second bullet whizzed by only inches from the stranger's ear, and he flinched. He gritted his teeth, hoisted Grace off her feet, and carried her off with him. He ran awkwardly down the sidewalk, away from the gun-toting kidnapper, with Grace fighting him every step of the way, using her hands to beat at his arms clamped tightly around her waist, crying hysterically for help.

Murdock staggered to his feet and stumbled around until his head began to clear. Then he heard the gunshot. He looked up and cursed when a violent pain sliced through his skull. When the second shot sounded, he saw G.W. wailing at the woman escaping over the shoulder of her rescuer. Ignoring the pain in his face, Murdock kicked himself into action. He ran up behind G.W. and smacked him hard on the head, then snatched the gun from his hands.

"What the fuck's the matter with you!" he yelled as he disarmed his partner.

"We're gonna die!" G.W. wailed.

"We sure will if you mark her!" he snapped. "Come on. She's the only way we're gonna get out of this alive."

Murdock chased after Grace and the man carrying her, running down the street with the gun in his hand. Behind him, G.W. cried like a child having a tantrum. He wailed over and over, tears on his face, "We're gonna die, we're gonna die!"

Approaching the alley, the young man tried to ignore Grace's wriggling, kicking, and battering against his back with her fists. He also tried to blank out the pain in his arm. But with every step he took, every beat of her hands against his back, every buck of her body, he felt the fiery pain jolt through it.

He wanted to curse her for her hysteria but there wasn't time for explanations. He reached the opening of the alley and saw it cut through the block along which he ran. It was dark and foreboding, but he knew the city well enough to know where this alley went. This one led to the street one block over, in the direction they would be seeking sanctuary. There were no obstacles in the way, no walls or fences to climb, nor any security measures for the businesses around them. He clutched Grace tightly and ducked into the darkness that immediately consumed them.

"No, please, no!" she cried, the tears streaming down her cheeks. She struggled more desperately, but her rescuer was too powerful to break free from. A pain began to build within her midsection. "Oh God, please, no!"

He paused a moment in the middle of the alley, where he looked back at the entrance, to the street behind them. Murdock skidded to a halt in front of the opening, considering the depth of the shadows, weighing the consequences of his pursuit into the dark alley.

"You motherfucker!" Murdock yelled. "I'll kill you!"

The stranger dropped Grace to her feet. He held her close to his body and clamped a hand over her mouth. When he bent to speak to her, he said, "For God's sake, please be quiet."

Something in the desperation of his voice made her settle down. She allowed him to drag her to the wall without resistance, realizing with sudden clarity that this kid who held her so tenaciously was there as her savior, the only person in a city of a million and a half people who would help her. She should have seen that from the beginning, when he suddenly appeared out of nowhere to thwart her abduction. It was the men who were now chasing them who were the bad guys. They were the ones who'd tried to hurt her—not this kid, who had only interfered at great personal risk to his own life.

She felt herself bump against his body as he backed into the wall. He sidled along it for the deeper shadows of the alley. She was mindful of his movements and relaxed enough so her body fell in place with his. Her hand slid down his wrist to hold loosely onto his arm, finding comfort in it.

At the mouth of the alley, Murdock grimaced and tightened his grip around the gun. He took his first step into the alley and felt the darkness overwhelm him. A shiver of uncertainty crawled up his spine, and he felt his limbs trembling, a primal sense of self-preservation warning him not to go any deeper. Sucking up his determination, Murdock headed more urgently into the alley, jogging along, seeing nothing more than the blackness ahead. He knew he was going in blind and would have to rely on his hearing alone, and because of that, he was forced to step more lightly to cut down on the noise he made.

In the shadows ahead, the young man holding Grace against his body slid along the wall until he reached the corner of the alley. It was shaped like a T, where a traversing drive ran along the middle of the businesses in which garbage trucks drove through to reach individual Dumpsters. From there, he and Grace would be able to run out of any number of short driveways.

When they reached the central drive, the young man turned into it and cut across to the other side. He found an alcove where an industrial-sized Dumpster was and squeezed himself and Grace between it and a brick wall. The smell was nauseating and overpowering, and the debris from the overspill shuffled underfoot. They made it to the wall against which the Dumpster was pushed and pressed up against it. There he crouched down and brought Grace onto his lap, where he held her tightly, one arm still wrapped around her waist and the other clamped over her mouth, gently now, more as a reminder than a restriction. He wrapped his legs around her shins to prevent her from kicking out—if that was what she intended to do—and brought his face next to hers, his lips so close to her ear that his breath was warm when he blew against it.

"Shhh," he said quietly, his voice only a whisper against her cheek.

Grace felt oddly safe in his arms, even though he used them to restrict her movement. She was vaguely aware that she might have misjudged him after their initial encounter and again just recently. She had pegged him to be a homeless person, but now she felt the strength in his arms and the definition of his chest and knew he had to be eating well to maintain such a physique. She smelled the faint scent of clean laundry and soap, and the underlying aroma of something unusual but not unpleasant. Something that brought back memories of a time she couldn't pinpoint, something homey and nostalgic. This kid—this stranger who had come to her rescue not once, but twice—wasn't a bum who was a stranger to cleanliness and nutrition. He kept up his own grooming even though his wardrobe was a bit out of the ordinary.

Grace nodded to let him know she understood the danger they were in. Slowly, the hand came away and she felt it come to rest more comfortably around her waist. Surprisingly, she felt safe and protected within his embrace.

A noise brought both their attention to the sound of footsteps near the entrance of the alcove. Grace tensed as her champion drew one of his arms away from her and groped for something behind her back. He tugged the gun free from between their bodies and held it down on the ground, under his palm.

The darkness in the alcove was complete and foreboding, but Grace found it comforting nonetheless. If she found it to be that way, then her pursuer might also feel how ominous it was.

The young man's keen eyes—far more used to the night than day—made out the shadow of Murdock passing through the alley, his steps cautious and slow, his gun sweeping back and forth. He paused in front of their hiding place and listened, then moved on, entirely too slow.

******

With his head falling against the brick wall, Grace's rescuer forced himself to remain still and silent for a while longer. A sickening fear began to form in his gut. The bats were now overhead, circling, sensing where their quarry was. His fingers curled around the gun but didn't pick it up yet.

Moments passed as he fought down the building terror of immobility. He felt like a sitting duck waiting for the hunter to rise from the marshes and fire upon him. He didn't want to fight two battles at once. Soon, the birds would arrive to pick the bats out of the sky. But until then, he would have to protect the woman on his own.

CHAPTER FIFTEEN

Sergeant Markey sat at a counter of a nearly deserted diner, picking the top half of a bun off his chicken filet sandwich. He stared at it with a critical eye, wondering what condiment he could add to mask the flavor of what looked like a chunk of gristle with a few token strands of meat clinging to it. Then he reasoned that gristle really had no taste and he shouldn't worry about masking something flavorless to begin with, so he dropped the bun back in place and picked up the whole sandwich, wincing when he ventured his first bite.

The police radio sitting on the seat next to him chattered incessantly with one emergency dispatched after another. He'd taken the radio from his back pocket to sit more comfortably on the stool and had ignored it for the most part. Until, that is, he began to pick out a certain pattern of emergency and priority calls being dispatched. They were consistent, and with each one, Markey listened more intently to the radio traffic, picking out a discernible pattern to the calls.

Almost all of the available units working that night were being dispatched to the suburbs north of the city. Fires and fights had broken out, which seemed to prelude another riot that might erupt after more of the contagious behavior caught on with the city's lowliest citizens. The city had been experiencing such outbreaks of violence on more or less infrequent occasions during the past two years, which put a strain on the city's emergency personnel, both on the spot and in the aftermath. Houses were broken into and businesses looted. People unlucky enough to be caught out on the street were attacked and beaten. Cars were fire-bombed and rocked and bottled. The cops and fire fighters were run ragged throughout the night, chasing shadows as well as real thugs, tending to the injured, and dousing raging fires. Crime scene preservation fell by the wayside until later.

The world was becoming a more violent place to live in, so why should this city be any different. He remembered a time when it wasn't so bad, but in light of other epochal changes in history, this change had occurred within the blink of an eye, some sudden shift in the world's luck, he supposed. All things considering, since there didn't seem to be any one significant cause other than a change in politics, the best thing to do was to go with the flow. Tread the water and hope to come out in the end a better world for what trials and tribulations it experienced.

Markey just hoped the violence in his corner of the world this time wouldn't escalate to the extent it had over a year ago, when the rural farms on the west end of town had been razed and plundered by unknown vandals.

He struggled through his blue plate special with gulps of soda in between bland bites. As he did, he turned up the volume on his radio and listened more intently as the units assigned to the Sixth District were pulled from their area of assignment and sent to the suburbs to assist the already overburdened squad there. The tempo picked up, the frantic voices of the officers causing the dispatcher to respond with her own distress. She called for more officers from the Ninth District, where most of the business center was, and sent them to the suburbs.

Markey shook his head and pitied the boys working the road. He had done his time in uniform before he'd reached Homicide and didn't miss the excitement those duties entailed. Homicide provided him more of an investigative experience than the heat-of-the-moment excitement, which suited him just fine. At thirty-nine, he wasn't as spry as he used to be.

In short order, he finished his dinner and pulled out his wallet. His attention shot to the radio when his ears picked out a call being dispatched to an area not too far away. A woman screaming over on Seventeenth Street. Right in the business district, where most of the officers had been pulled from. Only a few blocks away.

Markey answered the dispatcher's plea for someone to check out the call. Other than himself there were no other available units. He told the dispatcher that he was in the area and would take the call himself. As he gathered his wallet and radio, he imagined it was probably just a weekend domestic dispute that had carried over into the street.

But in the middle of the business district? Where nothing was open and no real apartments were located? Maybe it was someone staying at one of the hotels.

He got into his car and drove a few blocks up and over to Seventeenth Street. The roads were glistening from a misty rain that had fallen earlier, and the sodium lamps reflected yellow light sickly off the pavement. The buildings were all dark and ominous in the deserted night, with only the trappings of their names illuminated near the rooftops. At one time, the skyline had been a bejeweled panorama of extravagance, but times had changed and so had the skyline. The traffic lights at intersections were set on flash, even though there was no traffic in the area. A Sunday night in the business district represented an eerie contrast to the bustle there would be Monday morning.

Markey put the car in park and looked around, not surprised to find nothing in the intersection, up the avenue, or down the street. No woman screaming. No disturbance as reported by the dispatcher.

He got out of the car to justify his presence and listened to the quiet beyond the thrumming of his car's engine. The silence that met his ears was frightening in a way he couldn't explain. A chill ran up his spine and caused him to hesitate. The wind blew swiftly and flapped the canvas of a bistro's awning across the street. A few discarded flyers in the gutter raced along the culvert, while a loose sign on a post marking the avenue rattled.

Markey cocked his head and listened more intently, as if by angling his head in a different way he might enhance his ability to hear.

Nothing.

He shook his head and started to slide back into the car. It was then that he heard the crack of a gunshot. Instinctively, he ducked and spun around, his hand going to his hip, where he felt the reassuring presence of his weapon. The echo of the shot convinced him to draw his own gun and try to get a bearing on where the shot had come from.

A woman's scream drew his attention to a dark alley not far from where he was parked. Another gunshot and another scream made him jump. Markey suffered an attack of anxiety as a sense of total aloneness made him realize he was completely on his own. He scowled to himself and considered what he should do. His radio was on the front seat of the car, which wasn't really so far away, but it would do him no good to call for help. He'd been the only one in the area when the call had been dispatched. All the other units were battling crime in the north suburbs.

Markey cursed and ran across the street. As he reached the mouth of the alley and slammed his back against the wall, it struck him that the majority of the city's officers were far away from this very spot. He wondered whether his willingness to die a heroic death in the line of duty would be enough to see him through his fear of going into the alley on his own.

Another scream from the woman, followed by another gunshot, resolved his conflict. He peered into the alley and saw nothing. The blackness in there was somewhat reassuring, and he gained some mettle from it. Something in the back of his mind told him that whoever was firing the gun might be able to see whatever it was he was shooting at, which meant there might be some source of light beyond the impenetrable blackness at the entrance.

Markey cocked his weapon and slid into the alley. His back grated against the wet brick as he inched his way quietly, cautiously, along, his heart pounding as he began to hear things. Nothing distinguishable, but there was something, a sense of *something* definitely ahead, something out of place, out of the ordinary.

He fought the urge to hurry forward, even when he heard the woman shriek again, a long, drawn out squeal followed by a thud, and then another, and another. Despite knowing that he should have called and waited for back-up—and his rational mind telling him that he should slow down and proceed with only the utmost caution—he found his feet were afflicted with the adrenaline now surging through his body.

He reached a corner leading into a central driveway running between a series of businesses. Here, visibility was more pronounced, lit by the moon passing directly overhead. Markey paused to allow his eyes to adjust, and then peeked around the corner.

He immediately pulled back and pressed his shoulders against the wall, readjusting his grip on the gun and quelling the heaviness of his breathing. He shook his head to deny what he saw, even though he knew his eyes couldn't possibly be playing tricks on him. He hadn't had anything alcoholic to drink, which might have caused him to imagine the late night Tales of the Crypt scenario he was witnessing if he had.

A man dressed in all dark clothing had his back toward Markey, facing the other way, using his body to shield a woman from something overhead. Dark, swirling forms of flitting shapes darted in haphazard patterns across the sky. Larger, swifter, and smoothly moving creatures were chasing the smaller ones, attacking them with a ferocity that was distinctly war-like, fighting a battle overhead. A few of the forms broke from the ranks and darted down to the asphalt, streaking for the two people below.

Grace's champion kept a hand clamped on her elbow, keeping her within reach and always behind him, his body the second shield of protection against the bats. He'd already shot three and overpowered another that had made its way past the birds' defenses, and now he was sighting his next target. Others would make it through in time, but there were more harriers on the way, along with blackbirds, owls, and blue jays, enough to contend with the bats already there and those coming as reinforcements. In the meantime, he would have to protect Grace with what he had on hand until his second wave of defenders arrived.

Another black creature flitted across his shoulder and tried to land behind him. Grace cried out a warning and pulled on his arm. He whirled around, spinning her behind him again and nearly throwing her off balance as he brought the gun up to fire at the metamorphosing demon. The gun thundered in his hand and Grace shrieked. The bullet took off half the creature's face, and the demon flew backward against the wall, hitting it and crumpling into its bat form, its small hideous face nothing but pulp and bone now. The young man spun again, aimed, and fired, the shot ringing in his ears and echoing in the corridor between the two rows of buildings.

Grace flinched at the deafening sound and covered her ears with her hands. Two more shapes dropped from the fire escape to their left, one landing in front of them while the other landed behind. The young man twisted to keep each in view, fired once, then twice, and managed to place a gaping hole in each of the creatures' hollow, hairy chests. Both staggered backward and toppled, leaving nothing of their presence but their bat-shaped corpses.

Behind him, Grace screamed, and the man called Slash spun around to see a demon embrace her within its bony arms, then envelope her completely within its leathery wings. The beast faced him with a vicious hissing that sounded like grease dripping on a hot griddle. It rolled its lips back to expose wicked fangs looking like old scrimshaw sharpened to a deadly point. Its eyes gleamed like red embers sparked from the furnaces of Hell, and there was a sour odor of pungent ammonia with the power to cause the eyes to water and the throat to gag. Grace cried out as she furtively beat against the coriaceous membranes wrapped around her, but her words were muffled.

Slash swung the gun up and pulled the trigger.

The hammer fell on an empty chamber. He cursed and hurled the gun away, then dug into the folds of his coat for a long-bladed knife he felt more comfortable with anyway. He launched himself at the creature, moving swiftly and unerringly silent, his movements efficient and economical. With one swipe, he sliced the wing, creating a gap in the membrane by which Grace could breathe and struggle through. Then he swiped the dagger across the creature's throat and slammed a fist into its ugly face. Its head snapped back, wrenching the gash even wider. Black ichor pumped like a burst oil drill. Slash groped through the leathery tissue and found Grace's head. Knotting his fingers in her tousled hair, and without concern for tenderness or etiquette, he yanked her free of the toppling demon, throwing her to the ground even as she collapsed there on her own.

"Freeze! Police!"

Slash spun around and froze, his hands staying away from his coat to show that he would make no further moves. In the back of his mind, he recognized the meaning of the order and respected it, realizing quickly enough that disobeying it might result in a more devastating consequence than he wanted to deal with at the moment.

The officer came out of the darkness, moving with reluctance and uncertainty, his approach hesitant and awkward. Slash could see him clearly enough. The gun he held at full extension with tension-stiffened arms looked like an ineffectual threat, mostly because the fear was so starkly etched on the officer's face. His saucer-shaped eyes darted back and forth across the alley, then glanced quickly upward at the battle still raging above, and finally at Grace, where she lay crumpled on the ground in a state of catatonic shock.

"What's going on here?" Markey shouted, stepping forward and looking around, expecting to see evidence of a slaughter. "What the hell is going on here?"

Slash threw out a hand to warn off Markey's approach. "You don't want to be here right now."

"I heard a woman screaming," Markey started. "And gunshots. Now I come in here and find a woman in need of medical attention, with you standing over her. Step away from her."

"I was protecting her," the young man said. "She was in danger. She still is."

"I said get away from her," Markey ordered, growing angry and insistent.

A black shape fell from above and darted behind Markey, its sudden movement drawing his attention for but a second. Enough to give Grace's champion time to react but not enough for Markey to turn around to face the creature landing behind him. In a split second—shorter in duration than the blink of an eye—the thing drew up to its full height, erupting like a rising leviathan, its yawning mouth widening with dripping fangs poised at Markey's exposed throat.

The intelligence of the demon wasn't impressive but this one had reacted with a calculating reasoning that was intriguing and a bit frightening. Its decision to land behind the officer had forced Slash's hand, which would expose him to the officer's instinctive reaction of self-defense.

Regardless, he had no choice; not if he wanted the unfortunate officer to live to see another day.

With unerring speed, he snatched a dagger from his sleeve and hurled it at the creature, in the same direction the officer stood, who saw the dagger pinioning toward him and cursed, and at the same time, squeezed off a shot as he ducked the whirling blade.

The dagger buried itself in the throat of the demon, severing vessels carrying life-sustaining fluid to its brain. As it did, the officer tripped awkwardly away and staggered for balance, then spun around to regain sight of the young man in the alley, the very one he would have sworn had just openly attacked him with a deadly weapon.

Markey's bullet whizzed by Slash's ear with a hot hiss, followed by a solid *plunk* in the brick wall behind him. He instinctively snatched another dagger from his sleeve and held it ready for another bat to break through the ranks of his battle-weary harriers.

"Drop the knife!"

"Put your gun down."

"I said drop the knife!"

"I'm not trying to hurt you."

"You threw a fucking knife at me!"

"I was protecting her."

Markey looked at the unconscious woman lying on the ground and suddenly recognized her. His face drew on an expression of perplexity, his eyes narrowing. "How do you know this woman?"

"She's in danger."

"You're in danger if you don't drop that goddamn knife!"

"Put your gun down."

"Drop it!"

"I'm not here to hurt her. Or you, for that matter."

"Drop it!"

"You have to trust me on this."

"It's not my job to trust anyone."

Slash let his eyes roam up to the sky, where the added forces of a few great horned owls, combined with a flock of blackbirds and a few out-of-place ospreys, finally kept the bats concerned with their own survival for the moment. Still, at any time, one of them might break free and attack at ground level, transforming into a state the birds were not fit to fight.

He scoffed with disgust and allowed the dagger to fall from his slack fingers.

Markey rushed forward. He drove his gun into the young man's face and forced him to step back, until he was flush against the wall. The kid held his hands away in a gesture of surrender, but Markey's fury at having seen the knife spiral toward his face had put him on the edge of violence. His free hand slammed into the young man's chest and pushed him hard against the wall, cracking the back of his head against the brick. With an incredible effort, Markey restrained himself from indulging his compulsion for violence any farther.

Grace's would-be rescuer allowed himself to be manhandled against the wall, all the while keeping a vigilant account of the battle overhead. "I trusted you."

"I didn't ask you to."

"She needs protection."

"She'll get it."

"You can't protect her."

"Buddy, where you're going, neither can you." Markey grabbed the kid's shoulder and spun him around to face the wall. He kicked his feet apart so he was forced to widen his stance. "Put your hands on the wall and spread your legs."

"You don't understand."

Markey pressed the barrel of his gun against the young man's spine, insisting that he do as he was told. Slash immediately placed his hands on the wall in surrender, waiting for Markey to reach behind him for his handcuffs before he made his move. When he heard the chatter of the metal, he pushed himself off the wall, whirled, and smacked Markey's gun aside. With his other hand curled into a fist, he landed a punch on the detective's face, dropping him flat on his back.

Slash hesitated only long enough to see if the officer would get up, regretting that he had to go to such lengths just to do what he had to in order to protect the woman. The detective was out cold, and that was good enough. As for himself, he wasted no time rushing to where Grace lay crumpled on the ground. He bent at her side and felt for a pulse, which he found was thready and weak but at least there. He had no idea what injuries she might have or what might have been done to her in her capture, but he knew she needed protection. There was only one place he could go where he was sure the bats wouldn't follow.

With his own exhaustion setting in and a fiery reminder in his wounded arm, he lifted her up against his chest and hurried as he carried her out of the alley.

CHAPTER SIXTEEN

Christopher slammed the phone down in defeat. He grew increasingly more frustrated as he was rebuffed in his attempts to locate Malachi Drudge, or even anyone remotely associated with Spatial Industries. He'd tried the phone book, the operator, and the phone company, only to discover that each number he was given led to a voice recording stating that the company was closed for the weekend and would reopen at eight o'clock Monday morning.

He cursed out loud and slammed a fist on the calendar blotter, making a hollow sound and striking a nerve in his hand, adding injury to insult. The anxiety of the weekend was becoming increasingly more debilitating on his normally sturdy constitution. After his impromptu conversation with Robert Prescott, he'd experienced a bout of nausea and heartburn that just wouldn't go away, not even after drinking several glasses of Alka Seltzer and chewing Tums in rapid succession. Nothing seemed to help his condition, and it wasn't simply being hung over that was why he felt so poorly.

He knew what was wrong. It was the fact that everything in his life was suddenly in the hands of someone else. Everything he was currently working for—had worked for in the past and had ever achieved—was now at the mercy of another person. Whether he'd been allied to or pitted against this Malachi Drudge, Christopher found himself unable to draw himself away from the circumstances that wily bastard had detailed for him.

Drudge had told him he could have wealth and power, but he'd yet to explain what he wanted in return other than a rather ambiguous aspiration of owning the city. Up until now, Drudge had only defined the glory Christopher would achieve and the spoils he would reap. He offered the political backing of several powerful men to pull off the election and guaranteed a successful term in office. The only glitch thrown into the mix seemed to be the quizzical homicide in the room at the Rialto. And, of course, Grace.

Christopher pushed himself back from the desk and leaned wearily into his chair, folding his hands in his lap. He stared into space, considering his feelings about Grace's revelation.

I'm pregnant.

He tried to recall the impression she'd conveyed when she'd said those words. She hadn't cried when she'd told him about the news, nor had she shown any sign of regret for the mishap. The pregnancy hadn't caused her distress; his reaction had. Thinking back, he was sure she'd said those fateful words with a glimmer of haughty triumph. In fact, he was pretty sure she didn't find being pregnant distasteful. And to prove it, he remembered how she'd argued vehemently against ending the pregnancy. No, Grace wanted this baby. She wanted to carry, deliver, and raise it just to spite him.

But what was the extent of her plans?. Had she wanted the child only as a bargaining chip for the wedge into his marriage? He'd never thought she would be so brazen as to bring an innocent life into play, but perhaps he'd misread her all along.

In retrospect, Christopher imagined he might have told her that he loved her, may even have alluded they would eventually have a future together. He may have even complained that his marriage was doomed to fail because it was loveless. He may even have told her that she was his world and his life and his reason for waking up in the morning. But she never should have made such a bold play for his affections without his consent.

He'd never come right out and promised her that he would divorce his wife and make her his life partner. Or rather, if he had, she should never have placed such a demanding timetable on him. She knew he had plans and ambitions. She knew he had a political career and a reputation that had to remain beyond reproach. No scandal or threat of one could touch him.

Grace had done this on purpose. She'd selfishly allowed herself to become pregnant so he might suffer a fit of paternal responsibility. Or perhaps she'd planned to play up on his childlessness in the hopes of trapping him with the desire for an offspring.

If she had, then she'd failed to realize his whole life had been geared toward this one event. He'd dreamed of entering the political arena and moving up the ranks to become one of the youngest statesmen in the city's history. Now she was throwing a monkey wrench into his plans, and he'd be damned if he would love and cherish a woman who'd place such restrictions on his life, career, and dreams.

Then this Malachi Drudge had come into the picture just when things seemed hopeless.

Who was this auspicious gentleman who offered to handle his problems and support him politically? Surely, he had to have some personal stake in the matter; every campaign contributor did. And if he did—which Christopher was nearly positive he must have—then it couldn't be entirely on the up and up. Not if Drudge was willing to go to the extent he'd already gone to put Christopher in a position where he had no choice but to align himself with a murderer. He was the District Attorney, for God's sake, and he stood on a strong platform of integrity and law enforcement. He had the backing of the police union, the school board, and the city commissioners, even the local newspapers. Despite all the other groups hitching themselves to his bandwagon, he could stand on those endorsements alone. He didn't need Drudge's vast wealth to bring his dreams to fruition. Which had left Drudge only one recourse to trap him. A scandal involving a homicide would certainly destroy him in more ways than just politically.

Drudge spoke about pursuing even more grandiose plans than him remaining as the city's mayor. Christopher found it hard to think so loftily without jinxing his dreams, much less considering what lengths he'd have to go to reach those heights. Yet he knew he was in a precarious position right now and thinking beyond the moment was nearly impossible. Of course he hadn't killed anyone, but no matter how he looked at it, he was still the number one suspect in the homicide of a businessman in his suite at the Rialto Friday night. That alone would destroy his run for mayor and blackball any further candidacy for political positions in the future. After all, he wasn't one of the Kennedys who could ride the coattails of the family name to get where he wanted to go.

Still, despite how he looked at it, it all came back to Grace. Drudge had promised to take care of the problem she posed. He wasn't proposing anything Christopher hadn't already suggested.

All day, Christopher had fought the urge to call her. Drudge had warned him that his phone bill might be scrutinized. Any number associated with her had to be avoided.

He'd spent the night wracking his brain, trying to remember every trinket and card he'd ever given her, trying to recall if he had signed his name or left a photograph of himself with her beside him. He had always been careful about that. Although he'd never foreseen such a monumental scandal as what he now faced, he'd always maintained his adulterous life separate from his marriage. He'd learned from his other friends' mistakes and garnered tricks of the trade from criminal cases he'd prosecuted. He fancied himself a master of marital deception. He'd never divulged a home number, always kept communications restricted to their office lines, bowed out of public events, signed endearing cards with a nickname kept private between the two of them, never entrusted her with a photo of himself, and never—never!—had one taken of the two of them together.

He felt relatively satisfied that he could maintain the charade of not having seen Grace in more than a year. If there were any forgotten trinkets or photos, they could always be passed off as gifts from that irresponsible period in his past. But the same thing couldn't be said for the child she carried. The baby growing within her was a written confession to all the lies and deceptions he was promoting. It explained just how recent their affair had been. And with that in the forefront, Grace's word would be given far more credibility than his.

Christopher smothered his face in his hands as he sighed with frustration. Drudge had promised to take care of that problem, had assured him there would be no reason for him to worry about the child ruining his chances for the election. But he also knew what that would entail, and although he'd urged Grace to consider aborting the child, Drudge's offer to see it done sounded far more ominous than a simple medical procedure.

Christopher had never before equated abortion to being evil; it was simply an acceptable means to an end. But when Drudge talked about it, there was a sinister quality to it, making it sound like a vicious monster was lurking in the shadows for an innocent to play as sacrifice to appease its hunger. He worried for Grace and wondered what Drudge would do to convince her to end her foolishness. Perhaps money would be his motivating force, or maybe threats to persuade her that this pregnancy wasn't an expression of love, but a childish act of selfishness. Eventually, whatever Drudge had planned, Christopher convinced himself that Grace had created her own consequences.

CHAPTER SEVENTEEN

Monsignor O'Dwyer murmured the prayers of benediction to turn the unleavened bread and wine into the body and blood of Christ. He was alone in the cathedral, but he still made the ritual gestures over the offerings, raising the chalice and imploring God to bless the wine, then the platen on which the wafer sat. He tasted from each and wiped the wine from his lips, using a white linen cloth he kissed and laid over the chalice when he was done. He turned to a gold-colored tabernacle behind the altar and stored the decanter and platen in the gilded cabinet, locking the door with a small key.

With the ceremony being as solemn as it was, O'Dwyer was startled by a spattering of knocking coming from the front doors of the cathedral. He turned and faced the noise, at first frightened by the loud intrusion. But then he shook himself out of his fright and looked at his watch, pushing the wide sleeve of his cassock up and exposing the dial. It was only 9:03 p.m.

Juveniles, he scowled. Neighborhood punks rapping on the church doors to see if he would answer, while they ran away giggling. There was no other reason for someone to be knocking on the doors at this time of night. The church remained opened to its parishioners until eleven o'clock, when he usually battened down the hatches for the day. Despite his wish for the church to stay open around the clock, there had been a few occasions when the poor box had been stolen and the sacristy vandalized. Even then, he wouldn't be inclined to lock the doors if he only knew the money stolen was going to feed the poor instead of someone's crack habit.

The pounding repeated itself, becoming louder and more urgent.

O'Dwyer frowned as he pocketed the key to the tabernacle. He descended the altar steps and strode down the main aisle, fuming with an old man's impatience for juvenile antics. He was prepared to give his own version of the Sermon on the Mount to those delinquents, or to chastise a wino who was unable to find his way home, when he hesitated at the thought that it might be a ruse by thieves waiting for him to answer the door. He imagined a group of rowdy thugs bursting into the cathedral right at the moment he opened the doors, thrusting him aside so they could plunder the church's riches. Then, chuckling to himself, O'Dwyer recovered his senses. No thief would have to knock on an already unlocked door. He was just being paranoid. Anyone with the intention of plundering the cathedral would only have to open the door on their own to do so.

Bam, bam, bam.

He shuffled forward with an urgency born out of his growing irritation for the impertinence of the visitor. Whoever was at that door would suffer through a lecture of common decency before his own needs were attended to.

Irately, O'Dwyer grasped the handle of one of the large oak doors and pulled it open. The late night caller wasted no time in shouldering the door open farther, slipping past the old man with his arms burdened by an unconscious woman.

Monsignor O'Dwyer shuffled backward in surprise. He opened his mouth in bafflement. "What . . .?"

"I need your help, Father," the young man said with urgency. He turned to face the priest, his face bearing an expression of dire need.

O'Dwyer didn't overlook the fear on his face or the unconscious woman in his arms. "What happened to her?"

"She was attacked. Close the door."

O'Dwyer hastily shut the door and followed the young man into the nave.

"Do you have somewhere I can lay her down?" the young man asked, looking at the wooden pews neatly lining the church proper but disdaining them as unsuitable. "Somewhere she'll be comfortable."

"Yes, yes," the old priest said, bustling forward and beckoning him to follow. He led him toward a side alcove, where a baptismal font was centered in the christening room, and then beyond. They slipped through a curtain leading to a corridor lined with doors to offices and rest rooms. At the last door, Monsignor O'Dwyer turned and waved him inside, allowing him to carry Grace into a small office. The priest brushed past him and opened a final door, which exposed a large office. Inside were a desk and an office chair, with a pair of simpler chairs in front of the desk. There were also filing cabinets, shelves, and a couch along the opposite wall.

The young man went to the couch and tenderly set Grace down. He arranged her arms gently across her waist so she appeared to be in peaceful repose. Before he pulled back, he took a moment to study her face.

Despite the dirt and grime streaked with tears on her cheeks, there was a certain beauty shining through all the filth. She seemed at peace now, no longer troubled by the human thugs who'd pursued her, nor the horrible creature that had embraced her before she fainted. It seemed that even in unconsciousness she knew she was safe.

"What happened to her?"

The young man tore himself away from staring at Grace's face. He looked over his shoulder, acknowledging the priest's presence. "She was attacked."

"Yes, you've said that already, but by whom?"

"She needs a doctor," he replied instead of answering the question, rising to his feet abruptly and causing O'Dwyer to take a few steps back. "She fell out of a van."

Monsignor O'Dwyer moved quickly for the desk. "I'll call an ambulance."

The young man lunged for him. "No!"

Startled, the priest withdrew his hand from the phone, frightened by the adamant tone in his voice. "You said she needs a doctor."

"Yes, but it's not safe to move her from here."

O'Dwyer's eyes screwed up with confusion. "The paramedics will be careful moving her."

He shook his head. "You don't understand. She's only safe here. In the cathedral."

The priest narrowed his eyes suspiciously. "You're right; I don't understand. What's happening here?"

"Do you know where to find a doctor?"

"Just a minute," O'Dwyer said. "You still haven't told me what happened."

Considering his options, the young man gazed thoughtfully at the priest before replying. When he spoke, it was with reluctance. "There's something chasing her. She's still in danger from it, but I can only protect her if you allow us to stay here until morning."

"Stay here until morning?" O'Dwyer echoed. "Who is she? What kind of trouble is she in?"

The young man seemed to wonder about those questions himself but he had no answers for the monsignor. "I don't know."

O'Dwyer was curiously affected by the confusion on his face. He walked over to where the woman lay and bent down to examine her injuries. "She needs a doctor."

The young man didn't remind him that he'd already made that assessment himself. Instead, he said, "Do you know where to find one?"

"Listen, son," O'Dwyer said resolutely, "Doctors don't usually go to people anymore; people go to them. We'll call an ambulance."

"No," he insisted, holding out his hand to keep the priest from reaching for the phone. "She can't leave the church until the morning."

"I think you'd better explain yourself," O'Dwyer insisted, folding his arms across his chest.

"Please, Father, she needs help now."

Monsignor O'Dwyer remained stoical and unperturbed. He faced the young man without saying a word, bearing out a determination to hold firm in his resolve. At the same time, his unexpected visitor remained staunch in keeping Grace from being moved from the church. Finally, O'Dwyer realized the well being of the woman was more important than how she received the care and slowly allowed his arms to unfold from his chest.

"The free clinic has a doctor on staff until ten," he said.

The young man looked at the clock on the wall. It was now 9:34. His attention shot back to the priest. "Would he come here?"

"I suppose you'd have to ask him before he could say yes or no."

"Would he come if you asked?"

"Me?"

"You'd have a better chance getting a doctor to come here than I would."

"You have a point there." O'Dwyer gave the young man's attire a critical look. He moved to a coat rack by the door and removed his scarf. Draping that over an arm, he took down a hat and trench coat. "When I get back, you and I are going to have a heart-to-heart talk."

The young man reluctantly nodded and watched as the priest left the rectory. An exhaustion beyond comprehension settled into his bones, muscles, and joints, and he allowed himself to slink down to the floor next to the couch. He leaned his head back against the padded upholstery of the armrest, and after checking in on the aerial defenses above the cathedral, finally allowed himself a brief rest.

O'Dwyer left the cathedral and turned up his collar to ward off the wind, which had picked up to a blustery gale since he'd stepped outside after mass and bid his parishioners good night. Leaves and leaflets blew across the street and caught in gutters, against fences, and under the wheels of parked cars. Tree limbs in the courtyard creaked and groaned as they bowed under the force. A keening sound sieved through the architectural eaves of the Gothic building and the old tenements surrounding it, grating on O'Dwyer's nerves.

He looked up at the sky before stepping down from the cathedral's steps, a habit he'd developed of sanctifying God as he breathed in His good graces. But tonight he didn't feel there were any graces in the air, good or otherwise. There was a palpable sense of wrongness in the briskly blowing wind. O'Dwyer shivered within his coat, curling his shoulders forward and pulling the brim of his hat low over his eyes to keep the grit from blowing into them.

Before trotting down to the sidewalk, he caught sight of several black shapes circling in the sky overhead, swirling in such an agitated manner that he thought of birds having seizures. He gave his head a little shake and started down the steps, then headed up the street toward the free clinic located in a dilapidated apartment house two blocks away.

It took him no longer than he expected to get there but he found the walk distressing. His bones were weary and his joints seemed gummed up by the wet chill in the air. Even with the wind blowing behind him, he felt hampered in his movement. Maybe it was the weather, or maybe it was the unexpected visit from the young man who often frequented the church for moments of private reflection, but there was an aura of malignancy in the night that had an ominous feel to it. He only first noticed it after he'd left the confines of the cathedral and absently wondered what would happen if he returned to the church; if he'd no longer feel that menacing presence. He tried to laugh it off as silly but it was a difficult impression to shake. Our Lady of the Blessed Virgin Mother had always brought a comforting sense of well being to him. While he had never felt distressed by the outside world, right now, as he walked through the streets of a neighborhood mostly populated with the city's somewhat undesirables, he felt strangely threatened. As if there were villains hiding in the shadows ahead of him, waiting for him to pass so they could jump out and attack.

He looked over his shoulder and scanned the way behind him, looking for just such unsavory characters. But the only things that met his eyes were the flat shadows of inanimate objects and buildings. Nothing moved or accosted him, and the farther he walked from the cathedral the more foolish he found himself to be.

Finally, he reached the litter-strewn stoop of the tenement building where the free clinic was housed. Leaves and papers were gathered in the corners of the stairs, and a mixed odor of cheap wine and human urine reeked from the sides of the building.

O'Dwyer climbed the steps and pulled the door open, its knob not really sitting solid in a strike plate that had long since disappeared. He ambled down the corridor until he stood outside a wooden door with a plastic plaque proclaiming the rooms beyond to belong to the community center's free clinic.

He checked his watch and saw that it was a quarter to ten. Given the circumstances, he hoped the skeletal staff hadn't yet left for the night.

The door was still unlocked when he tried it. He went in, walking into a small waiting area of several metal chairs and a desk situated against the opposite wall. No one was waiting in the room, but a young woman was flipping through files behind the desk. She looked up and smiled when he came in. Monsignor O'Dwyer recognized her as one of his parishioners. Politely, he removed his hat and held it between his hands in front of him. "Is the doctor still in, Angie?"

The receptionist set her files aside and looked at him with concern. "Are you ill, Father?"

"No, not me," he assured hastily. "But there's a young woman back at the cathedral who needs medical attention."

"Do you need me to call for an ambulance?" she asked, her hand going instantly for the phone, not too quick to realize that O'Dwyer would have been able to do that himself back at the cathedral.

"No, I need the doctor," he said with too much insistence. "Who's working tonight?"

"Doctor Perez. She was just finishing up before going over to the hospital."

Hope surged in the priest. "She's still here then?"

"Yes."

"Could you see if she'll make a quick stop at the cathedral on her way to the hospital?"

"Just a minute; I'll ask."

The girl got up and went into the back room, allowing the door to shut behind her so he remained alone and hopeful in the waiting room. He stood in front of the desk feeling asinine, wondering what he would say to the doctor if she questioned him about the specifics of his needs.

Fortunately, he knew Monica Perez, both personally and by reputation. She was well known in the community for her selfless work with the poor and the homeless, dedicating her life to serving those she'd grown up among. She was a strong woman who'd been raised in the area, gone to medical school on a scholarship, and returned to her childhood neighborhood after interning at the county hospital. She'd been raised by a devout Hispanic mother who'd seen to her Catholic upbringing all the way into her high school years. O'Dwyer had been the priest who'd baptized her and been present at her first communion. He'd heard many of her confessions, officiated at her confirmation, and finally given last rites to her mother on her deathbed. That had been the last time he'd seen the young woman in any ecclesiastic sense, although he'd seen her many times in the lay sense since she'd returned from college. Now she claimed a more secular outlook of the world and didn't seem to have room for faith anymore.

Monica Perez came out of the back room with her receptionist in tow. She was a young woman with strong Hispanic features. Dark brows pinched over dark almond eyes. She had an olive complexion and exotic bone structure, and an apple-shaped face framed by thick hair she kept tamed with a rubber band. She was an attractive woman with provocative expressions and cunning wit, but her no-nonsense attitude made her appear harsh and unapproachable. O'Dwyer sensed there was a lot of unresolved anger in her that kept the cheer out of her character, and he often regretted that he couldn't do anything to help her get over it.

"Angie tells me there's a woman at the cathedral who needs my help?" Monica said, slipping on her coat after throwing her medical bag on the table.

"Yes," he said, suddenly realizing he didn't know any more about the situation than that the woman had been attacked. He should have insisted on more information about what had happened before going for help. "She's unconscious."

"Why didn't you call for an ambulance?" Monica's tone was a bit condescending and unconcerned. She finished buttoning her coat and wound a light scarf around her neck, keeping her movements unhurried.

"Monica," he said gently, if not a little impatiently, "will you come? There's more to it than just that."

Monica hesitated. "Such as?"

"The man who brought her there won't let her leave. He's very adamant about her staying in the church."

"So he sent you to get me instead," she said with growing skepticism.

"Yes," he replied edgily.

"Did you ever wonder if it might be a ruse just to get you to leave so they could ransack the church?" she posed with gravity.

"Not this man; he wouldn't do such a thing. Will you come? She's earnestly in need of medical attention."

Monica considered it for a moment, then picked up her bag and headed for the door. "I'll look in on her. But if she needs more extensive medical care, I'll have to bring her to the hospital. My shift starts in ten minutes." She turned back to Angie. "Call the hospital and let Doctor Bernstein know I'll be a little late."

Monsignor O'Dwyer followed the woman out of the office and then the tenement building, down the stoop and onto the sidewalk. Monica walked briskly, heading into the blustery wind with a determination that was humiliating for the old priest to match. He had to hurry to keep up, his stride having grown more lumbering over the years, and the extra effort taxed his breathing.

"What seems to be wrong with her?" Monica asked as she walked, looking over her shoulder to see him suffer her pace. She noticed he was having a hard time keeping up but she didn't slow down to accommodate him.

"I'm not really sure," O'Dwyer huffed. "But this man who brought her in said she'd been attacked."

Monica stopped abruptly, turning to face the parish priest with obvious concern. It wasn't unusual to learn about a woman being attacked, but it was distressing to hear it was still unsafe to walk the streets alone in her own neighborhood. With O'Dwyer's revelation, she seemed to feel the ominous presence of an evil looming nearby. She, too, looked around at her surroundings, much as the priest had on his way over. Her attention was drawn to some strange activity in the sky over the cathedral.

"What's that?"

"Birds, I suppose," O'Dwyer replied.

"Birds attacking birds," Monica observed doubtfully.

He couldn't make out much from their distance but it did appeared as if there was an aggressive engagement going on up there.

"I suppose it could be some predatory migration thing or something," O'Dwyer answered lamely.

"Or something," she said distantly, looking away from the unnerving sight with a shiver. The chill from the wind created goose bumps on her arms despite the warm coat she wore. A few strands of hair broke loose from her ponytail to worry at her eyes.

O'Dwyer followed her quietly, saving his breath so he could work at maintaining her arduous pace. When they finally reached the cathedral, Monica stood aside and let him open the door for her, not so much for the sake of chivalry but because she was reluctant to take the first step back to her abandoned faith. O'Dwyer didn't notice her reluctance, or if he did, decided not to show it. He simply opened the door and led the way to a back office in the rectory. There, he opened another door to the inner office, where he'd left his uninvited guests.

The young man jerked awake when he heard the door open. He jumped to his feet, startled to have been caught off guard and asleep. He stood in front of Grace, shielding her from view, and faced O'Dwyer as the priest stood aside to allow the doctor to show herself. Seeing who it was, his heart skipped a beat and he instinctively looked away.

Monica froze when she saw who it was standing in the monsignor's office, striking on a memory of the young man from the hospital two nights ago. She snorted derisively. "You seem to come across a lot of women in distress," she said in an almost accusing manner.

He looked at her, knowing he wouldn't be able to avoid her for long. She would remember him if she had that kind of memory. Even now, her face showed a flicker of brief recognition, but he couldn't tell if it was from a short or long-term memory.

"I do know you," she said ponderously, reliving a memory as a savory piece of information from long ago. "About a year ago," she recalled. "Maybe longer."

She came forward, her strides quick and abrupt. He stepped back, but not by much, because his legs bumped into the couch and couldn't go any farther. Monica reached out for his hands and caught them, then brought them up to look at them. They were covered in strips of leather, one of which was bloodied. She pulled her eyes up to his.

"You showed up at the clinic with your hands in shreds back then. I stitched them up for you." She tried to pull the scarf away from his throat but he pulled back. In deference to his self-consciousness, she dropped her arms and stepped aside so she could look at the woman behind him.

"My God," she murmured as she pushed him aside dismissively. "What happened to her this time?"

He turned around to watch as Monica squatted before her patient. "She fell out of a van."

Monica snapped her eyes up to him, narrowing them with suspicion. "O'Dwyer said she was attacked."

He nodded. "The men who attacked her pulled her into the van. She was able to escape them, but only by falling out of it."

"I have to get her to the hospital." Monica rose to her feet. She moved hastily to the desk where the phone sat, but he stepped in front of her, blocking the way.

"No."

"What?"

"She can't leave until daybreak."

"What are you talking about?"

"It's not safe for her to leave."

"It's a hospital we're talking about," Monica said, as if speaking to a dolt. "She'll be safe in a hospital."

"I said no."

"She needs medical attention."

"Then give it to her."

"She needs special medical equipment I don't have here."

"Do the best you can."

"She needs to be in a hospital."

"She can't leave here."

"Why not?"

"You wouldn't understand."

"No, you don't understand," Monica said insistently, angrily. "This woman is pregnant."

That was the end of their short tête-à-tête. He had nothing to say to counter the bomb she'd just dropped. Instead, he looked at the woman on the couch. For the first time, he saw that she did have a certain look of radiance about her. Before, he'd thought she was just beautiful, with the look of an angel. But now, being privy to the information of her delicate condition, he began to recognize the slight nuances pregnant women exuded. The glow in her cheeks, the luster in her hair, the gleam in her eyes. All of it made sense where it had made none before.

Could this be the reason why she was being pursued by Drudge's minions? Did the child she carry create such attention that so many demons would fight to their deaths just to reach her?

He shook his head of its persistent and irritating uncertainty. "You know this for a fact?"

"You brought her to me Friday night," Monica said, her ire tempered by his wary concern. "She's ten weeks into the pregnancy."

He continued to stare at Grace, trying to divine what made her so special that a master of the minions would so brazenly send his forces after her. "What's her name?"

"Grace."

"Grace," he murmured, testing the name on his tongue and finding it apropos. She looked like a Grace, an angel full of grace, an angel of innocence. Abruptly, he turned to face Monica. "Do what you can for her." And he spun around to stalk to the desk, where the phone sat, which he disconnected by ripping the cord out of the wall jack.

Monica's back stiffened at the popping sound of the cord snapping, then winced at the violence with which he threw it aside. He suddenly strode to her and unclipped the cell phone from her belt.

"Hey!"

"I'll return it later."

Feeling her own anger sparked, she folded her arms across her chest. "You don't trust me?"

"I trust your concern is to give her the best care possible. But I can't allow you to take her out of here. Not before dawn."

Monica became incensed. She shuffled on her feet, her mouth working as if to form words of retaliation. But before she could say anything, the young man left the rectory, leaving Monsignor O'Dwyer to stare gape-mouthed at the closed door.

"You'll need to call an ambulance, Father," Monica said after a moment of speechless silence.

"He won't let me any nearer to a phone than he will you. But I'll talk to him."

Shambling toward the door, moving with the economy of reluctance, O'Dwyer left the office and went into the outer reception area, where he found the brooding young man perched on the edge of his secretary's desk. He looked weary and beaten, more in spirit than in body, but even his hooded eyes didn't rise to meet O'Dwyer's demanding attention. Instead, they were riveted to a space somewhere between his face and the floor, casting his gaze at some other dimensional plane residing in his subconscious.

O'Dwyer had known the young man for a few years now, from a time so disconnected from the present that it was almost from another era altogether, probably from the very dimension where the young man was staring back at the moment. He remembered the first time he'd met the imposing young man—more of a kid then than now—when he and his lovely bride-to-be had attended marriage classes together at the church. Father Bannerman had been enthusiastic about the couple's compatibility and even mentioned it to him, despite how young they were. But O'Dwyer believed Bannerman's enthusiasm about the couple was because he was an avid fan of the team the young man played on rather than the prospect of the couple's level of maturity.

Although the young wife was a devout Catholic and churchgoer, her betrothed made only infrequent appearances at church for major religious holidays and the baptism of their first-born child. Bannerman had officiated at that ceremony, spending most of his time with the doting father discussing the sport of hockey and not the young man's obligation of raising a Christian child. O'Dwyer didn't find it too distressing, though, since he had faith that the child's mother would oversee her religious upbringing.

The next time O'Dwyer had seen the young man outside of midnight mass on Christmas Eve and Easter Sunday was less than a year ago, when he'd appeared mysteriously to beg a favor. Father Bannerman had since been transferred to another diocese, so the young man had asked if O'Dwyer would retrieve the bodies of his wife and child from the city morgue. He had begged for his family to receive a proper Christian burial and paid for all the expenses in cash. He had asked for the mother to be buried with their child in her arms, so the two might lay in rest together. As for the grave marking, he wished only for a stone angel to watch over them.

O'Dwyer was so moved by the young family's tragedy that he did what he was asked. On a cold, gray evening, he laid the young mother and child to rest with only the sullen young man in attendance. When O'Dwyer had turned to give comfort and condolences to the grieving husband, he'd discovered that he'd slipped away into the shadows, giving no indication of where he might have gone.

It was several months later before he saw him again, kneeling in benediction at the altar. His hair had grown long and his body was dressed in all dark clothing. The top half of his face was hidden behind a cloth he'd wrapped around his forehead, and his hands were covered in strips of leather, running from his fingers to his wrists. He wore a dark brown scarf wrapped around his neck, and O'Dwyer knew it wasn't for warmth. He'd tried to start a conversation with him, but the young man's previous aloofness had since transformed into a downright cold-hearted reserve.

Over time, the young man had become a regular sight at the church, although O'Dwyer suspected he never really felt as if he belonged to it. He always stayed outside the realm of the congregation, despite O'Dwyer's attempts to draw him in. Soon, he became nothing more than a mysterious figure in the building, and O'Dwyer began to feel unerringly safe whenever he was around, as if his presence represented some kind of ward against the things that went bump in the night.

"Adam," O'Dwyer began gently, reverting to a solicitous tone he usually took whenever he spoke with the young man. "You need to explain yourself. You've brought me into something I don't know how to react to. For me to grant you the sanctuary you seek you have to tell me what's going on."

Adam remained contemplative for a while yet, staring at the space between himself and the floor. His expression was no longer one of resistance, but of consideration of how to begin explaining. Because of that, O'Dwyer gave him time to put his thoughts in order.

He fully expected Adam to take a deep breath before he began, but the young man gave no such prelude to his words. He simply said, "When you left the church, did you see them? In the sky?"

For a moment, O'Dwyer wondered what he was talking about, but then he recalled the unusual activity that had caused him such curiosity he'd even mentioned it to Monica. "You mean the birds?"

"Not birds," Adam said evenly. "Bats."

The priest shrugged. "Yes, I guess they could have been bats."

"They attacked her . . . Grace."

O'Dwyer blinked. "The bats?"

"I saw them. They were hunting her."

O'Dwyer shook his head and looked at Adam with newfound concern. "You believe these creatures—birds, bats, whatever they are—were hunting that young woman in there? Surely, you can't believe that."

"I know it for a fact, Father."

"How?"

"I hunt them."

"Excuse me?"

"They aren't what you think." Adam spoke evenly, maintaining a level tone, yet somehow his words and the inflection of them were imperative. "They're evil creatures with evil intentions. You felt it when you left the church. You felt something wrong, something dangerous. You didn't feel safe again until you were back here."

O'Dwyer inwardly—reluctantly—remembered the feeling of insecurity he'd felt when he'd stepped off the porch steps of the cathedral. He almost agreed with Adam, but then a stabilizing sense of rationale saved him from admitting such insanity. He was a man of the church. With his education and training, he understood the business end of good and evil; he knew they were simply a moral compass by which to live a good life. A lay person could easily misinterpret unnatural events as signs or the purveyance of doom, and such mistakes could lead a person astray. It was as much a part of his job to lead the faithful to God as it was to prevent them from drifting into fanaticism.

"I understand your fears of such vile seeming creatures, Adam, but I assure you, they're just as much a part of God's creation as you and I are."

That remark caused Adam to bring his head up, with his back stiffening and his eyes clarifying with resolve. "You're wrong there, Father. Those creatures were never created by any just and loving God. And they bow to no one but their own cruel master. I've seen them under his control, hunting and destroying, bringing nothing but terror and death." He paused as he seemed to consider going on, then took a deep breath and began, his words solemn and painful.

"That night, over a year ago, when Claire and Marie were killed, the bats were there, along with their master. I saw them, when the ranches were burning and the people and livestock were slaughtered. I found Claire already dead, in our home. Her back had been sliced open. Marie was still alive, but just barely, and I tried to get her to a hospital. She was in insulin shock. But they were there, outside the house, preventing us from leaving."

He didn't pause in his retelling, but his voice began to crack and lose its even keel. The pain of the memory etched itself so starkly on his face that it was sad to look at him.

"The bats fell from the sky and took the form of demons, taking their orders from a man who walked out of our burning barn. He admitted that he'd killed Claire and told me to take my revenge out on him. When I couldn't kill him, he tried to kill me, marked me before he did and said I'd be his when I reached the other side." Adam reached up and removed the scarf from his neck. "He hung me from a rafter in the stables. Then he laid Marie at my feet to die."

He stopped, his voice swollen in his throat so no more words could get out. His eyes glistened as he relived the painful memory of his family's murder, and his own survival against his desire to die.

O'Dwyer said nothing for a long time, reluctant to break into the young man's quiet reflection. Yet he also remembered that he was a man of the cloth and it was his mission to bring comfort to those in pain. On the other hand, he was hesitant to believe Adam's story of demons and devils. Surely, the young man had equated the villains who'd plundered his home as demonic incarnations.

"Adam," he said gently, "that was a terrible time for you, no doubt. For a lot of people. But you have to understand—"

"Father," Adam interrupted. "You know I wasn't a religious man. I followed Claire to church only because it made her happy. I was completely content to avoid the question of God in my life. I believed no more in the existence of the devil than I did in Santa Claus or the Tooth Fairy. But that night, when my family was taken from me, I saw a man so evil I was forced to believe in God, because I swear to you, I saw the devil. And I didn't just imagine what I saw. As much as I tried to avoid it, I only came back to the realization that there is a very tangible form of evil in the world."

"Perhaps you saw something you only believe to be evil," O'Dwyer reasoned. "What happened a year ago was a horrible crime you were forced to witness and endure, and you must have felt powerless to stop it. It's not unreasonable for you to equate those vicious men to demons."

Adam looked in earnest at O'Dwyer, as if trying to gauge the priest's limit of belief. Perhaps he assumed the monsignor, being a mature cleric in his church, might have insight into the ecclesiastic realm of God. But whereas O'Dwyer wore the robes of his appointment, he wasn't all-knowing, nor was he privy to the exact interpretations of God's word.

Slowly, Adam nodded, if only to have the priest feel less concerned about his sanity. "Maybe you're right," he muttered, unconsoled by the words he spoke. The burden of his fate suddenly bore down on him, until he felt almost crushed by it. Tears of frustration welled up in his eyes, and he brought his hands up to cover his face.

O'Dwyer took a hesitant step toward him, afraid he might have triggered a mental breakdown with his unintentional words. Yet he was reluctant to move too close to the man, afraid he'd sparked off a negative chord in what could be a very unstable mind. Father Bannerman had always exclaimed how Adam Mogilvy was an experienced fighter in his own right, a skill honed by the sport he played, and that kept coming to mind now. Dismally, O'Dwyer recognized his own lack of bravado and cursed himself.

Adam looked up as he pulled his hands away from his face. "I don't want to go to Hell, Father."

Those words drew O'Dwyer out of his hesitation, and his face slackened as he relaxed his tense limbs. "Adam, unless you've committed some heinous crime or mortal sin, you shouldn't worry about going to Hell. You simply need to welcome God into your heart and receive absolution for your sins."

Adam lifted his hands to show them to the priest, despite their leather wraps. "He said he marked me that night, that I belonged to him. That I would be his once I made it to the other side."

"A mark doesn't send a man to Hell, son. The intention of his actions and the actions themselves will determine how a man spends eternal life."

The door to the monsignor's office opened and Adam self-consciously lowered his hands. O'Dwyer turned his attention to Monica as she exited the room. "How is she?"

"She's resting. She doesn't seem to be hemorrhaging, so that's a good sign. But it's not conclusive. She should see her obstetrician in the morning. Make sure she does."

O'Dwyer nodded as Monica strode toward Adam, her stride quick and determined. Abruptly, Adam jumped off the desk and moved a few steps away, avoiding her approach.

Monica stopped and frowned at him, cocking her head to the side. "Are you afraid of me?"

Adam remained where he was without a reply. She completed the distance to him and reached out with both hands. For the briefest time, she hesitated, momentarily worried what his reaction would be if she touched him. But being the hardened cynic she was, she quickly overcame her fear. Taking his left hand, she brought it up to examine it, her interest completely professional and curious, particularly of the blood soaked into the leather wrappings. She followed the blood up the sleeve of his overcoat, and with a quick motion, slipped the coat off his shoulder and exposed the wound in his arm.

Bending forward to peer at it, she said, "If I had to wager a guess, I'd say this is a bullet wound."

He met her eyes. "I suppose it could be, if it was interpreted that way."

"I'm required by law to report all gunshot wounds."

"I'm aware of that."

Disturbed by his cavalier attitude, she opened her medical bag and selected the items she would need to clean and treat the injury, which were actually two wounds. The small puckered entrance wound, which hardly bled at all but had a few clothing fibers wedged into it, and the gaping exit wound, which had bled profusely and required stitching.

She worked dexterously, not unkindly, worrying about the fibers that needed to be plucked from the wound with care. In the end, she wrapped his arm with clean gauze and handed him a vial of pills. "Make sure you take one a day to ward off any infection."

She packed her equipment and snapped the bag shut. Gathering her hair between her hands, she quickly bound it with a rubber band, then cracked her spine by stretching back, working out the kinks that had found their way into her vertebra after a hard day of work.

"Now, I really have to get to the hospital," she said when she released her hair and straightened. "There's probably an angry resident waiting for me to relieve him."

Adam gathered his coat from the floor. His injury seemed to cause him no pain or hindrance, and he slid into the coat without effect. "I'll see that you get there safely."

CHAPTER EIGHTEEN

Sergeant Markey knew there were a lot of things in his life he wanted to do—ski the Alps, retire on a full pension, make lieutenant by the time he was forty, and find a nice girl to settle down with and marry—but opening his eyes at that particular moment was not one of them. The simple act of raising his eyelids wasn't only painful but debilitating. With each time they flickered open, he felt pounds of strength ebb from his body.

He knew there was one other thing he wanted to do before his life ended, and that was to get his hands on the kid who'd laid him out so easily. With two felled swoops, that kid had dropped him like a fly, proving that he was much younger and spryer than Markey could ever hope to be.

Markey finally managed to blink his eyes open, only to see he was laying supine on the wet cobblestones in the alley. The back of his clothes was already soaked from the puddles he'd fallen into. A pain throbbed in his head where his left cheek had stopped the kid's barreling fist, and Markey worried that his face might have shattered like a cartoon character's. He hesitated moving, thinking that if he did, only more pain would hit him. But even though he remained on his back, he knew he'd eventually have to get up.

"That boy sure do pack a powerful punch, don't 'e?"

Markey jerked up and scrambled around so he could see who spoke. In doing so, he found his heart had jumped up ahead of him and was lodged in his throat. If someone had been around him while he was unconscious, he'd have been at that person's mercy the entire time. He took a quick inventory of his body as he peered into the shadows of the alley for the origin of that voice.

He couldn't make out the details but he could see a vague shape. The shadows always seemed to drift around what could only be a man. Or maybe the man had purposely positioned himself among the shadows so he wouldn't be so easily seen.

"Who's there?" Markey demanded, trying to bring his legs beneath him as he scrambled to reach the wall for support. His jerky movements brought painful jolts to his body, especially to his face, where he could tell his cheek was so swollen that it stood out in his peripheral vision. Instead of getting to his feet, he braced his hands on the ground and moaned.

The gruff voice from the shadows chuckled. "I always said that kid was the best damn enforcer in the league."

Markey slowly lifted his head and peered more intently into the dark. Whether the moon was becoming brighter or his eyes were becoming keener, he could now make out more distinct features of the stranger. He was a large man, old and dirty, wearing layers of tattered clothes and reeking a foul bodily odor. His jaw worked continuously as if he was chewing something between his words, and a thick tangled beard bobbed up and down against his chest.

"Who are you?" Markey demanded.

"Name's Sophocles," the bum answered. He stuck his fingers into his mouth and sucked on them, one after the other, as if tasting the last flavor of fried chicken off them. "Slash asked me to watch over you 'til you regained your senses."

"Slash?" Markey said, pushing carefully off the ground and rising to his feet.

"Not a name I gave him, mind you. Something he already came with. The boy who laid you out like Sleeping Beauty." Sophocles laughed at his remark, then grew more serious. "He says he didn't mean to hurt you, but you were keeping him from gettin' the lady to safety."

"Grace Fitzpatrick," Markey said, hearing himself as if he was speaking in echoes. "Where is she?"

"She's safe, I reckon, if she's with him." Sophocles hopped off a stack of milk crates he'd been sitting on. He patted his hands against his bulging belly and smacked his lips together, looking around with interest.

"Where would that be?" Markey asked when the old bum didn't say anything else.

"If he said he's taking her to safety, then she's safe, and you shouldn't worry so much about 'er. He'll take care of 'er, awright."

"You know him?" Markey demanded. His head ached and he wanted to be home, but he had more questions to ask. "What's his business with Grace Fitzpatrick? Why's she so important to him?"

Sophocles chuckled to himself. Again, he grew solemn. "Depends on what you mean. But that kid is the only thing keeping Hell from breaking free on this Earth."

Markey watched as the old man started off down the alley, away from him, informally dismissing him. "Wait, what are you talking about? If you have information of where a fugitive is hiding, you can be arrested for not cooperating."

"They're not hiding from you, Detective," Sophocles said as he stopped and turned around. "When he needs you, you'll find him."

"When *he* needs *me*?" Markey echoed, taking a few steps toward the old man with the help of the alley wall. "I don't seem to remember agreeing to help him."

"You should see someone about that shiner," the old man advised. "He don't know his own strength sometimes."

In the space of time it took Markey to blink, the old man was gone, vanished into the shadows or into thin air. Markey didn't chase after him; he knew he didn't have the strength to make the effort, nor did he think it would do any good. He suspected the old man would offer nothing useful anyway.

However, the old man's words rang like a reminder, and Markey remembered that he'd only been passing time until Doctor Perez came on duty. He glanced at his watch and winced when he squinted to make out the time in the darkness. It was almost ten thirty.

Murdock cursed and slammed his fist against the brick wall of a building. He'd been frantically searching for the woman for the last hour, scouring the nooks and crannies in which a small person might hide, listening for sounds of frightened breathing, squeaks of panic, and the clatter of footsteps. But he heard nothing, found nothing.

After a while, he made his way to Gutter Row, a makeshift town within the inner city where the homeless people made their residences. Shacks made of cardboard boxes and corrugated siding, milk crates, and shopping carts from stores miles away. Fifty-five gallon drums were set up and burning rubbish to create light and warmth, providing a primitive social setting. Suspicious, sullen eyes peered out from beneath the water-swelled shelter of boxes. Dirt-smeared cheeks and chins of curious children poked out of the shadows for a glimpse of his passing. No one accosted him. Although he was clearly not one of their own, they still sensed his presence wasn't for them and they'd do well if they simply let him pass through unmolested.

Murdock did, but not kindly. He stuck his head into the box homes and shifted meager possessions aside to look into hiding places. He asked a few attentive men if a woman had been through there lately, but they were reluctant to tell him anything even if they knew. He left Gutter Row no wiser for his efforts, only angrier. He meandered through the streets for a few minutes more before he realized Grace Fitzpatrick was probably nowhere near where he was looking. She might be at home, for all he knew.

He turned around to get his bearings. He was no longer in the business district, but he wasn't far from it either. The area of the city he found himself in was the oldest part of town, where the original businesses and apartments were centered. The city had been built up around it and the old buildings had since been abandoned and left to fall in on themselves. Murdock had often wondered why enterprising corporations didn't just purchase the land and raze the ugly structures in order to put up more of their impressive skyscrapers. But he figured it had a lot to do with where the city would hide its numerous homeless and impoverished residents, so the mystery seemed solved. Right now, with the status quo remaining the same, each part of society understood its place in the city. The bums would no sooner set up a cardboard shack next to the Citicorp monolith than a limousine would dump a jewel-adorned passenger out on Gutter Row.

Pausing in thought, Murdock considered his next move. He knew he'd have to retrieve his van soon, regardless of where he'd strike up his search for the woman next. The van could leave a trail straight back to him. Then he'd have to explain why his car was found abandoned half on the sidewalk with its front windshield smashed once the area became active in the morning.

He struck out with a grimace. His work boots made hollow clumping sounds on the sidewalk as he walked. The huge walls of the buildings loomed over him in an ominous manner, like giant sentinels guarding the streets. The circle of light from the street lamps made a sickly sheen of glistening blackness in puddles along the curb.

Murdock was aware that he was the only person out at night in that area. The fact that he was by himself wasn't what was so disheartening. It was the idea of being the only person out to brave the night that made him realize there must be something out there keeping everyone else inside. As he entertained such a notion, he began to feel the subtleties of the night that were particularly intimidating to him. Unfamiliar and intangible reasons. Unnatural inhibitions that made him quicken his pace so he could cover the most distance before he spent too long out in the open.

Soon he realized how greatly he would appreciate any open door to seek refuge behind and began to look for a bar that still catered to the public. It might be best if he neglected the van and struck out in search of company, if only to experience a sense of companionship by the simple fact of being near other human beings. But the more desperate he became, the quicker his steps got and the deeper into the business district he went. He knew he was near enough to the van where it would be easier to retrieve it than turn back for the safety of numbers, but his legs had other ideas. As his footsteps increased, it suddenly occurred to him that he was running.

Murdock forced himself to slow his pace, huffing breathlessly as he struggled with his fear, a fear that Drudge might find disfavor with him and send the bats to punish him. A fear that he would experience the terror so many disagreeable associates had already suffered. A fear that he would become one of the damned creatures Drudge commanded.

Murdock shivered with a chill and ran. The heels of his boots resounded on the asphalt as he crossed the empty street. A splash of water geysered as he stomped in a puddle.

A black shape suddenly darted across his path. Murdock came to a halt, nearly skidding along the asphalt as he braked. His breath caught in his throat as he tried to discern what it was that had crossed in front of him. It might only have been a shadow from something behind him as he ran at a different angle to the moon, or a bird startled from its roost, or even his imagination. But deep in his heart he knew none of those explanations would explain what otherwise would be one of Drudge's minions.

A squeak of hysteria slipped from his throat. He found himself frozen in place, too terrified to make a decision of which way to flee. He thought if he turned around he'd only face one of the demons in its most hideous form. If he continued forward, he'd be headed in the direction the black form had gone.

Another shape took wing and danced in front of him, even as more appeared around him.

Two, three, four. Six. Ten.

Murdock fell to his knees in front of them and began to whimper.

Sergeant Markey walked into the commotion of St. Jude's emergency room and headed directly toward the admissions desk. There, a dark-skinned woman of indeterminate age hastily scribbled something on a form and tucked it into a file. She looked up as his shadow fell over her paperwork, then reached for the top clipboard of several in a stack. She thrust it at him and said, "Sign in."

Markey disregarded the proffered clipboard and said, "I'm here to see Doctor Perez."

"They all are. Now sign in and have a seat. I can see you're not in dire need just yet."

Markey grimaced at the nurse's disdain and gripped the edge of the counter. He leaned just a tad closer to the woman and pulled out his badge hanging from a chain around his neck. "I didn't come here for medical attention. I came to see Doctor Perez about a case."

"She's not in yet," the nurse said, matching his poor attitude with her own.

"Your afternoon crew said she comes on at ten."

"And she called a while ago to say she was running late. She'll be in later, but I don't know exactly when."

"Listen," Markey said, holding his voice on the verge of exploding. "I was here at seven o'clock and told to wait until ten. Now . . ." he glanced at his watch. ". . . it's almost eleven, and she's not here yet. I didn't make a big stink about it then, when I agreed to wait patiently. Then I got hit by a Mack truck and I still waited until Doctor Perez was supposed to be in. Isn't she the head of the emergency room on the midnight shift?"

"Sometimes," the nurse answered, a bit more sympathetically. "But she left word with the desk that she was going to be late coming in from the clinic. If you could wait a little longer, I'm sure she'll be here soon. Unless Doctor Bernstein could be of some assistance."

Feeling somewhat mollified by the nurse's more redeeming attitude, he relaxed. "No. Doctor Perez will have the information I'm looking for."

The nurse shrugged. "Then you'll have to wait if you want to talk to her. It shouldn't be too long. On nights she works the clinic she sometimes gets stuck with a late walk-in."

"I'll wait," he said, and walked over to the farthest seat against the wall in the waiting room, joining the ranks of the sick, injured, and uninsured. When he took his place in the uncomfortable plastic chair and leaned his head against the wall, it wasn't long before he drifted off to sleep.

CHAPTER NINETEEN

Murdock stumbled into the room after the door was opened and he was pushed through. He tripped and flailed with his arms to regain his balance and angrily gathered his feet beneath him. With a quick look around, he noticed the room wasn't so much a room as it was a chamber, and an odd one at that. It was of granite construction and circular in shape, having no windows and only the rough hewn wooden door he'd been pushed through.

The men who'd escorted him to the Spatial Tower entered the room and closed the door after them. They moved to either side of the door, preventing his escape if he should take it into his mind to try. Murdock glared at them with loathsome distaste. They were no better than common thugs, but they were dressed in Armani suits and Gucci shoes, their wrists adorned with gold watches and diamond-studded bracelets, and probably their pockets bulged with a thick wad of cash held together with a designer money clip. Alliance with Drudge and Spatial Industries had its merits, but failure bore its agony.

Murdock wanted more than ever to remind the two men who'd snatched him off the street and dragged him through the doors of the Tower that they'd once been no better than him, and no amount of trinkets or expensive clothing could ever change their dubious origins. But now, after proving themselves capable associates of Drudge, they were referred to as Mr. Bentley and Mr. Devereaux. Murdock had always known Mr. Bentley as Pick, a petty thief who roamed the streets and pilfered from the pockets of businessmen who strolled through the downtown area. He'd never been more than a shadow in a crowd, but now he was a trusted employee on Drudge's retainer.

Previously, Mr. Devereaux had been known on the streets as Big D, a low level drug dealer who stood on the street corner and hustled his wares to whores and crack addicts. Until now, the biggest thing in his life had been maintaining the perimeter of his territory free of encroachment from other drug dealers. He was a shady character who waged warfare through drive-by shootings and rampant machine-gun fire. He had no finesse, no bravado, and no honor; yet he, too, was a favored associate of Malachi Drudge.

Murdock, on the other hand, was merely an underling, an aspiring freelancer. He'd wanted to be called Mr. Murdock for the respect of it and have the opportunity to wear Gucci shoes and Armani suits, too. But more likely he would favor black crew neck shirts and tweed jackets, with pleated pants and leather-soled shoes, just to be different. The allure of the glamour Drudge offered was intoxicating, and he'd volunteered his services for initiation into the clan many times, even though the idea of aligning himself with the devil was terrifying even in his best nightmares.

Now, preparing to stand in judgment of his failure, he was having second thoughts. As he slowly turned to face the center of the room, where he'd seen the only accouterments to be, he saw two people sitting in chairs and nothing else. In one wooden chair, poised in elegant repose, was Malachi Drudge, his look impeccable and meticulous. He wore a classic suit of silver gray, with his hair styled straight back from his forehead and hanging loose against his neck. His legs were crossed and his hands lay placidly on one knee. He glared at Murdock with a curiosity more attributed to a parent considering the actions of an errant child than of someone furious with a poor employee.

Murdock couldn't bare the look on Drudge's face and shifted his eyes uneasily to the other chair. There, his partner was taped with massive amounts of duct tape on his wrists and ankles, and around his mouth, securing him to the chair, keeping him immobile. But the most startling feature on his partner's face was G.W.'s saucer-sized eyes plied wide open in panic.

"Aw, G.W.," Murdock moaned, knowing instinctively there was no salvation for his friend, and not much hope for himself.

"Good men are so hard to find," Drudge remarked, only his lips moving.

"Mr. Drudge, we had her. We were bringing her right to you when we ran into complications." Murdock spoke quickly and desperately. He was begging for his life—pathetically, at that—and knew the even-tempered facade Drudge was showing was nothing more than a mask of what really lay beneath.

"Yes, tell me about those complications," Drudge said with mock interest.

Murdock swallowed and looked at his partner, trying to gain some mettle from the mere fact that he was, at least, still capable of explaining himself. "Two men interfered. An old bum distracted us while another man—a younger one—slipped her out of the back of the van. We gave chase, but your bats came on too fast."

"Are you saying I dispatched my minions too early and caused Ms. Fitzpatrick's escape?" There was a twinge of anger flickering in Drudge's narrowing eyes.

"No, no!" Murdock quickly interjected, holding out his hand to placate the man's fury. "It was that son of a bitch, that kid with the fucking headband and long hair. He wanted to play hero."

"And did, I suppose."

Murdock shrugged his head to the side to concede the point. "There were extenuating circumstances . . ."

"Like your partner panicking and running away," Drudge said understandably. He glared at G.W. with distaste. "As I said, good men are so hard to find."

"Well, Mr. Drudge, in his defense—"

"Don't go there, Mr. Murdock," Drudge ordered, his head turning back to chide him with warning.

Murdock stuttered on what he would otherwise have said to defend his friend but finally chose the better part of discretion. He closed his mouth and made a straight line of his lips. For several minutes, they remained completely silent, except for G.W., who whimpered uncontrollably, knowing his fate was relatively sealed.

"Explain this to me," Drudge finally said, breaking the silence. "How does one man—and a kid, by your own recounting—overcome two accomplished street thugs armed with guns?"

"Mr. Drudge, you had to have been there," Murdock began. "The van was wrecked and we were a bit scrambled because of it. Before we even knew what happened, Ms. Fitzpatrick was gone."

"With this hapless hero," Drudge added sarcastically. "This *kid*."

"I can find him for you," Murdock insisted. "And if I find him, I'm sure I can find the woman."

"And how would you find this kid?"

"He's one of the homeless. I've seen the old man he was with. I know I can find the old man easily enough."

"Promises, promises."

"Mr. Drudge, please, I can find her for you. I can bring her here just like you wanted." His desperation began to show in the quickness of his speech.

"I know where she is!" Drudge snapped abruptly. "I know where they both are!"

Murdock took a step back at the violence in his shout. G.W.'s eyes grew wider, if that was at all possible. Drudge rose to his feet in one fluid motion and began to stride back and forth behind the chairs. Each time he drew close to G.W., the bound prisoner sobbed spastically, his body hitching.

"They took refuge at the cathedral on the west side, the one they call the Blessed Virgin Mother. Both of them, Ms. Fitzpatrick and her savior. He took her to the one place that was safe from my minions. They'll stay there until daybreak. The Rakshasas can't reach them while they're in the sanctuary of the church. Somehow, this *kid* knew that." Drudge paced back and forth, his hands clasped behind his back. "But you can enter the property and retrieve Ms. Fitzpatrick for me."

Murdock perked at the suggestion, a glimmer of hope that he might be able to walk out of the room—and the Tower—with his life still intact. "Yes, I can do that. I'll need help, though, because there are two of them, but G.W.—"

"Mr. Bentley and Mr. Devereaux will accompany you," Drudge said, cutting him off. "They're trusted associates of mine."

"But G.W.'s the man I usually work with," Murdock said, his voice taking on a whine in the hopes of saving his friend from an uncertain future.

Drudge stopped his pacing and looked hard at Murdock. "You want Mr. Wilson with you?"

Murdock suspected it was a trick question and chose not to answer.

Drudge walked toward G.W. and stood behind him. With one hand, he stroked the sweaty, grimy hair sticking out at all angles. G.W. squeezed his eyes shut and whined, his cheeks puffing as he hyperventilated. Slowly, Drudge's well-manicured fingers seemed to metamorphose, becoming claw-like, thin and bony, covered in scales. His nails turned into talons, and the digits clamped onto G.W.'s skull with a relentless and ever increasing intensity.

G.W.'s eyes snapped open in horror. Depressions formed where the pads of the talons compressed, the razor-sharp claws careful to lie against the flesh of G.W.'s skull. No expression passed Drudge's face as his fingers spread out in a spider-like fashion and crimped. Bones cracked as a muffled scream of agony tried to breach the gray tape of the gag. Blood seeped from the corners of G.W.'s eyes and ran in sinuous rivers along either side of his nose. Thick droplets formed within each nostril and suddenly broke into a trickle down the tape. With a sudden wrench, Drudge crushed G.W.'s skull in one hand.

Tears of absolute terror streamed down Murdock's cheeks as he watched his friend's brain compressed by the shards of his splintered skull. When Drudge calmly released him, his hand pulled away from the nest of G.W.'s tousled hair as a human hand again. He raised his eyes to glare resolutely at Murdock.

"Mr. Wilson will be there," he assured. "But he'll be among the minions."

Murdock's hand came up to cover his mouth, which was opening in a stretch of outrage and insanity. He clamped his palm against his lips so they wouldn't form words that would see him delivered into the same ranks to which G.W. had been condemned. He kept the presence of mind to realize such audacity would only lead to his own destruction.

Drudge glared at him with open challenge. "Do you have a problem with that?"

Murdock watched as G.W.'s head abruptly lolled forward, chin on chest. With nausea filling his stomach, Murdock managed to swallow his defiance. Weakly, he uttered, "No, no problem."

A loud clatter of metal on tile jolted Markey out of sleep. His head jerked up and sent a shiver of pain through his skull. There was a dull ache in his neck from the angle on which his head had been bowed. His hand went out unconsciously to the area where a crick had wedged its way into his spine. In addition to that, his face felt thick and swollen, and his nearsighted peripheral vision could clearly see the raised bruise growing under his left eye. A vicious headache throbbed at his temple, and he thought it would be a smart idea to ask for an aspirin, at least.

He glanced over to the receptionist's desk and saw that the noise had been caused by a collision between two nurses hustling trays of instruments in different directions. Both were busy retrieving their possessions and arguing over who had caused the accident.

Markey ignored them and got up, stretching his legs to restart circulation through them. Pins prickled his flesh until it got so bad his knees threatened to buckle. He waited the process out, knowing if he walked now it would only bring him down.

He looked at his watch and saw it was close to midnight. With feeling back in his legs, he started for the receptionist, who was still the same woman from earlier. She looked up with the same sullen expression she'd worn when he'd first come in.

"Is Doctor Perez in yet?"

The receptionist pounded on a stapler with the proficiency of a lumberjack. "She's been in for a while."

Markey waited for her to get up and show him the way, but she did no such thing. "May I speak with her?"

"She's with a patient right now."

"Yes, and I've been here five hours now, which is longer than anyone else, I'd wager. I'm tired, hurt, and getting irritable. I want to speak with Doctor Perez now."

"*Getting* irritable?" the receptionist remarked.

Markey resumed a less harsh tone. "I only need five minutes of her time."

"All right, Sergeant, I'll let her know you're here."

The woman graciously got up and disappeared behind a partition cutting off the triage area from the waiting room. In a few minutes, she returned and resumed her seat. "She'll be out when she finishes up with the patient she's with."

Markey nodded and remained standing at the receptionist's desk, a little off to the side so he wasn't in the way. He'd be damned if he was going to be forgotten again by moving out of sight.

After another ten minutes, the door to the emergency room opened and a pretty young woman dressed in a white doctor's coat emerged. She picked him out immediately and approached. "Are you the detective who wanted to speak with me?" There was a hint of impatience in Monica Perez's tone.

"Yes," he answered, a bit culled by her presence after so long a wait. "Do you have somewhere we can talk?"

"Listen, detective, this isn't a date, so ask your questions and let me get back to work."

He could definitely detect a level of irritability in her, if not in her direct words, then in her voice. Characteristically, he took offense to it. "It's about a woman who was brought in Friday night. A woman by the name of Grace Fitzpatrick."

Monica's eyes shadowed as her brow crinkled with concern. She looked around and beckoned him to follow her. She led him out of the waiting area and into the triage room, where she pulled aside one of the curtains from an empty work station. Markey followed her without a word, until she finally turned on him once she gained the privacy she was hoping for.

"What about her?" she asked, folding her arms across her chest.

"There was a homicide Friday night and we know Ms. Fitzpatrick was on the scene, either before, during, or after the crime. I'm trying to determine which that was."

"And how can I help you?"

"The admitting forms reflect that she was brought in at 11:54 p.m."

"That sounds about right," she agreed, nodding.

"I've got about an hour and a half gap I'm worried about. I have to account for where she was during that time."

"Have you asked her?" she asked sardonically.

"Of course. She says she was walking through the streets after an argument with her boyfriend. Up until now, she hasn't provided us with anyone who can corroborate her story."

"Do you think she killed that person?"

"She could have," Markey admitted, unbiased in any way as to Grace Fitzpatrick's guilt or innocence. "But I want the person who did it, not just someone who happened to be in the same room where the victim was found."

Monica considered the detective's concern and seemed satisfied that there was no entrapment in his questioning. "She was brought in by a young man who may or may not be able to account for that questionable period of time you're concerned with."

Markey perked up. "Do you know who he is?"

She shook her head. "No. He didn't provide a name, and he was gone before we could ask him anything."

"He didn't explain what happened to her? Why she needed medical attention?"

"He only said that she'd been attacked."

"Do you suspect he might know *how* she was attacked?"

"I suppose he would have to, if he told us that much. She was unconscious when he brought her in."

Markey was intrigued. "I'd like to find this man, talk to him."

Monica remained silent for a minute, and Markey noticed she was chewing on her bottom lip, which piqued his curiosity. She seemed to be undergoing some sort of debate with herself. He allowed the quandary to bother her, hoping something would come of it.

Just as he hoped, she spoke without prodding. "Do you suppose this guy might have attacked Grace himself?"

"There's no telling what happened. Only Grace and that man can give us a true account of what happened Friday night. And she's not telling us anything."

"I guess what I'm trying to ask," Monica put otherwise, "is Grace in any danger from this person?"

"That would depend on whether or not he was the one who attacked her in the first place."

She mulled that over for a while. "Detective, I think I can tell you where you can find him." She balked before going on.

Markey waited. "If you know where he is, you'd only be helping Grace by leading me to him. He *is* the only one who can substantiate her alibi for the homicide, in the very least."

A look of appeasement crossed her face. "They're at Our Lady of the Blessed Virgin Mother."

Markey drew on a look of perplexity before he put two and two together. "She's with him? Tonight?"

"Yes."

"The man who brought her here Friday night?" he pressed.

"Yes," she said, narrowing her eyes warily.

"You know this for a fact?"

"I left them not more than an hour ago."

Markey released a breath of disbelief. "That son of a bitch did this to me."

Monica's eyes widened. "He attacked you?"

"He was out of control when I ran into him. He's a very violent young man."

"Oh God."

Markey headed out of the emergency room, his legs picking up the pace the closer he got to the door, his adrenaline in high gear. He felt a thrill of excitement at the thought of getting his hands on the kid who'd gotten the drop on him. Suddenly, the homicide investigation took a back seat to his vanity, and he bolted from the hospital like a shot out of a cannon.

Grace slowly opened her eyes and turned her head to take in her surroundings. She'd regained consciousness earlier, when Doctor Perez had snapped smelling salts under her nose, but she had since fallen back to sleep. Seeing the doctor had caused her to wonder about where she was, and Doctor Perez had told her all she could. Grace had then turned the focus of her worry on to the condition of her baby. After a cursory exam, she was told it appeared—that being the key word—that the baby was safe. She would still have to see her obstetrician in the morning to be sure but she shouldn't worry too much now. Exhausted, Grace had fallen asleep after those comforting words, and finally, after indulging in sleep that was restful and dreamless, she'd awakened a second time.

She knew better than to get up too quickly. She was afraid that moving too abruptly might dislodge an already weakened fetus in her womb. She satisfied herself with turning her head instead, and saw with a twinge of unspecified delight that the person she'd been looking so desperately for was sitting in a chair behind the desk across the room.

He appeared to be resting, his eyes closed and his breathing easy. He still wore the same clothes he'd worn when she'd last seen him, but he didn't seem so ominous now. Instead, he looked peaceful and kind, a silent spirit of mysterious origins who seemed more ethereal than physical. But his physical presence wasn't to be dismissed either, because his posture in the chair made a formidable impression on her.

He slowly opened his eyes and looked at her, the smooth motion of his head turning in her direction startling her somewhat. He said nothing and allowed no expression to pass his face. The fact that he made no effort to initiate a conversation made her slightly uneasy. She had always been a social creature by nature but she felt especially inclined to develop a rapport with him.

She carefully pulled herself into a sitting position. "I feel horrible," she began cautiously. "You've saved my life twice, and I still don't know your name."

He fixed her with an apprehensive eye. "Most people on the street just call me Slash."

"That's what the old bum said." She immediately regretted referring to the old man as a bum. It seemed to her that the old man's intercession had been portentous for her rescue on both occasions. She owed him a great debt of gratitude.

Adam didn't take her remark offensively. "His name is Sophocles."

She offered him a slight smile, both in humor of the bum's name and because of what she remembered the old man had said about her champion. "He referred to you as an angel."

Adam turned aside, and Grace felt she'd said something that struck a sore spot. She wanted to say something to get him to look at her again, but he turned back to her without encouragement, his brow creased with worry.

"I have to ask you about the things that were after you."

Grace stuttered on words that wouldn't find the proper form of verbiage. Instead, she blinked repeatedly as she tried to focus on the simple words he spoke. Taking them in the context he'd used, she suspected he might already know what those horrible things were. He spoke in a manner as if he didn't need anyone to tell him about their origin, but of the reasons why they would be concerned with her.

"They usually hunt for a specific reason," he said. "And they've taken a particular interest in you, it seems."

She struggled with the concept of being the target of something so monstrous. She looked down at her hands wringing in her lap. Her head shook back and forth. "My life just sucks."

"Excuse me?"

She looked up and saw the utter confusion on his face. With all his personal knowledge of the grotesque creatures they were talking about, he must never have expected those words to come out of her mouth. She gave a little chuckle at his quizzical expression and tried to explain. "It all seemed to have started Friday night, after I told my boyfriend I was pregnant. After that, my life took a turn for the worse. He wanted me to have an abortion, blamed me for getting this way on purpose. We had a big fight and that was when I ran out on him. Literally."

Adam remained quiet as she told her story. She spoke without misgiving or fear of judgment.

"That was the first time one of those . . . things . . ." she faded out, uncertain how to divulge what exactly happened when the creature accosted her. "Well, you know; you were there. You saw what happened."

"Yes."

"Then, after I was released from the hospital Sunday morning, I went home and found the police searching my apartment. They brought me in for questioning on a homicide. They say someone was killed in the same hotel room I was supposed to be staying in with my boyfriend. The funny thing is I don't even know the man who was killed and I have no idea why he was in the room after I left. But apparently I'm a suspect in his murder. The police asked me to account for my whereabouts during the night, and I told them about being attacked by a mugger and how you came to my rescue."

She paused and smiled at him, thinking this was a good time to express her gratitude. But by the look on his face, she sensed he wasn't pleased with her mentioning him to the police.

"I was looking for you tonight when those men dragged me into their van." Her face grew perplexed as she tried to understand what their purpose was in attacking her. "But you showed up just in the nick of time. Again."

"You still haven't explained why the minions are after you."

"The who?"

"The minions. The creatures that attacked you."

She narrowed her eyes. "You seem to know more about them than I do. Why don't *you* tell me what they are?"

"Exactly what you suspect them to be. Demonic servants of an even greater monster. A manifestation of evil. An incarnation of what people blind themselves from seeing. But you see them. You don't understand them, but you know they exist."

She wondered about that. "I know I've seen them, but I don't know what they are. Or why they're picking on me."

"Your baby," he said abruptly. When she blinked obtusely at him, he said, "This all started after you told your boyfriend you were pregnant. It seems the father of this child doesn't want your baby to live."

A look of appall crossed her face and her complexion paled. Unconsciously, her hand went to her abdomen to reassure herself that the baby was still there. Although she couldn't feel any swell in her belly yet, she sensed the baby's heart still beat strongly within her. She knew Christopher had suggested she have an abortion, but she couldn't believe he would be so ruthless as to abduct her for that very purpose. Christopher was the District Attorney. He'd vowed his life to the pursuit of justice. He wouldn't forsake his scruples because of a mistake in judgment.

She shook her head to refute his theory. "He wouldn't stoop to such tactics. He's a good man. Basically."

"No man associated with the minions has any good left in him."

"He's not affiliated with those . . . whatever you call them." Tears welled up in her eyes as she thought about Christopher ordering men to do her harm. Even though she argued that he couldn't have such control over those awful creatures, she wondered why common street thugs had entered the picture.

Adam said nothing. Instead of pursuing his line of questioning, he leaned back in his chair and closed his own eyes.

Outside, around the perimeter of the cathedral, the bats flew in constant vigil of the two refugees hiding within the building. But there was something strange happening. Something that made Adam watch the events with quiet concern. For some inexplicable reason, the bats were being called off, although not completely away. To be cautious, Adam ordered a slew of pigeons to follow them as they flew to perches several buildings away.

". . . do I do?"

He opened his eyes and glanced at Grace. She had recovered somewhat from her silent weeping to ask him what she should do. What could he say to her, a woman he knew nothing about, pursued by demons for reasons he wasn't entirely sure of. He had no assurances that she wasn't being sought by the minions to protect her. He wondered briefly if she was actually in danger of forces other than evil, and that Drudge was moving to protect her and the child she carried, not the other way around.

He couldn't trust uncertainties. He had to choose sides carefully.

A simple fact suddenly fell into place for him, and he shot out of the chair like a canon. His unexpected movement startled Grace, and she shifted uneasily on the couch. Adam came around the desk and hurried toward her, his overbearing presence causing her to flinch.

"We have to go."

"What . . .?"

"We're not safe here any longer. I thought there were two forces at work, but there's only one. He sent the men in the van *and* the minions."

"What are you talking about?" she said, growing more frightened than she'd been. His spurious words, accompanied by his sudden zeal, made her realize he might know more about the situation than she would ever be able to understand.

"The bats can only fly at night, in the dark," he explained. "So the men in the van were supposed to take you before the sun went down. When they didn't bring you back before nightfall, Drudge sent his minions to find you."

"I don't understand . . ."

He grabbed her elbow and tried to bring her to her feet. When she resisted, he spoke quickly. "The minions can't cross onto holy ground, so we're safe from them here. But that won't stop Drudge's people from coming after you. The ones from the van."

Grace's eyes grew wide when she suddenly understood what he was getting at. "The men from the van? They're coming?"

"The bats are going to roost. Drudge is clearing the way for his people."

"Oh my God."

"We have to get out of here."

She pulled on a look of panic. "Is it safe to leave the church?"

"I know a way."

She balked at that, remaining firm on the couch even though he held out his hand for her to take. She slowly shook her head. "I don't want to leave here."

"We have to go. If Drudge sends his men, we'll be trapped."

"But the bats are out there," she sobbed.

"Don't worry about them. I won't let anything happen to you."

She made a juvenile show of sliding her hands under her thighs so he couldn't take hold of them. "They don't know we're here."

"The bats know, which means Drudge knows. And if he knows, then so does his hitmen." He struggled to remain calm but firm. "When they come, there'll be more of them, and they'll be armed. I can't fight off everyone."

"I don't want to leave," she moaned petulantly. "I feel safe here."

"I'm telling you that you won't be safe here much longer."

In truth, there was only one place he would feel absolutely safe, but he hadn't brought her there because he didn't want to reveal his own sanctuary. Instead, he'd opted for the cathedral because it could provide immediate and unquestionable protection against the bats. Only he'd failed to factor in the presence of mortal men.

Adam knelt in front of her, his face even with her own. "I didn't come this far to let anything happen to you. You have to trust me on this."

Grace peered into his eyes and tried to see any reason why she shouldn't believe him. She had no reason to trust him, but neither did she have any reason to stop believing in him. Tentatively, she reached out and took his hand.

CHAPTER TWENTY

Back in his unmarked car, Markey called the homicide office and asked to speak to Detective Lumas. He knew Lumas would be there; he'd been assigned to look into Charles Driskell's background for other possible suspects in his murder, and that would take some time. Lumas would be pulling long hours tackling the task.

After a short wait, the detective picked up and grumbled, "Lumas here."

"Pete, I need you to get a car and meet me at Our Lady of the Blessed Virgin Mother, pronto."

"What's up?"

"I think I might have a handle on what happened in the Driskell case. I don't think Grace Fitzpatrick is a suspect after all, but I have a feeling she's in trouble."

"Ooh, a damsel in distress. What's going on?"

Markey handled the phone with one hand as he started the car. "I think we're dealing with a love triangle. There's a boyfriend I met tonight who seems to have a lot of unresolved anger issues."

"And he's seeking absolution in the church?" Lumas asked sarcastically.

"I have it from a reliable source that he's holding Grace Fitzpatrick against her will." Trying to drive one-handed, he turned the corner awkwardly and hit the curb. With frustration, he wedged the phone against his shoulder and gripped the steering wheel with both hands. He was driving like a madman, and it was all he could do to bring himself under control, but he felt the pressing urge to get to the cathedral quickly.

What was it that made him feel the compulsion to run into a relatively dangerous situation without thinking it through first? He'd already been bested by this man once; did he think he could go hand to hand with Grace's homicidal boyfriend again? Even his gun tucked faithfully in its holster didn't reassure him as much as he would have liked, not after he'd been embarrassingly disarmed once already.

"I'll be right there."

Markey disconnected the call and tossed the phone on the passenger seat. He calculated the time it would take him to reach the cathedral to be less than five minutes, but it would take Lumas about ten minutes to get a car and another fifteen to make it across town. He was just grateful it was a Sunday night after midnight. Lumas wouldn't be hindered by the usual gridlock traffic associated with the area during business hours. Traffic was nonexistent, and his own frantic driving was enough for even the casual observer to wonder about his sobriety, if there were any motorists out and about. He wasn't worried about the public image he portrayed with his poor driving skills; he was just anxious to get to the church as quickly as possible. Still, once he got there, he'd have to wait until Lumas arrived before he made any attempt to approach the building. Going in on his own would be sheer folly.

He finally turned onto the street where the cathedral was and shut off his lights, coasting up to the curb a few buildings away from the Gothic-influenced structure. The massive granite church was impressive and daunting all at once. Mammoth-cut stones set on top of each other, cantilevered cornices, and intricately carved marble columns all led up to buttresses gilded with gold leaf. Multicolored stained-glass windows lined the front facade of the cathedral next to the huge double doors carved in Greco-Roman relief. A large rosette dormer looked out over the street just below the multi-gabled roof. Gargoyles hunched along the parapet like heretical guardians against evil, chiseled wings and malicious faces giving the building an Old World flavor. The cathedral's construction was incongruous with the surrounding buildings of a more contemporary and practical design. The neighborhood was old, dating back over two hundred years, but only the cathedral was recognized as a historical landmark. The other structures—tenements and old office buildings—remained in disfavor with the city's developers and saw no money for restoration. As such, the area had quickly fallen into disrepair.

Markey turned off the engine and leaned back in the seat, his eyes focused intently on the front doors at the top of the cathedral steps. The car was quiet except for the tick of the cooling engine. Regardless, he turned up the volume on his police radio and listened to the eerie events happening in the north end of town. Unit after unit was being cleared to respond to one emergency after another. Haphazard rescue efforts were being attempted in one situation or another. Markey recalled the lessons the city had learned over a year ago, when the disgruntled masses of the crack neighborhoods had expressed their discord against the outlaying ranches west of the city, burning them to the ground, assaulting the homeowners, and even killing a few. Socioeconomists had blamed the recession and budget cuts in social programs to be the cause of frustration in the lower economic strata. That had essentially increased to volatile proportions, until finally some unidentified spark had triggered that explosive night. Much like the Chicago fire, the violence had simply gotten out of hand.

At least that was how the current political administration had explained it to the public after the constituents demanded answers for the sudden eruption of violence. Everyone knew it could have happened anywhere, and it was only unfortunate that anyone had to suffer the losses they had; but hey, let's face it, they said in private, it could happen again, anytime and anywhere, and everyone quietly worried about their own safety. But Markey—along with the rest of the police force who'd worked that night or listened to the tales of their comrades who had—knew a different story. No self-respecting, hard working member of the lower class by virtue of bad circumstances would ever have been a party to the massacre that night. The people who had burned, looted, and killed in the ranches had been nothing more than an organized band of thugs taking advantage of a collective effort to pillage for valuables and vent their violent tendencies against human victims. The fact that such a systematic and senseless attack had avoided prosecution all along was a mystery and an embarrassment the police department hadn't been able to get over. Although a few known criminals were brought up on charges pertaining to the crimes committed that night, none of the ones arrested had ever admitted who their ring leader was.

Markey experienced a sense of déjà vu and knew tomorrow would be a terrible day. When the fires were doused and the rubble was cleared, when the bodies were counted and the wounded were treated, the entire Homicide Bureau would be put on sixteen-hour shifts to discover who was at the bottom of it.

Since that tragic night when a handful of people had been brutally murdered, three separate disturbances had occurred in various outlaying areas of the city. Those had been relatively contained, and only one person had died as a result of the violence. The police department had developed a successful new approach to civil unrest and raved about their quick response and immediate action when the violence broke out. A curfew ordinance was drawn up to invoke at the slightest scent of civil disobedience and a no-tolerance enforcement policy was promoted when it was clear that any small disturbance was going to escalate into a full-blown riot. Those measures had proved to be successful to prevent the last three incidents from getting out of hand, and the city government believed it had everything under control.

Tonight, though, Markey believed otherwise. Listening to the radio chatter, he felt for the officers-turned-foot soldiers going head to head with urban terrorists. The protocol for these crazy nights was to settle immediate conflicts, remove hazards, and render medical attention. Any crimes committed were preserved until the morning, when the investigative units could work without being disturbed. Markey's turn to deal with the madness would come tomorrow, along with the tirades from the command staff about why nothing had been done to prevent their recurrence in the first place.

That would all be in the morning. Right now, all Markey wanted was to close his eyes and get twenty winks. But he knew he had to keep an eye on the front of the church. He wished he was more familiar with the layout of the building, but he was too much of an atheist to ever have set foot in a church, much less such an eminent house of worship as Our Lady of the Blessed Virgin Mother.

It was entirely possible this Slash fellow had already taken Grace out of the building by now, even though Doctor Perez had insisted he wouldn't leave until morning.

Headlights reflected on the intersection in front of him, and Markey perked up, thinking Lumas had arrived relatively fast. But he could tell by the sight of the car turning in the intersection, shutting off its headlights and coasting up to the cathedral steps, that it was not a departmentally-issued unmarked car. It was a brand-new sleek black Cadillac with wire rims and dark-tinted windows. Not the type of roadster to be found in the police department's fleet.

He watched as three of the four doors opened like wings of an insect and three men came out with an inane curiosity of what lurked on the street. Instinctively, Markey slouched down in the driver's seat, ducking low enough that the newcomers wouldn't be able to tell if the lone car across the street had any occupants. He peered over the dash and watched with bated breath for what they would do next.

The men seemed satisfied that no one was watching and walked to the trunk of the car. One man opened it and pulled out three shotguns, which he passed to his companions.

Markey's eyes widened at the sight of the artillery coming out of the trunk. A sharp memory triggered something in his mind, and he remembered the old man from the alley professing how the man holding Grace hostage—the man he referred to as Slash—was the best damn enforcer in his league. A hitman? That might explain why these men were armed to the teeth. If they were there for the same man Markey was, they were ready to do some serious business with the boy.

Markey began to rethink his theory about the murder at the Rialto. If this Slash character had killed Charles Driskell, would he have angered people who were partial to the businessman? Was Driskell tied to the underworld, and had Slash's arrogance clouded his judgment?

For whatever reason, Grace Fitzpatrick was going to get caught in the middle of a mob war.

Markey snatched up his radio and begged for the dispatcher's attention. He sputtered off his location and radio number. "I've got three armed gunman at Our Lady of the Blessed Virgin Mother. I need backup."

When the dispatcher responded, she seemed surprised. "Verifying Our Lady of the Blessed Virgin on Seventeenth?"

"That's right, downtown."

She paused for a minute, possibly looking over her screen to find the closest available unit to send to him. But Markey knew there would be no one in the area. All the working road units had been sent to the north suburbs. Had this all been planned, he wondered insanely, ruing his luck. He'd been convinced the whole time that the riots had always been orchestrated by an organized force. It wouldn't be too far a stretch of the imagination to relate that force with the underworld.

"I don't have anyone in the area. It might take some time to clear a unit."

A familiar voice broke through the transmissions. "Homicide Two-Fourteen."

Markey smiled. Lumas's baritone voice sounded self-important and reliable.

"Homicide Two-Fourteen," the dispatcher acknowledged.

"Show me en route to the cathedral. I've got Unit One Hundred with me."

Markey wracked his brain for who Unit One Hundred might be, then gasped in dismay. The old desk sergeant, Joe Fiskett, lovingly known as Smoky, was coming to be his backup. The ancient officer was reported to have more time on the department than anyone else and was looking at mandatory retirement by the end of the year. He hadn't seen action for the last ten years, at best, and Markey knew his hearing, if not his eyesight, was shot.

Markey peeked over the dashboard and watched in horror as the three men pumped their shotguns and marched up the steps. Their gait was definitely professional and there was no mistaking their intention. One stood on either side of the door, while the third stood in front of it. That one leveled his shotgun at the strike plate and triggered a round off. Even in his car, with the windows rolled up, Markey felt the concussion of that shot.

* * * * * *

It took Adam another ten minutes to convince Grace that she would be safer elsewhere. She stood up with his support, on shaky legs, wobbling like a newborn foal, only to find herself thrown into a paroxysm of uncontrollable hyperventilations. Adam settled her back on the couch, patted her hesitantly on the shoulder, and looked around.

She eventually regained a normal rhythm to her breathing and nodded for him to help her try again. Slowly, with an arm linked through his elbow, she allowed him to guide her to the door. She stepped gingerly, as if the slightest jostle would either throw her into another fit of tears; or worse, dislodge the baby from its anchor in her womb. They left the room, passed through the secretary's office, went into the corridor, and headed back to the church proper. Grace didn't question Adam's direction but trusted him implicitly.

Adam felt the need for urgency and coaxed her to pick up her pace. They made it to the christening alcove and into the church proper, where they passed in front of the altar, to the opposite side of the cathedral. Adam paused before the large crucifix on the wall above the tabernacle and genuflected, crossing himself reverently, muttering a prayer that they make it to sanctuary without mishap.

Perhaps God wasn't listening, or had just forsaken them to the wiles of fate, because a muffled blast went off directly behind them.

Adam spun around on one knee, coming to stand up straight and ready. The explosion came from the back of the cathedral, and he saw the door suddenly kicked in, the force of its impetus swinging it wide open. In the threshold stood a well-dressed black man with a shotgun held at hip height, his stance poised in anticipation of firing again. In one fluid motion, he wracked another shell into the chamber and glowered like one of the gargoyles sitting on the parapets outside.

Relying on instinct and better judgment, Adam grabbed Grace's elbow and bolted toward the alcove opposite the christening room, where rows of votive candles were lined up for benedictions. Some had already been lit by grieving relatives of passed away loved ones, while others remained dark. Beyond that lay a door to the dressing room for the choir and altar boys, the walls lined with white surplices and purple robes. Farther beyond lay another corridor, which led to several rooms, one of which was a stairwell leading down to a basement. That was where Adam meant to go.

Feeling the pull of Adam's insistent tugging, along with the nudge of terror pushing her on, Grace sobbed as she stumbled after him, her feet barely able to keep up with his longer strides. She cried out for him to wait but he was in no mood to slow down. The urgency in his tugging nearly pulled her off balance, until she finally did go down on one knee, barking out in pain and dragging him to a stop.

Adam turned when Grace fell, frustrated, then desperate when he glanced back at the doors of the cathedral. Three men had filtered into the building and were moving into the church proper. They fanned out at the back of the pews, the black man coming down the center aisle, while the man from the van ran toward the ambulatory where he could move up the side wall to the transept. A third man cut through a break in the pews to come straight toward Grace and him.

"Come on," Adam said, pulling Grace none to gently to her feet, not so much concerned about wrenching her arm out of its socket as when the intruders might start cranking off more rounds. The shotgun pellets would lose velocity the farther they had to travel, but as the men approached, the pellets would have greater penetrating ability. At that point, their spray pattern would make Grace and him an easy target to hit.

Grace cried out as if in pain. Reluctantly, Adam eased up on his tugging. Another explosion sounded, echoing with excruciating volume through the cavernous church. Both Adam and Grace flinched as splinters tore off the back of a pew only a few rows away. Adam ducked behind the closest, curling his shoulders and bowing his back to stay low. He knelt before Grace and held her shoulders so she wouldn't stand, shaking his head in the hopes that she would resist the urge to bolt, even though he felt it overpowering him as well. When he looked into her eyes, expecting to see wild fear and hysteria, he saw something else instead. She had such a beautiful face—in more ways than just the physical sense—it should be a crime to see it contorted by either pain or fear, much less both. Deeper than the fear for herself was the fear she felt for her unborn baby, and it was that similitude, the one that reminded him of Claire, that made him vow to see her survive the night, no matter what the cost. A clarity of what might be happening finally dawned on him, and he knew nothing as angelic as what was in her expression could ever be associated with the minions. Drudge's interest in her must surely have some evil lurking behind it.

"Will you trust me?" he asked.

She sniffed and nodded.

"I mean implicitly," he said. "Wherever I take you."

She seemed to worry briefly about that, but her only alternative was facing the three gunmen. "Yes."

"Come on, then."

He walked at a crouch along the first pew, toward the transept, keeping low so he wouldn't provide himself as a target. He no longer dragged or pulled Grace along; it was up to her if she would follow or not. Time was of the essence. If one of the gunmen made it to the altar before they made it to the transept, both he and Grace would be sitting ducks.

But thankfully, when he glanced over his shoulder, he saw her mimicking him, keeping up right behind him, to the point that one of her shoulders almost struck his hip. It was only twenty or more feet to the end of the pew and the anxiety to reach the transept was nerve-wracking. When they reached the end, they would be momentarily exposed, before they could duck into the chapel used for vespers for a brief moment of safety.

Before they got there, though, Murdock stepped into view, his body towering over Adam where he was crouched behind the pew. The shotgun swung around in Murdock's arms until it pointed directly at Adam's face.

Very carefully, Adam rose to full height. Murdock sneered as he stepped back and allowed the barrel of the shotgun to follow him up, redirecting the weapon to chest level.

"You made me look bad, sport," Murdock said, his tone malicious and vindictive. His eyes shifted to where Grace remained at a crouch behind Adam. When he peeled his lips back in a snarling grin, she shrank back even farther.

Adam raised his hands to show that they held no weapons, hoping to relax Murdock's grip on the shotgun. Then he glanced to his right to see one of the other hitmen skirting the pews and hurrying up the aisle. He knew if he was going to make any move it would have to be then.

His left hand slammed against the barrel of the shotgun and clasped the metal tube, directing the muzzle off to the side. With his right hand, he reached over and grasped the stock, then twisted both hands and flipped the shotgun stock over barrel.

Murdock's finger was caught within the trigger guard and unwittingly depressed it when the shotgun was jerked from his possession, firing a spray of pellets into the floor. Grace screamed, a terrified sound echoing off the high walls and mural ceiling, coming back at them twice before fading. Adam prayed she hadn't been struck by any part of the blast. At the same time, without a break in his initial maneuver, he caught Murdock's chin with the up-swinging stock. The connection caused a resounding crack of wood against bone, making a hollow, dead sound. Murdock's fingers went slack as his head snapped back, and he collapsed like a rag doll.

Adam took the shotgun and spun on the two remaining gunmen, ready to train the weapon on them. That was all he was willing to do, though, for he didn't have it in him to do violence in the cathedral. Not in a house of God. Regardless, the two men dove for cover behind the pews, having realized he'd now become armed and dangerous.

Worrying about how little time he had, Adam glanced down at where Grace still huddled. When she looked up, he reached down to bring her to her feet. Her small, delicate hand fit nicely into his palm and he raised her up, just as one of the gunmen popped up and fired a round from his shotgun. Adam only had time to flinch before the blast passed over his head, mere inches from taking it off. He grasped Grace's hand and bolted for the transept, just as another blast gouged splinters from a nearby pew.

Another gunman popped up to Adam's right and made a display of racking a round into the chamber. Adam skidded to a halt. He spun around to catch Grace against his body and propelled her with tremendous force toward the transept. Unencumbered, he dropped his shotgun in the direction of the assassin, remembering in the nick of time that he needed to put a round in the chamber.

"Police! Freeze!"

The two remaining gunmen turned away from Adam. Perhaps they sensed he had no round in the chamber, or that he wasn't a threat to them, or that the arrival of the police was more important to deal with than a mere shotgun blast; but both gunmen fired simultaneously at Markey standing at the entrance to the church proper. Adam gave the exchange a split second of attention before he used the distraction to his advantage and lunged into the transept after Grace.

Markey ducked behind a massive marble column for protection, the shotgun pellets pinging around him, chipping slivers of marble from the gleaming pillar. He covered his face with his raised arms while listening for a break in the blasts thundering one after the other his way. He could imagine the synchronized system of one gunman firing while the other racked a round into an empty chamber. He counted carefully, until he'd heard nine explosions, and then a stretch of silence.

He peeked around the column and saw powder and marble chips on the floor. The pungent odor of burnt gunpowder irritated his nose. With his heart in his throat, he leaned out from behind the cover of the pillar and panned his gun around the church, looking for assailants among the pews.

They'd laid suppression fire while they'd escaped.

Markey left the safety of the column and raced down the main aisle, vividly aware that the silence might be a ruse for him to do just such a stupid thing. He was ready to dive for cover, if necessary.

No one popped up from a hiding place among the wooden pews before he made it to the altar. He knew where the two men would have gone; after Grace and her boyfriend. And if they hadn't, Markey had more of a beef with this Slash fellow than he did with these underworld figures. In that respect, the odds were more in his favor.

He, too, ran toward the transept.

Adam led Grace through the dressing room of the church choir and out into a rear corridor. His hand, which had been holding hers, released it and went for something in one of his coat pockets. He produced a key just as he came up to a door near the end of the corridor. With one hand still holding the shotgun, he fitted the key in the lock and opened the door, then reached in and flicked on a light switch.

Grace came to stand beside him, her hand lingering on his arm for fear that the illusion of him would suddenly dissolve. She peered over his shoulder at the staircase descending into the hollows of the basement. Nervously, she looked at him.

"Trust me," he said and moved aside to allow her to descend.

Hesitantly, she did, trailing her hand along the wall for support.

Adam anxiously watched the corridor as Grace descended the stairs. When she was off the steps, he reached up with the barrel of the shotgun and broke the light bulb. As the delicate shards tinkled to the concrete steps, two men burst from the dressing room and spotted him. Adam stepped onto the stairs and closed the door behind him, fumbling to secure the lock.

He heard their uttered curses as they reached the door and discovered it was locked, then a shout for one to stand back while the other took aim against the strike plate. Adam bounded down the steps with an instinctive knowledge of exactly where to place his feet.

"Grace?" he whispered once he reached the bottom, turning in the pitch black to locate her.

"Here," she answered quickly, breathlessly.

He honed in on her voice and dragged her out of the perimeter of light that would spill from the upstairs corridor when the door finally opened. For the few seconds they had until that happened, between another deafening explosion and three successive kicks to break the door free, Adam drew her toward the wall.

He moved preternaturally, his knowledge of the underground cellar giving him confidence of where to place each step. Grace shuffled uneasily, unwilling to trust the blackness not to lead her into a wall or—God forbid—a cobweb. She knew without being told that she had to remain absolutely quiet, but she also knew she'd scream if a spider web suddenly caressed her face. The memory of the monster enveloping her in its foul, bristly embrace brought shivers to her body, and it would undoubtedly be the first thing her mind latched onto if she unexpectedly ran into a cobweb.

Adam brought her to a place where she was forced to stand motionless as the two gunmen cursed the dark and plodded awkwardly down the stairs. She could just make out their dim silhouettes as they descended, but after they reached the ground, she lost sight of them in the pitch blackness. Adam no longer held her hand, and her arms broke out in goose bumps. Frightened, she wanted to call out to him, but she also knew she shouldn't.

Then Adam reached for her, his hand searching for where she was, clasping her wrist when he struck her arm. He pulled her down to his level, which was apparently at a crouch, and urged her to move forward. Grace reached out with both hands to feel what she was being directed to and bumped her head against an overhang.

She bent lower to climb through an opening in the wall, trusting implicitly that the route her companion was leading her through was safe.

Once she'd made her way through, she was crawling on an uneven rocky downward slope. Carefully, she moved farther along the rocks, her fingers scrambling for purchase as she descended farther. Behind her, she sensed Adam following, his movements soundless and sure. He caught up with her as she precariously felt ahead for handholds. His fingers alighted over her arm, catching her elbow, and he helped her to her feet.

She stood uneasily, aware of a slope she was standing on. Adam moved ahead of her, walking with practiced steps until they reached level ground. There, he stopped and released her to do something she couldn't make out. She listened to a series of scratches, and then there was a tiny flare of light—exceedingly bright in the pitch black—and a *whoosh* of yellow flame became brilliant and blinding before her eyes. Adam held a lighted torch out ahead of him, leaving behind a box of matches on a crevasse of the rock wall, next to where several old torches lay.

"Sophocles showed me these tunnels when he brought me to live down here," he explained, his voice low but not exceedingly so. He struck out down the damp tunnel, retaking her hand to lead the way.

Grace had since come to accept the feel of his leather-wrapped palm against her bare skin. In fact, she thought she would surely panic if it wasn't there to reassure her anymore. She followed him with the confidence that no one pursued them. If he felt it was safe enough to light the way and speak out loud, then they must have managed to elude their pursuers. She felt a weight lift off her shoulders and the tension finally melt away. While he might have kept quiet and made no sound simply because it seemed to be his way, Grace allowed her feet to shuffle noisily, tiredly, no longer careful to maintain an absolute silence for the sheer exhaustion of it.

The tunnels were numerous and interconnected, and Adam seemed to move through them as if he knew their network. Water trickled down the sides of the rocky walls to pool in time-worn corners. Lichen grew in swatches on the outer perimeter of the puddles. Mice scurried underfoot at times, but Grace only jumped once, when the first one squeaked at their arrival in its otherwise private cavern. She felt no threat from the tiny creatures and even sensed they offered a little hope for the exhaustive night. She felt the ache in her limbs and the soreness at the bottom of her feet. Above all else, she wanted to stop and rest, but she wouldn't admit it. While they walked no more than a half hour, the trek was arduous and unforgiving.

Adam eventually stopped and fumbled with something in front of him, which his body blocked from view. When he moved aside, she saw it was a small door cut into the rock. She looked questioningly at him and saw him nod with reassurance.

"This is where I live now. You'll be safe here."

CHAPTER TWENTY-ONE

Markey cursed himself for his recklessness as he reached the end of the altar and took cover behind the corner of the transept. As he inched toward the alcove, he heard a blast from a shotgun coming from deep within the cathedral, beyond the transept, and he was encouraged by the idea that the gunmen were farther from him than he originally feared. He thought of Grace and the peril she was in, and wondered why he cared so much for her safety. It could possibly be that he only wanted to save someone from becoming one of the victims he encountered in the course of his job, or maybe he had a soft spot for abused women, but there was definitely more concern for her than the average victim. Perhaps he just didn't want to see this her fall prey to another psychopath's madness. Maybe that was all it was. He generally only had the opportunity to solve the mysteries of death only the bereaved appreciated, but this time, he had an opportunity to make a difference.

For once he wanted to be the hero who saved someone from some madman's obsession—or from an opportunist killer, or even from a crime of economic need—before the crime occurred. He wanted to intercede before fate claimed another life and left him with a bloody scene and cold body to work with, forcing him to put the pieces of the puzzle together with little regard for the life left behind. Dead men told no tales, nor did they have any say in the dispensation of their corpses.

He paused for a second as he gathered his resolve, his breathing heavy and labored. He clutched his gun to his chest and felt the cold stucco of the wall against his back, through the layers of his shirt and jacket. For him to feel that much his back had to be drenched in sweat. When he heard three quick thuds coming from the same area where the shotgun blast had sounded, he pushed away from the wall and entered the transept. Much as he suspected—and hoped—the alcove was empty and a door gaped open on what appeared to be a dressing room.

He stepped toward it with the utmost caution, aware that someone might be laying in wait. As he took his first step, something hard and unforgiving crashed into the side of his head and dropped him where he stood.

* * * * * *

Murdock watched with relief as the cop crumpled at his feet. He was just glad he'd come with a pistol along with the shotgun, after that had been ripped from his hands by the same kid who'd emasculated him on the street earlier in the evening. Enraged at the memory of being single-handedly overpowered, Murdock felt a certain displaced thrill in toppling the cop in the kid's place. He knew he was at risk of failing Drudge again and his only chance of redeeming himself was to join up with Devereaux and Bentley. He took a moment to relish this small victory over the cop who'd been stupid enough to stick his nose where it didn't belong.

After a bit of self-indulgence, Murdock remembered that there were more important things to do, and those involved going after Grace and her meddlesome friend. He was still armed and ready to do what had to be done, and he was pretty sure he could slip back in among Devereaux and Bentley without losing too much face.

Hopefully. If he was quick about it.

Carefully stepping over the inert form at his feet, Murdock hurried through the door to the dressing room, then into the corridor beyond. As he did, he heard the crash of a door and a shout coming from the nave. A man had called out someone's name—a muffled version of that name—then a word that sounded like *sergeant*.

More cops!

Murdock considered this new shift in circumstances. He ducked back into the dressing room and peeked out on the church proper. From there, he saw two men running up the main aisle from the front doors of the cathedral. The first man who jogged up the aisle was a portly man dressed in civilian clothes. Behind him was an older man—ancient, more like it—dressed in a police uniform. Both had their guns drawn and were ready for bear.

It wouldn't be long before they discovered their friend lying unconscious or dead on the floor near him. They'd bring in more cops, and then the cathedral would be swarming with them. Even though the north suburbs were experiencing a series of riots that drained the downtown district of its police force, there were always cops to be found to work the scene of a cop slaying.

Murdock slipped back into the dressing room and emerged in the back corridor, where he ran for the only door he saw standing open. He leaned into the darkened staircase. "Pick, Big D, time to blow this joint. Cops're here. More than just that dumb shit out there."

A curse and bumbling around, then more obscene words, and Devereaux came out from the shadows of the stairs. His face was glistening with sweat and his breath was labored. No doubt, he was livid with the way things had turned out.

"Mudder fucker," Devereaux cursed, stomping up the stairs and flailing his arms, his shotgun held barrel up in one hand. Murdock quickly stepped aside to let him pass, while Bentley trudged up the stairs next.

"We gotta get out of here," Murdock said.

"What the fuck . . . I ain't goin' back to the Tower without the bitch," Devereaux snapped. "Fuck that, I ain't gonna be one of his fuckin' bats."

It was clear from the man's hysteria that Devereaux had never failed Drudge before. He was unable to hide his fear behind his obvious fury. Murdock found it both amusing and daunting, but it was he who came up with an idea to save their lives. "I know what we can do to ease the pain of this fiasco, boys. Come on."

Murdock headed for the exit at the far end of the corridor. He looked back and saw that both Devereaux and Bentley were reluctant to trust anyone who wasn't in their employer's best graces. Frustrated, he returned to where they stood and repeated what he'd said, that he knew just what to do to save their asses, and their souls.

After a minute of considering their options, Bentley and Devereaux hurried after him.

Grace followed Adam through the basement the tunnels had opened up to, which was just as dark as the one in the cathedral and made doubly so when he extinguished the torch. He left that behind on a crevasse in a tunnel similar to the one he'd taken it from and guided her by holding her hand, which she found comforting despite trudging through a dark cellar with a man she had only a passing acquaintance with. That in itself didn't seem irrational to her in the least. She thought she might never trust anyone as completely as she trusted this man, although she didn't know why she placed her life entirely in his hands. Inexplicably, he stayed with her as if he'd been thrown into the predicament himself, with no other recourse to escape otherwise. She offered him nothing but trouble, no prospect of reward or recompense, only her undying gratitude. She didn't understand his determination to remain by her side, though she was reluctant to question his motives. Instead, she was terrified that he might suddenly suffer an epiphany of his own stupidity and leave her to her own devices.

Which, as yet, he hadn't.

He led her to a wooden staircase that he allowed her to negotiate at her own pace. At the top, he opened a door to a corridor no less lighted than the basement. He didn't speak, and she wondered if the silence was necessary. Under her feet, dirt and dust made scratching sounds as they strode through the inner bowels of the abandoned building.

Although her curiosity was piqued and she had several questions, she kept her silence in deference to his own. A twinge of compassion came over her when she considered his lonesome lifestyle, with no real home to walk into at the end of a hard day, no family to lean on for solace, no semblance of normalcy. Only a dilapidated building with dirty, dusty floors and cold, impersonal walls with plaster peeling from the junctures at the ceiling. She longed for her own apartment across town and the comfort of her bed, which she would have given anything to lay on just then.

They stopped at a spot he must have instinctively known was there. Grace's eyes had adjusted somewhat to the dark, but she could still only make out blacker shadows next to grayer ones. As she peered through the dark, he touched something, and a light illuminated the way ahead. Grace flinched at the brightness. She had to squint to adjust her eyes to the intrusion of the glare. When she was finally able to open her eyes again, she peeked past him to see a freight elevator in front of them.

"There's still electricity in the building," he explained. "At least enough to run the elevator and a few other things."

"How odd," she said, looking around and seeing how sparse and dilapidated the surroundings were. A thick layer of dust on the floor, curls of plaster in the corners, glimpses of lathing through the walls, sagging ceiling tiles, and mildew stains were everywhere. The light did nothing but highlight the miserable state of the building's interior. "Who pays for it?"

He ignored her question and turned to the elevator, swinging up the grating so they could enter. The light came from within the car, from a small bulb swinging from a wire in the ceiling, a shabby but functional contraption. Peering into the lift, Grace began to worry about fire hazards and the general soundness of the building's construction.

She tentatively entered the elevator when he motioned her to do so. He followed, slinging down the door with a resounding clatter, proving that noise didn't matter now. He pressed a button and the elevator groaned to life, then suddenly jolted as it lifted from the basement floor. Grace glanced ceiling-ward, trying to perceive the floors above, while Adam leaned against the wall and closed his eyes. His breathing was slow and shallow, and he appeared beaten and exhausted. He, too, only wanted the comfort of a familiar bed.

The elevator rose, passing floor after floor, giving only a brief glimpse of each level they passed with the light from the elevator bulb. The same dirty corridors with peeling plaster and dust bunnies the size of tumbleweeds seemed to climb with them. Grace tried to place the building in the city, but there was no way to figure out which abandoned monolith this might be. The city had dozens of just such structures that had gone bankrupt or been gutted by fire. Some were renovated, while others were razed to the ground to make room for more impressive high rises. But most of them remained only as an eyesore and a haven for rats and vermin alike.

Adam allowed himself the short time it took the elevator to climb to assess the world outside. By now, he was aware of the north suburbs being dealt a blow as a distraction for the minions' work in the inner city. It wasn't the first time Malachi

Drudge had drawn out the police in order to commit other heinous acts elsewhere. Again, Adam wondered if the senseless killing and destruction that had taken his family a year ago might have only been a distraction for something Drudge had done elsewhere in the city.

The elevator jolted to a halt and pulled Adam out of his meditation. He stepped forward to raise the grating and beckoned Grace out. She followed without hesitation, and he wondered why she did, showing no fear of him now. After all, he was a stranger to her yet, and the hell she'd been through should be enough to convince her to be on guard against everyone. But she wasn't, at least not with him, and that confused him.

The light from the elevator was only enough to cast a dim glow on a small space of floor outside the shaft. But it was enough to see that it was no corridor they walked onto, but a spacious studio. It was hard to tell what the layout of the floor plan was or how it was decorated, but there were windows comprising the three walls facing them. Large casement windows spanning from hip to ceiling were generously situated throughout the place. Sheer floor-length drapes hung on each window with their panels pulled apart. That was all that could be made out in the dark, until Adam led Grace to a bed.

"I hope you don't mind sharing," he said. "It's all I have to offer and the floor isn't comfortable."

Grace stuttered on what to say, unable to discern his face in the dark. "No, please, do whatever you want. This is your home."

"You don't have anything to worry about here," he said as he slowly sat, then laid on one side of the bed. He kept near the edge, not wanting to offend her or set her nerves on edge. He let out a restrained sigh as his body succumbed to weariness, sinking into the softly concaving mattress.

"Trust me," she said. "You're the only person I'm not afraid of at this point." And to show how true her words were, she climbed on the other side of the bed and slid down under the covers.

CHAPTER TWENTY-TWO

Grace didn't know how long she lay asleep even after the sun streamed through the windows, but she figured it must have been quite a while, since the room was suffused with a radiant glow indicating a time far later than dawn when she finally awoke. At first she couldn't see a thing. Sunlight streamed in all around her, making it almost painful to use her eyes. Then her vision grew accustomed to the natural ambient light and eventually accepted it, and she was able to see more clearly. She lifted her head from the pillow and pushed herself up on her elbows, looking around curiously.

She remembered briefly how her rescuer had brought her to this place during the night, when only the light of the moon through the shutterless windows had created silhouettes of what had been in the room. Now, with the help of daylight, she could see that the windows bore no shutters at all, only sheer drapes pulled aside and which billowed freely in the breeze. She was barely able to make it out herself because her view was hampered by a sheer netting hanging in folds over the canopy of the bed. She hadn't noticed it before, when she'd climbed exhausted beneath the covers, but she thought it might have been because she'd been more tired than she first suspected. Now she saw how the netting—which must have been pulled back last night—was dropped in place about her. She also saw that she was alone, and a brief spasm of fear and desertion speared her, compelling her to pull aside the netting and slip out of bed—then abruptly freeze in place, captivated by amazement.

Birds. Dozens of them perched on beams where ceiling tiles had once been, and on window sills. Several finches flitted from one perch to another, sharing their outcroppings with more aggressive birds of prey. Sweet warbling made her take in the entire expanse of the studio with an incredible sense of awe, and she saw the myriad array of winged creatures occupying the room. Thrushes, grackles, robins, and pigeons. A handful of budgies and a spattering of jays. More than a few sparrows and a few more blackbirds. A white dove took flight from a ceiling beam and swooped out an open window, making her realize there was no glass in the window frames and the birds came and went as they pleased. During the night, her mysterious host must have dropped the netting on the bed so she could sleep undisturbed.

As for her sleep, it had been restful and dreamless. With her body exhausted and her mind driven to the brink of insanity, sleep had been her only source of convalescence. Her trust in this enigmatic man as her savior and that she was safe in his world had been enough to rid her sleep of nightmares. The soft symphony of chirruping birds and the susurration of a soothing breeze through the billowing curtains must have been enough to lull her deeper into sweet slumber. The sunlight only chased away any remaining fear and swept her off to a sublime state of which she felt herself buoyed on tranquil waves.

Now that mood returned and she took a few tentative steps away from the bed, her hand trailing through the netting in an oblivious state of enchantment. Somewhere in the back of her mind she thought she should avoid all sudden movement. If she spooked the birds, she might send them into a chaotic panic that would only destroy the magical illusion she felt herself a part of. At the moment, the birds only eyed her with mild curiosity. The finches continued their nervous flitting, while the others remained in place, some fluffing their feathers and others making only the minimum of moves. Around her, the room was suffused with a white and radiant luminescence, and as she strode languidly through columns of streaming sunlight, she felt that she must surely be in a world of surreal design, where sharp edges and primary colors were subdued by the gentle toning of paler hues.

Drawn inexorably forward, Grace walked toward the closest window, drifting closer as if pulled by a sense of undeniable inquisitiveness. As she approached, she reached out and grasped the edge of the sheer drape, clutching it in case she felt an overwhelming urge to throw herself out of the absent window. She closed in on the gaping opening until her knees pressed against the sill, preventing her from taking extra steps; and yet her body leaned forward, canting past the window frame.

Gazing down, she saw that she was truly at an impressive height, dozens of stories above the ground. The immensity of the building made her feel small and trivial, with the grandiose window opening hugely about her. She let her eyes sweep around the world outside, realizing how someone could live relatively undetected from the world so high up. The people who walked on the sidewalk beneath her, in their bustle to get to work or be about on errands, seemed like small creatures of insignificance, and as she peered down on them, she felt intrinsic to greatness, almost as if she were an angel in heaven.

After a while, she found she had to get away from the window before the euphoric vertigo she was experiencing drew her completely through the opening. She felt slightly dazed and intoxicated, and struggled with herself to let go of the drapes in search of stability in her own legs. Faintly, she wiped a hand across her face and sighed, relieved to be able to break the spell she'd briefly been under.

Replacing that, instead, was another sensation, and she stiffened, momentarily paralyzed by the impression of someone watching her. Abruptly, she turned around.

Across the room was the young man she'd come to believe was her hero. He was sitting on the edge of a table, watching her with quiet perplexity. A hawk was perched on his shoulder, nobly watching her with bright and expressive eyes. In contrast, the young man's eyes were hooded under a white cloth tied around his forehead, and the look she caught him giving her made her feel slightly discomforted. Then his features softened, and she imagined she must have misread his expression, even though he remained utterly silent as they exchanged a level gaze for several seconds.

It was Grace who broke the stare before her unease could return. In the past two days, she'd become accustomed to his somber moods and silent presence. She believed it must be a character flaw that had its place at times. He didn't appear menacing or malevolent, but on the contrary, benign and heroic, since he'd saved her from certain death on more than one occasion. It wasn't just his features that had changed, but his attire. He no longer wore the dark coat or scarf he'd worn the night before, only a black T-shirt and jeans. However, he kept his hands still wrapped in strips of leather.

Hesitantly, Grace took a few steps forward, hoping to show that she appreciated his hospitality by showing she had no fear of him. Although he made no move to hold her back, she got the distinct impression that he was uneasy with her coming too close.

When she made it to within a few feet of him, she hesitated, cowed by the edge of tension growing more palpable the nearer she got. He said nothing to hold her back, yet there was a warning aura he exuded, cautioning her to tread carefully; she was encroaching on space that was terribly personal and well-guarded. Even so—knowing this—she glided even closer, until she finally stood before him. On his shoulder, the hawk's small head swiveled in jerky pivots to assess her from all angles, its feathers so silky they appeared to float about its breast.

Her eyes unwittingly left his face and traveled down to his neck, where the scars of a rope had once scored themselves into his flesh. Startled concern overtook her expression. She felt compelled to reach out and touch the angry welts. When she did, probing with trembling fingers, his hand shot up and snatched her wrist, forbidding her, and she gave a little cry of alarm.

His eyes locked with hers and maintained them without reproach. Grace wanted to say something to temper his fierce scrutiny, but her fear of offending him wouldn't let her, and she began to pray that he'd initiate some sort of response on his own.

Or at least let her arm go.

But he maintained his grip on her wrist, and even though it didn't hurt, it made her feel uneasy. She tugged experimentally on it and found her arm came away only at her insistence. Consequently, she took a step back only to show that she respected his need for distance.

"What would make you do such an awful thing to yourself?" she asked. She was shocked by the words, even though they came out before she knew what she was saying. What right did she have to ask questions about his personal tragedies, especially when hers might seem equally appalling to him?

He continued to stare at her without changing his expression, which worried her somewhat. Someone who was so outwardly unaffected by the history of their own misfortune must also be afflicted by a form of instability or antisocial behavior.

But then his face cracked so his mouth could work, and what he said was hollow. "I didn't do it to myself."

Surprised by what he said, Grace took his words as permission to speak freely, even though she didn't know quite what to say. Instead, she waited for him to explain further, but he remained infuriatingly silent, until she thought it would be up to her to draw out more of the mysteries he was hoarding. Shaking her head, she reached out again to touch the marks. This time, he let her fingers lay lightly against the ragged lines of his scored flesh.

Her touch was soft and cool on his skin, which had since become fevered by his anxiety of her scrutiny. His hands, which had been lying along the edge of the table, now clutched more tightly at it.

Meditatively, Grace let her hand drift up to his face to trace the outline of his jaw, her thumb grazing the line of a scar under its ridge. Where she touched, his flesh shivered, but not because she left a cold trail. It was more the intimateness of the contact that affected him. She could tell that he fought with himself not to react hostilely, and she appreciated the rare opportunity he allowed her. She sensed that he only permitted her exploration to ease her fear of his turbulent character, although it also nurtured a fear in him that he worried he wouldn't be able to master.

After some time, she noticed his growing agitation and decided it was enough. She dropped her hand and stepped away, offering a tender smile to soften her judgment, hoping he would understand that she wasn't distressed by what she saw.

She didn't know if he was offended by her examination. Instead of speaking, he launched himself off the table and strode across the room, to one of the windows. The hawk compensated only minutely for his sudden movement. When he reached the window, he stared out at a great black monolith across the street.

"That building wasn't there two years ago," he said, standing motionless. The sunlight didn't stream in as directly through this window as the ones facing east, but it still created a nimbus around his body, defining how strong and imposing a figure he struck.

Grace came up behind him to see which building he meant. She thought she might know it without even looking, but she felt she had to see it for herself to confirm which one he was talking about. Standing beside him, she saw that she was right in her assumption. He was staring blankly at a massive obsidian structure gleaming with polished black walls that seemed to absorb the sunlight rather than reflect it. A fascination in itself, Spatial Tower was an architectural marvel. It had been erected in record time on a plot of land purchased by a multimillionaire entrepreneur when the city's lease from the county expired. The city had declined to option the land for the expansion of a park in lieu of business growth. For the most part, no one really understood what Spatial Industries did, but it had been explained during the war for surveying contracts to be an industrial contingent for the brokering of intangible commodities.

What the hell was that supposed to mean, she often wondered, although she'd kept her lack of cosmopolitan sense private and merely nodded knowingly at the office.

Now she stood at Adam's side and eyed his moody contemplation of the black structure. Her eyes wandered to the building as well, and she shivered unexpectedly with cold fear. Something about its appearance from the window of this surreal world made it appear sinister and malevolent, like a leviathan rising from the earth, tensing to strike. She pulled her eyes away from it and looked intently at her gracious host, once again feeling safe and secure in his company.

"I don't like it," she said with juvenile petulance.

"I don't blame you."

They remained where they were for a few minutes, he looking thoughtfully at the building across the park and she gazing at him. She thought he would break his concentration first, once he felt her eyes upon him, but he never did. Instead, he seemed drawn by the power of the Tower, and she feared he might be in the thrall of it.

"What happened to you?" she asked tentatively, wishing to draw his attention away from the bleak and foreboding structure, even if it meant focusing his attention on his sullen past.

His eyes returned to her, and she had no qualms about inquiring more about him. His expression broke slowly, gradually, dissolving into slack features that didn't seem so much carved from granite anymore. Abruptly, he shifted his shoulders, as if shrugging, and the hawk flew off, going through the window, its impossibly long wingspan sweeping with graceful strokes to mount air currents that carried it off on some mission or whimsy.

Adam turned fully from the window to face her. "I was in the wrong place at the wrong time."

She laughed lightly, laying a hand on her midsection. "So was I."

He looked at her questioningly, then understood what she meant by her remark. "What does Malachi Drudge want with you anyway?"

Her eyebrows lifted, startled by the name accompanying his question. "Malachi

Drudge? *The* Malachi Drudge, of Spatial Industries? *That* Drudge?"

Adam gave her a look of curious speculation. "You know him?"

"I know *of* him," she said. "I work for an architectural firm that was salivating for the contract for Spatial Industries when they were going to build the Tower. But Drudge brought in his own talent. That was the big hoopla surrounding him. He didn't contract out for anything to build that ugly monolith. It created a bad taste in the business. One of the reasons the city allowed him to buy that tract of land was because it was supposed to bring in jobs for local workers. In the end, not only were the businesses snuffed but so where the workers. No one got a piece of it, and the union put up a stink about scabs taking jobs from local workers." She shrugged diffidently. "The argument was moot, though. The president of the union was killed in the middle of all the uproar, which might have raised an eye or two, but it was at the same time the riots took out a lot of people in the ranches last year. At that point, all of the city's focus turned to what happened in the ranches. No one really cared about another stupid building going up in the downtown area."

Adam's brow wrinkled. "He was killed the same night as the riot happened? This union president?"

"I'm not sure if it was the same night or just before, but he wasn't killed in the riot, if that's what you mean. I only remember it because it was all the talk in the business at the time." When she noticed his look of intentness, she added, "The construction business."

Adam continued to stare keenly at her, and Grace worried about what might make him think she was affiliated with such a powerful business mogul as the man who'd stunned the city with his financial imperialism. She certainly couldn't make the connection herself. "What would Malachi Drudge want with me? I've never even met him."

"Perhaps you don't know you've met him," Adam said, glancing down at her midsection.

She caught his look and meaning and suddenly stepped back. "Oh no, it's not what you think. I can guarantee this baby doesn't belong to Malachi Drudge."

His eyes narrowed as he brought them up to look at her. "I just assumed he was after you because you were pregnant."

"What makes you think Malachi Drudge wants me anyway? I haven't done anything to attract his attention."

"I don't know yet, but it's him."

Disturbed more by his growing anxiety than by what he'd said, Grace pressed on. "Why would a man like Malachi Drudge go to such lengths just to get a hold of me? With his reputation, he could just arrange an appointment through my employer."

She watched him for a response but he seemed distracted by his thoughts, and the absence of his awareness only perturbed her. Speaking more insistently, with a hint of impatience, she said, "Tell me why you think this Drudge guy would hire thugs to kidnap me."

"Because he did this to me." Adam turned his attention to her and touched his neck, startling her with his vehemence. "Drudge is evil, and he'll kill anyone in his way just to get what he wants. Only I don't know what he wants. That's the one thing that's always eluded me."

Grace could only stare back at him. She had a hard time accepting the idea of a rich and influential businessman committing such atrocities against her when she believed she'd never met him or had any third party dealings with him. She could fathom no reason why a man of Drudge's caliber would be interested in her anyway. The prospect of such a powerful corporate mogul using his vast resources to chase her down was frightening, to say the least, but she simply couldn't wrap her mind around it. Just the idea that it had happened—having been chased by thugs—alluded to the fact that *something* was happening. She just knew she would feel more comfortable—but only minimally so—if it was only a common criminal who pursued her; one who lacked the millions in capital and infinite resources to accomplish what he was after, instead of a person with the reputation and money Malachi Drudge had.

"Listen, I don't think I understand what this is all about, but I can honestly tell you that I'm tired of being chased. I just want to be left alone. Just because this baby is going to be an inconvenience to someone doesn't mean it has to die."

She turned away and began to pace about the room, her hands going up in forfeit. "I don't understand why it's so damaging for me to have this baby," she ranted, talking to herself more than to anyone else. "Just because it's putting *him* in an uncomfortable position doesn't mean this poor child has to suffer for it. Besides, I'm the mother and I'm carrying it. I've chosen to be responsible for its care. What right does that jerk have to make decisions for lives other than his own? Just because he's the district attorney doesn't make him God. I mean, he can put criminals in jail but he doesn't have the right to order an abortion on someone, even if it is his own child. That's a moral decision, isn't it?" She spun around to face Adam, glaring at him with a testy expression and expecting him to answer, defying him to dispute her.

Adam watched her fume, but when she suddenly focused on him for an opinion, he became mildly distressed. He stuttered on what to say even as her expression grew impatient for his answer.

"Isn't it?" she persisted.

"Well . . ." he began, uncertain how to answer to social dictates in a world beyond his understanding.

"You can't possibly think a child should have to die just for convenience sake," she said scornfully. "And if you do, why the hell are you helping me anyway?"

Adam recoiled from the unexpected venom in her challenge. "You're probably right."

Her stern look suddenly relaxed and the tension in her shoulders eased. There was only silence. Then she spoke, and her tone was gentle and untainted by her previous zeal. "So what's the deal with all the birds?"

Adam didn't immediately answer the question. Instead, he looked around the room populated with a myriad assortment of birds. They had remained quiet and unaffected by the emotional conversation sparked between him and Grace, remaining merely watchful and somewhat apprehensive. Now, one by one, then in pairs and trios, the birds flitted off their perches and flew to the nearest windows, streaking, flitting, and soaring through the openings. A few paused on the sills as if uncertain about venturing off over such a great abyss, but eventually they were all gone, leaving the room empty except for Adam and Grace. Their exodus had been done in such an orderly and un-chaotic manner that nothing other than the drapes stirring from a few brushing wings gave evidence of their leaving. None had gone near the window where Grace and Adam stood, but Grace watched in wordless wonder as the birds flocked trans-species out the windows in such an organized manner it reminded her of a seasonal migration.

"Drudge has his bats; I have the birds."

As the drapes settled from their slight disturbance, Grace got the impression the birds had never even been there at all, that she had imagined the spectacle as just a magical illusion brought on by her traumatic experience. She looked sideways at him, feeling distantly removed from reality, and said, "I saw birds in here."

As much as she wanted him to, he didn't smile, nor did he confirm her belief in seeing all those creatures. Instead, he shook his head dismally. "There has to be a balance, I guess. Against the bats."

She suddenly understood what he was talking about and shivered, remembering the malevolent creatures from the alley the night before. "Those weren't like any bats I've ever seen."

"No, but they're the closest thing to man that Drudge can find."

Her brow narrowed suspiciously, her gut turning cold. "Those things weren't really bats, then?"

"No."

"What were they?" she asked breathlessly, afraid to hear the answer but suspecting she already knew.

"The reincarnation of those who have sold their soul to him."

"Pardon me?" she sputtered, suddenly coming out of her remoteness, propelled back into reasoning by his unexpected explanation. Her body stiffened with a fear that she might have put her trust in someone who wasn't entirely sound of mind.

All of a sudden, she began to focus on the scars on his neck, wondering just how he'd gotten them, if perhaps—maybe—he'd inflicted them on himself.

"Drudge offers money, power, and fame for loyalty," Adam explained, unaware that he'd said anything to jeopardize her faith in him. "Most people don't believe what will ultimately be the price of their allegiance, but there are some who do. Those don't care, though, or have already gotten themselves too buried in debt to get themselves out."

"What are you saying?" she asked tentatively, skating lightly in case she might offend him. "That Malachi Drudge is some kind of devil?"

"A minor one. Yet he commands the minions."

"The minions?"

"The bats."

She offered him a friendly but dubious grin. "That's a little hard to swallow."

"You were in its arms," he reminded her. "You felt it around you, smelled it, maybe even sensed its evil. Twice. You can't deny that."

She shivered at the memory of the two events. Unwittingly, she re-experienced the revulsion she'd initially felt when those two creatures had held her in their leathery embrace. The palpable sensation of the memory was enough to make her believe in their evil origins. Hadn't she even equated them in her mind to being demons, professing them to be monsters to the staff at St. Jude's?

"Then how do you fit in?" she asked, desperately trying to dispute what was niggling in her mind, that he was right, the devil did exist and he was after her. "How do you know so much about them?"

Adam seemed to have been waiting for her to ask just such a question, although he didn't know how to respond to it. Rather simply, he answered, "I'm the one who got away."

CHAPTER TWENTY-THREE

Christopher was a wreck when he had his driver bring him to the front doors of the Spatial Tower. He hadn't been able to sleep all night for worrying about what he was going to do with his uncertain future. He was concerned about Grace's unstable state and whether she would expose their illicit affair and the fruits of their union. He'd been prepared to deny any accusation of infidelity, but he could hardly denounce a child when DNA tests proved the bastard was his. Such a minor indiscretion of passion shouldn't be enough to ruin a career or remove him from the running for city mayor. Especially when he was the best candidate qualified for the position. Just because of the whims of one flighty bimbo.

Grumbling to himself and ruminating over how he could stop Grace from destroying his life, he slipped from the back of his car with an unremitting exhaustion dragging on his limbs. When he looked up at the great black building, with its backdrop of a cerulean sky and the swiftly moving clouds behind it, he felt overwhelmed and nauseous. His hand reached out for the support of the car, hoping to steady himself after looking up and suffering the illusion of the building swaying back and forth. The magnificent structure made him feel insignificant and petty, and he suddenly thought it might be better if he tried to resolve his problems on his own instead of coming here. Such a building screamed of power and domination, and he was nothing but a little bug its great power might crush.

Resolving to overcome his ridiculous fear, Christopher stiffened his spine and brought his shoulders up, prepared to do battle with the Goliath behind those walls. Drudge had created a situation that was beyond Christopher's control, making promises he'd yet been able to keep. When it was more prudent for him to be meeting with his campaign manager and public image officer, Christopher had raced at the crack of dawn across town to demand just what could be done to salvage his life.

Despite his determination to stand firm against Drudge, Christopher was still exhausted from a night of insomnia and worry that left him seeking refuge in a bottle. It was hard to imagine how he'd spent the whole of Saturday in one form of unconsciousness or another and that it hadn't preserved him until Monday. Now he felt as if he was nothing more than a walking zombie, and he had to mentally prepare his body to cross the sidewalk and enter those foreboding glass doors.

But he did, and he found strength as he walked, remembering that he was Christopher Purcell, District Attorney, with more authority in this sprawling metropolitan city than most. How dare such an eccentric egomaniac toy with his life like some kind of pawn in a chess game.

There was no doubt in his mind that Drudge had arranged for the murder of Charles Driskell and had set him up as the patsy if he didn't do as he was told. The murder had been confirmed and the weapon existed—in Drudge's possession—but that wasn't what frightened Christopher the most. It was what Drudge wanted from him that made him sick. Belatedly, he thought he should have brought a small recording device so he could connive Drudge into an admission of guilt. But it was too late to turn back for one now.

Once Christopher made it through the front doors, wondering briefly just when he had passed through them, he walked up to the receptionist sitting high behind a raised dais. The ornate gold script of Spatial Industries was embossed on the wall behind her. She was a prissy thing, all sharp and angular features and snooty attitude. Her auburn hair was combed in a straight cascade down the sides of her face, like a waterfall, and her lips were painted a garish color the same as her fingernails. She was probably considered a beautiful woman by other men's standards, but she was far too severe for Christopher's taste, and he took an immediate dislike to her.

As he approached, he noticed she had a sleek headset on and her eyes were distant as she spoke in a sultry voice to the callers. One hand remained poised over a switchboard, while her fingers jabbed out expertly to engage different connections. When Christopher came up to the counter, he had to look up slightly to meet her eyes.

"I'd like to see Malachi Drudge," he said with authority.

A free finger came up to hold him at bay as she spoke to someone on the line, then tapped on an extension as she looked down at him, appraising him like something the cat had just dragged in. Sniffing disdainfully, she said, "May I help you?"

"I'd like to see Malachi Drudge," he repeated, bristling at her superior attitude.

"I'm afraid he's not in at the moment. May I have one of his associates help you?"

"No," Christopher replied stoutly. He reached into his coat, pulled out a gold card case, and flipped it open. "I'm Christopher Purcell, chief District Attorney. I need to speak to him on matters of extreme importance."

She didn't let his agitation slip past her notice, or the idea that the District Attorney had business with her boss. "I can have an associate sit with you until Mr. Drudge gets in, but—"

"Listen, young lady, if I'd wanted to discuss my business with an associate, I'd have called ahead and gotten an appointment. But as it stands, I have private matters to discuss with Mr. Drudge that might prove a little embarrassing if they were discussed among his associates. I'm aware of how damaging office politics can be."

She opened her mouth to speak but Christopher held up a hand to prevent her. "How long before you expect Mr. Drudge in?"

Her eyes drifted over his shoulder to look at something behind him, even as he heard a familiar voice.

"Christopher? Christopher Purcell?"

Christopher turned to see who addressed him and was more than a little surprised to see it was the same man he sought an audience with. Malachi Drudge strode toward him with confidence and official bearing, yet with a welcoming smile on his face. He wore his hair slicked back and gelled to a duck tail at the nape of his neck, which somehow distinguished him rather than made him appear sleazy. Complimenting his rather cosmopolitan look was an Italian suit that adoringly embraced his frame. He looked nothing like the jet-setter of the weekend; this morning, he was entirely no-nonsense and business-like.

Christopher turned fully on Drudge as the financier strode forward. Drudge stuck out his hand in greeting but Christopher balked at it. Drudge didn't miss a beat as he took Christopher's hand and pumped it enthusiastically, making eye contact that sucked the remaining strength right out of him. Drudge didn't let his hand go as he pulled Christopher toward him a couple of staggering steps.

"Get hold of yourself. You're being scrutinized."

Christopher looked around nervously. He felt himself wobble when Drudge suddenly let go. He hadn't realized he'd been supported by such a precarious hold on his arm, but when it was gone, he stumbled before he managed to regain his footing. Drudge threw a friendly arm around his shoulder to hide his cumbersomeness and guided him toward the elevators.

"Sophia, call my office and let them know my first appointment will have to wait. I have to discuss some campaign contributions with the city's next mayor."

"Yes, Mr. Drudge," Sophia said as her fingers lurched at the switchboard.

Drudge made sure Christopher was standing on solid legs before he released him. They waited for the ornate elevator doors to open, standing silently side by side. Although the reception area was becoming well-traversed by employees, no one chose to stand around the one elevator that was but one among many others. Christopher felt a bit uneasy about that, the feeling becoming even more pronounced when he and Drudge entered the elevator and the doors closed, cutting off any witnesses to what might happen inside.

The walls of the elevator were covered in smoky charcoal mirrors. Everywhere Christopher turned he saw Drudge surrounding him. The car lurched slightly as it rose, and Christopher reached out to steady himself against the brass railing.

"Really, Christopher, in order for you to remain unaccused of the horrible crime from the other night you must remain aloof and in control. As if nothing happened and you know nothing of what the police are talking about when they question you."

The abrupt reference to the murder at the Rialto threw Christopher further into a tizzy. He'd been all prepared to barge into the Tower and demand that Drudge go to the authorities and set them straight about what had happened, but now his courage spilled out of him like a milk carton split from a fall off the table. He could only concentrate on regaining a pattern of breath to adequately fill his lungs, but even that was difficult.

Drudge suddenly gripped Christopher's elbow and spun him toward the mirrored wall. "Look at yourself! You look like a despondent stockbroker on the verge of jumping off a ledge. You need a shower and a shave and a change of clothes. Your shoulders are stooped and your head is bowed like a whipped puppy. You're campaigning to be mayor of this city, damn it. You have a certain image to uphold. Not to mention your reputation, career, and your very freedom to keep intact."

Christopher stared at his reflection in the mirror and saw exactly what Drudge had pointed out. He saw a man who'd aged decades and given up on life. He saw how sunken his cheeks were from two days of fasting and how his eyes showed black hollows of sleeplessness. Stubble formed on his chin and cheeks, and he could just imagine what others must think of his reeking. He tried to remember if he'd even showered after coming home Sunday.

"I have every confidence that you can pull this off," Drudge said with simpering assurance. "Play along with the game plan and everything will be just fine. But remember, there are two things standing between you and a jail cell. One is the corkscrew I still have in my possession and the other is the baby in your woman's womb."

"She's not my woman," Christopher snapped, jerking his arm back. He staggered to stand on his own. "She's just a pretty face with great tits and a nice ass."

A grin crept up on Drudge's lips, apparently satisfied with the reaction he got. "I have that problem almost in hand."

"The police have already talked to her. She said I was in the hotel room when she left. She told them about our relationship."

"She's a woman in trouble who mentioned the name of an influential person to get the attention off her. It's your word against hers, and you have several people who will attest to the fact that you were nowhere near this city during the weekend. The only thing that will give credence to her story is that child she's carrying."

Christopher winced at the prospect of his life hanging on the existence of an unborn fetus, not even old enough to be viable on its own. The more he thought about it, the more he felt inclined to believe Drudge could use whatever means possible to take care of the problem. But Christopher still had the presence of mind to know he hadn't been a party to any crime yet and he was only the unfortunate victim of an unscrupulous blackmailer. He wouldn't condone any harm to Grace, even though she was wholly responsible for this fiasco. However, abortion was a legal remedy to the injustices that had been done to him; he could allow that much to happen without sacrificing his conscience.

"I don't want her to get hurt," he said, frightened of showing any kind of compassion toward Grace to a man like Malachi Drudge.

"Oh no," Drudge assured, patting him patronizingly on the back. "Hurting Grace would be the farthest thing from my mind. It would give the police something to wonder about if that happened."

The elevator doors opened after the car jolted to a stop. When Christopher looked out, he saw that they opened onto the lobby floor. Drudge's hand on his back pushed him forward. Christopher took a few stumbling steps out of the elevator and spun around to keep an eye on Drudge, who remained within the car. Drudge's hand came up in a sweeping gesture of shooing him away.

"Go tend to your personal grooming, Christopher. When you look respectable again, go to your office and tend to business as usual. This isn't supposed to rattle you."

Before he could say anything, the elevator doors closed, leaving Christopher to stare forlornly at the numbers changing as the elevator rose.

Drudge didn't move from his rigid position as the elevator rocketed toward one of the upper floors where his private offices were located. He stared at his reflection in the mirror and felt his fury rise in direct relation to the elevator's ascent. He'd been told earlier in the morning that Grace had eluded his men again. The interloper had succeeded in whisking her off to a safe haven neither his human associates nor his minions could find. Drudge had gone livid at the arrival of this news, but his fury had been tempered by the announcement that Devereaux, Bentley, and Murdock had found the old bum who'd worked in conjunction with the interloper. If anyone could locate Grace and her helpful companion, it would be his cohort. He was Drudge's first appointment in the morning.

He stepped off the elevator and walked through a gleaming black marble corridor toward his secretary's desk. The large lacquered wooden construction was set off by itself in the atrium. His secretary was a lovely young woman with silky blonde hair hanging in sculpted waves down her well-muscled back. Her bedroom eyes peered intelligently beneath long, curling lashes, dripping sexuality. Drudge had made her a fixture of his inner corporation for that alone. Human sexuality was a commodity to be exploited, and surrounding himself with manipulative measures proved to be in his best interest.

Slowing from a brisk stride, Drudge approached her desk at a more languid pace. Sliding behind it, he laid his fingers under her chin and stroked the curve of her throat. She sensually lolled her head against his pressing abdomen as his hands roved downward, under her loosely buttoned silk blouse, cupping her breasts and teasing her bare nipples. She moaned appreciatively, and then laughed.

"Mr. Drudge, please, I could own this company by simply reporting you for sexual harassment."

"And I could snap your neck with a twist of my wrist," he whispered back, blowing warm breath into her ear, licking its lobe with a flick of his tongue. "Which is what I would do before I'd let you attempt such a coup."

She stiffened for only a second, then allowed all the tension to dissipate from her body. She squirmed against his firmness as her hands caught his fingers beneath her blouse and pressed them against her breasts. "Would you give me eternal life so soon?"

"Hmm," he considered, slowly retracting his hands. "Before the first wrinkle of age ever mars your lovely face, my love. I promise you that much."

He came around the desk, all business-like then. "Has my first appointment arrived yet?"

"He's in the conference room now."

Drudge nodded and moved off down the hall, his strides long and sure, the heels of his shoes making resounding clicks on the marble floor. When he reached the door to the conference room, he opened it without hesitation, flinging it wide as if intending on making a grand entrance.

The room he walked into was unlike any corporate conference room normal businessmen were familiar with. This room had no glossy table surrounded by comfortably upholstered chairs and buffets, nor a white board or television/video combo for presentations. It didn't come with a pricey Berber carpet or inset track lighting, nor conference-equipped phones or intercoms. It was a room without dimensions, its parameters indeterminate. The distance of the walls was elusive and the height of the ceiling was imperceptible. A sense of illusionary reflections emanated from the polished surface of the walls, although there was no mirrored effect from the items or people within. Of the latter, three stood unbound inside the room, wearing expectant and hopeful expressions. The fourth person was the old bum from the street dressed in the same rank clothes he'd worn for the past month, with crumbs of week-old bread in his beard and old sores seeping pus. He was bound with his hands behind his back and appeared undisturbed by his predicament, staring off in the distance and focusing on something well out of sight, on something that probably existed only within his withered mind.

"Well, well, well," Drudge said as he closed the door behind him, his eyes riveted on the derelict. Off to the side, his three henchmen waited with bated breath. He glanced at them and allowed a slight nod to tilt his head. "You did well."

A smirk crept up on each of their faces.

"Now get out," Drudge snapped, hissing.

Murdock, Bentley, and Devereaux hesitated only a moment, then lunged forward all at once to leave the room, sensing there was a terrible scene about to be played out that none of them were willing to witness. After they had gone, Drudge turned his full attention to the old man, a sneer raising the corners of his lips.

"Well, well, well," he snickered.

"Yes, you've said that already," the bum remarked levelly. He seemed unperturbed by the predicament, but at least he focused his attention on Drudge now.

Drudge gave a wry chuckle as he stepped forward. He moved around the man with a curious interest in his egregious features, sniffing disdainfully at the smell reeking from him. "Is this how God rewards you? With disease and putrescence and destitution? You've become nothing but a walking corpse."

"What rewards I gain from God are of no concern to you."

"Hmph," Drudge remarked, allowing his scorn to show. "I could have given you power, Sophocles. Or money and pleasure if that was what you preferred, if only you had come over to my side. I could have dressed you in the finest clothes and provided you the sleekest sports cars to drive around in. You could have smelled of two thousand dollar cologne instead of your own human stench, and had any woman you wanted instead of satisfying yourself with your own calloused hand. You could have lived in a luxurious penthouse instead of your cardboard shack in an alley. Instead, you have skin that flakes off you in layers and teeth rotted to the core. Everything about you screams of cancer. You are nothing but a corpse."

Sophocles remained silent, unmoved by Drudge's disparaging comments.

"You were once a worthy opponent, Paladin. You put up a good fight and kept me amused."

"I sent you whimpering back to your lair to lick your wounds for more than twenty years once," Sophocles corrected.

"And in my hiatus you must have let yourself go." While he considered Sophocles, Drudge suddenly had a revelation, flicking his finger up to point out his theory. "You've found yourself a replacement. The young man who has Grace Fitzpatrick; he's your protégé, isn't he? He's the one who's been killing my minions with his tiny little knives." He threw his head back and laughed, beginning to pace back and forth before the old man. "Do you believe this one paltry boy can do battle with me? Come now, Sophocles, do you think he can do more than a prick of damage with his insignificant little weapons? You haven't even told him what he's gotten himself into, have you? You're still reluctant to relinquish the mantle, eh, old friend?"

Sophocles lifted his face and bore the castigation without reaction. His mouth only resumed its characteristic masticating on his own thick saliva.

"Look at you. You're nothing but a disgusting example of humanity. You were once a remarkable warrior. Now you're nothing but a public nuisance."

Drudge studied Sophocles with narrow eyes. The unconcerned expression on the bum's face annoyed him. "I can give you what you want. I can return you to the valiant crusader you once were. I can make you young and strong again, if that's what you wish. You were such an admirable nemesis. I would miss life without you."

"Perhaps I choose to relinquish the mantle because I know you enjoy our rivalry too much," Sophocles remarked. "If I can't destroy you with might, perhaps I can with tedium."

"Yes, you would do that," Drudge said ruefully. "That does sound like something you would do just to annoy me." He paused for a few seconds. "But do you really want to end your life in such a pathetic state. You were once a god—"

"I was never a god," Sophocles refuted vehemently, lurching forward despite the ropes holding his hands and rendering him powerless. "I was only a pawn, a mortal man with the knowledge of what is evil on earth. I claim no miracles, no magical powers, no worshipers, and no congress with celestial beings—only those earthbound. I am nothing without His will. I exist only to serve His purpose."

"Blah, blah, blah, blah, blah," Drudge mocked, flipping his hand dismissively to wave aside his words. "And I serve myself."

"You set yourself up on a dais to be worshiped by His children, and that is where you and I are at odds."

"But *we* don't have to fight each other. God pitted you against me because His own vanity demanded it. He Himself bears the cardinal sin of pride. One of the seven deadly sins, and God is wrought with it."

"I won't engage you in a debate over my convictions. Your convoluted theories have no bearing on my faith."

"I can give you whatever you want, Paladin. Youth, power, virility, whatever you desire. The only thing I ask in return is your protégé and the woman he protects. You can resume your role as my adversary and we can commence with the battle again, to the death—for God—if you like. No other strings attached. Your holy crusade will remain intact."

"Yet by betraying the woman and her protector, you will have defeated me," Sophocles observed. "No, I honor my faith by remaining loyal to God."

"And if you die here—now—will your successor know what he's up against? Will he have the power and courage and resources to defeat me?"

"He'll know when he's ready."

"My minions will find him sooner or later. Surely before he's ready."

"Perhaps."

Drudge cocked his head curiously. "Are you willing to leave this world in the hands of an incompetent heir? You'd do just as well to sell me your soul right now."

"Perhaps."

"I'll slaughter them both," he promised vividly.

"I do believe you would kill him, yes—if you could. But you need the woman alive."

"For the moment, until this ugly mess with her child has been taken care of. Then she becomes dispensable."

"Oh, to fear the innocent babe," Sophocles remarked in a mocking tone. "The child you do not know will yet destroy you."

Fire flared in Drudge's eyes. He stepped forward, gaining in size as he drew closer. "Name your play, old fool. Will you accept my offer of redemption?"

"My redemption lies with God, not with you."

Infuriated, Drudge ended the parlay. He turned his eyes on the old man and resisted the urge—the unerringly vain compulsion—of showing the underside of his malevolence. The point would be moot; Sophocles had seen him at his worst, much worse than how he now appeared, and wouldn't be persuaded. He was as stout and resolved in his conviction as he'd always been.

"Then I beg your forgiveness," Drudge said almost forlornly, "for such an unheroic end."

Without pause, he strode to a wall and reached out with his hand. When his arm retracted, it seemed that he pulled a sword out of the oily black substance comprising the formidable boundaries of the room. He brandished it before Sophocles, its chrome-like blade refracting light from its double-edged length.

"I'm sorry to say, then, that I won't be seeing you on the other side."

CHAPTER TWENTY-FOUR

Much to her surprise, Grace discovered the expansive studio had running water and electricity. The darkness of the night before had prevented her from seeing the features of the mostly open flat. In the morning, enthralled by the glorious morning light and her fascination with her host and his flock of companionable birds, she hadn't noticed the far wall had a counter with a few appliances on it. A small refrigerator, an old stove, and a toaster completed his kitchen electrical amenities. A single-basin sink sat off to one side with its faucets coming from the wall.

Grace was amazed when clean water poured from the spigot, and was even more impressed when he pulled out a griddle and plugged the cord into an outlet.

"You don't have morning sickness, do you?" he asked.

She was slightly nauseous now that he mentioned it, but she'd be damned if she was going to turn down any attempt at ordinary function he might offer. If anything, seeing him whip up a batch of pancakes might just be the remedy she needed for her vacillating faith in him. "I'm fine."

Accepting her answer at face value, he set about making breakfast, keeping silent as he worked. Grace wandered to the table and found a chair beneath it. He seemed to prefer the silence, and she decided it was best for the moment. It seemed to make him a little less tense, as if he wasn't comfortable with company in his home and needed a task to distract him. While he worked, she watched him, fascinated with the minor nuances of his body's movement. He wasn't a large man, now that she had the opportunity to look him over, but he was a bit tall and rather lean, muscled in the arms and back, and apportioned in a formidable way. His hair was long and unruly, perhaps because it had dried from a shower without being combed. His face was hairless, though, and his clothes were clean. What he wore was still peculiar, especially the wrappings around his hands and the plain strip of cloth he wore around his forehead.

Whatever his taste in fashion was, Grace was just happy to see him involved in some ordinary domestic chore.

Adam worked fretfully under Grace's watchful eye, her scrutiny causing him no small amount of distress. Her quiet vigilance seemed to be one of rapture, which prompted him to maintain an awkward silence. If he looked at her, he would only experience a pang of overwhelming grief. Her face bore the hint of a smile that glowed in such a way as to remind him of Claire. It could have been her sitting at the table while he made pancakes, much as she had before it all happened, back when they'd had only the future to look forward to.

He remembered Claire in the early stages of pregnancy, the way her face glowed and her hair shined like silk. When he remarked on how beautiful she looked, she only passed it off as the benefits of prenatal vitamins. But he persisted, claiming her beauty was too intrinsic to be only on the surface. He'd never forgotten how breathtaking she'd been.

He barely made it through the first batch of pancakes before he excused himself and headed for a door set off the side of the kitchen. When he opened it, Grace could make out the features of a small bathroom inside. Then the door slammed and she nearly jumped at its abruptness.

In the bathroom, Adam fell against the hollow weight of the door and squeezed his eyes shut. Tears welled up and slipped from the crevasses of his tightly closed lids. The memory of his family always overwhelmed him. In the past, the studio proved to be the only place where he could shed his tears unseen, uncriticized. But now he wasn't alone. He couldn't afford this misery when Grace might walk in on him. Such weakness deserved the privacy of a lonely bolt hole, a place where he could feel comfortable that he wasn't exposed to the human frailties of his character.

At some point, he pushed away from the door and staggered to the sink, which he gripped in an attempt to hold himself upright. He found his legs weak and rubbery, and they threatened to buckle if he didn't hold himself up. With his head bowed, a tear dripped from his cheek and fell to the ceramic basin, its clear globule bursting into smaller droplets on impact. Wearily, he lifted his head and gazed at his eyes in the mirror, strangely unfamiliar with the blue coloring of his Nordic ancestry. The white corneas rimmed his glass-like irises with a tint of red and made the blue a stark contrast in comparison. The blackness of his pupils looked like chips of obsidian. As he looked at himself, he no longer gazed at the whole of his face, but into his eyes, closer and closer, until he was focusing only on the glistening wetness of the black set within the blue set within the red. Out of that intense scrutiny, the flat reflection of shadows from a world hidden within his eyes seemed to swell and take over his whole face, and then the mirror, until he lost all sight of any peripheral image.

A figure moved into focus, as if Adam was only an observer approaching whatever stood within view. The figure grew larger and larger, until Adam could finally see who it was.

Sophocles stood bound before him, his face familiar and comforting despite the hideous pustules and sores seeping sickness in runny gel-like pus. The calmness in his eyes was enough to make Adam release the tension in his own body, but the binds holding the old man were more than a little cause for worry. Adam watched the scene unfold before him and tensed when the vision exposed someone else walking toward his erstwhile mentor. Although he couldn't see the newcomer distinctly, he knew the second figure was Malachi Drudge.

There was nothing he could do to protect the old man at that point, despite seeing it all happen in front of him. Adam's fingers clutched the edge of the sink in a bone-wrenching clench, the flesh of his fingers turning white and the muscles of his forearms going rigid. Cords of tendons became pronounced on his neck as his jaw clenched in frightened desperation. He watched in dread fascination as Drudge confronted the old man and criticized him with his condescending diatribe. Sophocles held his own against the ridicule, professing his faith and loyalty to God and deriding Drudge for tempting him with lies. Adam held his breath during the encounter, afraid his mentor would point directly at him despite the ropes restraining him. But Sophocles remained flaccid in expression and act and denied becoming a party to any such treachery.

Adam mouthed words of denial when Drudge retrieved a sword from the inky depths of his vision. His fingers became rigid as claws on the sink, his arms trembling with the fierceness of his grip. As Drudge walked up on Sophocles, Adam became more vocal in his disbelief, mumbling over and over the words of denial. He watched helplessly as the lord of the minions—dressed in all his finery and groomed to exquisite perfection—took an offensive stance behind the old man's back and rammed the point of the sword through him, skewering Sophocles on the impossibly long and brutal blade. Silvery crimson streaks gleamed on the protruding end of the sword, while the hilt was barely visible behind Sophocles' acutely arched shoulders. On the old man's face, though, was a placid expression of acceptance.

At the same time Drudge committed this murderous act in the Tower, Adam felt a blinding agony pierce his own body. The sudden blaze of pain through his spine surprised him with such brutal force that a scream was wrenched from his throat the likes he'd never uttered before. His knees buckled as his legs went numb, and he crumpled to the floor in a heap, his hands still gripping the sink, trying to prevent himself from cracking his head on the floor. As he went down, his hands were wrenched free of their hold. He groped blindly behind his back, searching for the illusory sword he felt lancing his spine and liver, piercing a lung and nicking a kidney. He felt nothing tangible, but neither could he relieve the agonizing pain afflicting his body through some metaphysical transference of events.

Adam became vaguely aware of a furtive knocking on the door. Slowly, gradually, the pain subsided and the feeling came back to his legs, even as the realization struck him that Sophocles was dead. As the physical agony dissolved into a horrible comprehension of his total aloneness in the world, anger raged through him like a torrid storm. His body reacted violently in defiance and he flung his arms wildly.

Furiously, he scrambled to his feet and beat his fists against the cold porcelain sink, its unyielding hardness matching his wrath. He spun around and picked up a towel post with a heavy base and crashed it into the mirror, shattering that with a profusion of shards spurting back at him. He grasped the top of the post and flung it at the shower door, creating a spider web crack in the upper half of the panel. The fact that it didn't shatter only fueled his fury all the more, and he kicked his foot at the bottom half, once, twice, three times, until it finally shattered. He turned into the tiled wall and beat his fists against it, his pounding making only mockingly soft thuds. All the while, he wailed, tears streaming down his face from a barrier that crumbled like brittle clay under a deluge. Eventually, exhausted, he slumped to the floor, his back sliding along the wall as his knees slowly bent.

Memories cascaded over him like a waterfall of trickling drops, teasing him with scenes of faithful sacrifice. Visions of his first glimpse of Sophocles as he looked up from a stinking gutter, at a time when his hair was a tangled mess and he stank of body odor and cheap wine. The reaching hand and the condescending monologue as Sophocles berated him for his lack of spirit and faith. Adam had wanted to send the old man straight to hell then, and had weakly fended him off with batting hands. But the old man was remarkably stronger than he looked and more insistent and had controlled him easily. Images of the weeks it had taken Sophocles to dry him out—chained, at first, then simply disoriented and afraid to leave his dank prison—the pain-wracking effects of withdrawal turning him into a bitter monster. He'd never been much of a drinker, even though he'd spent plenty nights nursing a beer with friends. Even then he'd learned that a body's tolerance couldn't necessarily be perfected if it just wasn't meant to be.

As the tears came, Adam struck the floor intermittently with a fist. He smacked his head against the unforgiving wall in his frustration with fate and squeezed his eyes shut. But by some chink in his armor, the tears still filtered through, becoming pure fiery pain as they furrowed down his cheeks.

Hearing the terrible wail from behind the door, Grace jumped to her feet. She froze, not knowing what to do. Silence then reigned beyond the barrier, until she heard a horrendous commotion erupt. It seemed to go on forever, until it suddenly died into silence again. Grace remained paralyzed, uncertain what to make of it. It wasn't until she realized she had to do something that she moved forward again.

She rapped lightly on the door. There was no response, so she laid a wary hand on the knob. The door cracked open and Grace peeked inside, shivering with the expectation of seeing the after-images of a battle waged within. But all she saw was the man she'd come to know as stoical and unemotional, now torn to shreds by some unknown force. She worried about that, wondering if it was the result of some chemical imbalance medication usually kept in check. She wondered if he'd missed a dose and suddenly had a brain infarction, or if the bats had somehow snuck into this enclosed room and attacked him?

Then she saw how he cried and thought there was something more disconcerting at work.

"Please," she said softly, trying to draw his attention away from whatever was causing his anguish. "Are you all right?"

He made no indication that he'd heard her. Instead, he slammed his head even harder against the wall, hard enough for her to worry that he might be doing damage to his brain. She whispered her plea again, barely able to bring up enough breath for the word to form and issue from her lips. And maybe it didn't, because he continued to ignore her until she began to cry herself.

"Adam, please," she begged, a bit louder. "Please stop; you're scaring me."

He snapped his eyes open and whipped his head around to face her. With that, she was startled by the starkness of his expression. It wasn't predominantly sorrow that marked his face, but fury. With such an expression of anger, she realized just how dangerous he was, how violent he'd been and how explosive he could suddenly become.

"How do you know my name?" he demanded. His face was a granite mask of distrust. "I never told you what my name was."

She stuttered on what to say, afraid that whatever she gave in the way of an explanation would be inadequate. But she had to say something. He was barely holding his temper in check. "The wine goblets in the cabinet. Adam and Claire. You were married to her, weren't you? To Claire."

The fury on his face quickly dissolved as he closed his eyes and moaned in anguish. His head leaned against the wall and made intermittent smacks against the tile, this time not so hard, only reminiscent of self-flagellation.

"You're scaring me," she repeated, her fear showing in the tremor of her voice and the quiver of her lips. She sobbed also, with tears of desperation.

Adam remained quiet and emotionally distant from her. The longer he remained that way the more frightened she became. "Please, Adam, say you're all right. Say this is nothing I should worry about and everything is fine. I need you to say that. I need to hear it from you."

But his expression was blank and he gave the impression that he'd been frozen in time. She pushed the door fully open, walked in, and crouched before him, finding the courage to make the approach. Yet she didn't reach out to him. Physical contact might trigger off a violent spark and send him into another tirade where she might get hurt. As much as she wanted to help him, she didn't want to put herself at risk by doing so.

"You're supposed to be the only sane one in this mad world," she cried. "Tell me you are. Please, I need to know you're not crazy, too."

He blinked, and the simple gesture was enough to make him appear human again. "But I am," he said miserably. "I am crazy."

"No," she moaned. Then she did reach out, touching his bent knee and confiding in the gesture that she believed in him, believed in the strength of his character, even though she didn't know him at all. "No, you're not. Please don't say that. You're all I have to depend on now."

He leaned his head against the wall and suddenly felt the physical pain he'd caused himself. His eyes closed as he sat in repose. "You can't depend on anyone. There's no one to trust now. No good to rely on anymore."

"Don't say that," she simpered.

"This is all just a big joke God is playing on us. A terrible prank."

"No," she said in a desperate whisper. "That's not true."

"It is," he said in a daunting tone. "It's all just a joke to Him. Just look at the birds. Look at how they gather here and cater to me. I was once told that when God created the earth and its creatures, He was pleased. He gave the birds their wings so they could fly up to Heaven and be His messengers. But I know now they're not His messengers; they're His pranksters."

She shook her head, swiping at her eyes with frustration. "You're talking crazy. Something happened to you in here that's making you talk this way."

"It's all gone," he said, shaking his head as his eyes focused on a faraway thought, nothing quite discernible, but rather an intangible conviction. "All of it. It's all gone."

"No." She gripped his knee as she fell to her own, crawling closer to him to beg his understanding. "I don't understand what happened in here. I don't understand what brought you to this point, but I know you're wrong. God would never play us for fools."

"He allowed it all to be destroyed."

"What? What was destroyed?"

"Love," he said, turning his head to look at her, forlorn and remorseful.

The look he gave her was omniscient, and she recoiled from the simplicity of it. His irises were a bright blue within the blood red of his tear-stained eyes. There was shame in his weeping, which glimmered in his sudden blinking. A large tear collected in the corner of one eye and slipped over the rim of its lower lid.

Grace's heart wrenched at the sight of it. "No," she said, shaking her head. "No, that's not true. Love can never be destroyed. I won't believe that. I won't accept it." She gulped and plunged on. "Just because Claire's gone doesn't mean your love was destroyed."

His hand grasped her wrist. The expression he offered was one of pure rage.

She braced herself to keep from falling forward, placing a hand on his leg. "She was your wife, wasn't she? You were married on May 5th. You lost her to Malachi Drudge. Something happened and now she's gone. Please, I'm just trying to understand."

There was pain reflected in her warbling, frightened voice. She was terrified of him but she wouldn't pull back. She spoke quickly to convince him that she meant no offense—no harm—in what she said. Regardless of his shame, he still brutishly thrust her wrist aside, unwilling to let her come any closer.

"Is that what happened?" she asked softly. "Drudge took her from you. Left you with nothing? Only a loss like that could drive a person . . ."

She allowed her words to trail off, afraid she might have gone too far in what she was suggesting. But he caught her meaning and struggled to his feet, leaving her kneeling on the floor. Stepping around her, he stalked out of the room, dismissing her without even the courtesy of excusing himself. Grace stood up and hurried after him, following with small steps that were prepared to stop in the event he suddenly turned on her.

He strode to one of the windows looking out at the Spatial Tower and gripped the framework in a death grip. Coming up behind him, Grace worried that he might launch himself from the casement. She knew she could do nothing to prevent him from doing so—if that was his intention—but she was prepared to talk him down from the ledge if he should step up on it.

But Adam stayed where he was, staring with determined hatred across the park, toward the abhorrent building. For a while, he remained silent, contemplative, and the longer he remained so, Grace began to relax.

Finally, he spoke, and his words were strong and familiar, spoken with a clarity of mind and intention Grace found comforting. "I have to go somewhere. If you stay here, you'll be safe."

"Where are you going?"

"To the cathedral. I have to do something there."

When he turned toward her, his face was devoid of all the disturbance it had been subjected to minutes ago. Once again, he appeared to be the strong hero she had come to rely on. Only now she didn't have such uncontested faith in him. She now worried he might do something rash, or that she would never see him again.

Then she remembered where it was he said he was going, and the tension in her shoulders relaxed. What evil could lurk in the cathedral? "You'll be back?"

"In a little while. But I have to do this."

He walked away from the window and came to stand close to her. Oddly, she didn't flinch or step away. He reached out and touched her cheek. "I promise, I'll be back soon."

When she looked into his eyes, she was sure she could trust him to return.

CHAPTER TWENTY-FIVE

His first concern when he stepped out of the transept, into the church proper, was how much damage had been done by the assault on the cathedral the night before. He remembered where the spray from the shotgun pellets had pulverized the marble columns and the wooden pews, and moved tentatively about, inspecting the defacement. He felt responsible for the damage, despite having been the target of the attack instead of the cause behind it. As he walked in front of the altar, genuflecting once before the crucifix, he understood what he was doing by inspecting the damage; he was delaying why he'd come here.

Wearily, with an ache in his head from all the pounding he'd done it against the bathroom wall, Adam slid into the first pew. His hands were tucked into his coat's pockets. Once again, the scarf was wrapped around his neck, the length of cloth around his brow. His hands were covered in leather strips, hiding the scars he'd received nearly a year ago. He leaned his head back and closed his eyes, savoring the peace in the cathedral. His mind was battered by thoughts crowding his brain, which he only wanted to dismiss. He wanted nothing but the peace that was supposed to come with faith, even though his restlessness wouldn't allow him to reconcile his worries—or his sins.

Failing to resolve the contention in his mind, Adam opened his eyes and looked at the iconic figure hanging on the cross. The carved image of Christ was rendered in dramatic detail. The painful anguish of the piercing of hands, feet, and ribs contorted with the baleful sorrow on its face. The flexed muscles and strained tendons showed the physical distress of the torture done to the man. Streams of blood were painted in frighteningly realistic crimson and trailed in droplets at various angles along the body. A young but haggard face, lean body, tousled hair, eyes showing a vast wisdom of eternal secrets; it was a sculpture Adam had looked upon many times before but which still gave him pause. He stared at it now, working out the confusion of its meaning with brief glimpses of insight and wisps of comprehension floating on the periphery of his mind. Never enough to fully understand; never enough to feel completely comfortable accepting the faith.

Adam blinked and broke his reflection. His mind jerked back to the secular order of the hard wood and cold marble of the cathedral. He pulled himself up and slipped from the pew, genuflecting in the direction of the tabernacle. With lingering strides, he moved into the christening area and through the door leading to the rectory. He passed no one as he walked through the back passage, all the while wondering if the priest might not be out on rounds to the elderly parishioners and shut-ins. Perhaps he wouldn't be able to find the monsignor when he needed him the most, but that would be the all-telling sign that he'd truly been abandoned.

He opened the door to the secretary's office but hesitated at the look of alarm on her face. Hoping to stem off her panic, he held out a hand in apology. "I'm sorry; I'm looking for Monsignor O'Dwyer."

She gave him a hasty once over, eyeing his unusual attire. With apprehension, she swallowed, showing her unease with his appearance.

When her hand inched toward the phone, Adam added, "I need to speak with him. He helped me last night."

"He's been busy filling out police reports," the old woman stuttered, her hand wavering over the telephone handset.

Adam dropped his eyes and relaxed his body in the hopes she'd sense he meant no harm to either her or the monsignor. He looked over at the door to O'Dwyer's office. "Is he in?"

She went for the phone again. "May I ask who's calling?"

Adam knew her ploy to pick up the phone might simply be to call the police. "Just tell him it's Adam."

The name was enough to set her at ease, a biblical name sounding of goodness. Her hand fell away from the phone as the lines on her face slackened. "You're the young man the monsignor talks about."

"Excuse me?"

"I'm sorry," she said with a kind smile. "Monsignor O'Dwyer said there was a young man who comes to the cathedral to pray. He said you keep your own hours." She laughed out of nervousness. "He described you as a bit frightening." When he raised his eyes inquisitively, she waved her hand dismissively. "But he said you were harmless. Oh, I don't mean it that way. He said you dress a little on the broody side and . . . um, he said I shouldn't be alarmed if I saw you in the church. You were only a little . . . Oh, hell, why don't I just tell the monsignor you're here."

She bolted out of her seat and waddled to the door to the monsignor's office, where she knocked, peeked her head inside, and mumbled something. She nodded and opened the door wide, then motioned for Adam to go in.

Monsignor O'Dwyer stood up when he entered, a little too quickly for Adam not to notice there might be some apprehension in the priest. In response, Adam hesitated just within the doorway, forcing the secretary to edge around him in order to leave them alone. The two men remained motionless, looking at each other, each waiting for the other to speak first.

After a while, Adam did. "Sophocles is dead."

O'Dwyer's apprehensive look slipped away as shock replaced it. His mouth quivered in a form of failed vocalization. Finally, he swallowed hard and recovered a sense of the duties of his office. "Life is just too hard for the older folk living out on the street."

Silence followed his remark. Adam didn't have anything to say, and O'Dwyer found that he couldn't add anything else that would be appropriate. Yet Adam stood his ground, expecting words of consolation to follow. When none came, he said, "He deserves a Christian burial."

O'Dwyer looked up and blinked, then nodded emphatically. "Yes. Certainly. I'll call the coroner's office and make the arrangements. He'll be buried in a Christian cemetery."

Appeased, Adam's shoulders relaxed. He didn't know how to explain to the monsignor how there was little chance of finding Sophocles' body. Knowing Drudge's cruel nature, the lord of the minions was sure to have burned his corpse out of sheer spite. Yet it was still good to hear that the church would tend to its own, if it could. Perhaps it was good enough for God to know that the intention was there to bury him in a righteous manner for it to have any affect.

Adam walked toward the desk. "I came to apologize for whatever damage was done last night."

"It must have been a spectacular show."

"I'll pay for the repairs."

"It's not the damage I'm worried about. It's the violence I'm afraid will encroach upon the church as a result of what happened yesterday."

Adam was sure Drudge's people would refrain from causing any further public spectacle after last night. "There's no need to worry about that."

Monsignor O'Dwyer nodded gravely. He retook his seat behind the desk, leaning back and folding his hands on his lap. "How's Grace?"

"Fine."

"Is she going to see her obstetrician?"

"I haven't asked her."

"Doctor Perez insisted on it."

"I heard her."

"I suppose she's safe, wherever she is."

"Yes."

"You came here for a reason," O'Dwyer said abruptly. "To pay for the damages, you said."

"Not solely."

"Then . . .?"

"I came . . ." He paused, then asked, "Can you explain something to me?"

"If I can."

"Explain God to me."

Monsignor O'Dwyer only stared dumbly at him, blinking once or twice before finally sighing. "That's quite a topic. You understand that mankind has been trying to explain God for thousands of years."

"Surely there's a theological view of what God is."

O'Dwyer gave a little laugh. "The Church's views on God have already filled volumes. What exactly are you looking for?"

Adam hesitated again, uncertain if he should ask the question plaguing him the most. But it was a question that had an answer, and the answer would determine what course of action he would take.

"Did God create Drudge?"

"Who?" O'Dwyer asked quizzically.

Adam shook his head, berating himself for phrasing the question in a manner the priest couldn't understand. The monsignor hadn't been willing to accept the supposition that evil existed in human form, and it was best not to push the man's precarious belief in his sanity.

"Did God create the devil?" he rephrased.

O'Dwyer sighed as he leaned back in his chair, steepling his fingers in front of him. "God is believed to have created the angel who fell from grace and became known as the devil, yes. The Bible constantly alludes to the devil as a tempter, from enticing Eve in the Garden of Eden to tempting Christ in the desert. He is recognized more as the evil that men do rather than any one individual."

"But the Church also acknowledges that demons exist," Adam remarked.

O'Dwyer looked more intently at him, considering the course the conversation was taking. He didn't seem to be in favor of debating theological dogma with a young man he believed was misguided, at best; someone hinged on a volatile ledge of stability. "Adam, what is it you really want?"

Sighing, Adam ran his hands through his hair, pacing about the office with a nervous reluctance to answer the question. He finally turned around and came to a halt, his face showing a confusion of emotions that rallied for dominance. "I'd like you to hear my confession."

O'Dwyer opened his mouth but found no sound coming from it. He blinked once and gave his head a little shake. He had asked countless times to hear Adam's confession, only to be turned down. Adam had never given a convincing reason for his reluctance to open up, and he believed O'Dwyer only continued to make his offer in an effort to learn more about the curious machinations of his mind. But now he was asking for absolution at the expense of confessing his most heinous sins, no matter what the priest thought of him.

"Of course, absolutely," O'Dwyer said, trying to restrain himself from showing too much enthusiasm. He stood up and came around the desk, straightening his white collar in order to distract Adam from his eagerness. "If it's more comfortable for you, we can do this in the confessional. It usually helps when you don't have to see the face of the person hearing your sins."

Adam considered the offer and nodded, finding it more appealing not to have to face a condescending look.

"Let me get my robe. I'll meet you in the number four confessional." He smiled amiably. "I have a preference for number four. The back of the chair has more support and rocks back rather comfortably."

Wordlessly, Adam preceded the priest from the office. The older man motioned for him to go on ahead when they reached the room where the vestments hung. Adam obligingly slipped out and headed along the ambulatory, toward the confessionals. He hesitated outside the cubicle O'Dwyer had a preference for. After a brief debate, he finally gripped the knob and stepped inside.

When the door shut, the light went out and the room was immersed in darkness. Adam knew there was a kneeler beneath a slide partition and dropped to his knees on the springboard. A glimmer of light came on under the kneeler from a trigger on the plank.

He waited in silence until he heard the door to the next cubicle open and movement as O'Dwyer settled in. The partition slid open between their rooms, revealing an opaque perforated screen. Adam felt sweat film the back of his neck despite a chill shivering up his spine. He heard O'Dwyer mumble benedictions, then dwindle into silence. An expectant lapse extended uncomfortably when he had no idea how to begin.

"There's no need for ceremony," O'Dwyer said. "Just list your sins and ask God for His forgiveness."

Another length of silence stretched as Adam struggled with the order in which he should admit his sins, wondering if it was important to prioritize them so the priest could gauge his sense of repentance.

"There's no formula to figure out," O'Dwyer prompted, apparently intuitive to Adam's hesitation.

"I've struggled with this faith, Father," Adam reluctantly started, swallowing with difficulty. "I'm ashamed to admit that I'm here only because of Claire."

"To follow the righteousness of another is nothing to be ashamed of."

"But my sole reason for accepting this faith is her, not God."

"She was a good woman and a good Catholic. She brought you to the church even before tragedy struck your family. You had already accepted God."

"In a sense," Adam said, conceding to a slight truth. He had believed in God and the basic tenets of religion but he hadn't dedicated much time to the actual worship of the faith. "After the funeral, though, I gave up on Him. I became nothing but an alcoholic, living in the gutter, wallowing in my own misery. I lost whatever goodness Claire had given me."

"But you found your way back."

"Because of Sophocles." Adam paused. He dropped his head reverently, feeling the weight of the old man's death press heavily against the nape of his neck. "He gave me some understanding as to why things happened the way they did. He told me God was the only way to defeat the evil that took Claire and Marie away."

In his cubicle, O'Dwyer shook his head. Sophocles had frequently visited the cathedral and spent time in prayer in the back pews, much as Adam had taken to doing. Unfortunately, Sophocles' senility might have grown in his old age, and his edification of faith to the people on the street had suffered as a result of it.

O'Dwyer was about to challenge Sophocles' right to preach when he heard something outside the confessional. A bump jogged the doorknob. O'Dwyer cocked his head to listen more intently. He wondered only for a second if it was someone who'd passed by and checked the knob, but then he heard a loud scuffle in the room next to his. He reached for the doorknob and twisted it, only to find it turned but wouldn't open.

Adam was gathering his thoughts when he heard a thump outside the room. He wondered briefly if maybe the priest had left the room for some reason, but then the door to his cubicle exploded open and two men lunged in. He didn't have time to gather his feet beneath him before the intruders ran him into the back wall and pinned him there, his legs twisted up beneath him. The first punch to his stomach drove the air from his lungs, while the second prevented any breath from filling his chest. A hand gripped a length of his hair and slammed his head into the wall, while another covered his mouth. All the while, two other fists pummeled him.

Eventually, the two hands that drilled his body grabbed his coat. Clutching folds of it, they dragged him from the confessional. His head was pulled back, far enough that he couldn't see forward or regain his balance. His arms were yanked behind his back as another man came at him from the other side, grabbing and propelling him forward until his knees met the back of the last pew. The hands knotted in his hair jerked his body downward, moving in such a quick fashion that he couldn't orient himself at the same time. His legs were then abruptly kicked out from under him.

Adam fell, his midsection connecting with the top of the pew. Again, the breath was knocked from his lungs and pain radiated through his body. His head was forced down and his face was smashed into the bench, while his hands were lashed behind his back. His head was suddenly yanked up and a swatch of sticky tape slapped over his mouth. Finally, a black hood was tugged over his head. With urgent roughness, he was hauled to his feet and dragged away.

He tried to fight back but his arms were useless. Instead, he struggled to regain his footing to use his legs, but he was never allowed to manage it. He became aware of being dragged outside, sensing a change in the ambient temperature around him, and he tripped on the steps in the urgency to leave the church. He almost went down on his knees, but the hands on his arms were strong and determined and he was hoisted up again. He heard the screech of tires and a car door open, and then felt himself tossed and jammed inside a car, where a man to either side of him shoved his body down to the floorboards.

With a growing sense of panic, Adam worked on remaining calm. Despite the hood covering his eyes, he was sure who his attackers were. It wasn't hard to figure out that the men who'd attacked the cathedral last night were the same ones in the car with him now. Even as he thought this, one of them spoke next to his ear.

"You fucking son of a bitch." It was the one he remembered from the van. "You messed where you shouldn't never have messed. When I'm done with you, there won't be anything left of you but an echo of you screaming."

Adam twisted slightly to ease the pain of the front seat pressing into his bruised midsection. When a fist punched the back of his head, his brain threatened to black out. He stopped moving. He would need to remain conscious in order to deal with the problem. With some effort, he allowed himself to relax, hoping his assailants would think he'd gone unconscious. He knew there were at least three of them, and where they believed they had blinded him, he would soon have the eyes of another.

They came at his behest, a flock of sparrows that had been roosting in the cathedral's belfry. Through their collective sight, Adam saw the car speeding away from the curb, tearing up the pavement as if the hordes of Hell were hot on its tail. Adam's first thought was that they would take him straight to the Spatial Tower. But he was a bit confused when the car turned east and headed toward the waterfront instead.

CHAPTER TWENTY-SIX

The first hint that something was wrong was the birds. Grace was lying on the bed when the birds—which had returned almost immediately after Adam left for the cathedral—became agitated and then frantic. As a group, they began chirping, squawking, screeching, peeping, hooting, and warbling, each species caterwauling in their own specific dialect, making no sense other than what could easily be discerned from their cacophony—that something was wrong. Their wings lifted in sporadic but ineffectual flits, as if they intended to fly off but were held back by something more imperative. Instead, their feathers ruffled and bristled from some form of avian-afflicted anxiety that only exacerbated the tension building in the room.

After Adam had left, Grace had cleaned up the breakfast dishes and put them away, then straightened the mess in the bathroom. With that done, she found a closet and rifled through it, picking through the clean clothes for something to wear. She found a pullover shirt and a pair of sweat pants, and carried them into the bathroom to take a shower, creating quite a puddle on the floor because the shower door existed only in pieces in the kitchen garbage. Once she was dressed, she slipped back into bed and hugged the pillows tightly to her body, suffering an influx of emotions that swirled inside her head. She tried to pick them apart and set them in order but she was still nothing but confused and exhausted when she finally dozed off.

Since then, she'd been napping. Then the birds suddenly erupted into their riotous gabbing, and Grace just as quickly lurched up in case what was happening was another attack from Drudge's hired henchmen. A quick scan of the expansive apartment assured her that no one was in the room with her—other than the agitated birds—and she managed to relax a bit, falling back on her elbows. For a short time, she watched the smaller birds dart nervously about, as if attempting to spark the larger ones into action. But those only remained on whatever perch they had selected, bristling and ruffling in a way that implied uncertainty and agitation. Grace thought at first they were just worried about encroaching bad weather, but then she noticed how the sun was shining just as strongly through the windows as when she'd awoken in the morning. Finally, as she wondered about their odd behavior, a few of the smaller birds gave up the ghost and darted out the windows, leaving altogether.

Grace looked around with concern, inexplicably disturbed by the birds' anxiety. As much as she tried, she couldn't see what would cause them to worry, much less herself. But she also wasn't about to dismiss their fretfulness without further explanation. Sluggishly, she eased herself up against the headboard and wiped the sleep out of her eyes, hoping the meager gesture might be enough to clear her vision so she could see more clearly. As she did, the birds' behavior evolved into a more frenetic state, and more flew from the rafters, darting out the windows. The smaller ones—the finches, sparrows, and lorries—flew about the studio with restlessness, while the larger, more predatory ones disappeared altogether.

Growing more concerned about what might be going on, Grace climbed out of bed and hurried to one of the windows, ignoring the fact that the birds were darting about in a mad whirlwind of fluttering, sweeping, and flitting wings behind her. As chaotic as their flurry was, none of them brushed against her in her dash across the room. Instead, they parted to let her pass, rising high enough so she didn't disrupt their wake, until she sidled up to the window to look out, her attention drawn immediately to the daunting view of the Tower across the greensward. Almost at once, an icy shiver crept up her spine.

There was no denying the sense of foreboding emanating off the ugly and imposing structure. She could see why Adam would look at it as a sort of perdition. But truly it was only a building, constructed of concrete and steel, girded the same way as any other building in the city, complying with the same building codes. It seemed peculiar that Adam would pick this building across from the monolith to be his home if he believed the Tower was a construction of evil. But she wasn't entirely convinced that Adam was of sound mind either.

Considering that, she leaned out the window to watch the swirling mass of birds flocking eastward, spiriting toward some destination that seemed to draw them with an all-consuming purpose. Although she couldn't make out where they were going, they were headed in the same direction, pinioning as one collective mass toward a common destination. Intuitively, she knew it had to be a bad thing but she wasn't sure why she knew or what it was. She only knew there was turmoil among the birds and it could only be the harbinger of bad things to come.

She suddenly grew worried for Adam, sensing whatever was wrong had something to do with him. The birds were his, he'd said, and even though it sounded crazy, she believed him. Whether they were tame or wild, they were still his companions, roosting in his home with a respect that was uncannily hospitable. For whatever it was worth, they seemed to be linked to him in a way she didn't understand. Deep down inside, she knew the birds were acting out of sorts because Adam must have suffered some terrible misfortune.

Reluctantly, she forced herself to look across the park, sensing the brooding evil inside the Tower. The niggling feeling was still there, leaving her repulsed and anxious about her own proximity to the building. Unfortunately, her eyes couldn't discern anything more than a polished monolith of gleaming granite cut with narrow windows glazed with black reflective glass. She ventured even further out over the sill to glance at the sidewalk in front of the building, seeing people moving in and out of its front doors with hurried airs. A normal business day, a scene reminding her it was Monday morning and she was supposed to be at her desk at Demars, Braxton, and Hilfinger.

Afflicted with a sense of conscionable work ethic, Grace spun away from the window to look for a phone, realizing she was horribly—terribly—late for work. Yet if there was a phone anywhere in this place, it must have been one of those novelty pieces disguised as something else—a shoe or football, or maybe even a duck—because she couldn't find it.

Damn.

With the baby on the way and no reliable presumption that Christopher would be responsible without court encouragement, Grace couldn't afford to lose her job. It was hard enough to find employment in a field where even a monkey could do what she did, but it would be next to impossible to find another job when a prospective employer had to consider hiring a temp once she went out on maternity leave. Considering the big picture, she would have to protect herself financially as well as physically.

Grimly, she glanced down at herself and frowned at the clothes she wore. She couldn't show up late for work in a pullover and sweatpants. That would be two strikes against her before she even got a chance to explain herself. On the other hand, she wasn't comfortable going home by herself to change. Realistically, she worried that her apartment would be under surveillance by the men who'd pursued her yesterday. She even suspected Adam might be furious with her to learn that she'd gone out on her own after he'd told her to stay put.

Adam . . .

Grace forgot about work and her troubles. For the most part, the birds were gone, leaving only the smaller ones to remain as her unseemly guardians. Their continued peeping, chirping, and cheeping was enough for her to worry that whatever was happening outside this tranquil haven was far more problematic than missing a day of work. She didn't think she could live with herself if she didn't do something to help him.

Although Adam was surprised to discover that he wasn't being taken to the Spatial Tower, listening to the three men arguing over why he wasn't explained the reason behind their motives. In actuality, they had no idea who he was and simply pegged him as a homeless person who'd gotten caught up in a situation beyond his comprehension. They had no idea how far off the mark they were. Instead, they considered him their only source of finding Grace and were anxious to retrieve her on their own. There was money at stake—and favor—and it seemed they had some redeeming to do for all the mistakes they'd already made.

Adam thanked God for small favors, knowing all too well he wasn't ready to confront Drudge on his terms just yet. His thirst for revenge wasn't enough to make him eager to race towards almost certain failure. Not just yet. When he finally decided it was time to go up against Malachi Drudge, he knew he had to be ready to die, because that was exactly what would happen. Adopting such a fatalistic approach to their next encounter was necessary, since when he squared off with the ageless minion lord, he knew his own end was certain. Yet there was a positive side to this idea, and that was when it happened, he'd be taking Drudge with him.

Over the past several months, since Sophocles found him on the streets and dragged him down to the underground passages beneath the city, he'd been weaned to fulfill his role in the endgame. The old man's tutelage had hinged on explaining the truth and fiction behind good and evil. It had been easy to understand when Adam listened to the old man's philosophies told in the even-keeled fashion of an emotionless lecture of how there was a distinct separation of what existed as a manifestation of evil and the formidable bastion of righteousness. Conversely, the details of Sophocles' lifelong battle against that evil were private and untold, and Adam respected the pain his mentor chose not to share with him. In return, Sophocles never asked Adam to speak about the night Claire and Marie had been killed, and it remained as a personal and private pain.

The car he was in drove into the business district, through the slums of the inner city, and then toward the waterfront, where fish canneries and storage warehouses existed. Seagulls and pelicans watched from the docks and pilings as the Cadillac whispered along the boardwalk, disturbing none of them. At the north end of the docks, local fishermen haggled with distributors over the price of their catches. The smell of the river and dead crustaceans was noxious and unappealing. Fish oils and guts having previously dripped onto the cement boarder and dried under the baking sun made for a nauseating stench. The tang of salt in the air did nothing to subdue the unpleasant odor of the not so far off ocean.

The Cadillac negotiated its way around dock hands, merchant marines, fishermen hosing down trawlers, and old men pulling long lines up to check their meager catch. The trespassing Cadillac hardly seemed congruous with the decrepit state of the pier, but its passage was given only a haphazard glimpse of concern from those people on the wharf. The men who worked the area knew what it meant for such a car to travel along the boardwalk and minded their own business. Another poor sap must have angered or interfered with one of the many crime bosses of the city and was about the become fish fodder. With the putrid state of the inlet and its muddy depths, many a body had been consigned to the dark waters beneath the wharf with little hope of discovery. Some of the older men would cast their nets around the south end of the pier tomorrow in the hopes they'd find the exact location where the body had been dumped, and with any luck, they would eat well that night.

Adam watched through his remote eyesight as the Cadillac drove past the working canneries and into the dilapidated south point of the docks, where the buildings were abandoned and in such a state of disrepair that no one ever ventured this far down the wharf. The car approached one of the warehouses constructed of rusted corrugated metal and afflicted with a myriad of windows coated in various shades of opaque glass caused by years of weathering or grossly encrusted with crud. As the car stopped in front of one of its closed hangar-style doors, Adam watched a few grackles fly through a couple of broken windows to perch on rafters inside.

Seeing the inside of the building from the grackles' viewpoint, Adam saw that nothing remained within the rundown building except shards of broken windows, dust motes coruscating in the streaming light, and wads of crumpled paper wedged along the walls. Sunlight filtered in various forms of brightness through the window panes, while a kaleidoscope of particles danced in rays cast in a version of sublimely golden beams.

This was where he would have to make his escape. His arms were bound behind his back, but even though they were tight, the rope wouldn't be immune to the edge of a blade. The foolishness of his attackers had been when they assumed he was nothing but a street urchin and hadn't bothered to search him for weapons.

One of the men got out of the car and hurried to the large warehouse door. It proved to be secured by a formidable padlock, and the man fumbled in his pocket for a key. With it, he worked to open the door, showing no concern for anyone who might be spying on his villainous activities. That only worried Adam all the more, and he used the opportunity to work his hands very slowly toward a pocket in his coat, where he slipped a hidden knife out of its sheath and palmed it around in his hand.

The car drove into the warehouse after the padlock was removed. Once the Cadillac had passed through, the door was closed and relocked. The driver carefully negotiated the support columns as he drove into the building, while the man who'd opened and closed the hangar door jogged across the warehouse and rejoined his companions where the car finally stopped. There the two remaining men got out.

There was some discussion among them, then arguing. Murdock made a wild gesture and uttered a foul remark, then walked toward the car's back door. He reached in, grabbed Adam's coat and wrenched him up from the floorboards.

"Come on, you stupid bastard, time to face the music."

Adam worked as best he could to get out of the car. He saw through the grackles' eyes how the other two men were moving in, and he waited for them to move even closer still. The lives of Grace and her unborn child depended on how successful he was in escaping his abductors, and he would only have one shot at it. Otherwise, he knew no amount of reasoning with these men would win his release.

After some bumping and squirming, Adam finally managed to get out and stand on his own. Regardless, Murdock held his elbow as he pressed a gun against his temple, drilling it harshly into the hollow beside his left eye. "You wanted to be a fucking hero, asshole. Well, this is what happens to heroes."

Even if he hadn't had the help of his remote eyesight from the birds, Adam would have known exactly where the gun was with it pressed against his temple. Knowing that, he reacted fast, giving his captors no chance to get comfortable with their advantage. He jerked his head to the side as he reached up with his suddenly unbound hands to grab the gun, while at the same time, spinning to ram his knee into Murdock's crotch.

Pain exploded in Murdock's abdomen as his legs went into immediate spasms. His fingers slackened as blood drained from his extremities. Adam was able to pluck the gun effortlessly from his fingers. Nearly fainting, Murdock doubled over and clutched his swollen testicles, moaning and wheezing as his face took on a ghastly hint of pallor.

Adam ripped the hood from his head and swung the gun around, pointing it in the direction of the two other men. The whole maneuver had taken him less than three seconds, and he managed to catch the others off guard as they hastily fumbled in their pockets for their own weapons.

"Don't!" he ordered, thrusting the gun at them.

Seeing how he now held them at bay, the other two men pulled their hands away from their pockets to show them to be harmless. Adam glanced about anxiously, uncomfortable with the openness around him. He sidled several feet away from Murdock in case the man suddenly recovered.

"You don't want to do that, man," Bentley said, his hand going out to hold Adam off. He inched a few steps toward the car, coming closer but angling away from Devereaux, separating from him but trying to keep his move surreptitious. "You got no place to go, my friend. The door's locked and there's no way out."

"There's always a way out," Adam said, eyeing his surroundings without actually taking his eyes off his assailants. There didn't seem to be any easy way out of the warehouse except for the broken windows, but the panes were actually smaller than what he'd thought when he'd seen them through the grackles' eyes. Seeing that now, he knew there was no way he'd be able to fit through them even if he made it to the wall.

"Give me the keys," Adam demanded, holding out one hand.

Devereaux glanced at his partner, then held out a pair of keys on a simple round ring—the keys to the padlock on the door. "You mean these?"

"The car keys," Adam said.

"What?"

"I said the car keys."

"That's *my* mudder fucking car," Devereaux said petulantly, his voice slipping into the uncultured tone of a street punk. "You think I'm gonna let you take my Caddy, you out of your mudder fucking mind."

"Give me the keys!" Adam insisted, his voice growing more urgent and strident. Beside him, he saw Murdock regaining his senses, and the look on the man's face was growing increasingly more dangerous as he recovered.

Devereaux flung his arms up as he stomped his feet in anger. "You're piss headed crazy, you think I'm gonna let you take my car, you mudder fuckin' asshole." Abruptly, he spun on Murdock. "You fuckhead, you better straighten this shit out! You da one who let him get the drop on you. Ain't no way I'm lettin' him take my sled."

Facing the infuriated and overbearing gangster, Adam hesitated, not really sure how he should deal with the man's tempestuous anger. If anything could be learned from it, it was that there was no way he was going to get the keys to the car *or* the padlock now. Instead, he'd have to think of an alternate way out of the building, even though it seemed fairly pressing for him to come up with a plan right away. The standoff wasn't going to last long, not if the Caddy owner had anything to say about it.

There was only one possible way he might be able to get out. Along the far back wall was a staircase leading up to a series of offices, and Adam begged the sight of the birds outside to see what type of window was there. Almost immediately, the birds responded in a reflexive mirage of images, each one passing the information to him without regard for the staccato pulsing it caused in his brain. He swallowed the resulting nausea and fought off the vertiginous effect until he was able to sort through them. There were large casement windows he could easily break through and make a twenty-foot drop to the ground outside. It was an easy way out if he could only get to the offices on the second floor.

In the meantime, Murdock regained his senses enough to realize what had happened. For the third time in not even as many days, he'd been duped by Adam, having been taken for a fool and gotten pulverized. At the moment, he couldn't think straight with Devereaux yelling wildly at him and the pain in his balls throbbing maddeningly. "Shut up!"

"Fuck you!" Devereaux shouted back, his face contorted into a twisted rictus of corded facial muscles and tendons. Seeming to come to his own conclusion of how the situation would best be handled, Devereaux reached into his coat for his own weapon.

Murdock instinctively dropped behind the Cadillac and Bentley ran for cover behind a nearby support column. Adam's eyes widened as a fully automatic machine gun came smoothly out of Devereaux's pocket. It flowed out of his coat like quicksilver, proving that the gangster was familiar with just such a maneuver and had probably practiced it several times in the past. Even as it came out, it was firing, spraying bullets across the floor, toward Adam's feet.

Murdock crouched into a tight ball, throwing his arms over his head as an ineffectual shield against the high caliber rounds. At the same time, he screamed shrilly at Devereaux, yelling insane recriminations of how they needed the kid alive.

But the report of gunfire was too loud and his words were muffled under the ceaseless *cht-cht-cht-chting* of the machine gun. Even as Devereaux kept up the staccato burst, Murdock ventured to peek through the window of the Cadillac. Amazingly, he saw Adam running instead of firing back with his own meager weapon, which was probably the smartest thing to do. Instead, he headed for the staircase against the far wall, while Devereaux continued to release a continuous spurt of rounds in his direction. When the firing pin finally landed on an empty chamber, Devereaux coolly dropped the magazine and jammed in a fresh one, the break in the bursts lasting only two seconds at best.

All the while, Adam ran just ahead of the spray of bullets, thinking that if he stopped or slowed he would be easily picked off with a lucky hit to an ankle or hip. In the back of his mind he knew he couldn't take shelter behind one of the columns, although he passed several in his sprint toward the back of the warehouse. He knew if he did, his three abductors would only skirt around and flank him from either side, then take him out at their leisure. He had to make it to the offices on the second floor. There he could make a stand against them, without anyone creeping up from behind.

He added a burst of energy to his legs and sprinted across the open floor. Bullets *plinked* off the columns and metal girders as they followed him toward the staircase. He gave a silent prayer for luck and wondered if it was blasphemous to ask God for good fortune. The stairs loomed in front of him only a few strides away, and he bounded for them, then up them with an impressive speed, which if the others watching him wondered about would only believe it was because he felt the demon of terror nipping at his heels. Adam's hand grasped the banister and hauled him more quickly upward. He felt the rickety steps shimmy with the pounding of his footfalls but he kept his eyes on his goal, which was the top riser. He tried not to focus on the sound of the bullets thumping into the wood behind him.

It wasn't a bullet hitting him that suddenly caused him to worry; it was the dilapidated wooden staircase eaten through by termites. Rotten sawdust sifted down with each stride, and a creak accompanied each foot stomping down on the risers. A creak, groan, and crack sounded as his foot stepped on the second to last one. The staircase shimmied and jarred. His hand reached out to steady himself on the banister but the wooden railing was even less secure than the steps. A length of wood under his hand pulled from its mooring, causing him to shift to the side and flail for something solid to brace onto. But there was nothing there and his hand grasped only empty air. In the last moment, he flung himself away from the dangerous opening, toward the wall, and found himself momentarily safe. But his foot came down on the final riser and stomped right through it, the rotten wood making more of an impressive crack than the reports of gunfire behind him. He groped for balance on the railing but found it buckled, while his leg fell through the gaping hole up to his knee. He tried to pull himself away from the opening, but as he put his weight on the top landing, that too broke through, jostling him to fall face first against the staircase.

The sudden jolt loosened the last precarious moorings of the rotten staircase. Adam's one hand clasped the protruding ledge of the second floor landing. His other hand joined the first as his legs fell out from under him. He hung dangling from the ledge, the force of his body swinging back and forth prying his grip loose inch by inch. Despite readjusting his hands a few times, his fingers became strained and weakened, until they finally slipped.

He tried to keep his legs down and his head up for the landing, but beneath the broken stairway were crates stacked ten feet high. His feet hit and broke through the top one, then caught on the second, upsetting his smooth fall. His back connected with the shattered remnants of the first crates and the crumbled debris of the staircase, and then his head.

CHAPTER TWENTY-SEVEN

As the morning wore on, Grace became increasingly more concerned about Adam's whereabouts. The birds had left for the most part, leaving one by one, as if they were rats on a sinking ship, and she felt terribly vulnerable because of their departure. Only a few finches remained—meager defenses for the bastion—and those flitted nervously about, offering no help for her growing anxiety.

In the time it had taken the birds to fly the coop, Grace had made a pact with herself to wait until noon before she officially began to panic. If Adam hadn't returned by then, she'd make a decision for what she should do.

But when noon came and Adam still hadn't returned, Grace decided she would wait another half hour just for good measure. When that deadline came close and Adam still hadn't come back, she figured she should honestly start thinking about her options. Finally, when another bird left the room—this one putting her to shame because it was a tiny creature that could provide little help in any crisis—Grace's sense of cowardice redoubled. She knew now, beyond any doubt, that Adam was in trouble and it would be up to her to do something about it. After all, what could a motley flock of birds do when it came right down to it?

But Grace didn't know where to start looking or how to go about initiating a search, so she decided to give it yet another half hour.

By one thirty, she was pacing the room. At irregular intervals, she peered out the window and scanned the sidewalk below, hoping to catch a glimpse of him on his way back. When she couldn't find him among all the others pedestrians, she suspected it was because she was so far up. There were people crowding the streets, walking from one building to the next, briefcases and laptops swinging at their sides, all anonymously cloaked in distance. They walked briskly and purposefully, without apprehension of being out in public, putting a realistic bent on her predicament. With the sun pouring down to illuminate all the hidden nooks and crannies that otherwise—at night—might harbor frightening creatures and ill-meaning criminals, it was hard to accept that something bad might have happened to her unlikely champion. By focusing on the routine and ordinary activities of people in public, she was able to loosen her disabling grip on pessimism. After a while, she convinced herself that she was over-reacting. There was no connection between the birds' behavior and what might be keeping Adam from returning to the loft. It was only her fear of being alone that made her imagine trouble befalling her newfound friend. She was just being silly. He was fine, and he would return when he was finished with whatever it was he was up to.

After a short while, Grace figured Adam probably wouldn't be walking out in the open anyway. He would likely be using the tunnels if he was afraid people were looking for him.

Again she wondered where he would have gone after such an emotional breakdown. He'd said he was going to the cathedral, but surely he couldn't have spent all morning there.

Or could he? She didn't know much about him, but if she was pressed to make a guess, she would have to say he *was* at the cathedral. His preoccupation with religion and his predilection to seek refuge there the night before—not to mention the route he seemed intimately familiar with through the tunnels—made her think Our Lady of the Blessed Virgin Mother was the most likely choice for where he might have gone in a time of emotional crisis. But to her embarrassment, she caught herself agreeing to wait yet another hour before doing anything about his absence.

She angrily stomped her foot in disgust. Adam had been there every time she'd needed help. He was the reason she was still alive and her baby was still nesting insider her. He'd sheltered her in his own home, even when he didn't know the first thing about her. She'd been nothing but a passing stranger, and it wouldn't have surprised her if he'd done nothing to help her at any point over the weekend. But he had, and for that, she owed him immensely, more than she could ever hope to repay him.

Grace pulled back from the window and looked around the room, hoping to dissolve the fantasy she was keeping of everything being all right. She was afraid of going out in the open, even though she knew she had to make some effort to find him, if only to relieve the guilt plaguing her.

She went to his closet and fumbled through the items on the shelves until she found a cap with a logo on it. Although she wasn't much of a sports fan, she recognized the emblem as belonging to one of the city's hometown teams. With growing apprehension, she gathered up the loose ends of her hair and piled them atop her head, then slapped the cap on and pulled the bill down over her brow so her immediate features were somewhat disguised. With the bulky pullover and baggy sweatpants, people would be hard pressed to pick her out of a crowd.

Reluctantly, she headed for the lift elevator and pressed the button to bring it up. The car rose slowly and clumsily, making her wait interminable minutes as she fought with her trepidation. She owed Adam more than just accepting his hospitality with graciousness. If he was in trouble, she had to try to help. For whatever it was worth, if she couldn't help him herself, she had to find someone who could.

The elevator clanged to a stop. Grace struggled with the heavy gates to lift them and then pulled them down after entering the car. The old contraption jolted as it began its weary descent to the first floor.

She knew she wouldn't be leaving the building the way she'd come into it. She'd never be able to find her way through the underground tunnels on her own, nor would she be able to find the entrance into them. Instead, she'd have to look for a more ordinary route out, hoping the building had an exit she could use.

On the ground floor, when the elevator jarred to a halt, Grace suffered another fit of nervousness at leaving the building. She hadn't been aware of how safe she'd actually felt in Adam's strange world. The prospect of going out into the city—a world that had proved itself to be aggressive and predatory in just the last few days—was daunting. But what other choice did she have if she was going to help him.

The elevator opened onto a corridor, which in turn, after a length, led to an eerily deserted atrium of marble and polished wood, albeit dusty and aged. The glass windows making up the front of the building were boarded up with sturdy planks of plywood. The front door was also barred by panels of wood. Light came in through slivers of space between them, creating slices of sunbeams that made her think of laser lights.

Grace took a few tentative steps into the atrium and peered about, wondering if Adam had left her so easily because he knew she had no way of leaving the building. But then she got a grip on herself. The fortress was probably more to keep *him* safe than her.

Huffing with sporadic breaths, she forced herself to overcome her anxiety and get about her business. With a bit of sleuthing, she tried to identify what this building might have been in its day by studying it from the inside. Although it was constructed of materials alluding to a certain amount of luxury, she couldn't picture what it had been before its demise.

She knew something of architectural coding and forced herself to brave the dark corridors leading toward the back, where the maintenance facilities were usually located. She had to feel her way along in the dark, cursing herself for not having had the foresight to look for a flashlight before leaving Adam's aerie loft. She felt blindly along the wall, her hand running across the peeling wallpaper and intermittent door jambs until she met corners at intersections and crossed over them, all in an attempt to find a door at an exterior wall, somewhere leading her out to a back alley, an obscure location away from the offices, near the end of a corridor perhaps, or in a stairwell.

Then she found it, a metal fire door with a push bar to open it. Per code, these doors usually opened only from the inside—in the event of a fire—and remained locked from the outside. She was betting Adam would have a ground access to the city streets despite his underground network of tunnels, and this might be it. With a breath of hope, she pushed on the bar, using all her weight.

The bar depressed and the door gave way, opening up to the brilliance of a sun-speckled alley running behind the building. Grace rushed through the door and let it close behind her, knowing it would be locked if she tried to regain entry into the building. She glanced up and down the alley and found it deserted, then hurried up the cobbled pavement toward the sidewalk. As she paused at the entrance to the alley, she stared at the pedestrians walking past her with their hurried and self-indulging airs. She stepped out amid the crowd and concealed herself among their bustling, keeping her head down and her shoulders hunched as she headed in the direction of Our Lady of the Blessed Virgin Mother.

Sergeant Markey found it hard to believe the priest's story. The old man kept insisting he'd been locked inside the cubicle while thugs attacked and apparently kidnapped one of his parishioners. Markey had agreed to investigate the crime only because of its particular connection to the cathedral, even though it didn't involve a homicide. Last night's assault had drawn his attention in more ways than one. The young man the old bum had called Slash had sought refuge here—so Doctor Perez had said—which meant there was a connection between the church and the kid. Markey was inclined to believe the connection lay with the mob. Whether it was one of allegiance or extortion, Markey hadn't figured that out yet, but he planned on doing so soon.

Last night, Monsignor O'Dwyer had claimed he hadn't seen the people who'd waged an armed assault on the cathedral, either. When he was questioned why he hadn't heard the shotgun blasts, the priest had merely explained that he'd been in a tiny house behind the cathedral, out of earshot. Although Markey wasn't a religious man and subscribed to no God himself, he was still reluctant to call the old man a liar. At least, not to his face.

"If you didn't see who came in, how do you know anyone came in at all?" Peter Lumas asked. "This man you were hearing confession from could have staged the whole incident."

"For what purpose?" O'Dwyer asked. "If anything, this man cherishes his privacy. He's not a man who craves attention."

"I don't know," Markey said meditatively, "he seemed to attract a lot of it. How well do you know this kid?"

O'Dwyer hesitated as if considering his answer. "He likes to frequent the church for personal prayer and reflection," he said simply.

"You mean he doesn't go to mass," Markey interpreted. "But he still comes here."

"You might say that."

Markey nodded and gave Lumas a sidelong glance. Lumas's eyes shifted over his shoulder and past him, which caused Markey to turn to see what he was looking at.

A woman had walked into the church and was glancing around, as if trying to locate someone. When she saw the three of them, she became excited and hurriedly approached. She focused intently on the priest as she ran directly to him.

Markey saw through her hastily thrown-together disguise only once she came close. "Grace!"

Grace abruptly stopped when she saw who she was approaching. With confusion, she blinked, her mouth opening and closing on unspoken words of surprise. "What are you doing here?"

"I was going to ask you the same thing," Markey said, his tone more authoritative all of a sudden. "I have the entire police force looking for you."

"Am I a fugitive now?" she asked.

Markey jabbered on an answer, surprised by her pervasive tone. "I saw . . . you were in trouble last night."

Her eyes narrowed suspiciously. As if she suddenly remembered why she'd come to the church in the first place, she turned her attention to the priest, dismissing Markey and his partner. "Father, has Adam come by today? He left awhile ago and said he'd be right back. It's been hours but he hasn't come back yet."

O'Dwyer's eyes darted over to Markey and Lumas. The look was not lost on them, and Markey picked up on the apprehension in Grace's voice. "Adam?"

She offered an impatient glance his way, as if conveying to him that she didn't appreciate his interruption. Then she addressed O'Dwyer again. "Did he come by this morning?"

O'Dwyer clutched her hand and held it supportively. "I'm sorry, Grace, but something terrible has happened."

"Oh no," she moaned, trying to take a step back and withdraw her hand. She attempted to break the handhold, but O'Dwyer kept her hand in a firm grip.

"I was hearing his confession when some people attacked. They locked me in my confessional and assaulted him. When one of the parishioners finally released me, Adam was nowhere to be found."

"Oh my God, they took him," she whispered.

"Who?" Markey demanded, leaning close, intending to assert himself in the conversation, regardless of her earlier dismissal. He was fed up with being relegated to the outside of his own investigation.

Grace turned to Markey and suddenly saw him as an officer of the law, a man to be depended on when there were times of trouble. "I don't know who *they* are, but Adam seems to know."

"Of course he knows," Markey said. "He's apparently pissed off some pretty big guns when he killed Charles Driskell Friday night."

"What?" O'Dwyer barked, taking sudden offense to the allegation. Beside him, Grace blinked dumbly at Markey, trying to interpret his words into a language she could understand, place faces to names, anything to make sense out of what he'd just said. But she couldn't, and the blank look of confusion must have given away her perplexity.

"Your boyfriend seems to have started a mob war," Markey supplied, ignoring the priest's interruption and addressing Grace instead.

She blinked again, but this time it was to bat away the look of confusion. In its place, her face showed a growing sense of disturbance. "Mob war? Boyfriend?"

"The old homeless guy in the alley called him Slash."

"What's all this talk about killing someone," O'Dwyer sputtered, releasing Grace's hand and flagging his own at Markey, who patently ignored him.

Grace's eyes continued to flutter with rapid blinking. "You think Adam is my boyfriend?"

It was Markey's turn to blink. "He's not?"

"No," she snapped.

"Then who is he?"

"He's just someone who wanted to help." When Markey eyed her doubtfully—finding it wholly impossible to assume anyone in the world might be willing to help another human being—she glared back at him with challenge. Then, with impatience and insistence, she said, "He's not my boyfriend."

"Officer, I demand an explanation," O'Dwyer said, interjecting himself into the conversation.

"It's sergeant," Markey said, proving that he'd heard the priest's demand but wasn't concerned with it. He kept his attention on Grace. "I guess that just proves you're the unluckiest person in this city. Getting caught up in the middle of a mob war because the guy you think only wanted to help you happens to be a hitman."

"What *are* you talking about?" she demanded.

"Have you any idea who those men were last night?" Markey asked.

She narrowed her eyes dubiously. "No."

"We suspect one of them was John Murdock, a petty street thug who takes on small jobs for chump change. But as far as I know, he hasn't done a contract killing yet. We found his van crashed a couple blocks from where your boy . . ." he trailed off before he was corrected with another acidic denial. "Anyway, Murdock's been associated with jobs connected with members of the mob, usually as a secondary mule or lookout."

"And you seem to think I know what you're talking about."

Markey sighed with exasperation. "We assume," he began with careful enunciation, as if speaking to a child who had comprehension problems, "that this Slash fellow is responsible for killing Charles Driskell at the Rialto Friday night and upsetting members of an opposing crime family. We haven't figured out who's who yet, but we will once we get a hold of either this Slash or Murdock."

Grace looked at him with an expression of utter disbelief. "And you're making this assumption based on what?"

"The elements of what occurred in the last couple of days," Markey replied. "In fact, the old bum in the alley even called this kid the best enforcer in his league."

Off to the side, keeping out of the conversation, Peter Lumas suddenly perked up. He looked sharply at Markey, who was in heated debate with the woman. He shifted his eyes over to her and noticed the emblem on her cap.

"Hockey," Lumas murmured, mulling something over.

Markey snapped his attention to his otherwise silent partner. "What?"

"Enforcer's a hockey term," Lumas remarked. "It refers to the player who takes care of business on the ice when the other team's playing nasty." He turned to Grace. "You called this guy Adam. Otherwise referred to as Slash. Are you talking about Adam Mogilvy?"

Grace recalled the name inscribed on the wine goblets back at the loft and nodded.

Enlightenment dawned on Lumas's face as a shadow of déjà vu clouded over Markey's. Monsignor O'Dwyer's expression became one of alarm as an entrusted secret became exposed.

"We're talking about Adam Mogilvy?" Lumas queried to no one in particular. "I should have made the connection sooner. Sarge, you remember him. He lost his family in the riots out at the ranches last year. He was arguably the best damn enforcer in the majors, up until he disappeared. Remember? His nickname on the ice was Slash. He has a scar under his chin from a slash he took from one of his own teammates. Took over a hundred stitches to close. Everyone thought at the time it was his jugular that got cut."

Not much of a hockey follower, something else did take root. The memories of an exhaustive and tragic investigation began to unravel in Markey's mind, and names and faces slowly fell into place. He recalled how they'd tried to locate the young man in the ensuing months but had found nothing. Adam Mogilvy had simply disappeared after the deaths of his family. Even the team's management had been looking for him.

"What are you saying, Pete?" Markey asked sarcastically. "That the team who holds his contract snatched him this morning to put him back on the ice?"

"Maybe that's not so far from the truth," Lumas replied evenly. "The mob has always been involved in sports. Maybe there's a connection somehow."

Markey held his tongue and considered the new theory Lumas was spinning, trying to resolve the issue of the death of Charles Driskell in the meantime. He hadn't dug too deeply into Driskell's past or associates, but it might turn out that the murdered man had ties with the team or someone related to the mob. It was definitely something to look into.

"Excuse me," Grace said insolently, "but what about Adam? He's still missing. What are you going to do to find him?"

Markey and Lumas exchanged looks.

"We've got nothing to work with right now." Markey gestured to O'Dwyer, his motion one of accusation. "The good father here said he didn't see anything."

O'Dwyer's expression turned to contrite sorrow when he looked to Grace. "I was locked in the confessional when I heard the struggle."

Her frustration suddenly erupted, and she stomped her foot. "I don't care what you do, just do something! He was only trying to help me. He doesn't deserve any of this."

Surprisingly, Markey felt humbled by her forceful demand. He sighed and shook his head to dismiss the desperation of the situation. "He could be anywhere in the city—or outside of it, for that matter. Maybe even dead." When the dreaded look on her face wouldn't be appeased, he continued with another sigh. "I guess we can start with John Murdock. We'll need you to look at some mug shots to verify if it was Murdock who was involved in the incident yesterday, maybe even pick out the other two men he was with."

"Anything," she answered eagerly.

Markey addressed the monsignor at last. "I gave you my card earlier. If you think of anything that might help, please give me a call."

A bit addled over all the information and accusations issued since Grace's arrival, O'Dwyer nodded. Satisfied, Markey, Grace, and Lumas headed for the cathedral exit.

Grace walked between Markey and Lumas, feeling safer among them than in the crowd of businessmen and women she had hurried among on her way over. Yet she still felt as if she was being watched when she walked out onto the steps of the cathedral and worried that a shot might ring out and put an end to her life. She still didn't understand why her world had spun into such turmoil, causing her to give up her ordinary life for that of a victim on the run, but she was sure there was a rational explanation for it. Even though Adam had tried to explain it, she couldn't quite accept the fact that devils and demons were the source of all her problems.

Markey and Lumas drew to a stop halfway down the steps. Markey uttered an expression of disbelief while Lumas only laughed. Grace looked in the same direction they did and gasped when she felt her heart skip a beat.

On the hood of Markey's unmarked police sedan was a stout and dubious pelican. Its shy eyes glistened at the top of its white head, while its sinewy neck twisted to consider her, its long slender beak tucked along the length of its neck and chest. Its eyes, which blinked balefully, seemed to focus solely on her.

"What the hell?" Markey said, trotting down the remainder of the cathedral steps. He pointed at the bird and looked back at Lumas. "That's a pelican."

"I see."

"We're nowhere near the water. He's miles from where he should be."

"I guess."

Markey shook his head as he completed the distance to the car. He tried to shoo the bird off the hood but it merely twisted its head to watch him, shuffling on its webbed feet and ruffling its mousy brown feathers. Markey then tried to sweep it off the car, but the pelican made a jab at him with its sword-like beak. Markey pulled his hands out of reach and glanced at Lumas, at a loss for what to do.

Grace came down to the curb in a daze. She locked eyes with the bird and tried to fathom its thoughts, wondering if it was one of Adam's flock. She hadn't seen any pelicans in the loft but that didn't mean anything.

While Grace considered the bird, Markey took advantage of its distraction and grabbed it from behind, throwing it down to the sidewalk. The pelican honked its displeasure and waddled away, flapping its wings to resettle its ruffled feathers.

"Come on," Markey said, opening the driver's door and sliding in behind the wheel.

Lumas opened the back door and allowed Grace to slide into the back seat. She pressed her face close to the window and kept an eye on the pelican as it moved to stand guard over her from the sidewalk. Without concern for whatever mission the bird had been sent on, Markey started the car and pulled away from the curb.

"You know, Grace, I thought I had this all figured out, but events keep popping up that warp whatever theory I'm currently working."

She dragged her eyes away from the pelican shrinking in the distance. "Adam didn't kill anyone."

"You seem sure about that. I thought you weren't even in the hotel at the time."

"I wasn't," she assured. "But neither was he."

Markey stared at her reflection in the rearview mirror. He remained quiet as she kept her eyes cast out the side window, watching the city as it passed.

When he returned his full attention to the street, Grace spoke. "He said he knows who's responsible for the riots that killed his family."

Markey's eyes shot back to the rearview mirror, studying her intently, while Lumas turned directly around to look at her.

"If that's true," Markey said, "then I really do want to find him."

"If that's true," Lumas said, "you may never find him."

CHAPTER TWENTY-EIGHT

Christopher Purcell spent the Monday workday in his office, practically barricaded from everyone for fear they would notice the anxiety wearing on his appearance. Earlier that morning, Drudge had commented about that very same thing, and from that moment, Christopher was especially self-conscious about how he looked. He took every opportunity to study his features in whatever reflective surface happened to be around, from car windows of passing traffic to storefronts along the sidewalk, provided they weren't slathered with promotional posters or advertisements.

His first stop once he got to the office was to visit the men's room and do a thorough assessment of his appearance. He looked a little haggard, but he believed he could pass that off to a working weekend with little sleep. When he put his face almost against the mirror, he thought he spied a few more wrinkles, a little more gray streaked through his hair, and . . . were those liver spots he'd first mistaken for freckles?

He touched his face in a dreamy manner, as if he was touching a phantasmagoria of himself from later years, after hard times, maybe even trying times, but certainly a face that wasn't what he was used to seeing when he gazed in the mirror. Instead, he thought he was actually . . . aging poorly.

I'm pregnant.

A small mewling sound escaped him as he heard the ghostly voice of Grace's fateful words. A shiver went up his spine that sent a rapid and reflexive quiver through his limbs. His legs felt numb and unsupportive, and he had to grip the men's room sink to keep from slipping to the floor. He almost glanced in the mirror again but averted his eyes in time, suddenly afraid to see the man who might look back. A Dorian Grey portrait of his own.

He tried to flee the bathroom then, his fingers failing to grasp the handle and nearly running into the door before he realized he hadn't really pulled it open. At the same time, another employee of the office, someone whose name he couldn't recall but knew he should have known, pushed the door in and pulled up sharply before they collided.

The unremembered underling was quick with his apologies and even laughed at the little blunder before awkwardly moving around Christopher, who seemed confused and uncertain about his business in the room. When the man asked him if he was all right, Christopher quickly recovered his composure, straightened his suit, and swept a hand through his hair. He pulled on a thin smile and said, "Quite. Glorious day, isn't it? Refreshing after all that rain this weekend."

The man relaxed his posture and acquired an agreeable expression. For a moment, Christopher wondered what the man's name was, then decided it really didn't matter. What should he care what this man's name was when he had his own seemingly insurmountable problems to contend with.

I'm pregnant.

Christopher had to get out of the bathroom and out of sight. His stomach felt nauseous and tumultuous, and he thought inordinately how he should be ducking back into one of the stalls if he was going to vomit. But he didn't want to be around this man—whatever his goddamn name was—because he could see his reflection in the brass push plate on the door. Despite the metallic patina of the image, he could see every vivid line, crease, and liver spot on his face. Even the gray in his hair was distinctly obvious in the reflection.

The unimportant man muttered something in response to his comment about the weather, then grew concerned about his look and mentioned something again about Christopher being all right. Christopher pushed past him and darted down the hall, clutching his stomach as if everything he'd eaten in the last week would come up with ungainly vehemence. The only thing he could be sure of was that he hadn't had anything to eat recently for there to be much of a mess to make. But he was certain the stomach acid that came up in its place would be vile.

In hurrying to his office, Christopher ran into a temp and upended a stack of files she was carrying. She gave a cry of alarm that seemed a little too theatrical for Christopher's tastes, and he immediately decided the D.A.'s office didn't need such flighty bimbos working around monumental landmark cases. He made a mental note to himself to learn her name and have her fired, and by damn, maybe have a few words with whoever hired her in the first place.

I'm pregnant.

It seemed to take forever for him to get to his office, but once there, he slammed the door and twisted the lock to secure it. He was just shy of pushing a credenza in front of the door when he realized he was acting completely out of sorts. Usually, he was a self-composed individual who was well-known for being meticulous and methodical, and oftentimes commended for his patience and temperance. But this little monkey wrench thrown into his carefully laid plans had thrown him for quite a loop. He certainly wasn't happy with the way he was handling the matter.

I'm pregnant.

Two measly words with a magical gist to them, uttered by a bewitching Jezebel.

He should have known from the start that the little trollop was after more than just a good time. Hadn't she put way too much emphasis on their tryst for it to be innocent, whispering innuendos of a life together, slyly conspiring to connive Anne out of the picture, spinning her web to ensnare him, and finally getting pregnant so he would have to make a decision. He should have known she was just a gold-digging bitch hoping to latch on to his gravy train.

He spent much of the day locked in his office, at first answering the calls from his secretary to stave off coming out of his office, delegating tasks he should be doing himself to other less capable subordinates, declining invitations to lunch, and finally telling his secretary to hold all his calls; he would be working on a case requiring his undivided attention and couldn't be interrupted. The old sow had the audacity to inquire about his well-being and suggested he leave early, since he wasn't looking all too good, but he told her that he was fine. He muttered something about having spent much of the weekend researching and preparing for the case before he remembered his little ditty wasn't the story Drudge had told him to use. He was supposed to have been out of town campaigning, not researching a case.

Damn, he cursed, then quickly decided it wouldn't matter. He could always tell the authorities questioning his discrepancy later that he'd told her what he had so she wouldn't worry about him biting off more than he could chew with his run for the mayor's seat. She was, after all, just a doting old bat, anyway.

And stupid and unreliable, he learned when she rang him midway through the afternoon to announce that he had a visitor who was insisting to see him with the utmost urgency. When Christopher asked who it was, he was floored to learn it was Robert Prescott.

"Send him in," Christopher said stoutly, slamming down the phone and running to the door to unlock it. It wouldn't be good for Prescott to discover the door locked. It would look entirely too suspicious for him.

I'm pregnant.

Guilt, he suddenly thought, pulling the door open to invite Prescott in with a wholly professional and astute manner. Was he really the father of Grace's spawning imp just because she insisted he was? Hadn't they been especially careful? She could just be pulling his leg about the whole pregnancy fantasy. Or, perhaps, she was pregnant by someone else and he was just the luckless patsy.

"Robert, good to see you," Christopher said, thrusting out his arm and grabbing his visitor's hand in a firm grasp, pumping it heartily. "How's Deborah?"

Robert seemed to be taken aback by the warm welcome and the inquiry into his wife's health. He sputtered awkwardly as he allowed his hand to be pumped. "F-fine. And, um, Anne, how is she?"

"Fabulous, absolutely fabulous. We're planning on having a little shindig to kick off the campaign run, and you and Deborah are on the A-list. I do hope you can make it?"

"I . . . well, I guess, maybe, sure, I think we can make it. When is it?"

Christopher still held onto Robert's hand and pulled him sturdily into the office, guiding the assistant district attorney to a chair in front of the desk. "We haven't come up with a date yet, but Anne's in charge of all that. I'm sure she'll have all the details put together soon. Please, sit down, take a load off."

Robert recovered his arm and sat uncomfortably in the chair as Christopher maneuvered around his desk to take a seat. The smile on Christopher's face was every ounce the politician he hoped to perfect, a little friendly and a little reptilian.

"But tell me, Robert, what brings you to my office?" He cocked his head and gave a little wink. "Not asking for a raise, I hope? We're union, you know. Out of my hands." He threw his arms up in apologetic forfeit, curling his lower lip in a gesture of petulant commiseration.

"No, um, Mr. Purcell, not a raise, I'm afraid," Prescott said, coughing and shifting uneasily in his chair. He clasped his hands together, fiddled his thumbs, noticed this, and pulled his hands apart, shoving them under his thighs to keep them still. "I've come to ask, um—" cough, sputter, croak, "—if you'd, perhaps, maybe . . ." His eyes roamed uncomfortably around the desk, the wall behind Christopher, even the ceiling. ". . . you'd come down to the police station and . . ." He snapped his head to the side so his neck cracked on its own, pulled one hand out from under his leg and used it to fumble with his tie, ". . . have your fingerprints taken," he mumbled almost inaudibly.

"Excuse me?" Christopher said, having only heard *come down to the police station*. Nothing else could be good after that. "Speak up, Robert, what is it you need?"

Robert coughed again, sounding phlegmy, and spoke louder. "The police would like to take your fingerprints."

Christopher smiled against all the enmity he felt. This time the smile was more serpentine than friendly. "My fingerprints? What would you need my fingerprints for?"

"Well, um, do you remember the case I picked up?" Robert struggled to get out.

"Yes, the murder at the hotel. Which one was it?"

"The Rialto."

"Ah, yes, the Rialto. Yes, I recall the phone conversation. A woman with a silly story about having an affair with me, at the Rialto, when I was out of town campaigning," he said, authenticating his alibi with pertinent emphasis in certain areas. "Need I provide you with the times and locations where I was during the weekend? Or should I only worry about Friday night?"

"I'm sorry, sir, but it's just a formality," Prescott said, gaining some mettle from somewhere to drop his discomfort and carry himself with a little dignity and decorum. "The police believe it will be for the best if we have a set of elimination prints from you."

"Generally elimination prints are from people who have a right to be in the area where you're printing," Christopher said, showing no sign of his inner turmoil about his fingerprints being everywhere in the suite at the Rialto. The bathroom alone would show him having been over every ceramic, marble, and veneer surface. Suddenly, the words *I'm pregnant* didn't have that much power over him. His own fingerprints would be his downfall. "Are we giving some credence to this woman's confabulated story? What was her name again? Faith?"

"Grace, sir. Grace Fitzpatrick."

"And are you?"

"What?"

"Giving credence to her story?" Christopher asked with hooded concern.

"Myself, sir, no. I believe whole-heartedly that you had nothing to do with this case. But the police brought up a good point. This investigation promises to be a high-profile case because of the accusations. We need to prove conclusively that you are not in any way involved."

"I would prefer my name not even be mentioned in relation to the case," Christopher hinted.

"I do understand your need for discretion, but we can't muffle this woman. She's bound to go to the press if we charge her in relation to the crime. We can prevent any negative repercussions just by having all our ducks in a row. Sort of cut her off at the pass, if you will."

Christopher was silent and outwardly thoughtful of the strategy. Inside, he was screaming at himself for not having anticipated the possibility of his prints being left behind. So obvious and damaging. How had Drudge not thought of that?

But he must have. He couldn't have been that specific in his blackmail that the only evidence to convict him of murder—one he hadn't committed—existed only on the murder weapon. His fingerprints on the corkscrew were enough to place him in the hotel room and within proximity to the victim to commit the crime. Drudge wouldn't have hoarded the corkscrew if he hadn't made sure it was the only damaging piece of evidence to hold over him.

Except for Grace and her demon-seed child.

He had to speak to Drudge and confirm that the bastard had sanitized the hotel suite of his fingerprints. He had to make sure he wasn't walking into his own trap.

"No problem, Robert," he said convivially, smiling winsomely and nodding. "I can see how you're thinking. Brilliant. I should have thought of it myself. I'll swing by the police station when I leave work tonight. Who's handling the case?"

"Roy Markey and Peter Lumas," Robert said with relief. "Either one should be able to take your prints."

"I'll see one or the other tonight." He rose abruptly, leaving his fingertips resting lightly on the desktop, the incriminating fingers to a crime he hadn't committed. "Do remember to keep Anne and me in mind when your invitation arrives. We'd love to see you and Deborah again."

Robert got to his feet as well. "I will, Mr. Purcell. I certainly will."

Christopher kept his Cheshire cat smile on until the door closed behind Robert. Then it slid off his face like a melted timepiece in a Dali painting. Even his jowls drooped as he considered his next order of business.

Drudge.

Adam came awake to an incredible pain pulling through his shoulders. He tried to adjust his arms to accommodate the ache but they were wrenched at horribly obtuse angles. Opening his eyes to look to either side of him, he saw that he was bound between two columns, and the ache in his shoulders was from his body hanging limply from his arms. In order to ease the pain, he brought his feet up beneath him to support his weight and managed to relieve the ache somewhat. At the same time, he noticed he'd been stripped of his coat and now it lay on the floor, several feet away.

"He's awake."

The voice sounded far away, and Adam's eyes drifted over to the three men who'd brought him to the warehouse. It was Bentley who spoke, and he drew the attention of his two companions from their passé conversation.

Murdock got up from where he sat on an upturned crate and walked toward Adam, who eyed his approach with weary concern.

Strutting like a peacock, Murdock sauntered near the outer edge of Adam's reach. He tried to maintain his dignity and sense of fearlessness, but a muffled chuckle from behind told him that Bentley and Devereaux saw right through his charade. In response, he faced Adam with increasing outrage, although he withheld his anger for the moment as he optioned for reason.

"You took a nasty fall there, my friend," Murdock observed. "I apologize for my associate's overreaction. He gets a little quirky where his car's concerned. He was afraid you were going to take it and ram it through that locked door."

"I was," Adam answered evenly, looking Murdock straight in the eye.

Murdock ignored the reply in an effort to remain unaffected by it. Instead, he gloated that Adam was tied before him like a fatted calf, ready for slaughter.

"Let me explain things before the situation gets any farther out of hand," Murdock continued in an even-keel tone, almost congenial, in fact. "My friends and I were hired by a third party to resolve a domestic dispute. Our employer has this friend who happened to learn some distressing news this weekend about his lady love. Seems this lady love told him that she's in a delicate condition now. You follow me?"

Adam nodded once, dealing with the ache ebbing through his shoulders.

"It was an unplanned event. Angry words were exchanged and everyone said something I'm sure they later regretted. Anyway, my employer is a bit of a matchmaker and he really doesn't want to see these two kids quarreling, so he hired us to make it right. We were sent to find Ms. Fitzpatrick and bring her back so she and her beau could work things out." He leaned in conspiratorially. "You know how women are. Emotional and temperamental. Throw in the fact that she's pregnant and bam, you got dynamite. An explosive combination. It's next to impossible to have a rational conversation with them. But my employer believes these two kids have got a future as a couple and he's interested in getting them back together."

Adam stared at Murdock, knowing he was feeding him bullshit, probably knowing the man knew he knew it was bullshit but he was going to feed it to him anyway. It was a shot, and Murdock was going for the easy way to get the information he wanted before he turned the interrogation over to one of the other two professionals waiting for their chance at him. "So what does this have to do with me?"

Murdock pulled back and nodded understandably. "Right, right. Well, you got caught up in this little love story." He held up his hand to beg for patience. "Don't get me wrong, I understand where you were coming from, damsel in distress and all. You heard the girl screaming and thought the worst. Thought maybe we were going to do something ungentlemanly. So you reacted as any civic-minded gentleman would. You jumped to her rescue, misreading all the while that we were only trying to bring her back to the man she loves."

"She didn't quite explain it that way."

"No, I don't suppose she did," Murdock assured. "But you have to remember that she had a nasty argument and was a little emotional. Talking to her significant other was the last thing she wanted to do, I'm sure."

"And what was the rationale behind attacking me in the cathedral today?" Adam asked, playing along.

"Well," Murdock said, splaying his hands guiltily, "your interference created a bit of discord between my associates and our employer. You made us look bad. Today, you just got what you had coming. Sorry 'bout that."

"At least you're being honest," Adam conceded facetiously.

Murdock smiled. "That's the difference between men and women. Two men can get together and discuss things without having an emotional breakdown."

"Then why am I tied up now?"

Murdock's expression faltered. He obviously had no response prepared for the question. "Just a precaution. You're a dangerous young man."

"Only when I have to be."

"I just wanted to explain things to you on a rational level."

"Okay, you've explained; now cut me down."

"Do we have your cooperation to find Ms. Fitzpatrick?"

"No."

Murdock's face blanched. "No?"

"No."

"Fuck this," Devereaux barked from his perch on the bumper of the Cadillac. He pulled out his pistol and strode toward Adam, until they were within inches of each other. He took a threatening stance and put the barrel of the gun against Adam's forehead. "I'm sick of this pussy bullshit. I'll get it out of him."

Adam pulled away from the cold metal of the gun, worrying about the volatility of the desperate trio. Death had recently become a phobia for him. Where he'd once been inured to the possibility of dying, he now knew it was more a reality than just a growing concern. What would happen to him once he died promised to be a rebirth into something else in Hell. Drudge had marked him as his own. Adam wasn't sure how the system of eternal judgment worked, but he feared Drudge had already laid claim to his soul. He didn't know if Claire's forgiving God would forsake him just because he bore the marks of a demon, or would his own self-inflicted mark in God's name override Drudge's stake on him. Whatever the case may be, he wasn't prepared to challenge that possibility just yet. He needed time to figure it all out, make an exact science of it, and do whatever it took to redeem himself in God's eyes.

"Wait!" Bentley shouted, coming up to Devereaux and laying a restraining hand on his arm. "You blow his head off, we don't learn shit."

Devereaux snarled and pulled the gun a few inches away. His long dreadlocks trembled as his head shook with fury. "Mudderfucker! He's the reason we'll all be sleeping in a cave tonight."

Adam suddenly registered what the man said. The three of them knew about the minions and were afraid of becoming like them. They were terrified of Drudge. If they failed him, they would become nothing but the wretched servants of a cruel master, bound to the nightly commands of his malevolent contrivings. Much as he himself was slated for in the not so distant future.

"I know more about this than you think," Adam said, drawing their attention back to him, feeling their stark eyes suction on him. "I know Drudge hired you to be his daytime henchmen because his minions are restricted to flying at night."

Their faces seemed to inch closer to him, while their brows narrowed suspiciously. It was Murdock who spoke first. "What do you know about Mr. Drudge?"

Adam considered his position carefully. Although these men obviously feared Drudge, they were still his paid henchmen. Drudge had opted to use money to enlist their loyalty. "I know he's a dangerous man, to say the least. I know he's not about to let that baby live any longer than he has to. And I know the extent of his power and what he commands."

The three hired guns pulled back to study him more intently, now puzzled and confused. Fear speckled their faces in the pasty ashen color of their flesh. Even Devereaux had visibly paled.

"Who are you?" Bentley demanded in a reverent whisper.

"Someone he's already laid claim to."

They all took several steps back from him, as if he'd suddenly become engulfed in fire. Bentley glanced at his companions and their theatrical antics. He drew up his shoulders to regain a sense of dignity and barked, "Bullshit! He would'a told us about you."

"If you don't believe me, look at my hand." Adam opened his right fist and bared his palm to them, which was still layered in leather strips.

Murdock hurried to the place where Adam's coat had been tossed. He rummaged in the folds for one of the knives they had found when they'd searched him after his fall. He gripped the edge of Adam's fingers and peeled them back, baring his hand. He wheedled the tip of the knife under the strips of leather. With a violent motion, he cut away the thongs, then leaned forward to stare in open amazement at the precise scars on Adam's exposed palm. Five healed slashes laid in perfect depiction of Drudge's preference, similar to the Spatial Industries logo, were scored into his flesh. Its mundane commercial meaning was hidden in the haunting connotation of its evil depiction.

"Fuck," Murdock breathed, releasing Adam's fingers and tossing the knife to the floor. It clattered resonantly on the bare concrete before laying still and silent.

Devereaux and Bentley exchanged fearful glances. Adam felt he'd gained a slight edge, which depended on how deeply rooted their fear of Drudge was.

"Did you ever think I might have been with her for a reason?" he said, alluding to possibilities they hadn't fathomed yet. "Did you ever think Drudge might be furious with you because you interfered with me?"

"Oh, my God," Murdock whispered, stepping back and seeming to consider everything they'd done so far, which had been on their own accord. Might Drudge have sent this man to retrieve the woman, just as he and G.W. had been racing toward the Tower to recover their ten thousand dollar bonus? Murdock's constant harassment had driven Grace and her escort farther and farther from actually arriving at the Tower. Instead, they'd gone to . . .

His brow furrowed as he rose up in defiance to the ruse Adam attempted. "You're lying!"

He reached out to snatch the cloth wrapped around Adam's forehead, which was buried under his long hair. Adam moved back to avoid him, but Murdock stepped into his approach. He viciously caught Adam's hair in one hand and yanked the cloth off with the other. Beneath it, above the bridge between Adam's eyes, was a black crucifix tattooed on his forehead, its long base ending in the double-edged blade of a dagger.

"What the fuck . . ." Devereaux uttered, leaning forward to see through the strands of hair falling across Adam's forehead. "You some fucking Jesus freak?"

Adam would never admit that he'd covered the tattoo because he was ashamed he'd put it there in the first place. It had been a desperate measure to put God's mark on him in lieu of Drudge's claim. Driven to such extreme measures by grief and day-long drinking binges, he'd lain under the dirty needle of an unlicensed tattoo artist as it was inked onto his forehead. Weeks later, when he'd finally sobered up and looked at his face in a mirror, he thought he might have truly descended into the deepest levels of insanity. Since that day, he'd hidden the mark from God and man, afraid his supposition to offer his services to God had been enough to seal his fate in Hell.

"I don't know who he is," Murdock announced with fury, pushing Devereaux aside and delivering a punch to Adam's midsection, doubling him over only to the point where his arms allowed him to. "But he ain't one of Drudge's people, that's for sure." He slammed another fist into Adam's ribs and then one into his chin, wincing when his knuckles met the bone of Adam's jaw, but also rejoicing in the wave of euphoria he got from pummeling him. "The motherfucker went into the church. Drudge said his bats couldn't go onto holy ground."

Adam took the hits with helpless acceptance, trying to guess which part of his body would receive the next assault, moving slightly aside to accommodate the attack. But nowhere he moved could help him escape the fury with which the man delivered his blows.

Devereaux and Bentley watched with expressed fascination as Murdock pounded out his frustration on the body that soon hung bruised and limp from the ropes. It wasn't until Adam's head lolled forward and his legs went slack that they realized Murdock may have gone too far with the abuse. Anxiously, they pulled Murdock back and struggled to control his flailing arms.

"You stupid shit, he can't talk now," Bentley screamed. Devereaux stomped about with frantic desperation, wincing and whining about their dubious fate. "Now we're fucked. Boy, are we ever fucked."

Murdock blinked away his uncontrollable anger as he staggered back from the limp figure. He hadn't known how mad he was until he saw the battered and bruised body before him. Amazing how the mind reacts when faced with death, Murdock thought, realizing it was his own death he was now facing if they couldn't find the woman.

"Fuck him!" Murdock barked back. "Fuck him!"

"What do we do with him now?" Bentley demanded.

"Leave him," Murdock said. "Leave him for the fucking bats. It's what Drudge expects anyway. They can deal with him."

CHAPTER TWENTY-NINE

Grace was able to confirm that the driver of the van was its owner, John Murphy Murdock, and she was currently combing through stacks of mug shots for his kidnapping accomplice and the two men who'd joined him in the assault on the cathedral. Peter Lumas and Sergeant Markey were at separate desks, speaking with different contacts and detectives of other bureaus of the department, digging up leads on Murdock. In the meantime, Grace flipped through page after page of booking photos, becoming familiar with the generic features emanating from all criminal photographs. Arrogance and defiance. Lips pursed, jowls slack, cords standing out on necks, throbbing temple veins, flaring nostrils, narrowed eyes. Looks of derision and challenge. Gleams of vengeance. She saw it all, her naiveté bombarded by the two dimensional visages of hatred and wrath. She saw nothing of remorse or regret, or of innocence that had been mistaken for guilt. Their eyes seemed to glare at her, and they all became dangerous villains who might someday stalk her outside these safe walls. The only reason she could fathom why she continued to pour through the pictures at all was to familiarize herself with the faces she may one day have to avoid on the street.

After a while, her attention began to lag. Her eyes shifted around the office, their muscles needing the slight distraction from their intense concentration. Desks intermittently occupied by plainclothes detectives were scattered with a myriad of papers, files, and photographs. Curiosity drove her to peek at the pictures, but they were always at an angle that defied more than a cursory view. Men got up and moved about without any interest in her other than an appreciative glance her way. They came and went, on their own business, unconcerned with how they could help her. They knew she was Markey's problem, and they apparently had their own to deal with.

Her eyes drifted over to Markey, where he sat with his jacket off and his tie pulled out of its restraining knot. He was on the phone with his feet propped up on the desk. He seemed to be enjoying the conversation he was having. There was jovial banter and chuckles, and gestures the other party couldn't see but emphasized his end of the conversation. Her eyes remained on him, her current champion in Adam's absence, someone who offered her shelter and protection, even though it was only civic-minded. It didn't matter to her that he was being paid for the job; he was still coming up against impossible odds in her defense. He'd even confronted them in battle already.

But ultimately his interest in her was strictly professional. He only wanted to protect her so she might lead him to a killer he was hunting. Adam, on the other hand, had nobler motives.

Which brought her back to worrying about him. The new information she'd learned only made her desperate to know more about him. Her interest in sports only bordered on recognizing some of the teams in major league football and baseball, and she only had a self-preserving knowledge of the riots that had sparked off the string of disturbances that followed afterward. Perhaps she'd been too much in love with Christopher to focus on anything other than her own happiness; had not openly recognized the tragedies occurring around her in her own town; had not even realized people had lost their homes, suffered tragic losses, and died that night. Instead, she had ignored the grief-stricken faces of the victims she'd passed on the street simply because she was in love. Or so she had presumed.

Tears filmed her eyes as she watched the pages turn mechanically before her. She blinked and tried to reason the phenomenon away to eye strain. But the reality of it was a self-loathing she couldn't hide from. Couldn't escape no matter how harassed she assumed her life to be. Her plight with these desperate criminals seemed trivial in light of the tragedy that had befallen the man who'd saved her from their villainy. She wasn't sure what happened that night, the night his family had been taken from him, but she sensed it must have been horrible.

A fat drop of crystal saline broke free from the corner of her eye. It fell in lazy sympathy on the page she now half-mindedly considered, creating a discolored circle on the filmed paper. Its appearance surprised her, and she drew back with distaste, ashamed that she'd fallen prey so easily to her own shame. But neither could she prevent the next one from following its predecessor, landing only a quarter of an inch from the first one. She sniffled as the tears tried to flow freely, just barely able to keep the deluge from coming. Knowing she was fighting a losing battle, she tucked her chin and allowed her hair to hang on either side of her face so no one in the room could witness her weakness.

Markey took that moment to hang up and move over to an unoccupied seat in front of the desk she was at. He made an audible expression of weary helplessness as he sat down. When he glanced at her, he could make out nothing of her face, which was conspicuously averted. Unnervingly, he leaned forward and peered at her from an angle. "Are you crying?"

She drew her head up defiantly and swiped at her eyes, shrugging indifferently. After a furtive effort to remove all signs of weeping, she blinked and coughed to obscure the squeak in her voice. "I'm under a lot of stress right now."

Markey nodded understandably. When he spoke again, he did so with just a slight amount of sympathy. "It doesn't look good for Mogilvy. We found out Murdock's held every kind of job you can think of. From being a dishwasher in a Greek restaurant to a merchant marine on the docks, even a butcher in a slaughterhouse. He's done it all. Right now he's not pulling in any paycheck that would require a W-2 form, but he's picking up money from somewhere. He's got a moderately priced apartment on the south end and is up to date on all his bills. Our Vice Enforcement Unit keeps a file on him because of his outer edge connection to the mob. There's no open investigation concerning him, per se, because he's considered just a low-level freelancer, but they still siphon information into his file when they come across it."

Grace wiped away the last of the tears and stiffened her shoulders, regaining some composure in the gesture. "You have to find him," she insisted.

"I'm working on it. I'm sending men out to the various places Murdock's been connected with to see if he's been around recently. Maybe we can locate him that way. He's not at his apartment, and we have no current place of business to check with, so we're hoping someone will pop up who can tell us where to find him. Once we do, we can bring him in for questioning."

Her voice was alarmed. "But that could take days."

Markey shrugged. "Most of my men are out in the north suburbs. The riots last night are on the top on the city's political agenda right now. I'm relying on help from Vice and Narcotics, even though they're stretched pretty thin as it is. The problem is that we're working too many leads with not enough men. I'll be honest with you; I think your boyfriend is already out of time."

Grace glared at him. "How many times do I have to tell you, he's not my boyfriend."

Markey sighed dubiously. "Look, Grace, I'm finding that a little hard to swallow. Why would a man you have no history with involve himself in a life-and-death war with the mob?"

"Because his wife was killed by the same man he believes wants to hurt me," she replied.

Intrigued by that bit of information, Markey straightened in his chair. "And who would that be?"

Grace hesitated, not wanting to admit what Adam had told her, realizing it would sound too ludicrous. But whatever her reservations were, she knew Sergeant Markey would insist on an answer. With a deep breath, she said, "Malachi Drudge."

Markey stared speechlessly at her for a time, then gave a dubious shake to his head. "You don't seem to understand what's going on here, do you?"

She raised her eyes uncertainly.

He took a moment to consider what he was going to say. "This man you've so unquestioningly placed your trust in may have been responsible for his own wife and kid's death." When her face showed a look of derision, Markey continued. "I was there the day after the riots happened, investigating the homicides. We learned that Mogilvy left Chicago on a flight earlier than the rest of his team. We know he made it home during the night because we found his car in the driveway, with his duffel bag still in it. We found his wife on the kitchen floor. She'd been impaled by some sort of cutting instrument—sound familiar. The baby was in the stables, dead from complications of a medical condition. I forget exactly what, but it constituted felony child neglect any way you look at it. Mogilvy was nowhere to be found, and I mean nowhere. He dropped out of sight and out of hockey. His team reported having no contact with him whatsoever. We began to consider him a suspect in the deaths of his family. We were doubtful he was responsible for the riots, but we believe he might have taken advantage of the chaos to commit those two crimes, at least."

During Markey's discourse, Grace's eyes had narrowed to shards of chilly rim rock, taking on hard edges with each word he spoke. Disbelief consumed her. "No way," she insisted. "He loved her. He would never have killed her. The pain I saw in his face was genuine. If there was anything else in him, it was vengeance. He believes Malachi Drudge was responsible for what happened, and I believe him. *He* can explain it to you—when you find him."

"Well, there's the problem," Markey said. "But you tell me. Why do *you* believe him?"

Grace held off answering right away. She wondered if she should say anything about the demons that had attacked her and were the product of Drudge's malicious recruiting. Should she explain that she'd stood at the window overlooking the Spatial Tower and felt the palpable evil exuding from the black monolith? Should she describe her encounter with the old bum who'd spoken so prophetically to her, to explain how this would have to be a delusion shared by another person? Should she explain how Adam had an uncanny connection with the birds of the city? Should she . . .

"Oh my God," she breathed.

"What?"

Her eyes suddenly became bright with hope. "The pelican."

"What?"

"Where do you think you'd find a pelican?"

Markey squinted dubiously. "I beg your pardon?"

"Pelicans. Where would you find them in this city?"

He blinked. "Well . . . I guess by the water," he answered. "Wherever the boats come in with their daily catch, I know that much."

"That's where he is," she announced, standing up.

"What?" he demanded, glaring at her with a mounting sense of confusion. He found it uncomfortable looking up at her, so he stood. "What are you getting at?"

"Adam," she insisted. "He's there, where you said the fishing boats come in."

"The docks?"

"If that's where it is."

"Because of a pelican on my car?" he asked doubtfully.

"Why not?" she demanded. "Do you see many pelicans in the inner city? I never have. Listen, didn't you say Murdock was a merchant marine. They work on the docks, right?"

"You're stretching this."

"Would it hurt to check?" she demanded. "You said you were having people check out all his past jobs. Couldn't you just go down to the docks yourself?"

Markey pursed his lips dismally. Grace Fitzpatrick was beautiful in her own right, but with those pretty cow eyes turning big and baleful, accompanied by the expectant tilt of her head, he was putty in her hands. "I guess Pete and I can take a run down there."

"Thank God."

"But I'm telling you this right now. If I had to lay a wager, I'd say Mogilvy's already dead and in the water by now."

CHAPTER THIRTY

As much as they dreaded it, Murdock, Devereaux, and Bentley sped through the city toward the Spatial Tower. They had only one way to redeem themselves, and it wasn't a guarantee that Drudge would find their ineptitude forgivable this time.

Devereaux drove while Bentley sat like a stone statue in the front passenger seat. Even his pasty complexion mimicked being cast in plaster. Murdock sat behind them, gnawing on a knuckle as he stared out the window, watching the buildings roll idly by. The sun was setting like a red fireball, unusually impotent for its lack of brilliance. They all knew they would arrive in the basement of the monolith just as the sun disappeared from the horizon. The significance of the timing was chillingly ominous. The business aspect of the Tower would have concluded for the day, the last of its employees having left more than an hour ago. Only a skeletal crew of servants remained to attend to the needs of the master . . . and the hundreds of mammalian demons roosting in the upper reaches of the building.

Neither Bentley nor Murdock spoke as Devereaux drove, although Devereaux muttered unenlightened curses as he negotiated his way through traffic. Murdock's eyes shifted over to him every time he barked out an unsolicited expletive, until Murdock became more and more annoyed with his utterances. Eventually, he snapped his own remark. "Will you shut the fuck up!"

Devereaux jerked, his hands pulling the steering wheel to the right. A panel van in the next lane honked angrily at his impertinence for fishtailing into its lane, and Devereaux offered another colorful curse as he corrected his course. In response, he glared back at Murdock with a look of violence contorting his face. "What the fuck did you say?"

"I said shut the fuck up," Murdock snarled. He felt incredibly daring at the moment, unafraid of anything. The terrible panic he harbored for how Drudge would receive them made all his other fears seem trivial.

Surprisingly, Devereaux chose to dismiss Murdock's retort, returning his attention to the road instead. Bentley hadn't even followed the short exchange, but continued to watch the landmarks as they passed. The silence grew thick and sour in the car, with an odor of sweat and fear becoming a film upon the surface of the dashboard, instrument panel, windows, and upholstery.

The Cadillac finally turned onto the street in front of the Spatial Tower, driving beside the park that had been cut in half by the sale of the city's property. It turned into a service drive leading to a side ramp going down into the basement garage. With a remote, Devereaux opened the metal gate and drove into the Tower, feeling dread set in. Murdock considered telling him to turn around and drive out, but he dismissed the idea at once. He knew—like his unfortunate cohorts with him—that their only chance of surviving the night, and each night thereafter, was to come clean with Drudge. If they chose to run, they would only be inviting his inevitable wrath.

Devereaux parked the car and sat waiting for someone else to initiate the move to get out. Murdock forced himself to make the effort, the simple act of pulling on the door handle being the most difficult move of his life. But he was then joined by Bentley and Devereaux, who both assumed the same inevitable fate.

They traveled as one across the garage, went into the elevator, and rode it up to one of the upper levels that acted as Drudge's private quarters. There they encountered an aged doorman as they stepped out of the elevator, a sentinel at an archway into the amazingly resplendent chambers beyond. Fabulous pieces of art and sculpture hung from the walls or sat on marble pedestals under focused recessed lights. Brocaded tapestries covered empty wall spaces between ornately framed paintings. Runners of gilded carpet protected cool slabs of marble. Alabaster moldings trimmed corners, ledges, and eaves. Elaborate silk wallpaper highlighted the hedonistic style, and an evil permeated the walls in the tiny crevasses of its print. Looking too closely might show hideous creatures depicted in awful acts of torture and murder—in remarkably minute detail—much like a floral pattern might detail the verve of a flourishing bush.

The doorman didn't offer any greeting as he nodded and moved into the parlor of the apartment. He motioned for them to stay in the room while he disappeared through an archway, leaving the trio to feel the unerring discomfort that came with being watched—but watched by what, they didn't know, although they were pretty sure it wasn't by security cameras. Murdock's hands twisted easily with the film of sweat coating his palms, and Devereaux's nervousness manifested itself in his rocking on the balls of his feet. Bentley's eyes shifted all around him, taking in every nuance of the apartment, every trace of Drudge, every hint of corruption, until he shivered.

The doorman returned as if out of the ether and silently beckoned them to follow. He led them through the archway, along an art-lined marble corridor, under identical triple-tiered chandeliers, through another archway, and into an expansive room littered with priceless icons of art and culture. A magnificent winding staircase with a gilded iron balustrade led them up to a second level. Closed doors of thick mahogany lined the corridor. The doorman chose one and came to a stop. He looked over his followers and counted them, as if he was afraid one might have strayed or declined the summons. When he was satisfied with the number, he reached out for the ornate brass handle and thumbed the latch.

Murdock gulped and looked at Devereaux, then at Bentley. They looked back at him in turn, then at each other, their brows lifting as they invited each other to go ahead, then made insistent nudging gestures with their heads. The doorman waited with interminable patience as they debated who should enter first.

"I'm waiting," a voice boomed from within the room.

Murdock, Devereaux, and Bentley jumped in unison, and then turned their attention to the interior of the chamber. There was nothing inside the room except blackness. The walls appeared to be non-existent, the ceiling so high it showed no discernible dimension. The floor itself glimmered with such reflective polish that it seemed to be nothing more than a black pool of water under the moonlight. The room appeared to be unoccupied, except for the voice echoing from within.

Murdock made the first move to step into the chamber, feeling chilled by the cold space he assumed would be similar to thousands of miles above the earth's orbit. His feet detected no surface beneath his shoes as he crossed the threshold, and he felt as if his body had lost all sense of gravity. He peered deeply into the depths of the chamber's dimensions and tried to pick out the flatness of the walls, the angle of a corner, the slight contrast of the ceiling to the walls, but he could determine nothing. Nothing that described the boundaries of the room. Its vastness was frightening, as if there were no distinct limits to it and he might slip away into nothing at the slightest tip of the room.

Devereaux and Bentley shuffled in after him, crowding Murdock in an effort to feed off his slightly higher level of daring. But they, too, sensed the immensity of space once they joined him. The coldness in the chamber was an eerie climate not associated with earthly weather. It was the chill of dead space, of the absence of heat, of lifelessness . . . of nothing. The blanket of this ambience smothered them and a pressure of dread swelled their lungs.

A loud boom sounded as the door closed behind them.

"I have only one question for you," the voice intoned, its sound carried not on the particles of dust in the air, but on the waves of inter-dimensional energies. "Have you located Ms. Fitzpatrick?"

Devereaux, Bentley, and Murdock exchanged looks of accusation and insistence to answer the question, but none chose to act as the spokesman for the group.

A darkness moved from the shadows of the void. A figure took shape and Drudge became visible. He wore his usual black business suit of rare daytime exposure and his hair was pulled back from his face. His stern visage was one of daunting powerfulness, deep furrows interlacing lines across his brow. His eyes were drawn high at the outer corners and narrowed at the bridge of his nose. He appeared completely volatile and entirely capable of rending them limb from limb all on his own. He wouldn't need the help of his minions to do his dirty work.

"It would behoove you in the most profound way to answer my question," he warned.

"Um . . . uh," Murdock started, realizing he would rather plead for his own life if it was about to be forfeit. "Um, well, sort of."

"Sort of," Drudge repeated slowly and precisely, as if savoring each word in its own right. "Sort of. What the hell does that mean?"

"We found the man who was protecting her," Murdock hurried.

Drudge's brow eased considerably as his eyes gained symmetry. He cocked his head slightly to one side, and a crack of a grin lifted one corner of his mouth. "Really?"

"Yes, sir," Murdock said, noticing the delight gleaming on Drudge's face.

"You brought him here then?" Drudge asked hopefully.

Drudge's anxiousness was not lost on Murdock. He shivered with a sudden sense of wrong for having left the man on the edge of death back at the docks. They had discussed it among themselves and decided that Drudge might not appreciate an uninvited guest brought to his Tower, so they'd left him where he was for disposal by the bats.

"We thought it might be best if we kept the guy from coming here. You're still quite removed from being identified in this mess," Murdock said respectfully, hoping his concern for details wouldn't be overlooked.

"You decided this on the basis of what?" Drudge demanded, showing a burning cauldron of fire in the way his mouth curled around his words. "That this boy has the bleakest chance of surviving any encounter with me?"

Murdock's mouth opened and closed, unable to form a reply. Devereaux noticed the difficulty Murdock was having and jumped in. "Mr. Drudge," he started respectfully, "we're not capable of making those decisions for you. At the time, it seemed the right thing to do. But it's easy enough to retrieve him, if you want us to. He's not going anywhere where he is."

Drudge's eyes turned to his trustworthy lieutenant. He seemed to garner the sincerity of such a response and thought this could be the most intelligent decision they could have made on their own. "Did he tell you where the woman was?"

Devereaux shook his head as he cast his eyes to the floor, then immediately lifted them when vertigo set in. The room's lack of boundaries forced its occupants to focus entirely on each other rather than feel the nothingness encroaching in on them.

"He said he knows you're behind it, though," Bentley broke in.

"Does he now?" Drudge asked with curiosity. "What else did he say?"

"He didn't talk much," Murdock said quickly, hoping Bentley would get the idea about keeping the abusive beating quiet, which had driven the man into irretrievable unconsciousness. "We came here to tell you this because you'd given us a deadline. Even though he admitted knowing you were responsible, we didn't know if he was lying."

"And did he tell you how he came about this pearl of wisdom?"

"No," Murdock replied. "But he mentioned that you'd already laid claim to him." At Drudge's curious expression, he continued. "He bore the scars of your company on his hand."

Drudge's brow narrowed with perplexity. He seemed completely puzzled. "Did he now?"

"He also had a tattoo of a cross on his forehead," Murdock added, trying to help identify the man for Drudge's easy recollection. "In the form of a dagger."

Drudge's countenance exposed an expression that wasn't often seen on him. "A man with my mark on his hand? And a cross on his forehead?"

The three henchmen nodded in concert. Devereaux spoke first. "He's tied up tight and locked away at the wharf."

Drudge cocked his head. "My mark on him, you say? Puzzling."

They made no gesture of assent; Drudge was only talking out loud to himself.

"Well," he said abruptly, coming to a decision on his own. "I guess if he bares my mark, then he's mine. I'll have to retrieve him. Strays shouldn't be allowed to roam free. They apparently think they have a right to run amok."

"We can have him back here within the hour," Devereaux said with assurance.

Drudge shifted his attention to his lieutenant. "I don't think so. A man who bares my mark is a rare thing. There's no telling what his talents are."

CHAPTER THIRTY-ONE

Cold and heat. That was what he first became aware of. The prickly cold of a netherworld swirling with the implosion of heat within regions of organic cells. He only remembered that. That and the agony. The cold of shock suffusing with the heat of deep-seated damage. He was no stranger to pain, his body tolerant to the abuses of a vengeful sport. But that had been a protected and attended pain, all his aches promptly diagnosed and treated. He'd been a valuable person then, and a contract had protected his body; his joints and ligaments, bones and soft tissue alike, even his head and knees. But now he was nothing. An unknown soul lost in the vortex of a city that was fodder for devils. A token sacrifice to a lord of pain and suffering, delivered before a god on a bounty of grime and dust.

Adam peeled his eyelids open and barely had enough energy to keep them that way. Sharp pain blazed through dull, throbbing aches. Joints stretched against ligaments and tendons. Muscles cried out from deep bruising. He tried to lift his head but his neck had been bent too long. A yolk of pressure weighed down on his shoulders and the nape of his neck, extending to the very edges of his extremities. His eyes strained to the side, only to see that he still hung from the ropes tied between two columns. The cold he felt wasn't the familiar cold coming off the ice of an arena, but the coldness of an empty void, the abandoned vastness of the deserted warehouse on the wharf. Darkness permeated the weak light from the rising moon outside, which was hiding behind a thin fog rolling in.

Numbness had already settled into his hands. He tried to lift his feet beneath him so he could ease the pain in his shoulders. His legs were too weak to support him, so in a gesture of surrender, he allowed his lower limbs to hang limply. The individual spots of soreness coalesced into larger areas of pain, his torso becoming nothing more than a smoldering pot of agony. The bones in his face ached, but not by very much in light of the damage done to the rest of his body. His tormentors had learned early enough that using bare knuckles against surface bones was too painful to keep repeating.

His eyes dropped to the ground beneath his feet. He saw only his knees bent and then nothing. Again, he tried to bring his legs up under him, but failed. Hopelessness winked in and out of his consciousness. Déjà vu glistened like a coiled snake in the grass, his body hanging helplessly from another rope slung over a rafter. A similar shiver of desperation chilled his spine.

After some time, Adam pulled his head up with a great effort. The birds were outside the warehouse, perched on rooftops, broken sills, lamp posts, dock railings, and crates. They were restless and anticipatory, waiting for something—direction or declaration.

Adam closed his eyes and soothed them, letting them know he was still among the living, still breathing air into his tattered lungs. A collective response of caws, trills, hoots, and shrieks pierced through his mind like a blade, making him pinch his eyes shut and wince from the mental assault that came with the relay. Their worry made his head swim, and he tried to quell their calling. They were shrieking in such a cacophony of anxious chirps, squawks, and screeches that he finally had to break the connection, eliciting—he was sure—their scorn.

He heard a shriek pierce the hollow emptiness of the warehouse. Startled, Adam looked in the direction the echoing originated and spotted the red-tail hawk shooting through one of the broken windows. It came like an arrow, a brown mottled projectile with gracefully swooping wings. It flew low to the ground, almost skimming the concrete, then swept up and around him, all the while taking a matronly assessment of his condition. Finally, it landed on the floor several yards away, directly in front of him, and there considered him with a critical eye.

Adam tried to avoid its patronizing look, but he had no choice but to hang from his suspension like a fool in stocks. There was no way he could turn to avoid the public humiliation, no way to mask his helplessness. He wanted to tell the bird to go away, that he was tired and didn't want to be anyone's champion anymore, but he knew it wouldn't care about his minor concerns. It, too, was nothing but a pawn in a grander scheme, and it had accepted its role without compunction or complaint.

The bird's disproportionately long wings stretched and took to the air again, making a short jaunt across the distance to Adam, flying at an infuriatingly leisurely pace. It took roost on his right forearm, its talons gripping his flesh. Despite the numbness in his arms, he was aware of the deadly claws piercing the surface skin, close to puncturing it. Reluctantly, he turned his head to consider the bird, even as its black eyes glared back at him.

The hawk took a few painful steps along his forearm, to his wrist, where the rope was looped and knotted tight. The bird attacked the cord, its head mimicking the movement of a chicken in a coop at feeding time. Strand by strand, the hooked beak broke the length of each fiber, pecking at another, and then another, working meticulously despite the number of strands twisted into the cord. Its efforts were infuriatingly slow and tedious, but it continued until both of them simultaneously looked up and stared at the broken windows.

Outside, Drudge's minions were swarming in droves, swirling in the sky like cumulus clouds in the eye of a hurricane, collecting their consciousness into one mass for a full aerial attack. The blue-blackness of the night, speckled with the celestial and planetary bodies reflecting solar light from a sun halfway around the world, was suddenly inked out by the massive onslaught of fury about to be unleashed. It would only be minutes at best before the horde attacked, and that was too soon to be caught in such a compromising position. The hawk would need more time to work on the ropes hoisting him between the two columns, and Adam encouraged it to pick up the pace.

Then the invasion struck, far sooner than expected, like black rays of energy bursting from an erupting diseased core. Individual bats streaked from the whole conglomeration to barrage the docks on kamikaze strikes. Birds flew from their perches to engage the creatures in mid-flight, their clawed feet coming in from behind. Some were successful in cutting the leathery wings of their enemy and disabling them. Others were able to whisk the smaller ones out of the foray, while at the same time crushing the breath from their putrid lungs. But then the second wave engaged the defending warriors, taking them from behind, just as the birds had done to the first wave. Hundreds of bats flitted in uneven lines, crisscrossing each other in a network of winged ranks.

Adam cursed the hopelessness of the raging battle. He forced his feet to drag themselves up and redistribute his weight from hanging wholly on his arms. His knees resisted the command at first, but he concentrated hard enough for them to finally obey. As he stood, his weight lifted off his arms and he gained a little slack in the ropes holding him. The lengths of cord had been stretched by his body's weight bearing down on them, and his hands now had a little play as he stood. Even the loops around his wrists slackened and blood once again began to slip into his starved extremities.

Incredible pain wracked his fingers as fresh blood flooded the starved veins and arteries of his hands. He cried out as a prickly heat suffused his palms, making them seem as if they were swelling to the point of bursting. His fingers felt as if they were pumped full of napalm, and he desperately wished he had a valve on his wrists to allow the blood to trickle back in, saving him the awful feeling of revitalization. Instead, he waited interminably as his hands went through the process of regaining sensation and function, while their lividity-colored hue faded as the trapped blood escaped.

Feeling became less of an agony as the blood settled from a rush into a more systematic circulation. The prickly needles dulled to an ache around his wrist where the ropes had chaffed ugly welts into his flesh. He brought his eyes over to his coat lying several feet away, where it had been discarded by his abductors. The knife Murdock had used to slice away the leather strips on his hand now lay useless on the concrete a few feet away from where his other weapons lay hidden.

Adam instructed the hawk to stop working on the ropes. There was no way the bird would be able to sever the bonds on one arm, much less two, before the bats broke through his defending ranks. Instead, he sent the bird to the knife, where its practiced talons snagged the haft as if it were a field mouse in high grass.

The hawk rose and circled, scooping the air with languid sweeps of its wings. At the same time, Adam flexed his fingers, working furiously, hoping desperately to bring normal feeling back to his extremities. He watched the smooth flight of the hawk wing around the warehouse as it gained momentum to soar back toward him.

The bird swooped around in a wide arc at the end of the room, skimming the wall with the tip of its wing, heading back his way. It screeched as it approached, crying a warning or a preparatory instruction, Adam wasn't sure which. Either way, he didn't need any encouragement from the bird. He already knew he had to catch the knife in the transfer. His life depended on it.

The bird came as close to his hand as possible, its one front claw barely stroking his fingers. Adam strained his hand open, wincing at the pain the movement caused, and grasped the haft of the blade. As the hawk's talons released the weapon, Adam rejoiced in reclaiming it, feeling his heart quicken with hope. He had the blade—barely—but he had it.

For a brief second only, and then it slipped from his fingers and clattered to the floor.

Adam groaned in frustration. The effort had taxed his tortured fingers too much and he hadn't been able to maintain his grip.

The hawk shrieked back at him in criticism and Adam responded with his own curse of frustration. "I know, goddamn it!"

The hawk swooped in from behind and startled Adam with its quickness in snatching the blade off the ground. Impressed as he was, he knew it was up to him to complete the trick, like a family of trapeze artists who were nothing if they weren't in synch. He opened and closed his hand as the bird made its course across the warehouse, getting ready to head back his way. Murmuring his own words of encouragement to himself, Adam blocked the hawk's belittling recriminations from his mind.

Another shriek of warning, this one making it through the shroud he kept on his mind, forced him to realize the imperativeness of the catch. The birds were holding their own outside, but more of Drudge's reinforcement were pinioning toward the battlefield.

This time, when the hawk passed the weapon into his hand, Adam clamped his fingers around the edged blade, feeling not only the sharp metal cut into his palm but also the burning sensation of his revitalized flesh. This time he gritted his teeth through the pain and tightened his grip, wincing as the razor-sharp blade did more than just leave its impression on his fingers and palm. Crying out relieved a little of the pain, but he still had to work at making the weapon into a more formidable tool.

Adjusting the tightness of his grip on the blade, Adam had to be careful the slickness of his own blood didn't make it too slippery to work with. A cacophony of ear-splitting cries reminded him that he had to act fast. Fumbling awkwardly, he managed to slide the knife into his fingers and walk them up the length of the blade, to the handle, where he gripped it.

The battle outside was becoming a slaughter, with small bodies falling from the sky at a tremendous rate. Bats and birds both lay strewn on the docks as if they'd fallen like rain. Valiant efforts by birds with broken wings or ripped bodies to retake the air made Adam realize the futility of the battle on his behalf. With a sense of self-loathing, he turned his attention back to the rope and worked on it with the knife, sawing furiously.

A frantic shriek sounded from above. Adam's attention shot over to the hawk as it launched itself from a girder to meet a bat that had managed to flit through a broken window. The bird engaged the creature and dispatched it easily enough, its massive talons squeezing the life from the matted body, then dropping it dismissively from its clutch. Another black shape darted into the warehouse, followed by another and another, all from the third wave of attack that had come in as a tail guard.

Adam beckoned more of the birds to the wharf, hating himself for begging such noble creatures for help, knowing they would come to fight for him, and die on his account. Had it not been for his own fear of dying, he would have considered succumbing to the fangs aching to rip his throat out. But as despicable as he found it—and found himself—he knew if he let this life go so easily, he'd become nothing more than a slave to Drudge—and turned against his own birds. All chance at redemption would then be lost.

The hawk shot after the nearest bat and plucked it out of the air like a hand snatching a fly. With prejudice, the bird wrenched its neck apart and dropped it to the dusty floor. At the same time, Adam sawed furiously at the rope until he finally severed it. He twisted to attack the bindings on his left wrist and freed himself, only to turn and discover the bats were steadily filtering through the broken windows, one after the other, flitting about the warehouse until they were familiar with its layout through their echolocation. Some of the birds followed, but they were vastly outnumbered and not likely to get rid of them all.

Adam lunged for his coat and swept it up. As he ran toward the shattered stairs leading up to the abandoned offices, he threw it over his shoulders and jammed his arms through the sleeves. A black shape dropped several feet in front of him, exploding into a pillar of foul hair and coriaceous wings. The small head and feral face hissed and lurched at him, spitting venomous saliva his way. In response, Adam slashed with his knife and struck the demon in the throat, severing veins and arteries hidden beneath tendons and ligaments. Black ichor spurted from the gaping cleavage, pumping systematically to the beat of its wicked heart. The creature clutched at its neck and howled, its murderous intention suddenly quelled by its own desperate concern for survival.

Adam kicked the beast aside to bull his way through but pulled up short when he saw another monster behind it. As he raised his knife for another strike, the gargoyle shot out one of its impossibly long limbs and grabbed his arm in a vice-like grip. Adam's eyes focused on the claws of black bone clamped around his wrist, horrified at the length of their lethal fabrication. He became intimately aware of how such a formidable set of weapons could be used to disembowel a bear with a single swipe and suddenly realized he wasn't in the most advantageous position. With that in mind, he hastened for the inside of his coat with his free hand.

Before he could reach one of his other weapons, the demon wrenched his arm high, jerking him off the balls of his feet. His shoulder cried out against the pain, while the beast made a fist and launched a roundhouse punch to the side of his head.

Adam pulled his head back to avoid a direct hit but took the blow on the cheek hard enough to clack his teeth together and spin him into a daze. He wasn't aware the creature had released his arm and allowed him to tumble across the floor until he discovered his body sliding through the dust and slamming into one of the columns. Desperation made him shake his head clear and scramble to his feet, even as the demon made another lunge at him, seeming to take pleasure in batting him around like a cat toying with a mouse.

Before the demon could grab him again, the hawk shot between them and attacked with its outstretched talons. Eight sharp claws raked the hideous face of black tufted fur and red ember eyes. Eight sharp claws gouged into the sockets and orifices of its mouth and nose. Eight deadly talons clung to the chunks of flesh and anchors of bone while its wings beat furiously and its beak tore gobbets of flesh.

Adam watched in horror as the demon grabbed the bird from its face and wrung its body between its massive hands, then tossed it away. The hawk's body fell twisted and limp against a pile of crumpled advertisements, its black eyes glassy and vacant, lifeless. For a frozen and paralytic moment, Adam stared at the bird, devastated by guilt and an utter aloneness in the world.

And then by fury.

He slowly turned to the ravaged demon, barely aware it was busy patting gingerly at its grievous wounds. Adam had no pity for the monster, only infuriating hatred, and his blood burned in his veins like vitriolic acid. Incensed with vengeance, he reached with practiced ease into his pockets and pulled two knives. He moved with an uncanny grace that was lithe and nimble for any man. In a frenzy, he launched himself at the gargoyle and took his pound of flesh . . . then a length of innards and a flailing extremity. Finally, he parried into its chest with blind fury and cut out its quivering heart, flinging it off the edge of his blade to smack wetly against one of the columns.

The slaughter did nothing to appease his fury, and Adam slipped even further into his venomous rage. Around him, bats metamorphosed into their gargoyle counterparts, batting at the birds even as they fought valiantly on.

Adam bolted for one creature and barreled into its matted body, knocking it clear off its feet with his momentum. While it was stunned, he drew his right blade across its throat and jammed the left one into its gut, wrenching it high enough to cut the tip off its black heart. The bloodlust of the fight—nothing like the subdued stuff he felt when he'd been in on-ice scuffles—consumed him in a way he'd never experienced before. He spun from the dead beast and lurched out with swipes at another as it foolishly reached for him. One clawed hand separated from its crooked wrist, then the other followed suit, spinning overhead, two monkey paws adorned with wickedly long claws. For the coup de grâce, Adam slammed the point of his blade overhanded into the bulging eye of the screaming amputee.

More birds came through the windows, engaging those of the minions that remained as bats just before transformation. The upper stratum of the warehouse was a proliferation of them and the noise of the battle was excruciating loud. The piercing shrieks of the bats trying to orient themselves amid the chaos mixed with the cacophony of cries coming from the birds, to the point where it sounded like an asylum of lunatics off their meds.

None of the deafening din made any impression on Adam. He had only a mild idea of what motivated his actions. Escape. If he managed to get away, there would be no need to continue the engagement. The minions had come for him. Losing him would confound them and send them back to the Tower. The birds could quit their efforts to protect him and seek refuge to tend to their own wounds. All he had to do was make his way to one of the tunnel entrances where he could move anywhere in the city. But to do that he had to forge his way through the thickening crowd of demons obstructing his way. Beyond that, outside the warehouse, hundreds of bats waited as a secondary force in case he succeeded in escaping.

Some inner instinct guided his actions as he focused his attention on dealing with one beast at a time, one obstacle defeated after another. Survival was paramount. Not only was his soul in jeopardy, but the lives of the birds who continued to fight on his behalf.

The first demon to openly challenge him did so at its own peril. Adam dodged the charge and stepped under the unfurled wing, slicing it as he passed. The cut did no real damage but the pain distracted the creature. It howled and whirled on him, its jagged fangs dripping saliva, its mouth gaping wide with a putrid odor of rot carried on its breath. This one roared and lunged again, but Adam was already turning on his heel, sweeping around in a cyclonic spin to slam the point of his blade backhanded into its protruding chest. The air it had inhaled to let out a horrendous ululation escaped as a wheezing sigh through the gaping hole left behind when Adam wrenched the knife out.

Giving it no other thought, Adam sprinted for the opposite wall where the offices were, realizing the staircase was nothing but a collection of splintered timber that had collapsed during his previous attempt to escape. Yet his subconscious mind—that which was ruled by instinct and cunning—recognized a way up to the second floor landing, and he headed directly that way, where crates and oil drums were lined up beneath it.

A clawed hand with bristly fur clamped onto his shoulder when he was only halfway across the distance. The power behind the handhold brought him to a skidding halt that nearly took his legs out from under him. Adam spun around with the two knives sweeping upward in angry arcs, their handles slick and slimy with blood and gore. His grip on their rugged hafts was tight, and he slammed one blade into the ear of his attacker and the second up into its jaw, catching the beast's head in a vice-like trap. With a quick jerk of his arms, Adam snapped its neck with a resounding crack, then wrenched his weapons out of the resisting bones of its skull.

Whirling around, Adam took off again, sprinting toward his destination. His steps were sure and solid, his rubber-soled sneakers making no sound on the concrete floor. When he finally reached the end of the warehouse, he hastily sheathed his weapons and prepared himself to leap at the second floor landing. A quick glance over his shoulder showed him another monster was storming toward him, its claws outstretched and crimped. Its vestigial wings angled over its shoulders to streamline its body for greater momentum.

Adam knew he had no time to climb out of its reach before the creature finally closed in on him, so he took a few launching steps toward the demon, tucking his head and torso into a ball for a full-fledged body check. The demon crumpled over him, and Adam followed through with the impact by lifting the lower half of the beast over his shoulder and flipping it. He spun around and lashed out with a kick, catching the recovering creature squarely in the side of the face. Its head snapped back and quivered, what little brain sitting in its skull rattling against the cavity of its bones. Adam then barraged it with combination shots, until its eyes grew glassy and rolled back in their sockets.

Finally, he turned back to reaching the second floor landing. With all the adrenaline coursing through his body, he launched himself upward and caught the edge of the landing Using little effort, he gripped the ledge with one hand and lurched a leg up, then swung the rest of his body onto the landing. As he did, pain reminded him that he wasn't working at his best, nor could the chemicals in his body mask all his agonies.

Hurriedly, he regained his footing and tore for the closed door at the end of the balcony. The room beyond was bound to have windows overlooking the wharf, where management would have once watched what the employees were doing below.

When Adam reached the door, he kicked it in. The frame splintered into fragments of wooden matchsticks, never to be used again in the manner it was intended. Before entering the small office, he looked inside and saw the blessed windows he was hoping for, those with panes large enough for his body to fit through.

A black shape darted over his shoulder and landed on the floor behind an old metal desk. Adam flung himself at the piece of furniture and ran it across the floor, against the wall, smashing a wooden chair in his effort to crush the demon. But the demon was already transforming and the force of its metamorphosis exploded the desk out from under his hands, throwing him backward. Adam tumbled to the floor amid a scatter of old shipping invoices covered in rat droppings.

The creature tossed the desk aside and stood erect, its head swiveling to look for its prey. In seconds, it saw him as he rolled to his feet. With wicked hatred, it hissed, spraying spittle like a fountain. In a blind fury, it reached for a chair and hurled it at him.

Adam warded off the blow with his arm. The brittle frame splintered around him, encumbering him with its spindly wreckage. Before he could shake off the pieces, his left arm was seized in the beast's powerful grip, crushing the bones in his wrist. Adam retrieved a knife from his coat and swiped with it, catching the forearm of the monster, severing nerves, muscles, and tendons, but causing little effect in the overall strength of the vice. Fury spurred the creature to cuff him with a pulverizing backlash, catching his chin on the bristly knuckles of its hand. Adam's head snapped back. His teeth rattled and his consciousness wavered, but he forced himself to accept the pain.

Evaluation was his tantamount concern. At the moment, his arm gripped in the clawed vice was his most disabling problem. He flipped the knife over in his right hand and jammed it into the wrist of the demon's imprisoning claw. Then he wrenched it up the muscle between the radius and ulna bones, all the way to the elbow. Severed nerves made the beast's arm useless, and its fingers fell away like dead petals from a pistil. Adam pulled his arm free as he slammed the tip of the blade into the concave of the monster's throat, opening a cavern of meaty vessels.

He re-sheathed the knife as the creature clawed at its neck, trying to stem the pulsing blood from pumping out of the gash. Calling on reserves of strength, Adam snatched up a small two-drawer filing cabinet and hurled it at the window. The glass shattered and spewed from the frame in jagged fragments. With his elbow, he broke out the remaining shards.

Nothing existed below the window except twenty feet of open space. No cushioning tarps or netting, but also no deadly rusted machinery either. Only the scattered pieces of glass from the window strewn in a generous pattern on the ground and the file cabinet that had bounced away.

Another black shape twittered into the office. Adam caught its movement out of the corner of his eye just as he was swinging his feet over the sill and readying himself for the drop out of the window. He wasn't concerned for how well he landed; his adrenaline was too effective to feel any more pain than was already in his body. Without a second thought, he leapt.

His feet took the shock easily, his legs bending at the knees and landing with catlike agility. As he turned to flee down the wharf, calling the birds to end the war, headlights pinned him to the wall. Startled, he staggered backward in fear that the rapidly approaching car was going to crush him. But then it rocked to a sudden stop with a squeal of its burning tires. The two front doors burst open but Adam couldn't see beyond the blinding high beams to discern who was there. He didn't have long to ponder the possibilities before a figure on the passenger side ran up to the front bumper with a gun in his hand, aimed at his head, and with frantic excitement, shouted, "Freeze, asshole!"

CHAPTER THIRTY-TWO

Adam breathed easier when he recognized the man holding the gun to be the officer he'd met in the alley, the man he'd regrettably knocked unconscious and the one he'd sent Sophocles to watch over. He held up his hands in a surrendering gesture and glanced up at the broken window. It wouldn't take long for the demons to realize where he'd gone, or for them to follow him through the window.

"You, my friend, are under arrest," Markey said in a voice quavering with excitement.

"Fine, let's just get out of here." Adam hurried toward the detective, around him, and into the back seat of the sedan, slamming the door resoundingly.

As Adam approached and slipped into the car, Markey moved to keep him at bay, shifting awkwardly to stay out of reach. He looked curiously at Lumas, who only shrugged his poorly fitted shoulders and grinned. "I told you, he's just a hockey player."

Adam leaned over the front seat to peer out the open door. "We have to leave. Now."

Markey bent down to look at him. "You've got a lot of explaining to do, kid."

"And you're going to have to do a lot of shooting if you don't get us out of here," Adam countered, maintaining the detective's inimical glare. "Right now!"

A pillar of rippling muscle covered in black hair dropped from the overhead window, voluminous wings unfurling behind it for balance. Those stretches of leathery membranes fanned out on ribbed joints to exhibit the demon's full and sinister hideousness. Burning eyes of crimson fire sparked fury in the reflection of the car's headlights, which illuminated the gargoyle like an entertainer spotlighted on stage. The beast seemed infuriated by the bright light and howled its displeasure from only a few yards away, its shriek reverberating between the walls of corrugated metal.

Markey turned to stare in abject horror at the creature bellowing its raucous rage. He murmured breathlessly, "Good Lord."

"Oh buddy," Lumas moaned, almost in unison with Markey's comment.

"Get in!" Adam ordered, lurching over the seat to grab Markey's arm. He couldn't reach him and Markey was too stunned by the monster to move on his own.

Adam kicked the back door open and burst from the car. He came up behind the detective and grabbed the gun from his slack fingers, firing it at the demon's preening chest. The creature's howl became a shriek as it twitched and jerked in the death throes of the gunfire.

With little inclination for courtesy, Adam shoved Markey into the front seat as he barked at Lumas, whose eyes blinked clear when he registered the gunfire and how it punctured the shriveling creature. "Get us out of here!"

Adam slammed the front door on Markey and jumped into the back seat, still clutching the gun. Markey tried to untangle himself from his head-first dive into the car, while Lumas slid behind the wheel and slammed the gear shift into reverse. The tires spun wildly before they finally gripped the pavement, and the car shot backward along the dock. Dirty white smoke plumed up from the rear wheel wells as the tires squealed.

Adam was thrown forward against the front seat and Markey cried foul as he fell onto the floorboard, finding his body wedged tightly between the dash and the seat. He reached out for something to grab and hoisted himself up, while Lumas twisted around to look out the rear windshield to negotiate their retreat. The car wavered ever so slightly but Lumas maintained control of it. When he reached an intersection and passed it, he slammed on the brakes and twisted forward, slipping the gear into drive. The car turned right and barreled onto a street that would take them back to the city.

Markey cursed as he hauled himself back onto the seat. With trembling hands, he reached over his shoulder and tugged on his seat belt. He then ran his shaky fingers through his hair and drew a stabilizing breath, taking a moment to put things into perspective, calm his threatening hysterics, and quell his racing imagination. When Adam tapped him on the shoulder, he jerked and squealed, then twisted around and saw his gun offered on the flat of Adam's hand. Irrationally incensed, Markey snatched the weapon and jammed it into his shoulder holster.

"What the hell was that back there?" Markey demanded.

Adam considered his look of disbelief and said simply, "A monster."

"No shit," Markey remarked brashly and turned to face forward again, trembling.

"You know me," Adam said to Lumas.

The detective turned to regard him briefly. "Adam Mogilvy, defenseman. Twenty-three goals and thirty-three assists in one season, up until the time you disappeared. One hundred and thirty-two penalty minutes." He grinned in the rearview mirror. "The team could use you back this season."

Adam was silent, a little uneasy about his professional stats being quoted by a total stranger. That part of his life had ended eons ago, it seemed, and the amount of tragedy he'd suffered in the meantime made the year seem exponentially longer than it was. He didn't look with regret upon losing his career; Claire's and Marie's deaths had taken all the sting out of that. Instead, he barely remembered the life he'd had in hockey, and now it wasn't even something he longed to return to. Miserly, he muttered, "'fraid that's not gonna happen."

"Shame."

Adam watched the scenery pass by. He worried about what would happen next, if the minions would follow or return to the Tower, admitting defeat. He closed his eyes and watched as the battle back at the wharf slowly dissipated. One by one, the demons drew away from the foray, fluttering anxiously and in confusion. Some of the birds darted after them, but only halfheartedly, their ranks suffering grievous injuries, as well.

"Where are we going?" he asked after reopening his eyes.

"Headquarters," Markey answered, struggling to regain his composure after coming face to face with something he wasn't even sure he'd seen. As the minutes ticked by, it seemed he'd managed to convince himself that he hadn't actually seen what he'd thought he'd seen and it must just be that he was overworked and overwrought. "You're still under arrest for assaulting a police officer."

"Would you mind if we stopped by a hospital first?"

"Why?"

"I'm bleeding all over your back seat."

Markey turned sharply to see Adam bring his hand out from under his coat, red and slick and glistening in the light of a street lamp they were passing. His eyes surveyed Adam's body as he shucked off his coat, favoring his left shoulder. Blood glistened on the back seat as he leaned forward.

Having noticed the closest hospital would be St. Jude's, Adam decided to take advantage of serendipity. His father had been a police officer in Alberta, so he knew a little something about police procedures. He only hoped this one was universal among all departments, and before any interrogation could happen, the detectives would have to tend to his medical needs. Not that he needed anyone to see to them; he just wanted the diversion.

"Shit," Markey cursed, facing forward again. He hit his clenched fist on his thigh and spoke to Lumas. "The lieutenant would have our asses if we brought him in like this. We might as well swing him by a hospital. What's the closest one?"

"Hmm," Lumas mused, looking around at their surroundings, trying to orient himself. "We could go to County, but it's usually a madhouse. We'd be there for hours before we even got to see a doctor. We're pretty close to St. Jude's, though."

Markey hesitated. The hectic bustle in the hospital Lumas mentioned was much better than County. All the city's indigent citizens without insurance—which amounted to a large portion of the population—went or were transferred to the county hospital for medical care. And because of that, the quality of service was tolerable, at best. They didn't have the time—or the patience—to put up with obnoxious, arrogant, and inconsiderate county employees.

"Sarge?" Lumas prompted.

"Let's go to St. Jude's. Maybe we'll get lucky and it isn't busy."

Lumas made a right turn at the next intersection. Within minutes, the unmarked police car drove up to the emergency room entrance. Angrily, Markey burst out of the car and opened the back door. He made a dramatic motion to beckon Adam out.

"Come on, let's go. We've got things to do." When Adam gathered his coat and moved to get out, Markey said, "Leave the coat. You won't need it in there."

Reluctantly, Adam left the coat and got out. Brusquely, Markey turned him and frisked him. Finding nothing, he slapped a set of handcuffs on and grabbed his elbow, then dragged him roughly into the hospital.

"I need a doctor," Markey said to the first staff member he encountered, a young nurse pushing a wheelchair to the entrance with a discharged patient.

The young woman glanced irritably at them, then noticed their handcuffed prisoner. She seemed to decide at least one of them was a police officer—most likely the one who'd spoken—and tempered her tone with a measure of respect. "Give me a minute; I'll get someone."

Markey and Lumas stepped aside, tugging Adam to stand against the wall with them. They waited as the patient in the wheelchair was ejected from it to await a ride on the curb, and then the nurse hustled back.

"All right, who's the patient?" she asked, shifting her eyes back and forth between the three of them, rocking the chair for emphasis.

"I'll walk, thank you," Adam said.

"Suit yourself," she replied and shoved the wheelchair to the side. She beckoned them to follow her as she led them through the waiting room and into the back treatment area.

It was a slow night in the emergency room, not many people needing serious medical care, and even though St. Jude's took a number of uninsured patients with verifiable identification, there didn't seem to be a long wait ahead of them. The only patient competing for immediate attention was a young child being stabilized for surgery while her haggard parents mournfully clutched each other. The nurse beckoned the officers and their prisoner to the end of the curtained cubicles, into a room separate from the public area by a closed door. "I'll find a doctor to see you."

Markey pulled Adam to a gurney against the wall and uncuffed one of his wrists, then attached the bracelet to the metal rail. Adam glanced around the room and picked out certain items that were out of character for a hospital. A bench protruding from the wall itself had a metal ring bolted into the concrete block. A gun locker was near the door. A table with a utilitarian chair was next to a shelf with several pockets of forms. The room was obviously the secure holding cell for the medical treatment of prisoners or uncontrollable mental patients.

"Where's Grace?" he asked, breaking his silence. He'd learned from the birds that Grace had left his loft a long time ago, and although he'd instructed several of the smaller ones to be her guardians, they'd done only a half-hearted job of it because they were more concerned with his welfare.

"She's safe," Markey replied, offering no encouragement in expounding on what he meant.

Adam relaxed somewhat, sensing Markey's assurance was sincere. He glanced at the wall clock and saw it was a little after nine p.m. He was tired and beaten, driven past exhaustion, his body swollen with aches and bruises. In the rush to escape the warehouse, adrenaline had kept him pumped to the point where pain was not an issue. Now it was more than an issue; it was a concern of great proportions. He wondered again if the pummeling Murdock had done had left him bleeding in critical places. Had his liver been lacerated or his heart been pricked by a fractured sternum? Or had an artery been severed or his kidneys contused? Were his ribs broken or bruised, or were his lungs in danger of being pierced by a sliver of bone? He tried to focus on each part of his body, every major organ that had been subjected to the beating, but it was impossible to separate the individual aches from the whole miserable agony. Each one seemed to be absorbed into the collective mishmash of pain, a collated dispersion of aching throughout his entire body.

It was a quarter of an hour later before a doctor came in to see him. The man seemed entirely too young to have completed medical school from the look of his boyish features. In compliment to his fresh-faced appearance, he exuded an air of discomfort for having been chosen to attend a prisoner in police custody. With nervousness, he nodded to the two officers as he clutched a clipboard against his chest.

"What have we here now?" he asked, his voice a high octave that belied his attempt at bravado. When he looked at Adam and saw the tattoo of a cross and dagger on his forehead, he gave a little double-take to show just how inexperienced he was. In his mind, he probably believed the tattoo had been inked in a maximum security prison for only the most hardened criminals.

"You're gonna have to ask him," Markey said. "We're still a little in the dark about what happened ourselves."

The doctor sighed dismally and ran his hands through his hair, hesitating at first in approaching Adam, who only sat on the edge of the gurney. To the young intern, he didn't seem so much casually reclined as he seemed poised to attack. Taking in the brooding young man with his sharply focused eyes and disturbing tattoo, the doctor probably presumed him to be a seedy character of an underground culture wrought with violence and criminal vices. No amount of the Hippocratic Oath could ease the angst he felt dealing with him. But he had to deal with him, which was the bottom line, and he sighed again.

"Do you think we could move this along," Markey said impatiently, unsympathetic to the doctor's discomfort.

Slumping in forfeit, the young intern addressed Adam, "I'm Doctor Richards. What happened?"

"I got hit with a chair," Adam replied simply, offering no other explanation for what would otherwise be presumed to be an injury from a bar fight.

"All right," Richards said, motioning for Adam to position himself a certain way for the examination.

Adam complied with a sigh of his own, relaxing his body from its stiffened posture and somehow shedding the look of hostility he'd previously exuded.

As Richards approached, he seemed to regain some of his composure. He probed the wound gently, prodding around the perimeter of the ugly gash while hoping not to incense his patient with inflicting pain during his ministering.

Several deep and jagged slashes raked across Adam's shoulder, with pieces of splintered wood impaled in the edges of his skin. Richards searched in a nearby drawer and withdrew a pair of tweezers, which he used to pick out the shrapnel. He worked dexterously, daubing blood away with gauze soaked in alcohol. When he finally tossed aside the tweezers, he examined the flayed strips of flesh more closely, then pulled back and rubbed his eyes.

"I was hoping to get away with mostly butterflies bandages but you've got some nasty gouges. Let me get a nurse in here." He moved off quickly, whether out of fear or a natural hyper-tendency to move fast.

An hour later, after Richards had spent the majority of the time cleansing the lacerations, piecing together, and mending the slashes of skin and muscle, his work was finally done. Local anesthetic had been injected into several places to reduce the pain during his suturing, and a tetanus shot had been added for good measure. Swatches of gauze were taped to cover the ugly network of bristling thread.

Finally, Richards gave instructions on how to care for the injury, which Adam only half-heartedly listened to. The numbness of the anesthetic and the distant tug of the thread through his skin had made him drowsy. Exhaustion caused his eyelids to droop and finally close, and it was only the steady hand of the nurse on his shoulder that kept him sitting upright.

A voice sounded from far away, familiar and comforting, but disturbing somehow. Adam tried to shake his head clear, but it didn't shake so easily, and he felt a hardness against his cheek. When he opened his eyes, he did so slowly and sluggishly, and saw the wall in front of him. At some point, he must have lain down and fallen asleep.

"You're getting to be a regular around here, aren't you?"

Adam bolted up at the sound of Monica Perez's voice, his legs swinging over the side of the gurney, ready to leap off and run away. But he was still cuffed to the rail and couldn't go anywhere, so he faced her and saw that she received his presence with a measure of grudging tolerance. Her arms were crossed over her chest, her lips pursed in resolve, and she gave her head patronizing shake. Approaching the gurney, she took control of examining the work of the young intern and peeled the edge of the bandage back for a peek. Replacing them when she was done, she checked her own work from the previous night.

Amazed, Monica absently tossed aside the old bandages as she peered skeptically at the faint scar. Wrenching his arm farther up for a closer inspection, she felt the slightly rigid skin showing evidence of an injury, but evidence of what was an old injury. Twisting his arm around, she examined the same type of tissue replacing what should have been a wound only two days old. Her lips parted in amazement as her eyes slowly drifted up to his, which she found were watching her guardedly.

She abruptly released his elbow and took a step back. Stopping herself from drawing farther away, she slowly reached for his hand and turned it over, exposing the palm that wasn't covered in leather strips. A pair of wrinkles creased her brow. She reached for his other hand and slowly unwound the strip of leather. Her attention lifted to his face, curious and probing. His intense blue eyes drilled into her darker brown ones, accepting her wonderment of what must have been gnawing at her for over a year. He knew the question that came to mind now—a statement, actually—wouldn't hold its place on her tongue this time.

"These scars," she said, "are exactly alike. I didn't notice it back then. That night I . . ."

Adam only stared at her, offering no confirmation or denial, only agonizing under her befuddled reflection.

"They're deliberate," she observed tightly, shaking off some of her thoughtfulness and taking on a more speculative tone. "I thought they were defensive wounds from a knife attack, but . . . They're too precise. And it seems I've seen this design before."

Again, he gave her no explanation, no assurance that she was on the right track, no clue as to what the design was patterned after. Instead, he gently pulled his hands away and said, "You betrayed me."

Her eyes sparked with offense. "I did not."

"You told them where to find me last night."

"I told them where to find Grace," she stated defensively. "I told them she needed medical attention and you were refusing to let her go to a hospital."

"It's important for her baby to live."

"I'm trying to see that that happens."

"Some people would just as soon see it never be born."

She shook her head in frustration. "She should be in a hospital."

"So where is she now?"

Monica fell silent, a sense of guilt and fright showing for her lack of an answer. "Shit," she muttered and spun around, leaving the room with a smack on the door hard enough to fling it open. Once she was gone, the door slowly closed on the room.

Adam saw that he was alone. The detectives had left the room sometime during the time he slept. Not knowing how long he'd have, he hurried about his business, knowing the police wouldn't be gone for long.

He hopped off the gurney and pulled the wheeled table over a few feet to where a set of drawers was located in a counter. All he needed was one thin wire to do what he needed.

When he was a child, his father had taught him how to open handcuffs with nothing more than a paperclip. Fascinated, he had practiced the trick until he'd perfected it, mostly to amaze his friends. Although most of his friends found it thrilling to know that a paperclip separated most criminals from escape, Adam could use any sturdy piece of wire.

What he found was exactly what his father had used to teach him the trick, which was a paperclip holding a collection of papers together on the counter. With a dexterity he still retained from childhood, he straightened the paperclip and inserted one end of the wire into the keyhole, notched it to create a little tooth, and twisted it around with a practiced and delicate hand. It might have been years since he'd last delighted anyone with the trick, but his mischievousness paid off within seconds. Unlocking the one cuff from his wrist, he was then free.

Monica Perez strode up to the two detectives who were sipping coffee at the end of the hall, where they could still keep an eye on the door to the room where their prisoner was. At the moment, despite her curiosity for the young man's extraordinary healing abilities, she was now more concerned about someone else.

She'd worried the other night that Grace might have miscarried the baby. She'd argued to get the woman to the hospital, but the bull-headed young man holding her hostage in the cathedral had refused to let her leave the church. Monica had told Detective Markey where he might find her in the hopes that he'd see her safely to the hospital, where Grace might ask for the tests necessary to check on the condition of her baby. Markey apparently hadn't followed through with his end of the bargain, and for that she was furious.

"Detective Markey," Monica snapped angrily, "where's Grace Fitzpatrick?"

Markey turned to Monica with his own resolve. "She's safe."

"Safe? I told you she needed medical attention. Did she get it?"

"She's fine," he assured.

"She may appear fine to you, but the *baby* might not be."

Markey and Lumas said nothing as they absorbed what she'd just said, what twists it implied. Markey's mouth worked in perplexed silence as Monica gloated, her arms akimbo.

"Yes, *Detective*, she's pregnant."

"Oh," was all Markey could say.

"Well?"

"Well what?"

"The experiences Grace has been through have been extremely traumatic, if not physically exhausting. She needs a complete examination and ultrasound to check on the condition of the fetus."

"Wow," Markey said. He ran his hand through his hair while his other clutched his cup of coffee.

"That young man in there seems to think her baby may be the fulcrum of all her problems," Monica added, jerking her thumb over her shoulder.

Markey and Lumas shot their eyes in the direction she pointed. Cocking his head to one side, Markey said sardonically, "He does?"

"So he says."

"What threat could an unborn baby do anyone?" Markey wondered, lifting his head slightly and staring off into space. It didn't take long for him to come up with the answer himself, and he suddenly hit Lumas on the arm. "Proof that Grace Fitzpatrick was sleeping with a particular someone. And five'll get you ten that her baby has an illustrious paternity."

Lumas's eyes narrowed. At that moment, he seemed almost ape-like. "Charles Driskell?"

"I can't think of how a baby would be detrimental to Mr. Driskell's reputation. But it would be devastating to Christopher Purcell's."

Lumas grinned. "You think she really was boinking the district attorney?"

"The district attorney slash mayoral candidate," Markey corrected. He turned to Monica, who was trying to follow the exchange as closely as possible. "Would you be able to determine the father of that baby with DNA testing?"

"Probably," she replied, her curious eyes narrowing.

"How soon could you do the test?"

She shook her head. "That's a very personal and private decision. Some mothers might not want their children to know who their father is."

"Yeah, well, I'm not overly concerned about what the child might learn about his father. However, I am concerned that the district attorney might be involved in a homicide."

"I don't follow you," she said, shaking her head.

"You don't have to. If I bring Grace here, could you do the DNA test?"

"Wait a minute," she said. "If you think I'm going to be a party to any unwanted medical procedure, you're out of your mind."

"If I'm right, I'm betting Grace will be the one demanding the test be done."

"If that's the case, then that's a different story. But I'm not going to have her coerced into anything she doesn't want." She thrust a finger at the two detectives. "Just bring her in so I can check her out."

Markey nodded and turned to Lumas, his excitement complete. "Go to the office and get Grace. Don't let her in on the DNA test just yet. I'll explain it to her when she gets here."

Lumas trotted off in the direction of the exit. Markey followed at a distance, going to a courtesy phone to call the homicide office because his cell phone wasn't getting service inside. He wanted to have Grace prepared to go to the hospital as soon as possible. His own patience to learn the true lineage of the child was growing thin. Christopher Purcell had offered alibis for his whereabouts over the weekend, but he had also denied any affair with Grace. If they could prove Grace's baby was also Purcell's, his alibi would suffer a severe credibility attack. Getting Grace to agree to the test was only half the battle; the other half was getting Purcell to provide a DNA sample.

When Markey was through with his call, he hung up and faced Monica, who had moved in close to listen to his phone conversation. He acknowledged her curiosity with a slight nod of his head. "You'll be able to give her that exam when she gets here. Now, if you don't mind, I have a prisoner to interrogate."

He sidled around her and headed down the corridor, toward the door to the room where he'd left Adam Mogilvy. He grasped the handle and pulled, opening the door to expose a vacant room with only a discarded pair of handcuffs still hanging limply from the rail of the gurney.

CHAPTER THIRTY-THREE

Adam slipped quietly through the hospital basement where the morgue and archives were located and even deeper where the massive boiler, water pipes, and electrical conduits ran. He threaded his way through the hissing pipes and wet floors, feeling the heat encroach on him at various places, then the chilling cold. Forty-watt bulbs were lit at intervals of twenty feet along the ceiling, lighting the way, or seemingly so. Mice squeaked fretfully as his steps made hollow sounds on the concrete. Skittering nails scratched as the tiny creatures ran along the walls to get away. Pipes ticked as liquid or gas rushed through them. A steady thump sounded as machinery chugged.

He finally reached the lowest level of the basement, which was hardly traveled or visited except by maintenance workers, and then only infrequently. There he wormed his way behind a collection of machinery and pipes. The air was thick and hot back there, with steam rising off the joint seams. A steady hum sounded close by, letting him know the boiler was working and shouldn't be disturbed. Adam had no interest in the steaming contraption. Instead, he pulled aside a plank of wood covering a short door the size of the opening to a root cellar set securely in the lower half of the wall. He fumbled for the handle—an old bar rusted from all the moisture in the air—and wrenched on it with all his might. The barrier gave way with a groan and he crawled through, into the interlocking tunnels beneath the city.

Fumbling through the dark, he found a niche to his right bearing a box of matches and lit one of the torches taken from an alcove set just inside the door. Yellow-orange light flared as the pitch on the top caught fire from a single match. Smoky tendrils of licking flames lapped at the tip of the brand as a pungent odor of burnt pine drifted into his nostrils, making his nose wrinkle.

He held the torch out before him to light the way, walking through the tunnels as wisps of fire lost contact with the flame's core. His shoes tromped through grimy puddles, spewing stagnant water, while mice scurried away with squeaking surprise. The heat emanating from the torch barely dispelled the cold from the earth, but the light was enough to give him some meager comfort.

As he made his way through the tunnels, the fingers of his free hand skimmed along the pitted and rocky wall. He ducked under low hanging outcroppings and skipped over knobs in the earth. The path was well worn from several years of secret liaisons and traipsing, but it was still treacherous without some knowledge of the pitfalls and obstacles. It wasn't a problem for him; he'd been using the underground passages since the time Sophocles had dragged him down into them. He'd been a drunk then, his brain a swirl of liquor and guilt. During that bleak period, he hadn't believed he could get any lower than sleeping in the gutter and eating food from the trash. He wasn't even aware how long that period lasted—he was too drunk to count the days—before he suddenly found himself sobering up in the bowels beneath the city. Sophocles had kept him a prisoner then, forcing him to listen to his diatribe of religion and duty, feeding him insanity but insisting on allegiance, his discourse always one step away from brainwashing. At first, Adam thought the old man was a lunatic, but as he sobered up and began to listen, he started to hear the wisdom in his words. Sophocles wasn't talking so much about religion in a conventional sense, but about the difference between good and evil. Adam sensed there was more to what went on out in the open, above ground, than what the public perceived as reality. He felt the truth of it in the roiling of the earth, in how the world spoke to him through the birds. Even now, he could feel the discord growing inside the packed soil, limestone, and wet mud surrounding him.

He traveled for nearly an hour, crossing two and a half miles of tricky ground. He passed numerous side caverns and tunnels, knowing intimately where each intersection led. He'd been roaming these warrens for several months and had a sufficient understanding of where they went. He'd been lost several times in his first jaunts through the burrows alone—escape attempts when he was still drunk, then when he was in withdrawal and pain. On those occasions, Sophocles had hunted him down to reclaim him before his all-consuming paranoia inflicted permanent psychological damage to his brain; and that was something Adam suspected Sophocles wanted full rights to. Eventually, once Sophocles believed him to be fully convinced of the claptrap he preached, Adam was taught the ways of the tunnels, until he became comfortable with roaming the underground realm on his own.

He finally arrived at an opening to a large cavern. He thrust his torch out before him to light the way, streaking black smoke and an echo of yellow flame ahead of him. The air was cold and thin in the chamber, but it wasn't any more claustrophobic than it was in the passageways. He smelled familiar odors. Not pleasant but at least nostalgic. The musky smell of underground dirt, the fetid odor of human sweat, and the pungent reek of old food. It was a compilation of odors that would make most men gag, but not him.

Fully engulfed by memories, Adam stood in the chamber and looked around, a clutch of grief wrenching the muscles of his chest. A cot was pushed against the far wall, covered with tousled army blankets. There was a battered cooler where food had once been stored at the foot of the cot. A Coleman lantern with a can of kerosene sat on an upturned milk crate, next to a basket of tattered and well worn books. In one corner of the cavern was a cedar chest that still smelled fragrant but barely masked the other odors. That meager piece of furniture was the only thing forbidden to him, and in spite of all Sophocles' warnings, Adam now felt compelled to investigate its contents.

He walked gingerly around the chamber, his eyes closed but his other senses heightened, not touching anything but wishing to revel in the memory of his dead mentor. Sophocles' spirit had touched this small hole in the earth. His memories floated on drafts sweeping through the tunnels, finding home here. A soft whistle—barely audible—wavered with the air currents sidling into the cracks.

Adam spent a minute in quiet remembrance, then snapped his eyes open.

Knowing full well what he was doing, he strode over to the cedar chest and dropped to his knees, holding the torch high in one hand so he could keep the light overhead. Gingerly, he lifted the lid and looked inside, using the sweep of the flame to cast a yellow pall over its contents. Sophocles had refused him access to this chest, claiming he wasn't ready for what lay within it. But now the contents—the entire shabby remains of the old bum who'd saved his life—now belonged to him. Sophocles had no family to bequeath his priceless treasures to, no estate to pass it on, only him.

His stomach tightened as he thrust his hand into the chest and rifled through the soft knit blanket swaddling only a folded piece of parchment. Sophocles had told him that the weapon he would need to destroy Malachi Drudge lay within this chest. Despite Adam's persistence to know what it was, Sophocles had only shook his head and told him that he wasn't ready to know.

"Damn you, old man," he cursed as his fingers encountered nothing else in the folds of the blanket, and nothing beneath it, nothing but the piece of parchment. He snatched the crisply folded paper, thinking it would contain the directions to where such a weapon might lay, and opened it with his thumb, drawing it into the circle of the torch's light. All it said was: *Faith*.

Disappointed to the point of anger, Adam swiveled around and fell against the chest, weak-kneed and trembling. He dropped the torch and clutched the parchment in both hands, considering it for a time before his frustration grew to such an infuriating level it demanded release or it would suffocate him. He tore the paper in half, doubled it, and wrenched the pieces apart again. When he'd made confetti of it, he threw the shreds aside, letting them sprinkle down around him like fluttering petals caught on a soft summer breeze.

Tears welled up in his eyes as he remembered Claire and Marie, the image of them in their final minutes of life, the terror they must have felt, the hopelessness and desperation of that night quashing all the good memories he had of them. He wondered if Claire had cried out his name, whether in supplication or as a curse, when she discovered she was going to die. He imagined what she thought of him in those last minutes, taking the memories of their life together into herself for salvation. He was sure she would have accepted her fate boldly when it became clear her life was over. He knew she would have tried to save Marie; she would have begged for their daughter's life until finally she would have sheltered her with her own body.

His breath hitched on sobs he couldn't hold back. No one would care about his grief if he wallowed in it in this underground cavern. Not even the ghost of the hermit who'd once lived here, who'd rescued him from the gutter and a pathetic life of short-lived alcoholism and disease-ridden misery, who'd confided in him the secret horrors of the world. Not the specter of a man hinged on insanity because of the secrets he was privy to, who'd shared them with Adam because he knew his body and mind were on the decline, because he knew his work wasn't over even though he didn't have it in him anymore to fight the war. No, that disembodied soul had fled the world with the alacrity of a freed slave, leaving nothing but a pitiful heir to a horrible throne.

Adam didn't know how long he spent in the damp cavern before he realized it must have been longer than he'd expected to stay. His head throbbed with the nagging beginning of an ache. Even though he'd lost all consciousness of his immediate surroundings, he hadn't invited the birds inside with him. Their collective consciousness had been tapping at his brain, but he only shut them out and ignored them in deference to his own private commiseration. He didn't want to share his grief with them, even though their concern seemed to grow more imperative the longer he took with it.

Finally, he struggled to his feet, his shoe kicking the now dead torch in the dark. He hadn't even known the light had gone out, snuffed by the sooty layer of dirt on the floor. A momentary sense of panic worried him that he'd be encumbered by the dark, until he remembered the lantern sitting beside the cot.

He fumbled around until he had the lantern lit. The light filling the room was less primitive than the torch had been, more steady and white, and he used the new beacon to light his way as he hurried through the burrows.

The door he exited from was the same he'd led Grace through the previous night when they'd fled the cathedral. He left the Coleman on the outcropping of the wall just inside the tunnel. With a weary stride, he climbed the flight of stairs up from the basement and let himself out in the corridor, which was dark and foreboding, the windows looking out on a courtyard showing nothing but the deep black of night. He suspected it must be early Tuesday morning but he had no idea what the actual time was.

The church proper was always left with the lights burning, even though Monsignor O'Dwyer locked up late at night. Adam had often entered the church for his own period of meditation through the very way he did now.

Tonight, though, he didn't need the solace of private reflection; he needed to find the monsignor. With a genuflection before the altar and a gesture of crossing himself, he passed through the church and went through the opposite door, which led to the rectory office. He knew the priest wouldn't be in his office this late, but there was a door leading out to the west courtyard at the end of the corridor. There, a cottage provided residence for the attending pastor, a place Adam knew about but had never ventured.

A little apprehensive about infringing on the monsignor's privacy, Adam forced himself to overcome his uneasiness and rapped lightly on the door. The overhead stars were little prickles of sparkling light showing through the light gray clouds. A pale shadow stood at an angle to his body, his solidity casting phantoms on the grass. A dove flitted from a low-lying branch to perch boldly on his shoulder.

Adam jerked. Recovering from his momentary surprise, he peered ruefully back at the little creature. Its presence was a slight comfort in the lonely night.

When his first attempt at knocking didn't bring about its desired result, Adam realized he might not have knocked hard enough to wake a sleeping old man. This time he knocked harder, creating more resounding echoes. In a few seconds, a light turned on in the side window. Noise preceded another light being turned on behind the window of the living room. A fumbling of the dead bolt lock and then the doorknob twisted.

As the front door opened, the dove took off from Adam's shoulder and the priest appeared in the doorway. O'Dwyer was dressed in a bathrobe, his eyes squinting with sleepiness, his hair tousled. When he saw Adam, he blinked, and then swung the door wide open.

"Adam!"

"Father, I'm sorry to bother you . . ."

"No, no, come in. Hurry up, come in."

O'Dwyer stood aside and grabbed Adam's arm, pulling him inside and closing the door. He shuffled around in old slippers, examining the young man for injuries.

"You're hurt," he said, seeing the ugly bloody mess of his shirt.

"It's been taken care of," Adam assured. He felt awkward standing in the priest's living room, glancing around at the Spartan decor peppered with minimal icons of religious influence. The silence the old man perpetuated only served to make him more uncomfortable. Adam cleared his throat and turned to face him. "I'd like you to finish hearing my confession."

Monsignor O'Dwyer blinked, then nodded enthusiastically. "Yes, of course."

He disappeared into a back room. When he came back, he was wearing his black shirt and pants and his white clerical collar. In the interim, Adam had wandered slowly through the living room, letting his eyes sweep carefully over each and every item in the open, trying to draw out the time while O'Dwyer changed.

"If you'd like, we can finish up in here," O'Dwyer said, motioning toward the dining room. When Adam's uncertainty appeared on his face, O'Dwyer waved away his concern. "There's no need for ceremony. Absolution needs no rituals."

Adam peered into the depths of the darkened room and nodded. He followed the priest to the dining table and took a seat across from him. O'Dwyer crossed himself and kissed the inside of his bent index finger. For a moment, he seemed lost in quiet reflection, then he lifted his face to smile at Adam.

"All right, where were we?"

Adam shook his head. "I don't remember exactly."

"Then we'll start over." When he noticed the stricken look on Adam's face, he said, "Just follow along." He crossed himself, saying, "Bless me, Father, for I have sinned."

"Bless me, Father, for I have sinned," Adam echoed, mimicking the gesture.

"It has been so long since my last confession. You add how long."

"I've never had a confession."

Father O'Dwyer bowed his head reverently. "These are my sins."

"These are my sins."

Silence.

O'Dwyer looked up and saw Adam chewing on his lower lip, struggling with his conscience to admit his shortcomings, or wracking his memory to remember them.

"Start with the small stuff. It'll get easier as you go along."

But it didn't. Adam found it hard to start, to find something so trivial as to act as an opening. Everything he thought about seemed to swell in comparison to common, everyday transgressions. Yet he had to bring his sins out in the open for the monsignor to forgive him, to prepare him for what he was planning.

"Adam . . . ?"

"It . . . It's hard," he said apologetically.

"Let's see," O'Dwyer considered. "Let's start with the universal sins. Have you told lies?"

"No."

The old man raised one eye critically. "Really?"

"I don't talk to many people. But I suppose I have lied in the past, so yes, I must have lied at one point or another."

"Have you shown disrespect to your parents?"

"My mother died when I was young," he said regretfully. "And I haven't spoken to my father in over a year. I do regret that."

"All right, how about something off your own list."

"I've harbored hatred for a man. A man I've sworn to kill."

O'Dwyer looked quizzically at him. "Pardon me?"

"This man has to die, but I can't kill him if I hate him."

"I'm afraid you've lost me, son," O'Dwyer said uneasily. "And I must say, you're frightening me."

Adam hesitated, wondering if he should continue even though Sophocles had written what he'd often professed. *Faith.* How Sophocles had meant that, Adam wasn't sure. Was he supposed to have faith in God? Himself? O'Dwyer? Who, or what, did he mean? The old hermit's infuriating sense of the oblique followed him even after his death.

"This man I'm talking about killed my family," Adam said in a venomous tone. He motioned to the red scars on his neck. "He did this to me after he killed them. And he killed Sophocles. He'll kill Grace's baby, too, if someone doesn't stop him."

O'Dwyer slowly recoiled from Adam's angry words, realizing the gist of the confession had turned into an oath of desperation. When he finally found the words to speak, he did so gently, soothingly. "If that's true, then this man needs to be brought to justice."

"No justice can touch Malachi Drudge," Adam answered sullenly. "Only God's justice will have any effect on him."

"'Vengeance is mine, says the Lord'," O'Dwyer quoted. "You shouldn't presume to be the hand of God."

Adam gave him a look of unknown provocation. "I don't presume to think God will sanction anything I'm prepared to do. But I will kill this man. The only thing I ask is absolution before I do."

O'Dwyer stood up to pace the room. As he did, he swept his hand across his face and heaved a heavy sigh. He finally turned back to Adam, who had maintained a respectful silence as the priest struggled with his conviction. "I can understand your plight, Adam, but I can't condone your actions. You're talking about killing a man, taking vengeance out on someone when you know it's morally wrong."

"Is it?" Adam broke in. "Is it wrong to let someone live so they can continue their terrible crimes against humanity. What makes his life any more important than Grace's child's? Or Grace's, for that matter?"

"We must do everything we can to keep the child safe, yes, but we're not the ones to decide who lives or dies."

"And Drudge is?" Adam asked sarcastically.

"I'm not saying what he does is acceptable. I'm saying two wrongs won't make it right."

Adam closed his mouth on any further argument. He understood now why Sophocles had kept his incredible knowledge of the ethereal secret. Father O'Dwyer would only preach church dogma and scripture. Despite the priest's religious training, he wasn't capable of opening his mind to the terrible forces in effect around him.

"Will you forgive me?" Adam asked, his voice apprehensive.

"I can't condone your intentions to kill a man," O'Dwyer said.

Adam dropped his eyes to the table, feeling a pang in his heart that was on the verge of panic. When he looked up, his eyes were rimmed in red. "Claire told me that a man can't enter Heaven without God's forgiveness."

"Extreme unction is very important to people who haven't had the opportunity to give confession before passing," O'Dwyer said. "But someone who dies without the last rites can still enjoy eternal life if he's lived a virtuous life."

This didn't relieve Adam's fears. He shook his head, his expression crestfallen. "All I want is to be with them again. I don't give a damn about spending eternity with God. I never really subscribed to Him anyway. And to tell the truth, I'm only using Him to get back to them. But I still keep thinking about Grace and her baby, and I know I can't leave her with Drudge still alive. I don't understand why he wants to kill her baby, but—"

A loud bang sounded at the front window. Both Adam and the priest jumped. Adam found himself on his feet, suddenly moving toward the front door, brushing past O'Dwyer as if it was his home he had to keep safe. O'Dwyer hurried right behind him, worried that the same men who'd attacked the cathedral that morning were back.

Adam reached the door and pulled it open, showing no fear in the quickness with which he yanked it. In a second, he tripped down the porch steps and dropped to his knees on the wet grass. When O'Dwyer came up behind him, he glanced over Adam's shoulder and saw that he cradled a dove in his hands. The bird was dead, having tried to fly into the warm cottage through the closed window.

Adam felt the guilt for such a tiny tragedy, especially after all the lives lost on his behalf in the earlier battle. His dismissal of the bird's prodding thoughts had forced the little creature to smash itself into the window just to gain his attention. He was paying attention now, but there was no way he could bridge the gap between this world and eternity to hear what the poor soul had meant to tell him. Instead, he closed his eyes as much to connect with the collected discord of several birds now trying to relay something to him as to prevent the tears from pooling in his eyes.

Monsignor O'Dwyer was muttering his perplexity over the bird's sad fate when Adam suddenly sensed the old man was behind him. He gathered his resolve and got to his feet, cradling the tiny creature against his chest. He passed the bird to O'Dwyer. "Amazing how even the smallest creature can get into Heaven with a gesture of self-sacrifice but I can't even get a confession."

O'Dwyer looked intently at Adam and tried to read his expression.

"I appreciate all you've done," Adam whispered, "but I have to go."

"What?"

"There's no time to convince you about what I'm going to do. It's either now or never."

"For what?" O'Dwyer demanded, afraid he was going to hear something he wasn't prepared to deal with.

"It's time someone stops Drudge."

As Adam attempted to get absolution from Monsignor O'Dwyer, Christopher Purcell crawled on his hands and knees through a slathering of files and paperwork in the County Public Records Archives. It was well after dark and beyond business hours for county employees to still be at the facility, but Christopher had used his status as the District Attorney to remain in the building after hours. In fact, as he shuffled on his hands and knees through the litter he'd created from carefully catalogued and filed records, he was unaware of the time of night. His movements were jerky and sporadic, and a pathetic noise of his own making somewhat resembling the whine of a tortured soul warbled out of his throat. Listening closely, one might be able to make out exclamations—albeit softly uttered and deliriously disbelieving ones—of something not necessarily comprehensible. Whatever it was, it caused him great distress, and Christopher scurried hither and yon in the piles of paperwork in search of something substantial.

"No, can't be, isn't here," he mumbled and murmured, his head hanging low as his hand snatched another file, fanned through the documented and time-stamped papers before finally flinging them away. Around him, in no particular order, were cardboard boxes that had once housed the files he was now nesting in. Their lids were scattered about, some crushed under his hands and knees as he tromped over them.

"Can't be. Gotta be something. Something. No one just doesn't exist. Bullshit. BULLSHIT!" he bellowed and flung papers every which way, his fury no match for their patient sifting down to others already strewn before them. Christopher sat back on his haunches and stared with something close to clarity—the closest he had gotten the whole time in his search through the public archives for dirt on Malachi Drudge. He was an attorney and knew how to peruse seemingly innocuous documents for suspicious wheelings and dealings. String a series of records together, those that didn't appear together on their own, and one could get a good view of plans, schemes, and underhandedness. That was what Christopher was attempting to do before confronting the bastard and demanding control back in his life. But the more Christopher delved into the public persona of Malachi Drudge the more he learned the man was as elusive and unconventional as anyone could get. There was no history of the business mogul other than his appearance on the scene less than two years ago, when he'd politicked and purchased land reserved for city beautification; in this case, a public park. Money had won that war at the promise of increased commerce and an influx of jobs. After all, how could a park employing only a smattering of employees contend with a skyscraper that would bring not only business in its construction, but in continued employment for clerical, management, sales, and whatnot people. There was no competition, and Drudge's acquisition of this piece of prime real estate went through without even the hint of a scandal. It had been a time-honored maneuver of bringing a better offer to the table.

So while Drudge was able to steal the land out from under the city's nose at a purchase price over the value of the parcel zoned as a park but well under its fair market value if it was rezoned as commercial, he appeared not to have committed any crime. And while he'd built his eyesore of a monolith to the deviation of every building code on the books, there were genuine permits in records to vouch for their legality. Drudge had a knack for getting his way, even if it wasn't the acceptable way for things to be done. Perhaps with time Christopher could delve deeper into the connivings of Drudge's real estate deal to find unscrupulous practices of blackmail and graft, but until he had that time, he had nothing to go on.

Christopher dropped his head in dejection. He'd come to the public records archives on a mission, sure he would be able to divine Drudge's nefarious scheme within the city. But after hours of pillaging and scrutinizing county records, he hadn't discovered anything of value. Everything according to the paperwork was on the up and up. He wouldn't be able to snare the mogul in such manipulative measures without speaking to the people Drudge had dealt with firsthand. Instead, he'd have to come up with something more tangible than conducting business through a little graft and gratuity.

It was a while before Christopher resigned himself to failure; at which point, he remembered Prescott's solicitation for his fingerprints. Christopher had promised the assistant D.A. that he'd provide his prints to the two detectives by the end of the day. Well, the day was over and they were now well into the night. Perhaps he should consider addressing that issue before it got too late. If Prescott learned that he'd balked at providing his fingerprints, he might begin to worry that Christopher had something to hide. And it wasn't like they couldn't get his fingerprints in a more circumspect manner, although cooperation would speak volumes for his façade of innocence.

But first he had to ask Drudge if he'd thought of everything the night he'd killed the man at the Rialto. Had the bastard erased all his fingerprints to keep the only piece of incriminating evidence in his possession? It reasoned that he should have, but Christopher had to be absolutely sure.

CHAPTER THIRTY-FOUR

An hour and a half earlier, Grace was awakened by one of the nameless detectives who'd stayed in the office with her. She was told she had a phone call. Up until then, she'd been napping in the lounge, oblivious to any of the detectives who walked quietly in to get a cup of coffee.

The person on the phone had been Detective Markey, and he'd told her that he was sending his partner by to pick her up and bring her to the hospital. He'd run into Monica Perez and learned of her delicate condition. Doctor Perez had scolded him about his lack of concern for her health and suggested very strongly that he bring her in for a complete examination.

Detective Lumas arrived twenty minutes later and hurried her out of the office. She asked him to stop by her apartment for a change of clothes, thinking that a chance to slip into something from her own wardrobe would make her feel much better. Unfortunately, Detective Lumas said it would be too dangerous, so she'd grudgingly conceded. After some babbling about just trying to bring a sense of normalcy back to her life, Lumas suggested sending an officer to her apartment to pack a bag and bring it to the hospital.

Lumas escorted her to the same sedan she'd ridden in earlier, the one the pelican had been on. She slid sleepily into the front seat and fastened her seat belt as the portly officer went around to the driver's side. He maintained a respectful silence in regard to her dreamy mood and offered only a smile when their eyes met.

Grace settled in and closed her eyes, knowing the drive would take no more than twenty minutes to get to the hospital. The gentle rumbling of the passing roads and the sway of easy turns soon coaxed her into a light doze. When the car finally stopped longer than the cycling of a traffic light, she instinctively sensed an end to the ride and opened her eyes.

She glanced around and noticed none of the features of the hospital she'd been in Friday night. Instead, what appeared before the car was the opening mouth of a secured underground parking garage. She bent her head to peer through the windshield and gasped when she saw the smooth black siding of the obelisk tower.

"Easy now, Grace," Lumas said, catching her wrist in a restraining grip. He offered her the same smile he'd used to comfort her when they'd first gotten into the car, only now it seemed more menacing than soothing. "There's a lot of money to be made if you only play your cards right."

"But . . . you're a police officer," she whispered, her voice hoarse and tremulous.

"And the pay ain't so great these days. Listen, Mr. Drudge doesn't want to hurt you. He has a proposition for you, that's all. That's what all this running around has been about."

No matter what he meant, his words didn't settle her. She tried to pull her arm away but his hold was unyielding, and with some fumbling with the use of only one hand, he drove into the parking garage. Once the metal gate rolled down behind them, he let her go, and her elbow hit her ribs with the force by which she pulled it back.

The parking garage was eerily deserted and silent but for the fluorescent lights humming overhead. Lumas pulled into a parking space near the elevators and shut the engine off.

"You have to believe me, Grace," he said. "I wouldn't do anything to jeopardize your life. But we're talking about a lot of money, for the both of us. Enough for you to be set for the rest of your life. You won't have to work another day in your life. No more drab little apartment or public transportation to get around the city. All you have to do is keep your mouth shut."

She pressed herself against the door to get as far away from him as possible, suddenly repulsed by him. His slovenly appearance and offensive body odor could no longer be overlooked by the fact that he held an estimable position on the police force. Instead, it made him as repugnant as any of the thugs who'd tried to abduct her off the street over the weekend.

"It's gotta be this way," Lumas said desperately, feeling a bit uneasy because of how she was reacting. "If you don't take him up on his proposition, he'll just as easily kill you. Don't kid yourself; he's not disinclined to do something like that. It's a pretty easy decision for you to make."

"You . . . you know he kills people?" she stuttered.

"He's a powerful man," Lumas explained. "He always lets people make their own decisions. We create our own futures."

"My God," she moaned. "Do you really believe that?"

She could see it in his eyes that he was having a hard time with his own bullshit, and he lowered his face so she couldn't see his guilt.

"We're at that point now, Grace. It's your decision."

"He killed Adam's family," she accused with venomous outrage. "You're a homicide detective. You should be putting him in jail, not helping him."

Lumas's head snapped up. "Don't preach to me, sweet cheeks. I've been living just above poverty level my entire life. This is my one chance to get ahead. I'm not going to retire at fifty-five with a seventy percent pension and ulcers eating at my guts. I'm getting out of here with a big chunk of change and enough years left to enjoy my life. Whatever you choose for yourself is your own business."

"Please don't do this," she begged, trading righteous indignation for tears. "Adam told me about him. He wants my baby."

"I don't know anything about that. I only found out you were pregnant when that doctor said something about it this evening. But you shouldn't worry about Adam Mogilvy. He's not so far from being committed to an institution."

She stared at him with solemn, red-rimmed eyes. The power of money could be a huge influence in the motivation of a lot of people, but it was hard for her to believe she could be so significant to anyone's plans that murder and extortion had to come into play. As she sniffed back tears, she began to wonder what harm it could do just to take the money and run. She couldn't think of a reason sufficient enough to dismiss Adam's warning about Malachi Drudge, but if her choices were to take the money and keep her silence, or die, she would surely have to think about it.

"Will you come up on your own, or do I have to help you?"

Grudgingly accepting her fate for the moment, she nodded and reached for the door handle herself.

Sergeant Markey looked at his watch and cursed under his breath. He paced back and forth in the emergency room, looking toward the doors each time they opened. It had been an hour and a half since Lumas had gone to pick up Grace and he hadn't so much as called to explain his delay. If it had taken twenty minutes to get to the office and twenty minutes to get back, they should have returned forty-five minutes ago. Markey had called the office and learned that Lumas had retrieved Grace already, so they were lost somewhere between the headquarters building and the hospital. He knew Lumas was responsible enough to contact him if there was an unnecessary delay, but now, with no word from him, he began to worry that there might be some underhanded sabotage at play.

Resolved to get to the bottom of the mystery, Markey contacted dispatch and requested she try Lumas's car radio. As with the information from the office and trying his cell phone, there was no response from the police radio. As a last resort, he set off Lumas's pager; but after ten minutes, when there was no return call, Markey wondered how he might try to contact him otherwise.

Five minutes later, his own pager went off, startling him, and he jumped at the sudden vibration thrumming excitedly at his belt. He snatched at the device and looked at the display, but he couldn't place the numbers as any he recognized. That much didn't matter, since Lumas might be calling from a foreign number, and Markey rushed to the nurse's station to ask to burrow her phone.

"Someone paged me," he said to the person who answered the line.

"Sergeant Markey, it's Monsignor O'Dwyer. I'm afraid something terrible is going to happen and you're the only person I could think of to call."

"What is it, Father?"

"Adam was just here. He was talking nonsense, about how a man named Malachi Drudge had killed his family and was after Grace's baby. He mentioned that he was going after him. He asked me to hear his confession, and from what I gather, I suspect he might be prepared to die tonight."

"What?" Markey transferred the phone to his other ear in order to turn around and face the emergency room door. The need for Lumas to show up right then was growing more and more imperative by the minute. He didn't want to miss the overweight, uncouth brute when he made his dramatic entrance. "Is he still there?"

"He left about five minutes ago. I think he's headed for wherever this Drudge fellow might be."

Like a lot of people with an interest in the power base of the city, Markey knew who Malachi Drudge was and where he lived, which was in the Spatial Tower. He also knew the building was virtually impregnable. He wasn't so much worried about the business mogul's personal safety as he was interested in finding Adam Mogilvy. That kid had escaped from him three times in two days, and it was becoming a matter of personal pride and professional vanity to track him down. When he finally got his hands on that slippery young man, he was going to have him bound hand and foot. After that, he wasn't going to let him go until he was processed at the county jail.

"What makes you think he's prepared to die?" Markey asked, anxiety and excitement building in his gut.

"Perhaps you don't understand the significance of the confession, Sergeant, but Adam expressed a desire to be absolved of his sins."

"You're right, Father, I don't understand the significance; but if it's significant to you, then I can appreciate it. If he happens to show up again, would you call me immediately?"

"Yes, of course," he assured, then tempered his tone to a more fearful demeanor. "I'm concerned about Adam's mental state. I don't want to see him get hurt."

"If you can arrange his peaceful surrender, I'll guarantee he's taken safely into custody. He won't get hurt that way."

"I'll do what I can."

Markey hung up and glanced at the entrance to the emergency room, hoping for Lumas to walk through the door at that moment; or the next, or even the one after that. But certainly not five or ten minutes from now, or—God forbid—thirty or forty from then. He needed Grace to be safe in Doctor Perez's hands and Lumas by his side when he went after Mogilvy, and he didn't have the time or patience to be playing stupid games like this.

He waited only another minute before he snatched up the phone. He called the police complaint desk and asked for a patrol car to be sent to the hospital.

The complaint desk operator stuttered on a reply. "I'm sorry, Sergeant, but we don't have a free unit available. The rioting started up again toward the north part of town. We've put the district on alert and have the day shift being called in early."

Shit, he thought, dropping the phone back in its cradle. Two nights in only so many days. The riots had never happened within such short intervals of each other before. Things must be heating up somewhere.

But for now, he had to get to the Tower, and it looked like a taxi would be the best route.

Adam exited the tunnels through a door sealed from inside the underground passageways. He'd spent several precious minutes working at the rocks and debris blocking the accessway. Once he breached the gap, he suddenly found himself in the bowels of the basement of the Spatial Tower. It was his first time ever to attempt such an invasion, and he understood there would be no turning back once he was inside. Malachi Drudge would probably know his every move from here on out. He was probably reveling at this new turn of events, goaded into the challenge by the audacity of someone breaking into his realm. But Adam was dead-set on reaching Drudge despite any obstacles placed in his way, and he forged on without hesitation.

With his ears on high alert for the slightest sound, he wended his way through the twists and turns of the monolith's subterranean levels. It was cold in the deepest depths of the sinister building and he was dressed in nothing but a torn shirt and pants. The cold easily permeated his meager clothes and winnowed its way into his body. His sneakers hardly made any noise as he raced through the empty and desolate corridors lacking any semblance to the luxurious structure still several levels above. As he reached the darkened stairwell leading up to a door, he hesitated only long enough to search out the dangers he could sense. Above, in the parking garage, several pigeons had flown through the bars of the parking garage gate and perched on water and ventilation pipes. From their vantage point, he saw nothing laying in ambush behind the door at the top of the stairwell.

He hurried up the steps and pushed experimentally on the bar, fearing it would be locked. But the door swung open, taking him with it until he stood in the silent parking garage. Slowly, he stepped away from the door and let it swing shut behind him, clanging resoundingly. He glanced around and took in the total desolation of the shadowed depths, feeling chilled by more than just the cold climate. There was only one car parked near the elevators across the stretch of the garage. Outside, a deluge had begun to fall, and the sound of streaming water pouring through the gutter made for a confining ambience.

With his senses attuned to the birds stationed around him, his eyes focused on the lone vehicle in the garage. He recognized it as the police sedan he'd been in earlier that night. Staring at it, he suddenly understood that an alliance must exist between Drudge and the police. It infuriated him that he'd been betrayed by the law everyone believe to be incorruptible. He himself had been raised in a home where the police were respected and revered. By God, he'd always held them to be next to infallible in their judgment and virtues. But here was proof that his faith had been displaced, his belief that the men who upheld the law in this city wouldn't sacrifice their principles for material gain.

He reached the car without incident. Each door was locked but he could see his coat still on the back seat. With a sense of rage building, he lashed out with his foot and kicked in the back window, and from the back seat, retrieved his coat and checked how many weapons still remained. Not as many as he would have preferred but enough to arm himself against Drudge. After all, that was why he'd come.

He slipped his arms into the familiar sleeves and shrugged the coat over his wounded shoulder, relishing the warmth it brought. One less thing to worry about as he strode toward the elevators.

Where he suffered a sudden apprehension about entering one of those mechanical contraptions. If he took the elevator to the upper levels of the Tower, he wouldn't have the benefit of the birds around him.

Feeling the ominous power of the elevator drawing him toward its invitation, Adam backed away. He glanced at the door to the stairwell instead. The door itself wasn't locked, which built on his anxiety. When he looked up into the darkened reaches of the stairwell, with only an intermittent bulb set at each landing, he decided there wasn't any safe way to call Drudge out.

He shook his head of its nagging sense of warning and attacked the stairs with a determination that sent energy surging through his bruised and battered body. He wasn't sure which level he should stop at, but he knew the lower floors were merely a ruse for a functioning business. The higher levels—much higher than he was treading past now—were where Drudge's true enterprise existed. That was where he would find the minion lord.

He climbed higher and higher, using the cold metal railing to haul himself up, taking two steps at a time. He kept his ears pricked for doors opening or an ambush setting up on the higher landings, but nothing came at him. His eyes remained on the dim lighting of the next level as he trudged even higher still.

Sergeant Markey had the cab drop him off in front of the Spatial Tower. He hesitated getting out in the pouring rain and cursed the weather forecasters for not warning him to bring a coat. Reluctantly, he got out and ran for the awning covering the front doors, seeking shelter from the rain. There he shook out his hair and futilely wiped at the wetness spattering his suit. Grimacing, he turned to the dark recesses of the smoked-glass front door and cupped his hand over his eyes to peer into the lobby.

It was deathly quiet within, and Markey wondered if he might not be on the wrong track. Adam Mogilvy might have professed an interest in killing Malachi Drudge but there was no way he could breach the security of such a finely appointed building. With the rain at its most torrential, it was possible the young man might have postponed his assassination attempt for a drier time.

Regardless, Markey had to make sure the kid wasn't lurking anywhere around the building, staking it out or surveilling it. He pulled out his gun and held it ready, not about to be taken by surprise this time. Traffic of any kind was non-existent, and Markey hugged the building as he left the protection of the awning. Without the protective canvas overhead, he was immediately drenched by the falling deluge.

He skirted a corner to a small intersecting side street. That too was deserted. Only a small stretch of pavement lay before him as it led to another main road behind the Tower. There was another entrance to the building on that side of the street and he'd have to check it before he felt completely satisfied that Adam Mogilvy wasn't around.

When he entered the side street, he was slightly relieved to find that the rain wasn't as brutal here as it was on windward side of the building, although it still drilled down in sheets from the parapet. A ramp led down into the parking garage, and Markey paused to make sure the door and gate were secure before moving on. He peered through the bars to make sure there was nothing amiss and drew up short.

He clutched the bars with his free hand as he stared at the police sedan parked near the elevators. The rear passenger window was smashed out and shards of glass were lying on the floor like diamonds in the fluorescent lights.

"Fuck me," Markey cursed.

He tried to lift the metal gate but it wouldn't budge. Once again, he cursed and stepped back to look around. His eyes settled on a door with a small window beside the garage gate. Wire mesh acted as a security feature for the window. There were probably contacts in the glass to an alarm system in case the glass was broken, as well as contacts on the door jamb, which was just fine with him. He could use a little backup right about now.

He pointed his pistol at the strike plate and fired three rounds at it. Three loud blasts resounded in the small side street between the two buildings. Wood splintered and metal sparked where the bullets dug out a hole in the jamb and distorted the lock. He pulled on the door and found it still held, although it rattled in its frame. Another well-placed shot further warped the locking mechanism, and the door pulled free from the frame.

With a feeling of dread, Markey stepped into the parking garage, out of the rain. He trotted across the vast empty space, toward the sedan, rain dripping from his sodden clothes, his shoes squishing loudly. He held out his gun to cover the inside of the car as he sidled cautiously up to it, aware that at any minute someone might pop up and shower him with a hail of bullets. But the interior of the car was empty, the back seat sparkling with the thick shards of glass.

Markey spun around, looking intently at the ominous shadows formed by the support pillars and alcoves. He listened to detect any movement. Only the water from his sopped clothes dripping to the cold concrete made any noise. He shrugged out of his wet coat and threw it on the hood of the car, then ran to the bank of elevators.

Christopher hurried out the back door of the county public archives and allowed the door to lock behind him. He pulled up short as the rain pelted him like eggs thrown by mischievous kids. Sputtering at the shock, he stepped back under the eaves until he realized it wasn't eggs being thrown, but harmless rain.

He looked around the side street at the torrential downpour and caught his driver sitting behind the wheel of the car, reading a paperback. Christopher hailed him with a shout and a wave, but just then a peal of thunder drowned him out. Cursing, he tried his call again, only to learn that the rumble of thunder hadn't made any difference in whether or not his driver heard him the first time. The man was oblivious to his presence.

"Lazy slob," Christopher cursed as he bundled up inside his business jacket and darted out from under the eaves, wincing as the cold rain struck the back of his neck and sent chills directly into his bones. He ran awkwardly to the car, reached the back door, and pulled on the handle. The door resisted his tug.

Christopher screeched and pounded on the car's roof to demand admittance. There was a momentary delay as his driver put his book down and ducked just enough to look out the side window to see who was making such a racket. When he saw who it was, he popped the door locks and allowed Christopher to clamber into the car with vehement curses.

"Sir, why didn't phone ahead so I could pick you up at the door," the driver said, looking back at him ingratiatingly.

"No matter, William," Christopher said, needing to keep his temper in check. He wasn't supposed to seem rattled by recent events. He shivered like a dog shaking off water and fluffed his jacket out around him, sweeping his hands down his sleeves as if he was simply smoothing out the creases. His jacket was in worse shape than having hung wrong from a coat hanger and it would need more than a cursory swiping.

"Home, sir?"

Christopher thought about that. It would seem the natural response at this point. But there were still many things to do before the night was over. Eventually, he had to supply his fingerprints to the police, but before that, he had to speak to Drudge. He had to tell the man that the police were demanding his prints for comparison to those found in the suite at the Rialto. If Drudge hadn't sanitized the room, Christopher was going to take his chances with the police and come clean, incriminating evidence in Drudge's possession be damned.

"No, William, I've still got some research to do. No rest for the weary, and all," he muttered, looking out the window at the black, soggy night and wishing it would end. He dreaded his visit to the Tower.

"Then we're off, sir?"

"What, um, yes," he said, snapping back to attention. "I need to make a stop at the Spatial Tower, if you can manage that."

"Yes, sir, I think I can," William said, putting the car in drive and pulling away from the curb.

There wasn't much traffic in the area, and Christopher wondered why. He glanced anxiously around and muttered something to that effect. His driver glanced curiously in the rearview mirror. When Christopher caught his look, he abruptly shut up.

"What was that, sir?" William queried politely.

"Nothing, William, just talking to myself. Nothing important."

"If you say so, sir," he replied and returned his eyes to the road.

"I was just wondering where all the traffic was," Christopher said, feeling uneasy for having been caught muttering.

"This late at night, sir? And with all this rain? It's a wonder anyone's still out."

Christopher glanced out the window and saw for the first time that deep night had truly fallen. He checked his watch and was surprised by the time. Somehow, it had gotten away from him while he was in the county archives. No wonder William had been engrossed in his book. He'd simply grown bored waiting for him.

William attended his driving from that point forward, without any interest in his employer, while Christopher studied him with growing concern. Something niggled at the back of his mind, and it took a while before it came to the forefront. When it did, Christopher lurched forward and gripped the front seat with an untenable grasp. "You're in on it."

"Pardon me, sir?" William said judiciously, keeping his eyes on the road, his hands at a professionally sound two and ten o'clock.

"Drudge said you'd confirm that I was out of town for the weekend," Christopher accused, scooting closer to the edge of his seat. "He said you would vouch for my alibi,"

"Sir, I apologize for the misunderstanding, if there is one," William said with unmitigated courtesy. "But I don't know what you're talking about."

"Of course you do," Christopher countered with growing frustration. "Drudge said you'd cover for me for the weekend."

"Yes, sir, I always cover for you during your . . . trips out of town. I hope my loyalty is not being brought into question."

"You bastard," Christopher railed, slamming his hands down on the back of the driver's seat, jostling William a little. "How dare you conspire against me? I pay your salary. I've given you end of the year bonuses. I've sent your family Thanksgiving turkeys, you ingrate!"

"But, sir," William countered, finally struggling with driving and arguing, while at the same time trying to remain professional. "I've not conspired against you. I don't understand what you're talking about. I only know what I'm told."

"And what were you told, Brutus?" Christopher challenged acidly.

"About this weekend?" William sputtered.

"Yes, you dolt, about this weekend," Christopher shouted, his hands again wrenching on the driver's seat, giving it a rattle. When William looked in the rearview mirror, he saw something of a madman in the reflection of the district attorney's face.

"I was told you were unexpectedly called out of town by an opportunistic encounter with a Texas businessman. The gentleman was interested in expanding his coffeehouse franchise in the city and wanted to talk politics with you. I inquired if I would be needed to return Mrs. Fitzpatrick home, but I was told that had already been taken care of. I hadn't thought there was a problem with that."

Christopher stared fitfully at William's stricken expression in the mirror, his own eyes bobbing in their sockets. He remembered what Drudge had said about his driver's corroboration and what William said now. The man could have been duped, as well. After all, he was just an underling, a servant, someone of no importance at all.

"Um, of course, I'm sorry, William, I'm mistaken. I thought . . ." he struggled over what to say, realizing he should come up with an explanation to excuse his pre-emptive behavior, but he was unable to think of one. He shamefully sank back in his seat and crossed his arms, not defensively, but in abashment. "I didn't mean those gruff words. They were said in anger. I profusely apologize."

"No worries, sir," William said, returning to his well-known efficiency as a highly referred chauffeur. "Miscommunications happen."

"Yes, they do," Christopher concurred quickly, hoping to smooth things over. He pulled his wet coat around him and shrank into it, feeling no warmer for its embrace.

In short order, they arrived at the Spatial Tower. The rain was still a deluge. William reached for an umbrella and made to get out of the car, but Christopher touched him on the shoulder and held him back. "Don't bother, William, I'll handle it. Just let me take the umbrella myself."

"You'll get sopped, sir," William protested.

"I'm already sopped; it'll make no difference now. And I don't want the public to perceive me as a dandy," he said with recovery.

"No, sir, you wouldn't want that. But the building looks deserted for the evening," he observed.

"It's not," Christopher said, taking the umbrella and preparing to use it as his shield when he finally exited the car. He knew Drudge had residences in the tower and should be in attendance on a night like this. In the very least, his servants would be there. Christopher would find a way into the building if he had to break in to do so. "Wait for me, William. We'll have one more stop after this before we call it a night."

"Yes, sir."

CHAPTER THIRTY-FIVE

Grace hesitated leaving the elevator, even though Lumas stood off to the side and motioned for her to do so. She gave him a scathing look of accusation. Gritting her teeth, she stepped into a brightly lit and lushly carpeted corridor. Great oak doors were set in alabaster walls, and elaborate crystal fixtures in the walls replaced recessed lighting in the ceiling. She had to admit that she was overwhelmed by the sense of grandeur, even as Lumas walked up to her.

"Pretty fancy, huh?" he said.

She showed her disconsolation with a bitter sidelong glance. With a sigh of resignation, he held his hand out for her to walk down the hall, toward a pair of ornate double doors at the end of the corridor. As she approached them, they seemed to grow larger and more impressive, and she felt herself dwindle in proportion to them.

Lumas hastened ahead of her and knocked loudly. In no time, both doors opened inward, grasped at the carved handles by a large gentleman dressed in a smart black business suit. He said nothing in welcome but stepped aside as Lumas officiously took Grace's elbow and guided her into the room.

Grace stared in awe at the luxury surrounding her: the rich gleaming marble her soles squeaked on; the high ceiling of pristine white; the alabaster columns supporting sculpted busts and pieces of art; the gently scrolled walls covered with priceless paintings and tapestries; and the brocaded furnishings from Queen Anne's period. White and gold surrounded colors of accent. Light was provided by track lighting fixtures, but a massive chandelier of hundreds of tear drop crystals hung from a chain in the center of the receiving room. Grace's face turned up to stare at the million dollar trappings, shamefully aware that she was wearing a pullover and sweat pants that didn't even belong to her.

Lumas brought her dazed meandering to a halt once they were fully within the room. He looked dutifully around for someone to greet them other than the servant. There was no one but the man who'd opened the door, and when Lumas turned around to ask him where Drudge was, he found that the door was now shut and the man had disappeared. He looked over to another door leading to other rooms and then to a recessed alcove where a parlor appeared to be. Nothing.

He motioned for Grace to stay where she was while he moved to a terrace overlooking the city above the park.

Grace shivered from a fear of the silence. She'd felt minimally comforted by Lumas's hand on her arm but became less so the farther he walked away. She watched him intently as he pulled aside thick gold drapes and glanced out the glass.

A cold hand suddenly lay upon Grace's arm. She shrieked and spun around to face the man who'd touched her, startling her so abruptly. Her hand went up to still her fluttering heart while she tried to catch her breath. Frozen, she stared with open-eyed fear and awe at the man who stood before her.

He had a beautifully etched face of white skin, with sharp, angular features and a high forehead. Gleaming black hair combed back from a face that was chiseled perfect and caught at the nape of a delicate and sinuous neck. Slightly exotic features made him appear partly Mediterranean, although he was too pale to pull that heritage off completely. He was dressed in a black crew neck shirt with no emblem denoting his family crest or monogram. Black pleated slacks fit a narrow waist. His shoulders were powerful and broad, and his chest filled his shirt with well-defined musculature. His age was indeterminate, yet not as old as she would have expected him to be for such a colossal business magnate.

"Forgive me, I didn't mean to give you such a start," Malachi Drudge apologized. His voice was musical, cultured, and smooth. A slight accent of European origin confirmed that he might be from the Mediterranean after all.

"You didn't," she stuttered defensively, her eyes riveted to the exquisiteness of his face. She tried to fathom the evil in him—to see the cruel manifestation of viciousness Adam insisted was in him. But by the casual way his face was set and how he blinked so naturally, she couldn't imagine him as anything but an arrogant multi-millionaire with eccentricities. Adam must have mistaken Drudge's hand in his family's death; and Grace began to wonder if her erstwhile champion of the past few days might actually suffer from delusions and have imagined it all.

"You must forgive me for all the misunderstanding," he said as he casually motioned for her to take a seat on a brocaded couch. He moved with her, laying a hand on the small of her back as they walked. Where he made contact, Grace felt a shiver of excitement run up her spine. "I had no idea the measures by which my ill-advised men would act in carrying out my requests." He waited until she took a seat in one corner of the couch and then gracefully settled on the other end himself. "My meaning was taken out of context by my incompetent employees. I wish I could take back all the pain and confusion you had to suffer because of them."

Grace suddenly felt compelled to relieve him of his guilt, which was evident on his face. "I guess two many cooks in the kitchen truly can spoil the pot."

He smiled bright white and perfect teeth. "Simply put. May I get you something to drink? A bite to eat? You must be famished."

He turned to Lumas as the detective slowly made his way into the sitting area, coming back from the window. "Detective Lumas, would you care for something to drink?"

Lumas shook his head, saying nothing. It was apparent that he didn't want to stay any longer than he had to. In fact, not even to receive his blood money.

"Then let me settle up with you so you can be on your way," Drudge said. "Mr. Bentley!"

A man in a suit and tie came in from the parlor. "Yes, Mr. Drudge?"

"Would you see Detective Lumas down and settle up with him?"

"Yes, sir, of course," Bentley said, motioning slightly with his hand for Lumas to follow him out of the apartment.

Lumas pressed his elbow against the gun nestled in his shoulder holster. "Mr. Drudge," he said tremulously, "I've left word at my office where I've gone.

"Good for you," Drudge answered patronizingly, leaving Lumas feeling stupid for saying anything of the sort.

Lumas dropped his head and walked toward the front door, falling in step behind Bentley as he exited.

"Strange and paranoid police officer," Drudge said lightly, as if to himself. Then, addressing Grace, he said, "But you never said if you wanted anything to drink?"

"No," she answered quickly, afraid to accept anything from Drudge for fear it would mean she was entering into some undefined pact to do something she normally wouldn't agree to.

"If you should change your mind, just let me know," he said. He allowed a silence to pass between them, a silence that was serene and comfortable as he leaned back and relaxed his body.

From her rigid position, Grace watched his languid posture and was reminded of a cat. When he spoke again, his head was resting against the back of the couch, his eyes staring at the ceiling, at a Renaissance mural painted with classical strokes in the detailed rendition of masters. "I'm just a businessman, Grace. A ruthless businessman, I'll admit. Some people even call me a devil of a scoundrel, but I'm just a businessman. And a successful one to boot."

She merely looked at him without knowing what to say. He seemed weary all of a sudden, and a sigh escaped him as he lifted his head to look at her. She held his eyes as an act of defiance, even though she didn't understand what she was opposing.

"I can understand what Christopher sees in you, my dear. You have a beauty beyond compare; but you also exude an essence of strength and nobility. Qualities that cannot be acquired no matter how hard someone tries, but which are inherent only in certain people. You are truly a goddess."

Her mouth stuttered on what to say—her ego extolled with her humility tendered—so she said nothing. She feared if she said anything, she would dispel his compliments and pin herself as a babbling fool. Rather than do that, she opted for silence and lowered her eyes in a look of coquettish embarrassment.

Drudge leaned over and touched her hand, his gesture soliciting comfort. "I know he dismissed you when you truly needed him."

She looked up to meet his pandering gaze. His eyes were a deep black—depthless, in fact, but reflective on the surface—and she felt culled by them.

"A man should never reject a woman out of his own arrogance and fear."

The color of his eyes seemed to soften, although they remained black as night. But in softening, they appeared to take on a hue of midnight blue that swirled in the inky black like gasoline in water, shimmering with an iridescent glimmer too compelling to watch. Understanding and consolation were there, but so were cunning and manipulation, although she wasn't put off by them. She could easily presume those were attributed to his business savvy and ruthlessness, which must certainly be a side of him that made him successful in the corporate world. Consequently, he must have a private, personal side that was ruled by compassion and sincerity, and it was that side of him that she was—God forbid—attracted to.

"He needs to be held accountable for his actions," Drudge said. "He needs to make right what he believes to be wrong." The depths of his eyes and the lilt of his voice were intoxicating, and Grace nodded her head without realizing it. "But," Drudge said more ardently, sweeping an index finger up to get her attention and draw it away from her meditative, reflective state. "He's still the best man for the position of mayor in this grand city. He only needs to be held on a short leash."

Grace shook her head to clear her mind of confusion.

"Don't you think?"

She stammered on what to say—what to think—but there was a morass of sludge keeping clarity at bay. Slowly, she nodded. "Yes."

"As a businessman, I support local government that would sanction my own agenda—as do all voting constituents. I want the best man in office who will protect my interests in this city, and those interests are concentrated on promoting my success here." He gave her a look of unconscionable superiority when she only stared back at him gaped-mouthed. Sighing, he said, "Grace, just because a candidate is morally reprehensible doesn't mean he'll be a deplorable leader." She blinked vacuously at what he was saying. "I'll endorse the most availing candidate to my interests. At the moment, Christopher has the most shining qualities for that office. His campaign platform parallels my own needs. I'd stand to gain the most with him in office." He looked keenly at her. "As would you."

"Why's that?" she barely managed to get out.

"You hold the key to his success," Drudge said. "That tiny fetus you carry can ruin his chances for office. I propose we offer Christopher an option he can't refuse."

She looked at him, fascinated by his offer, although she couldn't understand why. "What option?"

"I'll endorse his campaign for office and support his child with generous stipends if he recognizes where his allegiance should be. As a matter of course, you'll be paid handsomely for your part in this. Consider yourself a very lucky woman to be a part of this endeavor."

"I don't feel lucky," she said, drawing some depth out of her shallow comprehension.

"Once again, my apologies."

"Are you proposing to blackmail him?"

"Business propositions and political endorsements are always based on the terms of blackmail. I'm going to accept a lifelong commitment in supporting his child if he'll only remember where that support comes from. I simply expect him to protect my interests in this magnificent city."

"And what are those interest?" she asked, her eyes narrowing. "If they're so benign, why would you need to blackmail him?"

"I'm sure Christopher wouldn't find my interests offensive or degenerative, but they might be contradictory to other supportive factions' interests. So let's just call the child my insurance." Drudge spoke smoothly, the talk of business easy and commonplace for him. "Grace, look at it this way. Christopher blames you for becoming pregnant and doesn't want anything to do with this child. He wants it aborted. I, on the other hand, want the child to live a long and fruitful life. Of course, the child is my ace in the hole, but we all benefit from this measure. Christopher gets to be mayor; your baby will be raised with all the comforts of high society; and you will be richly rewarded for your inconvenience. But more importantly, my interests in this city will be protected. What else could any of us want?"

"It's still blackmail," she said, although she wasn't vehement in her argument.

"Listen, Grace, the choice is yours. And Christopher's, of course. He can be mayor or remain simply the district attorney. That's his choice. You can have your child grow to full term and be delivered into a healthy environment, or you can give in to Christopher's demands and have it aborted. That's your choice. I can propose this to the both of you, or put my support behind another candidate and crush Christopher in the process. That's my choice. We all have choices to make."

"But you're *forcing* him to make a choice," she said resolutely, gaining mettle the more he talked.

"He would give *you* no choice," Drudge replied fiercely, his hand suddenly clutching hers, imposing passion to his argument. His touch was electric. His eyes softened to include sympathy for her predicament. "You have to understand that your relationship with him will never be what it used to be. A man who believes, even for the slightest moment, that a woman became pregnant to win him over will never trust her again."

"But I didn't!" she denied.

His grip grew tight and possessive, supportive. "I know, I know," he assured compassionately, his expression simpering with empathy.

Grace felt chilled by the whole prospect, thinking about the proposition. She would have the opportunity to live comfortably, the hazards of her working-class lifestyle removed by the regular delivery of a monthly stipend. Her child was guaranteed support by a means she didn't have the ability to provide herself. At best, she could only hope to live at poverty level, since she was barely above that with her dead-end job now. By accepting Malachi Drudge's proposal, she envisioned her child delivered by the best obstetrician, cared for by the best nannies, sent to the best schools. She reveled in the idea that she might never have to work again, that she could stay home and raise her child the way she wanted. She even envisioned finding love in the realms of the upper levels of society, since she was guaranteed a place there if she accepted Drudge's offer.

Drudge stroked her arm, his eyes dreamy and his head cocked to one side, admiring her. "You know, Grace, I've always envied Christopher. You're a lovely young woman. He's a fool for giving you up."

Again, she looked down, complimented by his words, yet feeling awkward because of them.

"It's hard for a man of my power and wealth to find a sincere relationship. It's difficult to separate the genuine from the artifice. I've watched you with Christopher for quite a while, I must admit. I could see how close you were to him, completely dedicated to what could only be described as your love for him—but to a fault." Her eyes lifted to his as he said seductively, "He's a fool."

She felt him moving closer, drifting forward and bringing a heat with him that made her gut quiver. His hand moved more surely up her arm, rubbing her shoulder, and then caressing her bare throat, sending an electric thrill through her body. His face leaned forward—boldly and brashly—and his lips brushed lightly against hers. She closed her eyes with a dreamy solicitation to prolong the moment. In response, his hand tickled the tiny hairs on the nape of her neck, enticing goose bumps to crop up on her arms and a heat to spread between her legs, embarrassing but unrepentant. His kiss became a gentle plying of his tongue across the swell of her lips, and her mouth opened partly, deliriously.

He pulled back and gave her a close look. "I could come to love supporting you, Grace."

His words brought bursts of emotions to her. Christopher had never used the word love before, and he had always left her lacking because of it.

"There's only one thing I'd like you to do for me." His expression was supplicating as his fingers stroked her cheek. "The young man who helped you avoid my invitation, would you tell me who he is?"

Grace pulled back from his suave seduction, her eyes shifting back and forth as she surveyed his face, noticing something intrinsic in its solicitation. Something frightening started warming inside her gut and it left her with an uncomfortable feeling—an eerie sensation that she was being manipulated and had no control over resisting his influence, which made her panic. A nudge in the back of her mind made her think of the man who'd risked his life for her several times over, with no reward for his daring. Although everyone seemed to think Adam was crazy, she felt, at worst, he was only misguided by the tragedy of his past.

But she wouldn't say his name. Somewhere inside her, she knew Adam's name in the hands of this man would be disastrous. However, despite knowing that, her lips formed a whisper of it, which parted on a breath.

Drudge pulled back abruptly, all of a sudden dropping his seduction. He smiled, and the curl of his lips and the opalescent gleam of his teeth made Grace shiver. "Adam? Adam *Mogilvy*? My prodigal son? I wondered why he'd never made it to the other side that day."

Grace gasped and clutched at the couch cushions. "How . . . I didn't say his name."

"Yes, you did," he said, his long manicured fingers reaching out like tentacles to stroke her face. Grace felt the coldness of his touch and wondered if there was any blood in him at all to warm his flesh—or his heart.

"Why do you want to know who he is? He can't be anything to you."

Again, Drudge grinned, as if he kept his secrets to himself. He leaned conspiratorially forward and said, "He's an old acquaintance of mine."

She looked at him through narrowly suspicious eyes, recalling Adam's story of his family's death. She wanted to know Drudge's own account of what happened that night. Needed to know it. "H-how is . . . he . . . an old acquaintance?"

Drudge pulled back to sit against the couch, settling in comfortably and crossing his legs. "We had a deal some time ago and he failed to keep his side of the bargain."

"Wh-what deal was that?" she asked hesitantly.

He waved aside her interest, finding it inconsequential. "Just a wager between two sportsmen."

But his elusiveness made her more curious, and bolder to inquire deeper. "What kind of wager?"

He shrugged noncommittally. "I gave him the first chance to kill me, but he couldn't do it." Thinking on something for a moment, as Grace gasped and stared in open-eyed horror, he finally said, "But it seems I missed my opportunity as well." He slapped his hands on his thighs and leaned forward on the couch. "I guess that means it's back to being his turn."

Grace's waxen expression was one of appall, pale and pasty in the brilliant lighting. She suddenly saw Drudge more capable of fitting the role Adam had portrayed for him than what she'd hoped he fit only minutes ago. "Did you kill his family?"

He looked at her with a sidelong glance, a crooked smile speaking for his unspoken reply. She whimpered once and buried her face in her hands, sobbing for all her foolishness, and her desperation at finding herself at Drudge's mercy.

With a snort of derision, Drudge said, "This should be easy."

Lumas entered the elevator when Bentley stood aside and waited for him to precede him into the car. In doing so, Lumas surreptitiously unbuttoned his coat and crossed his arms under his armpits, tucking both hands inside his jacket. His right hand unsnapped his gun holster and gripped the butt of his pistol. Behind him, Bentley strode into the car and turned to face the closing door at an angle.

The extravagance of the décor turned the two men into dozens of reflected images in the mirrored walls. As the doors came together, Muzak began to play, making for an eerie setting that was irritating and a bit histrionic. Lumas was sure the trip from the fifty-fourth floor to the parking garage would most likely result in one of their deaths, and he was determined if it was anyone's, it would be Bentley's.

The soft ding of the elevator passing each floor was annoying, as was the instrumental of an easily recognizable tune from the seventies. Lumas had to fight the urge to peek at the numbers. He knew as the numbers decreased the chances of a fateful opportunity for a showdown would increase. He tried to count the dings but soon lost count as he intently watched his escort watching him.

Bentley remained aloof in his casual posture, affording himself the luxury of watching the numbers tick off the floors as the elevator descended. He rocked back and forth on the balls of his feet, his movement distracting and annoying to Lumas, who desperately wanted to check the numbers but didn't dare take his eyes off the man. Bentley's liberty to be at ease irritated Lumas and made him even more nervous than if they were both wired tight.

Shortly, Bentley used his right hand to smooth back a lock of hair from his forehead, drawing Lumas's eyes up to focus on that hand. In that brief second of distraction, Bentley's whip-like arm produced a gun and extended it toward Lumas's face. The detective's expectant and practiced draw matched Bentley's to a nano-second. Beside the dozens of reflections, they mirrored each other except in their expressions. Bentley's vacant grin showed his lackadaisical attitude to the fatalistic confrontation, while Lumas's fear glistened on the perspiration of his forehead.

"I guess this comes down to who's got the greater trigger pull," Lumas said, his arm surprisingly level and steady.

Bentley's grin widened. Lumas wondered if there was even a brain in his thick skull to reason with. The dings of the passing floors continued and the Muzak of a Barry Manilow tune—sans vocals—unnerved him. Lumas's brain subconsciously calculated that the number of dings had far surpassed the number of floors they'd started from, but he didn't dwell too long on it. Instead, he focused intently on the finger controlling the trigger of his adversary's weapon. When it began to contract, Lumas knew it was over. His own finger fired off as many rounds as possible before Bentley's gun did the same.

"Virtue is just an option, Grace," Drudge said portentously. "You can take it or leave it."

Markey watched the flash of light illuminate the numbers above the elevator door as the car ascended. Accompanying him in his ride were the lilting sounds of

Muzak piped in from a hidden speaker in the corner. His own gun hung loosely at his side as he tried to decide which floor he should bring the elevator to a stop. He suspected Drudge's living quarters would be at the penthouse level, providing stunning and majestic views of the city, but there was no certainty of it. If the millionaire was as eccentric as everyone professed, he might have chosen to live in the basement, for all anyone knew.

The odds were more in his favor that the penthouse was where he would find Drudge. What he'd do once he got there was another thing. Surely, he would introduce himself and explain how Drudge's life was in danger, with a police detective and a homicide witness suspiciously missing from a police car parked in the locked garage creating quite a mystery to unravel. Markey suspected the business magnate might be angry at first, but when it was explained how his life was in jeopardy, Markey was sure Malachi Drudge would cooperate fully.

Or not.

As the elevator ascended, Markey glanced at his face reflected in the mirrored wall. It was a glass construction with the brightness of incandescent bulbs creating shimmering edges to the brass accents. He studied how haggard his features had become, the glistening bruise on his cheek, the hollows under his eyes, and the sharpness of his cheekbones from his lack of healthy eating. He needed a vacation. After this was all over, that was exactly what he was going to do.

As he was staring at his aged and beaten face, several gunshots thundered from close by. He jumped and spun in the direction of the blasts, immediately throwing his arms up to futilely shelter himself from the rounds crashing through the mirror. One right after the other, from the top of the elevator to the floor in a matter of one or two seconds. Then silence—except for the maudlin rendition of a classic Cher ballad—as he slowly removed his arms from his face and stared at the jagged succession of holes in the glass. The mirror was not shattered, but it reflected a series of similar holes on the opposite wall.

Markey regained his senses and punched the STOP button on the control panel. The elevator came to a quick jolt as he jabbed repeatedly at the OPEN button. His gun was ready and he waited to lunge from the elevator when the doors parted. Finally, the doors opened and Markey lurched out.

With horror, he saw the awesome space of nothingness just beyond the shaft even as he took his first step from the elevator.

Christopher pounded incessantly on the front doors of the Spatial Tower. He was gratefully saved from being drowned in the downpour by the canvas awning over the front sidewalk. Of course, no answer came from his knocking and he peered through the glass in the hopes of seeing someone—anyone—tending the lobby. But despite how desperately he looked through the glass, he couldn't see if the place was occupied and had to assume it wasn't. Grumbling to himself, he looked around and thought about his other options in breaching the Tower.

William was watching him curiously from the curb, waiting for him to give up and return to the car. The lout was probably hoping to make an early evening of it, despite the time-and-a-half Christopher was paying him past his regular hours. The lazy ingrate.

Christopher popped the umbrella over his head and sheltered himself under it, then darted from under the awning and ran along the length of the front of the building. When he got to the corner, he turned and hugged the edge of the foundation to keep the torrent from blowing in at him. He sidled along the side of the building, looking for an alternate way in, thinking there had to be a way if the building doubled as a residence for the owner. Drudge would need a way into and out of it during non-business hours. Maybe there was even an intercom he could use to hail the businessman in his apartments and request an audience. How else would the man receive visitors when everyone else had gone home for the evening? What if he wanted pizza delivered?

Rank puddles and sodden debris filled the side street where Christopher walked. His shoes were soggy by the time he reached a metal door beside the parking garage. He ignored the door and stood before the gate, peering into the building like a child outside Fenway Park. One hand clutched the bars and tried to pull it up, but it was well-rooted in place, impenetrable. Grimacing, he tossed the umbrella aside and used both hands to pull on the gate, only to get soaked for his efforts. His fingers curled tightly around the metal bars and gave a furious rattling to them as he screamed in anger and desperation. He even kicked at the bottom of the gate, but the tip of his shoe got lodged in a recess and held him tight. He suffered a momentary sense of panic when he thought he was caught in the hold of a bear trap and tugged desperately to free himself. His foot came out of the snare with vigor and nearly pitched him off balance. He looked furtively around to see if anyone had noticed his foolishness.

No one was around, and he tried to primp himself up under the pouring rain. Somehow the whole image of him being drenched didn't bring about an air of sophistication, which he wasn't aware of. He was only concerned with how he could breach the bastion. With little hope for the obvious, he grasped the knob of the door beside the gate and gave it a good wrench, certain it would resist his efforts. To his surprise, the door flung open and nearly crashed into his face. He just had time to catch it before it gave him a serious clout on the head and knocked him unconscious.

Despite his exhilaration at finding a way in, he studied the reason for why the door opened so easily, puzzling it over. The locking device and strike plate were destroyed, and he had no idea how or why.

A sense of hesitation pulled briefly on his initiative and held him back. If the door lock was damaged, it was possible someone was attempting a burglary of the business. Christopher didn't want to get caught in the middle of a break-in where violence might erupt. He'd only come to the Tower to talk to Drudge; to seek his advice. He'd meant no criminal intent in entering the building.

Then he figured the damage to the door could have happened any time in the past and it just hadn't been noticed or fixed, yet. Or, if there were burglars in the building, perhaps he wouldn't encounter them. It was a big building and he knew where he was headed. Chances were he wouldn't run into anyone looting where he was going. Besides, it was imperative he speak to Drudge before he went to the police station for fingerprinting.

With some trepidation, Christopher went into the Tower.

CHAPTER THIRTY-SIX

Energy was draining as exhaustion and anxiousness set in. Adam knew he could only maintain this level of exertion and anticipation for a limited amount of time before succumbing to doubt. Considering that he'd have to confront Drudge's forces sooner or later, in order to get to the master himself, he'd need to conserve a significant amount of strength for that encounter. But he was angry, and his anger forced his legs to churn more determinedly up the stairs, burning his stores of reserves far too quickly. Soon, as he mounted the fortieth landing, he paused and leaned against the wall in order to regain his breath. Propped up so, he was more aware of the damage he'd suffered in the past few days. His bruised ribs, battered kidneys, strained shoulders, all seemed to fight for attention for which hurt the worst. Other than satisfying his driving compulsion for revenge, his other desire was that he could climb into bed in his loft and drop the netting around him, allowing himself a few hours of sleep. That was all he would need to be as good as new. Just a few hours. The soft warbling of his songbirds always seemed to relax him, and he yearned for them now.

Adam closed his eyes and allowed his mind to accept the vision outside the Tower. The blackness of the early morning hours was scattered with a swirling collection of winged warriors. The mood from them was nearing hysteria, and again he was the cause of their dread. They were frightened for him, terrified that he was in the enemy stronghold on his own. The viciousness of the world was about to become augmented tenfold and the evil unleashed from the Tower. Adam's covetous aim to join Claire and Marie in the hereafter was about to end with his own metamorphosis into the demon he'd been marked for.

If he was going to be pulled into Hell, he wouldn't be going under the dominion of the master. Not if he could help it. If he was going there, he would be going *with* the bastard.

A series of distant and muffled explosions jerked him out of his reverie. His eyes shifted in an effort to pinpoint where the noise came from. Gunshots from below.

He worried for Grace, knowing she was the focal point of danger in the building now. But he sensed Drudge wouldn't reduce himself to using a gun when it came to harming someone. He had more personal means of dispatching his enemies, and a gun was too remote. Adam wasn't sure what part Grace played in Drudge's plans, or if she was even his enemy, but he knew he had to get her away from him. He also knew she would be higher up, where Drudge kept his lair protected from the infringement of his public business or a ground assault, and that was where he had to go now. The gunshots were only an indication of something happening elsewhere in the building. Whatever it was, he didn't have time to investigate it.

He pushed off the wall and began to climb, drawing himself up with a reluctance to leave behind the curious happenings below.

Grace sobbed into her hands as Drudge settled more comfortably into a position beside her. His arm went around her shoulder so he could nestle her against his chest. She was weak and unable to resist, knowing if she pulled away she'd only be jerked back. She might anger him and bring about a violence similar to that which had killed Adam's family. She didn't want to provoke him. Her own child's life was at stake, and she wasn't even sure Drudge's interest in keeping it alive was genuine. He seemed to enjoy toying with people; he might only have offered his proposal to set her at ease before actually devouring her like an insect in a Venus fly trap.

She was embarrassed and ashamed for allowing herself to be seduced by his dark beauty and suave charm. In retrospect, she wished she'd slapped him for his impertinence, or at least pulled back to deny him the kiss. But she'd succumbed to his magnetism and was more the fool for it. She'd reduced herself to tears and to a debility that refused to let her defend her honor. Now she would have to sit there with his cold arm embracing her while he gleefully waited for Adam to come for her.

* * * * * *

THE UNFAITHFUL

Markey's feet slipped out from under him as he tried to keep himself from leaving the elevator. His hands shot out for a hold on anything before he could tumble into nothingness, his gun thrown from his grasp so he could grab anything—anything, at all. The pistol sailed in an arc far from the elevator, flipping end over end until it disappeared into the darkness.

The swirling debris of the cosmos slowly coalesced in random patterns around him. A deep-space cold made his flesh chill so completely that the grip he gained on the edge of the elevator was precarious and painful to maintain. He groaned with the effort to keep himself from falling into oblivion and whimpered with his mind's inability to accept such a distortion of space and location. His feet swung wildly without the support of the ground that should have been there to mark the level of another floor. But there was nothing, and the emptiness of nothing was freezing.

Markey wondered why he still breathed oxygen if there was truly nothing outside the elevator. But then he thought that what he breathed was what air he brought with him in the elevator, and soon that would be gone as it dissipated into oblivion.

His mind forced itself to focus entirely on the physical aspect of this distraction. One of his hands had managed to grip the rubber bumper set in the door, while his other arm clutched the floor up to his armpit. His swinging legs either helped or hindered him, depending on how they swung under the elevator floor.

Groaning, he twisted slightly at the hips and forced his left leg to swing up. He missed the first two attempts to hook the floor. On the third try, with the strength in his arms strained and exhausted, he finally managed to catch a toe on the edge of the elevator. Frantically, he worked his foot up and then his leg, clutching more drastically at his handholds, his fingers straining to the point where he imagined they were actually physically stretching. He grunted with the effort, adding a primal urge to it, until he finally managed to draw himself back into the elevator.

Desperate to put distance between the nauseating sense of vertigo gagging him and the gaping maw of the cosmic abyss, Markey crawled to the far corner of the elevator and clutched at the mirrored wall. He panted frantically, drawing in as much breath as he could, heedless of the possibly limited oxygen supply at his disposal.

What the hell is this, his mind exploded all at once, staring with horror at the eerie cosmos beyond the elevator doors. He thought it might be some morbid illusion, some connotation of a mental breakdown caused by poisoned air maybe. Perhaps his need for a vacation was more than just a passing whimsy.

Hell, he cursed and struggled to his feet, his back sliding against the glass of the far wall. He forced his arm to stretch as far as it would reach so he could press the CLOSE button. Obediently, the two doors met at the middle. At their closure, an instrumental version of an Abba hit picked up in mid refrain.

With the macabre scenery shut out from sight, Markey was able to recover some of his senses. It wasn't long before he envisioned that he'd imagined the whole episode. He forced himself to put the terror of the incident behind him as he focused on what lay ahead. He couldn't afford to be distracted by ludicrous thoughts of the impossible.

Should he go down and try to see what had caused the gunshots, or should he continue his ascent to the top floor to find Malachi Drudge? He pondered the question for a few minutes, then leaned forward to the control panel and pushed the button for the top floor.

Christopher traipsed across the parking garage to reach the bank of elevators. His shoes made squishing noises as he tromped across the slick concrete. A buzzing from a fluorescent bulb going out accompanied his plodding. It wasn't difficult to spot the four-door sedan and recognize it as an unmarked police car, but he got all the way abreast of it before it registered to him as being there. He pulled up sharply then to study it, giving it his full consideration by circling it with keen interest. He noticed the broken window and seemed puzzled by it, and wondered if it might be the reason why burglars had broken into the garage. On second thought, burglarizing a car seemed to be a trivial reason to go to such extent as to break into a well-fortified building. Besides, it didn't look like there was much missing from the interior, and from the presence of the trunk-mount radio, he confirmed it was a police car.

His hopes suddenly soared and plummeted, a rapid spike and decline that had his head spinning, his legs wobbling, and his balance affected by vertigo. He had to reach out to steady himself against the car. At first, he thought the unmarked sedan—clearly a detective's car—meant Malachi Drudge was being investigated for something criminal and the police were there to arrest him. But after some pondering, struggling with the hope that it might be MURDER Drudge was being charged with, Christopher theorized it could be the exact opposite. The presence of one marked sedan meant a detective, yes, but only one or two at that. Only one or two wouldn't have come to arrest or interrogate Malachi Drudge by themselves, not in this bastion of power. If anything—if an arrest was imminent for the business mogul—the police would have come in force, certainly more than just one unmarked car, probably even with a paddy wagon.

No, Drudge must have invited the police to his fortress in order to . . .

"Oh no," he whimpered, imagining Drudge handing the corkscrew over to the police, the one reputedly with his fingerprints on it. He recalled everything Drudge had told him to do that morning and how he'd behaved deplorably throughout the day. He must have done something to set Drudge off. It couldn't be for any other reason than to turn over the fabricated evidence incriminating him for the murder of a man Christopher had never seen.

THE UNFAITHFUL

If that was the case, Christopher was going to come all out and tell them about the blackmail Malachi Drudge had tried to keep him in line once he became the city's new mayor, and that it was Drudge himself who had committed the crime. There wasn't a chance in hell he was going to go down without a fight.

Christopher stumbled to the bank of elevators and pressed the call button, shifting anxiously on his feet in his impatience to have one of the elevators open and allow him in. These elevators weren't graced with a display of numbers of where the cars were currently at, so he could only wonder how long the wait would be. With growing anxiety, he discovered that even the short time it took to wait for the elevator would give Drudge that much more time to convince the authorities that they should be looking closer to home for their murderer. For that reason alone, Christopher bolted for the staircase.

Shortly thereafter, the second elevator descended to the parking garage, slowing to a stop as it came even with the ground. The doors slid open silently, revealing two inert forms slumped on either side of the elevator floor. One was a portly figure with no face. The other was an ape-like goon with its throat blown half out, but with a vacant grin still pasted on its ashen face.

Adam finally reached the fifty-fourth floor, where he pulled up short of actually mounting the landing. A surge of fury infused every cell in his body as he considered how close he was to quenching his thirst for revenge, a need that was long overdue. A flush of heat formed on the surface of his face and an uncomfortable tightness crimped his chest, making breathing somewhat burdensome. Anger flourished in his soul, and he grimaced at the thought of vanquishing his misery through the sole application of violence. Had there been any other way—justice, maybe, whether it be by man's, God's, or fate's inclination—he would have felt vindicated. But after so long in waiting, he was now the only way it was going to happen.

With resignation and resolve, Adam composed himself and pushed the door open, which took him into a lushly carpeted hallway where the walls were papered in embossed silk and lined with gold light fixtures. He surveyed the area ahead before allowing the door to shut behind him. Closed doors lined the walls up to a point halfway down the hall, at which point only a pair of ornately carved wooden doors faced him at the end.

He strode toward the double doors with a determined but careful step, one hand clutching a knife within the folds of his coat, a formidable weapon in his hand to defend against anything he might encounter along the way. But not against Drudge, for sure.

When he reached the end of the hall, he paused and stood to the side, listening to the silence within the room. He cocked his head and strained to hear anything, even the slightest breath that might have made it past the crease of the threshold. But there was nothing.

Again, he closed his eyes and watched the collective frenzy of birds circling the Tower, their various flying patterns creating a stir-crazy dance among the clouds. The closer he came to Drudge the more frantic their mood grew. He knew Sophocles would have cursed him if he knew he was making such a foolhardy frontal assault. But his mentor's advice was distinctly absent now, and he had died without providing Adam the secrets of destroying the demon they had both fought. It was Sophocles' own fault that he was in this predicament alone, and damn him for hoarding his secrets.

Adam's hand felt oddly cold and separate from his body as he grasped the ornate brass handle. There was no need to knock for an invitation; his dead family was summons enough. The latch disengaged and the door moved smoothly inward, sweeping an arc along the marble floor of what appeared to be a lavish foyer lined with pedestals of marble busts and sculptures. Paintings hung in gold-gilded frames with track lights exposing the dramatic brush strokes and swirls of long dead artists.

With a modicum of dread, he took his first step onto the marble floor, his shoes making no sound as he moved. As he entered Drudge's private apartment, he left the door open, passing through the foyer into the great room.

At first he didn't see them. The extravagance of the room overwhelmed the eye and made him overlook the two figures sitting on the Queen Anne couch; until a gasp and sniffle brought his attention back to them. Adam's anger flared when he saw Drudge sitting with his arm around Grace's shoulders, the former bearing a smug look of triumph, while the latter tried not to let a flood of tears spill from her eyes.

Adam felt an incredible urge to launch himself at the demon lord right then, but he suspected Grace had been positioned in just such a manner as to protect Drudge in case he attempted an attack.

"Well, if it isn't the prodigal son returned," Drudge said.

"Grace," Adam beckoned. "Come away from him."

Grace's face blanched as Drudge's hand rubbed her shoulder, his lips looming close to her ear and murmuring words that apparently taunted her. The tears came then, as Drudge faced Adam squarely with a smirk. "She's promised to sell me her baby."

Adam took another step toward them, his free hand going out to Grace for her to take. His expression was one of earnest determination.

"Don't look so stricken, Adam," Drudge said. "Every woman will sell her child for the right price. Claire did." He sniffed disdainfully, his eyes rolling deprecatorily. "But your little whelp was too sick to keep."

Adam thrust out his hand, his cheeks and forehead flushing red, his lips set grim around tightly clenched teeth. "Grace, come away from him!"

Drudge bolted to his feet. "Don't you dare try to take from me what is mine, you pretentious excuse for a warrior!"

Adam took a step back despite hoping to appear undaunted.

"You belong to me yourself, boy! Instead of taking your place among my minions, you've spent the last year slaughtering your brethren! You've been a tedious thorn in my side, and I've brought you here to finally pluck you out!"

Grace brought her legs up to curl into a tight ball, shrinking in size as Adam backpedaled. She buried her face in her hands and sobbed.

"Grace," Adam called out, his voice trying to sound strident, but failing. "You have to come away from him on your own."

Drudge cocked his head as if to consider Adam's impertinence, then slowly turned to consider Grace. In a genteel voice, he said, "You'll have to excuse me, Grace. This boy seems to have mistaken my home as his own. I apologize that I have to tend to him in front of you."

He regarded Adam again, his forehead furrowed with creases as his eyes scowled. His mouth was pinched into a straight line. His shoulders set squarely as he seemed to rise up another foot, but his bearing only provided the illusion of immensity. His eyes glinted with fury as they landed on the outstretched hand Adam held out for Grace.

"Have you shown her the marks I gave you?" Drudge asked maliciously. "Have you told her how you came to bear them? How you sold yourself for a chance to kill me."

Adam's eyes shifted to meet Drudge's. He knew his anger would grow to unbearable proportions if he allowed Drudge to continue to speak. He had to get Grace out of the room before he launched his attack or she'd be caught in the middle. He had to give her the opportunity to escape the Tower.

He and Drudge shared a knowing look of contention, an exchange of a promise to defeat the other. Adam's was borne out of a vengeance of human frailty, while Drudge's was fueled by the fire of superiority and indignation, a scathing hatred complimented by an arrogant knowledge that he could destroy his enemy with little effort.

"You might have avoided joining my rookery before, but it's high time you finally took your place within it now." He held his hand out toward Adam, who quickly dropped his arm and canted his body to one side, assuming a defensive posture. Drudge smirked and waggled his fingers in an openly coaxing motion. "Come on now. Come to me."

Quickening with anger, Adam fingered the knife within his coat, steeling himself to make his move, regardless of Grace's proximity. But then he felt a tenuous stroke of evil sliver through his mind, an alien implication that wasn't a part of his own volition. It was a cold clasp on his brain that winnowed through the convolutions of gray matter to find the part that controlled his voluntary functions. A sickening rape of his will, an oily snake slithering its coils within his skull. A numbness suffused his body, as if the poison had infiltrated his nervous system, taken the route of his spine and ganglia, and commandeered his motor functions. The seditious toxin removed his bodily control from his own control and left him an unwilling puppet to a cruel master.

Again, Drudge beckoned silkily. "Come to me, boy."

Adam fought the urge his legs felt compelled to take. He winced when the pain wracked his muscles into a rigid contortion against Drudge's summons. His body felt a coldness permeate every cell, freeze its electrical impulses, and deliver control to a remote source. His arms went out toward Drudge in a gesture of acceptance, his fingers drawing themselves out of his coat and uncurling from the hilt of the knife.

A smile crept up on Drudge's patronizing face. He turned to Grace with a winning look. "See, my dear, he bears my mark."

Grace brought her hands only slightly away from her face to see what Drudge was talking about. When she saw Adam's arms drawn up and his face contorted into a painful grimace against the control exerted on him, she wept all the more.

A malicious contortion of Drudge's face exposed the fury he bore. He suddenly slammed his hand downward, slicing the air with a whistle. Adam's knees buckled as his body fell forward in obeisance. His traitorous palms barely caught him before his head smacked the cold marble floor. With every ounce of strength in his limbs, he tried to push himself to his feet. But he found his hands were frozen to the floor, his volition nothing but a preconceived notion having no bearing in reality.

Adam heard the click of footsteps as Drudge approached him, his shoes making ominous sounds on the marble like the tolling of a drum in a dirge. As Adam caught sight of the expensive Italian shoes coming into focus, a hand grabbed a shock of his hair and wrenched his face up, forcing him to stare into the blazing eyes of his oppressor. For the briefest moment there was anger before a cloud of curiosity played across Drudge's expression.

"What's this?" Drudge asked, then laughed, a ridiculing chortle that made Adam inwardly renew his regret in trusting a faith he hadn't fully embraced. Drudge wrenched his head back even farther, cranking his neck to within an inch of snapping. "Do you honestly think that putting such a silly tattoo on your forehead could dismiss my claim on you?"

"Please," Grace whimpered from the couch she'd burrowed into. Her hands were still clutching her face with her fingers almost tearing into her eyes. "You don't have to do this."

Drudge whipped his head around to look at her. "Do you have any idea who I am, Grace? What it is to defy me? Do you have any idea of the power I have?"

Her eyes remained riveted on him, her head giving a little shake, trembling. Whether out of fear or as an indication of answering his question, she was able to relay just that, that she really didn't know who he was or what kind of power he wielded, or even what it meant to defy him. But the man who'd been forced to kneel before the powerful businessman had sacrificed a lot to see that she remained safe, even though neither one of them could be called that right then.

Slowly, Grace pulled her hands away from her face. "I know you can hurt people," she stated with fierce accusation. "I know you buy and sell people like a cheap commodity and think you own them afterwards. I know you have a perverse sense of possessiveness, and that's terribly misplaced. So you're wrong. You have no right to do this."

"Really?" he demanded. He wrenched Adam's head back, keeping a firm hold on his hair. "Do you remember how I gave you a choice, Adam? And how you chose what you did? Do you know that I gave Claire an option also? Life is a gift, Adam, but virtue is just an option."

He angled Adam's head toward the side of the room. "Watch."

Adam's eyes blinked to clear away the painful tears misting his vision. What he saw made his gut kick violently. A spasm of nausea gagged in his throat.

The luxurious apartment gave way to expose what had once been the living room of the house he and Claire had shared. Gleaming white marble gave way to polished wood floors; the papered walls metamorphosed into oak paneling with pine accents; a bright illumination from cathedral lighting dimmed to the yellow incandescence of a shaded lamp left on a low setting. Queen Anne-style furniture shifted to the comfortable essence of bulky wood and overstuffed cushions. A pretty young woman sat rocking a sleeping baby in a rocker by a cold fireplace.

Adam moaned at the sight of Claire and Marie on the last night he remembered seeing them. His wife was dressed in a pullover and jeans, while Marie was still in her one-piece pajamas, swaddled in a blanket. Claire was waiting for him to come home so they could take the baby to the hospital together, and she was humming a soft lullaby to the sleeping child.

A creak sounded outside the imaginary front door. Claire called out Adam's name, expecting only him to come by. No one responded, but a second later the door crashed inward, startling her. She clutched the baby as a tall, dark figure stood within the threshold. The smell of smoke and fire was thick in the air, noxious and choking.

"What are you doing here?" Claire demanded, standing up defiantly and turning slightly so her baby wasn't fully exposed to the intruder. "You'd better get out of here before I call the police."

The figure strode into the house, his dark coat swirling around his calves as the wind blew his dark hair about his head. "Are you the lady of the house?"

"I said get out of here," she said strongly, unafraid for herself but fearing for her child, whom she had to protect with strength and defiance. She would have made an impressive show of it if she hadn't taken a step back.

Drudge stepped into the light of the lamp. His eyes caught sight of the bundle in Claire's arms, and he reached to move the blanket aside. Claire twisted her body away and covered Marie, clutching the baby closer and denying Drudge his inspection. Anger flared in his eyes at her boldness. He snatched her hair with his hand, holding her head in check while he made a show of looking at the child.

"Do you know what I am?" he finally asked.

Fear showed in Claire's stricken expression. She said nothing, but there was something in her eyes that exposed something of knowledge.

"People call me an ogre." He smiled a winsome smile, tilting her head to one side. "Do you know what an ogre does?"

Her eyes widened until the whites showed entirely around her pupils.

"They eat babies."

"No!" she screeched and wrenched her head away, leaving a lock of hair in his hand. She spun away and raced into the kitchen, cuddling Marie close to her breast. Drudge caught up with her at the archway into the kitchen, clamping a hand on her shoulder and drawing her to a skidding halt. He spun her around and slammed her into the wall.

"How much is this child worth to you?" he demanded, leering into her face.

"What . . . ?" she stammered, sobbing and shielding the baby with her arm.

"I asked you how much this child is worth to you?" he demanded, enunciating each word distinctly.

"She's . . . she's my entire life," Claire whimpered, tears streaming down her cheeks.

"Is she now?" Drudge asked petulantly. "Is she truly yours?"

"Please don't hurt her. She's just a baby."

"Is she yours?" he insisted curiously. "Or is she someone else's?" When Claire's expression collapsed into tears, Drudge changed his line of questioning. "Would you trade your life for hers?"

"Wh-what?"

"Would you give your life so she might live?"

Claire's eyes shifted back and forth with terror, her face ashen. "Wh-what?"

"If not your own—which wouldn't matter anyway—then would you trade the life of her father for her?"

Her eyes flashed fearfully. "Oh God, no, not Adam."

He cocked his head inquisitively. "Would you trade your dear sweet Adam's life for this baby's? That foolish boy you must love so dearly."

She shook her head slowly, tears streaming down her face with such sudden ferocity that she couldn't see any longer. "Oh God, this can't be happening. Please, please, just go away. Leave us be."

"Answer me," he demanded.

"No!"

Drudge pulled back his head in curious interest. "You wouldn't trade your husband for the life of this child?"

"No!"

"You would let this child die?"

"No," she whimpered, slumping wearily against the wall, nuzzling her cheek against Marie's head. "No."

"Would you try to stop me from taking her then?" he asked.

She snapped her eyes open, a fire burning in them. "I'd do everything in my power to stop you if you tried."

He laughed out loud, releasing her with a show of his hands. He seemed to enjoy his chuckle as he backed away, giving her room to move.

Claire sidled along the wall and into the kitchen, clutching Marie to her more tightly than before. When she gained the room, she turned and ran for the back door. In a bare second, Drudge was upon her, his sword appearing from the folds of his overcoat and skewering her through the back, severing her spine so she fell to the floor like a Raggedy Ann doll.

"*NNNOOO!*" Adam shrieked.

Tears seeped from his eyes with a vehemence that attested to experiencing the loss all over again. He couldn't move his head for the hold on his will, but he squeezed his eyes shut and begged for the image of Claire impaled on the end of a sword to dissolve from his memory as much as from his vision. A phantom patina remained in the darkness of his closed eyelids, where he believed it would remain forever. He saw every vivid detail of the crimson spread of blood on Claire's back, the arch of her shoulders, the silent expression of surprise, and the quiet bundle held aloft on her shoulder. He saw how weakly and helplessly Claire slid off the blade as her weight and gravity bore her to the ground, and then how her limbs just flailed limply as she crumpled to the floor.

"No," he moaned softly, his strength suddenly dwindling away to nothing.

CHAPTER THIRTY-SEVEN

Markey was more wary of opening elevator doors the next time the car came to a halt. As he ascended to what he hoped was the penthouse floor, he bent down to remove a snub-nosed .380 from his ankle holster, the only weapon he had left after tossing his service pistol into . . . wherever it had been he'd tossed it. He remained crouched low, holding the side of the car with one hand, watching the numbers as they slowly and methodically lit up, his breathing harsh but gradually coming under control. Finally, the elevator came to a smooth stop—just a barely perceptible gliding bump to indicate the end of the ride—and a cheerful ding sounded as the doors parted and a lamenting instrumental from Celine Dion cut off in mid-note. He gripped his gun in one hand, while the other hand firmly clutched the edge of the door, determined that he wasn't going anywhere this time unless he was sure of his footing—or that there was something solid to put his feet on.

Although the doors didn't open onto the boundless expanse of the cosmos this time, what he saw wasn't what he expected at all of a penthouse suite belonging to a multi-millionaire business tycoon owning a monolithic structure in the middle of a metropolitan city. Instead of a short entryway into the main quarters, where he imagined a set of ornate doors would bar his further entry until a butler of some sort answered his knock, the doors opened onto a cavernous chamber of gypsum and limestone walls, with aspiring stalagmite floors and dangling stalactite ceiling. The latter was raised to such a point that its true height was masked by the shadows of its sheer elevation.

There was a steady drip and dribble of water down several formations, pooling in glimmering and glistening puddles reflecting silvery-tinged black surfaces in a dull luminescent light. Otherwise, the ground was layered in a grainy thickness of dune-colored sand or silt that seemed to have been sifted evenly about but showed no evidence of anyone ever having walked through it. A bitter odor of sulfur crinkled Markey's nose, teasing him to sneeze despite his open-eyed bewilderment. He absently lifted his hand to cover his mouth and nose in case he breathed in toxic fumes. Steam hissed from hard-packed craters in the floor, probably the source of the smell, but also the source of a cloying moisture in the air, making it uncomfortably humid. Slits in the walls venting the gases out of the cavern and drawing in

THE UNFAITHFUL

oxygen also revealed slim strips of the black night outside.

The unique microcosm was a spelunker's wet dream. But that wasn't what blew Markey's mind to where he babbled incoherently to himself. It was the battle of birds and bats inside the cavern that made him rise fully up from his crouch and lower his gun to his side, his mouth falling open even farther in astonishment.

A various assortment of feathered combatants screeched and cawed as they flew on updrafts and down air currents to meet a battalion of black-bodied bats. Or, at least, what Markey assumed were bats from the way they screeched in high-pitched tones to orient themselves in the fracas, which they did with desperation. The leathery-winged creatures were frenetic, flitting about as they were plucked from the air one by one, their ugly heads rent from their disproportionate bodies and dropped to the ground without ceremony. A foul stench of ammonia filled the air as the bats pissed in their death throes, overwhelming the sulfuric odor. A few smaller birds were wrenched out of the air by a cadre of enemy coming in from behind, but it was mostly the birds who were more concerted in their endeavor—and more successful. Inert shapes fell from the air and thudded on the ground, littering the cavern with the bodies of friend and foe alike.

Markey stood paralyzed as the slaughter continued. He looked in mute astonishment at the edge of the elevator positioned in the craggy outcropping of the cavern. Thousands of bats still hung upside down from the roof of the cave, their sleepy arousal from the sonar echoing of their brethren slowly drawing them out of slumber. Leathery folds of wings twitched, then unfurled as they dropped from the ceiling to either be picked off by a predatory bird or engaged in aerial combat. Deafening shrieks of ear piercing screeches made Markey wince and wish he had more hands to cover his ears.

With a powerful effort to move his head from its rigid position, he turned to stare at the dark slits in the upper walls of the cavern—from a height of an impossible fifty or sixty feet above the ground. He noticed the birds were entering through the openings, coming and going as they pleased, engaging in battle and then zipping away. Markey couldn't tell why, but he supposed there was some sort of organized effort at play in the birds' assault; but for the life of him, he couldn't figure it out.

In his reverie of watching the onslaught—the sight somewhat daunting, yet exhilarating—he noticed how some of the bats had dropped to the floor on their own. Out of his peripheral vision, he spotted a large shape shoot up from behind one of the stalagmites; and because of its abrupt immensity, Markey turned his attention in its direction. What he saw had him frozen in absolute terror.

The creature had a hideous, protuberant face with razor-blade fangs and red feral eyes, a convoluted and cochlear nose, and stiffly pointed ears on the top of a towering body of unbelievably human-like construction. It had two arms—impossibly long and gangly—ending in claw-like extensions tipped with lethal-looking talons, and two legs, bending forward—but awkwardly, as if unsure of itself yet. These four limbs extended from joints at the hips and shoulders knobbed with bulbous, bony extrusions, giving the creature a malformed look. Even more malformed and disturbing were the wings quivering and attempting the flail open, convulsing spasmodically in an effort to portray the thing in all its monstrosity.

With jerking steps, it lurched forward, the creature spying the open elevator and the occupant standing like a wounded animal just within the threshold. It hissed with a stream of saliva dripping from its chin, while its vestigial wings finally managed to flare out, a complex and spindly skeletal structure comprising appendages stretching the membranes thin and voluminous.

Markey's mouth dropped as his jaw fell away in an expletive of disbelief. "Oh dear God in Heaven."

As the beast suddenly launched itself in the direction of the elevator, Markey gave a cry very much like a woman's. He pulled back from the open door, his fingers pounding on the CLOSE button, then punching all the buttons at random. The closer the creature came, the more frantic Markey jabbed and jabbered, cursing the slothful mechanics of the expensive piece of machinery.

"Shit, shit, shit!"

More beasts were rising from their huddled shapes on the ground, stretching tall to become full-fledged gargoyles. To hell with it, who was kidding who, Markey decided, they must be demons straight from the fiery pits of Hell.

Their wings twitched as they flexed their appendages, most having been awakened from a deep sleep under the roof of the cave and not yet limber or comfortable with their humanoid forms. The smell of ammonia was pungent and nauseating, and Markey felt as if he would gag. But his attention was more riveted to the slow responding elevator and the approaching creature that appeared as if it was capable of tearing him limb from limb.

The forgotten pistol, now remembered, flew up in a fluid and sudden motion even as Markey's brain triggered his finger to fire off three successive rounds. The loud reports rocked the cavern with explosive force, sending ripples through the echoing currents of the bats' sonar transmissions. The birds seemed to hesitate in their engagement as the reverberations of the gunshots dwindled.

Then the ensuing silence created a brief pause in the flurry, just before Markey watched in horror as the remaining bats hanging from the roof awoke and fell from the ceiling in sheets of hundreds—God forbid, maybe even thousands—screeching so loudly the sound was piercing and deafening. The multitude immediately overwhelmed the feathered enemy in their collective swirling masses, slaughtering them in a matter of less than a minute. The savagery was unbelievable, and although it seemed as if the birds had been the invaders, there was something terrifying about the way the bats defended their cave. It might have been the fact that the cavern was the home of such hideous demons converging on him at that very moment, intent to shred him to bits or devour him down to the bone—whatever it was those awful, vicious monsters did to people like him. Or it could just be the fact that bats were naturally repugnant creatures, considered vermin—rodents with wings—carrying all kinds of parasites and diseases. Whatever it was, whether it was based on a psychological terror or predisposition of disgust, there was something definitely disconcerting about the birds' forces being decimated.

The pungent smell of ammonia became overpowering, and Markey worried he was doing irreparable damage to his lungs by breathing in such noxious fumes.

The elevator doors finally closed as the nearest gargoyle developed a lithesome gracefulness and charged at him, its fury mounting as the doors shut off the avenue of escape for the lone figure of its hatred. Just as the doors were joining, the beast slammed into the thick metal flashing with a resounding crash, buckling the doors inward to the point where they didn't join cohesively. The creature pounded repeatedly at the barrier, wailing horrendously, sending shock waves through the car, making it reverberate in its confining shaft.

Markey fell victim to a series of violent tremors as he collapsed against the mirrored wall. He mumbled a prayer of his own making to a God he previously had no belief in, but now believed—BELIEVED, goddamn it!—wholeheartedly in because he had to know there was some counterbalancing force to what he'd just seen.

He huddled on the floor, groping for the railing that was now above him, to help support him from being tossed about the car by the tremendous abuse it was being subjected to. His mind was on the verge of snapping, his brain overwhelmed by the frantic workings of his imagination, reasoning, and new conversion to faith.

He suddenly shrieked when he felt the floor jog into a descent. The infernal Muzak picked up in the middle of an instrumental Neil Sedaka hit, something about an afternoon delight. Markey felt relief, albeit wary relief, and slumped with weakness. His gun hung limply from his quaking hand. He still smelled the horrible stench of the creatures' piss and venom, and the acrid odor of sulfur and copper. The hideous rictus of the demon's rage was permanently seared into his brain, as were the malodorous scents imprinted on his olfactory memory cells. He tried to regain a systematic pattern to his breathing, but the series of huffs and hiccups he was subjected to were reluctant to allow any semblance of normal respiration to return.

Struggling to quell his rampant trembling and hoping his heart didn't suddenly sputter into an arrhythmia, Markey forced himself to think rationally, equivocate what he'd seen with what made sense, even if it meant he was hallucinating from inhaling toxic fumes.

And that was what it was, he decided, as he felt himself come under control again, attributing his moment of panic to the physiological affects of a suspicious agent in the air. He would have to notify Haz-Mat to shut down the building and do an analysis of the air quality before allowing anyone else to enter, because, God forbid, a company of employees hallucinating dastardly things would amount to total pandemonium.

Yes, that was what had happened, he convinced himself. Hallucinations brought on by an airborne toxin. A terrorist act—whether political, ecological, or economic, but an attack all the same—intending to affect a major corporate headquarters for some unspecified public statement. He could believe that, because even though it was impossible at one time to believe the country could suffer such extreme devastation as the Oklahoma bombing and the Twin Towers tragedies, he had learned it could. The world had turned into a dangerous place, so he could believe a similar terrorist attack could happen—because they'd done it before. He could believe it.

So long as he didn't look at the elevator doors, punched inward at their juncture.

Markey refused to look and focused on other things instead, notifying Haz-Mat and the FBI and Homeland Security and . . .

He suddenly remembered why he'd come to the Tower. He'd intended to warn Malachi Drudge that his life was in danger; only now that danger had been augmented ten-fold with the suspicion of toxins in the air

Or a vastly cavernous portion of Hell residing in the upper reaches of the building.

At the time, when Markey had first entered the building and noticed his damaged car in the garage, along with Lumas missing, his goal had been motivated by personal concerns. Now it became more imperative that he attempt to save his own hide before he tried to find anyone else, even if it was Lumas, Grace, or Drudge. It would be more prudent to go back to the parking garage and call in the troops, send in the suits, both the fashionable ones worn by the Feds and those worn against contamination.

The elevator dinged softly as the car came to a smooth halt. Markey abruptly jerked in panic, unwilling to have the doors open on another insane level of madness, thereby proving that no amount of rationalization was going to convince the ego portion of his brain that he'd experienced a hallucination.

He lurched forward and jabbed the CLOSE button, nearly jamming his finger in the process, but the doors were already in the act of opening, the Muzak cutting off. All the buttons he'd hit when he'd tried to close the door would deliver him one by one to each of those floors before he could finally land at the basement level.

The doors opened infuriatingly slow. Markey brought his gun up in defense of what might greet him. He licked his lips and cracked a kink out of his neck by flicking his head to the side, then took a more advantageous stance against whatever lay beyond the elevator, readjusting his feet to shoulder-width apart, cocking his elbows slightly to absorb the recoil of the gun, and raising the weapon to a low-ready.

What appeared before him was no conceivable product of office space in any metropolitan skyscraper that could be found in this city.

The view was vaguely familiar, in a déjà vu sort of way. The sky was suffused with a hazy brownish-yellow light, and the smell of smoke was thick and choking. Its prickling in Markey's nostrils was powerful, and he coughed to clear out the first few breaths he'd mistakenly taken in his anticipation of encountering another scene that might bear a poisonous atmosphere, or none at all. But other than the smell of smoke, the air seemed breathable.

Curiosity made him throw his hand out and catch the door to keep it from closing. He thought he recognized the landscape—was sure of it—but he couldn't quite put a finger on it. The elevator seemed to be situated among a copse of pines, the sleepy needles hanging down in a canopy around the elevator, a few so bold as to sway into the car. Lush grass rolled in gentle slopes across a field fenced with creosote posts and barbed wire. Three structures appeared in the distance. A large white farmhouse with red trim, a red barn with white trim, and a white stable with black trim, all well-kept and looking elegant in their arrangement. A gravel path came in from a two-lane blacktop road, leading up to the house and its wraparound porch. The two other structures were set about a hundred yards from the house, with white fenced paddocks.

Markey took a step closer to the opening of the elevator, his feet a few inches from the gap existing between the mechanical contraption and the dewy wet grass. Again, the elevator doors tried to close, but his hand on the one sent both doors snapping back into their recesses.

Although the scene seemed to be improbable outside an elevator car, much less inside an obelisk structure in the middle of a well-populated city, it appeared non-threatening in its Norman Rockwell appearance. And still the view was frustratingly familiar.

Maybe if he saw the place from a different angle or in a different light he might recognize where he'd seen it before. But he was afraid to step out of the elevator for fear of not being able to return to it.

Then a woman's voice shrieked in the distance, coming from the direction of the house. A voice of distress and unrecognizable origins, but one surely at the edge of terror by the sound of its high-pitched octave. Markey cursed his inherent dedication to duty and took the first step out of the elevator.

Adam's head snapped forward as Drudge released his hold on his hair. He tried to pull his hands off the floor but Drudge kept them there with the sheer force of will. Drudge walked behind him and away, moving out of sight. Adam couldn't follow him with his eyes the way he was positioned so he turned to Grace, who was still cringed on the couch, her legs pulled up to her chest and her cheek pressed against her knees. Her eyes were shut to what she'd been watching, horrified to bear witness to the slaughter of his family, certain of her own doom hovering nearby. Adam's heart had torn to shreds with the worst memory of his life relived, but Grace had had her own convictions shattered as well. Up until then, she could have gotten away with believing he'd been deluded by an unfortunate tragedy; that everything was going to be just fine when all the misunderstandings were worked out. But now she understood that what he'd been saying all along had been true.

"Grace," he choked, a constriction in his throat tightening his voice

She blinked when she looked at him. Her swollen eyes were red, while her complexion was a mottled hue of pale shock.

He nodded encouragingly. "You have to get out of here. Get off the couch and leave."

She shook her head, wrapping her arms more tightly about her knees. The baggy pullover she'd borrowed from his closet bunched up around her shoulders, creating pockets in which she hid her face. Her hair hung in a loose curtain over her eyes.

"Grace!" he snapped. "Please."

She looked at him with one terrified eye. "Only if you come with me."

"I will," he said. "I'll be right behind you."

She shook her head more vehemently, seeing through his lie. She buried her face in her knees again. "You won't. I know it; you won't."

He hung his head, thinking of how he could convince her to leave. When he lifted his head again, he spoke only one word, her name, before something swung around his face and wrapped about his neck.

A coil of thick rope wound around his throat and cut off his words. He choked as Drudge grunted and hauled back on the line, ripping his hands from the marble floor and jerking him onto his backside.

Grace shrieked and released her knees, horrified at the violence of the attack but powerless to do anything to stop it. The look in Drudge's eyes was feral and violent, yet also triumphant and excited. He was like a shark in a feeding frenzy, and to get in his way would be to invite her own destruction.

With his hands now free, Adam grappled with the rope around his neck, attempting in vain to relieve the pressure choking him into near unconsciousness. He kicked with his feet to gain a purchase on the slick floor, but Drudge moved too quickly for him to keep up.

"How great a sacrifice was it when the Lord you chose to follow gave up his one earthly existence knowing he was yet still the Son of God?" Drudge posed as he dragged Adam backward, along the marble floor of the great room, then across the hard-packed earth of the ranch house's front lawn.

Adam's sneakers slipped in the dewy grass. He smelled the pungent odor of burning buildings and charred flesh. His hands clutched futilely at the rope at the back of his neck where it was twisted into a knot. He gurgled sickly, his vision becoming blurry with the thick smoke.

"Claire's sacrifice was far greater when she had only one life to give," Drudge intoned. "And she died for you, Adam. She wouldn't give you up even for the life of her child. A child who was sick and feeble."

Anger drilled into Adam with a ferocity nearly as choking as the rope. His feet kicked frantically for leverage but he could get no purchase.

"But the humor of it all," Drudge said comically, "is that you belong to me anyway."

Drudge jerked emphatically on the line, dragging Adam farther along the beaten footpath, through the grass, to the white building with black trim standing as the stables.

Adam recognized the house as his own when he passed into the back yard and saw the structure above him. His stomach convulsed and curdled, because he knew this time he would surely die. Still, he maintained the presence of mind to close his eyes and try to pick up any birds, any creature that would answer his call, but there were none. There were no living creatures in this illusion other than him and his tormentor.

"She had so much faith in you," Drudge barked, his tone brutally condemning yet revering of the woman he spoke of. "Only she didn't realize you had no faith in yourself. She was a fool to believe in you."

Tears streamed down Adam's cheeks. Tears from the burning smoke in the air, the pain he was suffering, the heartache he was forced to endure, and the desperation that he would never be able to defeat this evil as he'd been expected to. He wanted to shriek just such an admission at Drudge. At Sophocles and God. At anyone who would listen, but he had no voice beyond the constricting barrier of the rope. He barely had enough breath through the strangling noose to keep his mind functioning.

"This time, when you come back to take your place among your brethren, you'll understand misery for sure. Misery to see humanity again. Misery to know what you once were and what you will never be. Misery to never see your precious Claire and Marie again."

Adam kicked out violently, his fury overwhelming his need to survive. Muscles bulged in his arms as he walked his way up the rope, gaining some slack in the length between the knot at his neck and Drudge's hold. He tried to kick himself over, so he could gain leverage on his hands and knees and meet Drudge face on, but Drudge seemed to sense his intention and increased his efforts. With a might unparalleled to any other, Drudge hauled on the rope and jerked Adam off his feet again, dropping him onto his back, where he was dragged through the open stable door.

Drudge acted quickly. With incredible force, he flung the end of the rope over the same rafter he'd thrown it over that fateful day and wrenched on it with all his strength. The rope became taut, then rigid, and Adam was hauled off his feet. His legs scissored wildly as Drudge tied off the end on a stall post.

Adam clutched the rope and pulled up with all his reserves of energy, his shoulders straining despite the pain from his earlier beating. He gagged as the line wedged into his trachea. Drudge hadn't made a noose around his neck that would tighten as his weight pulled on it, but made a knot to prevent the rope from doing just that. Drudge didn't want him to suffocate all at once; he wanted to taunt him yet. However, it would only prolong the inevitable by minutes.

Drudge stepped into view, his face turned up with a smug expression. He cocked his head to one side to consider his captive. "I believe I owe you a child."

Anger swelled in Adam as he groped for a higher purchase on the rope. His arms were strong and he weighed less than when he'd been playing hockey, but he still knew he wouldn't be able to hold on much longer.

"I promised you that I wouldn't kill her—the pathetic little whelp of yours—but the poor thing must have died anyway." Drudge spoke snidely. "I'll make it up to you. When I come back, I'll bring you Grace's baby."

Adam twisted more wickedly, his arms actually lifting himself slightly off the pull of the rope. It was a brief respite from the cutting edge on his throat, but one that was short-lived. As Drudge gave a despairing chuckle and turned to walk out of the stables, Adam felt the burning pain in his arms begin to mount. He gathered as much of his strength as he could and poured it into the muscles of his left arm, while his right hand gave up its hold and fished frantically in his coat for a knife.

His weight pulled heavily on his one straining arm and he wasn't able to keep himself fully off the clutch of the rope. His fingers danced over the haft of a blade even as he felt the horrible swelling in his head from blood that couldn't pass the obstruction around his neck. He knew he'd have only one chance. If he didn't sever the line holding him aloft, he'd be dead in minutes.

As he pulled the knife from his coat, it caught on a fold of material and twisted out of his precarious grasp, flipping end over end to fall to the floor beneath his feet.

Markey ran headlong across the lawn to the ranch house, heedless of what dangers might be lurking within. The nagging impression of having seen this place—been here before—pestered him. The vivid stench of smoke, the feel of the dewy grass and gravel, the sound of his shoes thunking on the porch steps and then sliding to a halt at the front door, made him experience shivers of delirium. He paused only long enough to listen to anything moving within. With a curious restraint, he pushed the door open, looking around the edge to catch any response to his intrusion. But there was nothing, no barking dog, no shout of the homeowner that someone uninvited would try to enter. The lack of anything was frightening, and he handled his gun the way it was meant to be used by a seasoned law enforcement officer.

As he went into the house, Markey was again reminded of the similarities to memories he kept in the back of his mind. Flashes of visions flickered across his mind's eye but which were always out of reach. He became determined to satisfy his curiosity, an overpowering inquisitiveness that could surely lead him into a trap where he might not be able to retreat to the elevator. He felt like a cat coasting along on fate during the last of its nine lives.

Markey entered the foyer, shedding a sick light on the floor by letting in the peculiar light of the adulterated dawn. As he looked beyond, into the living room, he was suddenly struck with the revelation of where he'd seen this place before.

It was the Mogilvy residence, which had since been closed against trespassers, first by police tape and then by abandonment. He remembered it vividly then, the day after the riots that had decimated the ranches, the two-story home with large rooms, two stone fireplaces, and comfortable décor. The house had been fastidiously cared for, its rooms spotless and smelling of scented potpourri—vanilla spice, if he remembered correctly. Quilted covers lay over the back of the couch and love seat, and Markey recalled a plaid blanket tossed over the arm of a rocker as a homey enticement to sit a spell. He had wandered the rooms in the silence of the morning after the tragedy and marveled at how two kids just barely out of high school had managed to reach such bliss so early in their lives. Only he'd been mistaken to think such happiness could last forever.

Now Markey walked cautiously from the living room, past the dining room and into the kitchen. It was a spacious room with a generous number of cabinets and drawers, a pantry, and an island table with copper pots hanging overhead. Markey had loved the hominess of the room when he'd seen it a year ago but unfortunately he'd been turned off by the smell of death and tragedy overpowering even the old aromas of spices and good home cooking.

In retrospect, he realized he was walking the same route he'd taken when he'd examined the crime scene a year ago, and again, he went around the island table in much the same manner as before. Startlingly, he jolted to a halt when he saw the body of a woman sprawled on the floor, her arms wrapped around something under her. The position of the body was different from what he'd remembered in the actual homicide scene, but it was the same woman, he was sure. In that original setting, Claire Mogilvy had laid on her back in what appeared to be a peacefully supine position. Markey had suspected the body's position had been staged, and he was now aware that what he was looking at was the true position of the woman after she'd been murdered.

Markey cautiously approached the body and knelt beside it. His hand reached out as a shaky extension, fearful that the arms of the corpse would suddenly become animated and latch onto him. At this point, after seeing all the things he had, he wasn't sure of anything, not the constrictions of time and space, the ridiculous myth of monsters, nor the natural order of death and decay. But then his years in homicide rescued him from idiocy, with the numerous times he'd seen the sudden jerking of muscle spasms and opening eyelids, and he recovered his resolve. Any movement committed by the corpse could easily be explained with sound scientific principles he'd actually witnessed in action before. He wasn't about to be spooked by something so basic it was used to set up rookies for a laugh among veteran cops.

With the dexterity of a professional, he checked for a pulse just to make sure the woman was dead—despite the overwhelming mass of blood soaking the back of her shirt—and found nothing, just as he expected. The body was cold and clammy, and lividity was setting in; the forehead, cheeks and chin were turning purple from being face down on the cold tile. The gaping laceration in the back had bled profusely but had since stopped, now that no heart worked to pump the blood from the body.

A bittersweet sorrow sent a cold emanation through Markey's own body, with the icy tendrils of its influence wrapping wholly about him. He hadn't known this woman while she was alive and vital, but there were times when he had feelings about the spirit of a person. He felt that way about Claire Mogilvy. How her friends and family had spoken favorably about her; how her death had completely devastated her husband and driven him into a reclusive existence, to the point where no one knew where he'd gone; how the aura of her passing had left a specter of an extraordinary spirit Markey felt all about him now, a presence that left him feeling the willies. Once again, as on rare occasions, he wanted the liberty to weep for such a loss, to have the audacity to share in a communal mourning of familial survivors and ease the tightening grip clutching his throat and choking him up.

Markey was about to rise from his knees when he caught a glimpse of something unexpected beneath the woman. A tiny white hand with pudgy white fingers curled in a relaxed fist protruded only minimally into view. With a pang of fury, he realized the child belonging to Adam and Claire Mogilvy must have lain this way when the mother was killed.

Musingly, Markey reached out and slipped a finger into the curve of the tiny fist, feeling an urge to issue a prayer for her passing, however delayed it might be. But he nearly cried out when the little fist reflexively grasped his finger, not in a manner that was the result of a muscle spasm or atrophy, but from a concerted effort to actually clutch something—intently and with purpose.

Good Lord, Markey thought, the child's alive!

He heaved the body of Claire Mogilvy over and the child turned with her, still clutched to her mother's breast. Markey frantically tried to pry the infant from the mother's hold, and with some coaxing, finally gained possession of the baby, hugging her to his own chest. He felt the heat of a fevered illness emanating from her frail body and remembered she hadn't died from an injury that night, but from a medical condition left untreated. For the life of him, he couldn't remember what it had been.

"Looks like it's time we blow this Popsicle stand, little one," he murmured as he stroked the child's clammy brow and looked around. He would have to find the elevator again if he wanted to get out of this . . . whatever it was. He just didn't expect he would be very successful, considering how the day was turning out.

He stood up and moved to the back window, scanning the horizon for any sign of the elevator he'd ridden up in. The smell of smoke was acrid in his nose but he could see no fire in the area. If he remembered correctly, the neighbor's farm to the east of the Mogilvy ranch had gone up like a tinder box, the silo exploding like a ballistic missile misfiring in its hold. He should be able to see flames shooting over the copse of trees separating the two properties, but he didn't. Even the barn that had been nothing but charred kindling stood unmolested at the back of the house.

Markey hugged the child tightly to his chest and exited the house from the back door, walking carefully down the steps to a mulch path leading to both the barn and stables. The door to the stables was open and he caught sight of movement within, which startled him because he wasn't expecting it, nor did he want to deal with anything the place had to offer, especially if he had a sick child to deal with. But he was curious about the movement, which still occurred in a rhythmic way, casting a shadow across the stable floor. He opted to move into a position where he could get a better glimpse, yet remain far enough away where he could still react with either flight or fight instinct.

He stepped a few feet closer and saw something that caused him to bolt forward, running awkwardly with the child clutched to his chest, moving faster than he would have thought possible. When he finally reached the stable, he paused momentarily to stare in absurd fascination at the man he'd come to know as Adam Mogilvy—his fugitive at large—kicking wildly as he struggled to hold himself off the choking noose around his neck.

Markey quickly came to his senses and laid the child in a nestle of hay, then ran helplessly around the otherwise deserted stables, looking for something to cut Adam down before he suffocated.

"Hang on, kid, I'm gonna get you down," he said frantically as he looked into the stalls for something—anything—to prevent the inevitable, something he could put under the young man's wildly scissoring feet, something he could use to cut the rope he saw was tied in a tight knot on one of the stall posts, any goddamn thing at all. But not even a milking stool or a shovel was in sight.

"Shit!" He cursed the madness that set up the props in this freaked-out world—or the tidiness of its caretaker—and ran to stand before Adam. "Where's the tack room?"

Adam wrenched his eyes open at the sound of Markey's question. The detective was in front of him, yelling at him, asking him something, where the tack room was. Any blind fool could see the door was at the end of the stalls, but Adam had no voice to work with. And he couldn't afford to release one of his hands from his precarious hold to point in that direction.

Instead, Markey realized the futility of his question and took a few steps to look around in earnest. That was all he took before he kicked something with his foot and looked down to see the knife Adam had dropped earlier.

Markey took the knife as a miraculous omen and snatched it up. He ran to the end of the rope tied around the stall post. Holding onto the rope with one hand, he sawed furiously, hoping to bear the young man down easily. But when the rope snapped, it burned through his hand and Adam fell from the rafter. Markey himself fell against the stall with the force of whiplash; but he quickly recovered and scrambled to where Adam lay, gulping deep gasps of air.

"Hold still, kid, I got you."

Markey used the knife to saw at the noose around Adam's neck, his arm pumping madly to break through the stranglehold. When the two ends finally snapped, Adam ripped the coils off and hurled them away, his breathing stertorous and labored. His overtaxed arms tried to hold his body up, but they, too, collapsed and he fell face down in the hard-packed dirt.

"You okay?" Markey demanded, pulling Adam into a sitting position. "Are you all right?"

Adam tried to answer but he wasn't ready to give up his breath for talking just yet. After a few deep intakes of air, he managed to nod.

"Do you know what's going on here? Because I sure as hell don't. I was on an elevator one minute, the next I'm stepping into a crime scene from a year ago. This is one fucked-up building."

"Grace..."

"I know; she's somewhere in this freaking Tower, but hell if I know where." He looked around. "I'm afraid Grace is going to have to wait. We've got to get your daughter out of here."

Adam looked dumbly at Markey, unable to process what the detective had said. He blinked a few times until Markey scooted over to where he'd laid the child on a nest of old hay. Adam's eyes followed him until he saw Marie. At first, he only stared vacantly at the child, as if he thought he was hallucinating it, imagining the bundle Markey touched was his daughter when it was really something else, something inert and inconsequential. But then something must have clicked and he scrambled over to where the detective crouched.

Adam pushed him out of the way so he could take his daughter in his own arms, desperate to hold her one last time before he had to lay her to rest again. He choked back sobs that couldn't be dammed up any longer. Familiar tears welled up in his eyes as he hugged Marie's small body tightly to his chest, rocking her on his knees.

"She's sick, Adam," Markey said as he crawled up beside him. "I can't remember what caused her to die that night, but I know she's sick with it right now."

Adam's eyes shot over to stare at Markey. He cradled his daughter's head against his neck, nestling her fine down-covered head against his scarred throat. There was a heat coming off her that should be unnatural for a dead child. A heat that was familiar and frightening.

"What was wrong with her that night?" Markey pressed.

Adam pulled Marie away from his chest and looked at her tiny fevered face, the vision of her flushed innocence blurry through his sheen of tears. Shiny red cheeks made frighteningly fetching accents to her features. Her small pug nose had the barely detectable flare of breathing. Even her lips took that moment to open and close, a hint of a suckling instinct brought to bear. Adam swept a hand over her face, over her hair, his calloused palm encompassing her whole face. He felt the soft breath of life tickle the scar tissue of his hand.

"She's alive," Markey assured, touching his shoulder.

Adam suddenly burst into tears, overwhelmed with disbelief—and faith—and clutched his daughter tightly, burying his face against hers, feeling the frailty and smallness of her body, delighting in the fever of her skin because it meant she was alive. Close to death maybe, but still very much alive.

A tug on his shoulder and his name brought him back to the present. He looked up and saw Markey getting to his feet, tugging on his arm to get him moving. "She's still sick. If we're going to keep her alive, we have to get her help."

Adam said nothing as he rose to his feet and ran from the stables, toward the house, up the porch steps, and through the door, which he wrenched open with such strength it slammed against the wall. Markey ran after him, determined not to be left alone in this God-forsaken world. When he entered the kitchen, Adam was rummaging through the refrigerator with his daughter still against his shoulder. Abruptly, Adam took out a baby bottle. He uprighted it over his mouth and squeeze some of the liquid onto his tongue to taste, then adjusted the child in his arms so he could feed her.

"What is it?" Markey asked.

"Sugared milk," Adam said. "That night, Claire said her blood sugar was high. I thought she needed insulin, but now I know otherwise. Claire had given her insulin already. Marie was in insulin shock by the time I got home."

That's right; the baby had died from insulin shock. She could have been saved if she'd only gotten medical attention quickly enough. But she'd been left out in the elements far too long without help.

Adam let his back fall against the counter for support. His eyes drifted over to the body of his wife on the floor and another set of tears welled up. He forced himself to look away, feeling the weight of his child in his arms instead, her little hands coming up weakly to grasp the bottle as she sucked desperately at its contents.

"I'm sorry, Adam," Markey said shamefully. "I . . . I thought . . . you were responsible . . ."

Adam turned his eyes on the detective, his face flaccid and pale. "That night," he began, "I took an earlier flight out of Chicago because Claire said Marie was sick. I told her I'd meet her at the hospital, but Claire said she'd wait until I got home, keep an eye on her blood sugar. I called from the airport when I got in, to let her know I was coming and to see how Marie was doing. But there was no answer, so I assumed she'd already taken her to the hospital. I went home to see if there was a note or something, of where she might've gone. But she wasn't . . ."

Gone?

But she was. When Adam had come home that night, Claire was gone, in a more definitive way than he'd originally suspected.

"This is a replay of what happened that night?" Markey asked, watching the baby suck on the milk with a hunger that seemed unquenchable. Her tiny eyelids fluttered but didn't open.

Adam looked around, his expression taking on a grim reflection of what was happening. Again, his eyes alighted on Claire's body, and he squeezed his eyelids shut to cut out the image of her brutal death.

"Malachi Drudge is a part of this?" Markey demanded, remembering what Grace had told him. And who would know better what happened that night than the man who'd been there.

Adam's eyes snapped open and burned with a murderous conviction at the mention of Drudge's name. Marie pushed the bottle out of her mouth and took a noisy breath of air. Her eyelids fluttered weakly, and then opened to focus dreamily on the face of her father. Adam shifted her to his shoulder and tossed the bottle in the sink, as if someone would be washing it later. He rummaged in a drawer and took out a needle and syringe, shoved those in a pocket and went back to the refrigerator. He snatched up a small bottle of insulin and put it in his coat also. When he turned back to Markey, his face was the same determined and undaunted face as before.

"If this is that night all over again, those monsters will be out there." Adam nodded at Markey's hand, which still gripped the small .380. "Do you have enough rounds in that?"

Markey suddenly remembered the small automatic Adam indicated. He brought it up, ejected the magazine and checked the number of rounds still remaining. "Five."

Adam grimaced. He moved out of the kitchen, through the dining room and living room, and into the foyer. "I have a shotgun with a couple boxes of shells."

He opened the door to the closet and let Markey retrieve the weapon and ammunition. The detective broke the shotgun open and loaded all five shells into it, four into the feeding tube and one into the chamber. He flicked off the safety and shouldered the weapon.

"When I came home that night," Adam continued, "I found Claire in the kitchen . . . The way she is now. Marie was still alive. I knew I had to get her to the hospital. By the time I got her into the car, those things attacked. The things you saw at the wharf. They'll be out there now."

Markey gulped and hefted the shotgun higher on his shoulder. He hoped the gesture assured Adam that he was prepared for any battle against the spawns of Hell, as much as he hoped to convince himself. "I take it your car will start."

"I hope."

"You get her in the car. I'll cover you."

Adam nodded and wrenched the door open, hurrying down the steps with his daughter buried in the folds of his coat. He vaguely heard Markey's heavy footsteps following him down the wooden stairs as he raced for the car in the driveway. His eyes shot in all directions, all at once, gauging the shadows and the shifts in them. When he reached the car and opened the back door, he hurried to get Marie into the car seat, fumbling with the straps to snap them in place. As he did, he heard a curse and spun around.

Markey brought the shotgun fluidly to his shoulder and squeezed off a thunderous round at an advancing creature sprouting from a black shape on the ground. Its face disappeared in a splatter of blood, bone, and brain matter. The body crumpled to the ground and shifted back into the form of a headless bat.

"Jesus."

"They'll come now," Adam warned, twisting around and facing the shapes as they landed and exploded into their full demonic immensity.

Markey pumped a shell into the chamber and triggered off another round. The wad struck the creature at center mass and threw it several feet back. Markey pivoted on his heel, racked and fired another round into the abdomen of an accompanying monster.

Adam spotted two more as they landed and erupted into being. He directed Markey's attention to one while pinioning a knife at a second, impaling the beast in the hollow of its throat, the blade embedding itself up to the guard in the demon's blood vessels and windpipe. Markey twisted to cover their backs when he saw Adam's attacker go down with a croaking sound, efficiently neutralized. He noticed three others coming at them from one side of the car, and pumped a shot into the closest one's cheek, spinning its head around, its body following with the force of the impact. The two remaining creatures didn't even bat an eye before they hissed and launched themselves across the hood and trunk of the car. Markey flipped the shotgun over, grabbed its barrel and swung it like a baseball bat. The stock connected with the rodent-like head and crushed its skull. The demon flipped off the hood and rolled several feet away, where it remained stunned but still alive. Adam turned to the other and sliced at it with another knife he'd produced from his coat, leaving Markey to wonder why neither he nor Lumas had been conscientious enough to search the same coat before allowing Adam to keep it. Then he remembered how everything had happened so fast back at the wharf and they hadn't had the opportunity to search him before arriving at the hospital. By then, Adam had taken the coat off and left it on the back seat of the car. He must have retrieved it from the car when he'd stumbled over it in the parking garage.

"Get in!" Markey shouted as he returned the shotgun to the proper position at his shoulder. He shot a round into the head of the recovering demon and put an end to the possibility that it might cause any more problems.

Adam slid into the driver's seat and groped for the keys in the ignition, only to find them missing. "Shit!"

"What's wrong?"

"The keys."

"Where are they?"

"I . . ." Adam thought, trying desperately to remember what had happened to the keys that night.

"What did you do with the keys that night?" Markey asked intuitively, reading his mind without intending to.

"I . . ." he pondered, looking around, back at the house, around the yard. Suddenly, he lurched out of the car and began searching the dirt, kicking the ground, hurrying back and forth in a frantic search to find something he remembered might have been dropped there a year ago.

Markey watched with growing apprehension. He saw black shapes coming out of the stables, their twitching wings bringing them closer to the front of the house where they would . . . "Adam, hurry!"

Adam suddenly disappeared from view when he crouched down. When he popped back up, he displayed a ring of keys in his hand. He slid into the driver's seat and shoved the right one into the ignition. With a wrench, he had the engine revving and the car in reverse as Markey settled into the passenger seat, setting aside the shotgun and taking out his handgun. He looked around, then ducked to peer out the front windshield, at the sky.

The tires spun madly in the gravel, gained traction, and rocketed backward. Adam spun the wheel hard to one side and sent the car into a spin, braked, and threw the car into a forward course. He seemed to gain some sense of satisfaction when he caromed into a creature that believed it could stop the car with its body. There was a solid thump as the fender connected with the demon just before the car reached the asphalt road.

Adam spun the wheel to the left and pressed his foot against the pedal with such force he almost fishtailed out of control. Strobing red and blue lights could be seen in the distance, and both he and Markey experienced a thrill of triumph at the evidence of other people. Even though they weren't able to see them yet, they knew those colored lights meant other human beings—law enforcement officers, for God's sake. Maybe even trained paramedics.

Markey set his handgun aside and broke open a box of shotgun shells, which he fed into the tube. He thrust the remaining shells into a pocket of his coat, watching the scenery outside the car for hostile forces. Adam maneuvered the rearview mirror to an angle where he could keep Marie in sight, her head slumped to the side because she was held up and in place by the straps of the car seat.

"Is she . . . ?" he asked desperately. "Is she . . . all right?"

Markey looked at him, then at the child in the back seat. He reached back and touched the baby, fearing the worst as well. She sleepily pushed his hand away—annoyed with his prodding—and moved her head to the other side, heaving a sigh. Markey straightened in his seat and relaxed.

"Don't ask me how, but she's alive." He nodded up ahead, where they were approaching the color of blue and red lights reflecting off the street, trees, and houses. "There's help just up ahead."

"I'll let you out if you want, but I'm getting my daughter to a hospital. Every second may count, and I can't afford to get delayed with questions."

Markey gave him a wary look, then stared straight ahead. Something in him told him not to get separated from Adam Mogilvy. He suspected the kid might know more than what he was letting on, and that something might entail how to get out of this inexplicable history.

When they approached the first set of stopped police cars, they saw no one around. It was as if whoever had driven those cars—or whoever had called for assistance—had simply been transported elsewhere, leaving everything behind. There was an eerie sense of desertion in the area, and Markey didn't like it. He motioned for Adam to go on without stopping, and Adam gave him a look of uncertainty. But he drove the car through the throng of police cars at Markey's insistence and headed in the direction he knew would be the best help for Marie.

CHAPTER THIRTY-EIGHT

Sitting in the passenger seat, Markey maintained a vigilant eye on the surrounding panorama of the world passing by, while in the driver's seat, Adam focused on driving, his command of the wheel a precise determination to get to a specific place. Markey maintained his silence after he'd pointed out that a hospital lay on the edge of the city, only to have Adam dismiss it without explanation.

In the distance, the sun was an ugly ecru ball of haze as it rose over the horizon, bringing on an ill cast of light to the already appalling day. The smell of smoke was acrid in Adam's nose, and his eyes were stinging, but he kept on course, his excessive speed and perilous maneuvers drawing no attention from the already overburdened police, who had better things to do with their time than stop him for minor traffic infractions.

In short order, Adam pulled up to the emergency entrance of St. Jude's Hospital, one wheel hopping the curb in an effort to fit into the only space yet unoccupied by an emergency vehicle. People hastened in and out of the automatic doors with purpose or desperation, inquiring about relatives or friends who might have been brought in. Rescue units were backing out and making way for other ambulances. Someone barked at Adam that he couldn't park there, but Markey shoved his badge in the man's face as Adam pulled his daughter from the back seat. Her feverishly sweating body was nearly scalding, and Adam pressed her tight against his shoulder as he raced to the entrance.

Markey overtook him once they were inside. He plied his way through the throng of patients and waiting family members with an officiousness that seemed remarkably police-like. His blustering drew their scorn and rebuke, but he kept his badge up as a permit to by-pass all others.

Hospital staff worked in chaotic orderliness, passing off charts, equipment, and medication. Shouts of diagnoses, prescriptions, and commands never overrode any other. Wails of pain and grief were dampened by painkillers or a move to a private room. Names were being called for the next patient to come forward, while others were sternly told to retake their seats and wait their turn.

Markey pressed his way through the reception room and into the back treatment area, drawing the shouts of a chastising nurse dealing with a horde of angry people.

Both he and Adam ignored her, and she struggled out from behind a counter to run after them. In no time, she was overwhelmed by a throng of boisterous patients and family members awaiting their turn for attention.

"I need a doctor!" Markey shouted, his cry sounding demanding and obtrusive even in the chaotic flurry of activity.

Adam rushed about the treatment area, looking behind curtains and in and out of rooms, growing more frantic as time wore on. He knew she'd be somewhere in the emergency room—even at this hour—so it was just a matter of finding her. It was nearing the end of her shift by the time he and Markey had arrived at the hospital, but she'd have stayed to help with the overflow of casualties. He was sure of it.

Then he saw her popping up from behind a horseshoe desk where she'd been pulling out a handful of packaged catheters. Her hair was pulled back in a ponytail, but strands of it had pulled free and hung loose on either side of her face as evidence of how tiring and haggard her night had been. She checked the packaging on the equipment, then spun around to head out from behind the counter, where she ran into Adam.

"I need your help," he said urgently.

She looked at him, her eyes showing surprise at his sudden appearance, and then concern. Finally, her expression took on a look of indignation as she realized he must have slipped past the triage nurse. "You're not allowed back here."

"My daughter is diabetic. She needs help."

Abruptly, Monica Perez turned to the baby clamped tightly against his shoulder beneath his coat, her concern suddenly concentrated on the infant. She threw aside the equipment she'd been holding and reached out to pry the child away. Reluctantly, Adam relinquished Marie and gently placed her in Monica's care.

Markey joined them as Monica cradled the girl in her arms and began a quick and cursory exam. "She's burning up," she said and hastened over to an empty gurney.

Adam and Markey followed as Monica shouted for a blood sugar test kit. A nurse appeared almost instantly, producing the device. In response, Monica rattled off the child's vitals to the nurse, who quickly assumed the role of her assistant. Adam and Markey listened and watched as Monica gave orders and the nurse responded. Finally, Monica snatched a phone off the wall and punched a few buttons.

"This is Doctor Perez, from the ER. I've got a female infant in insulin shock. Who's attending up there? . . . Let him know I'm going to do what I can to stabilize her down here. Just get a place cleared out for her."

She hung up and started an intravenous line going into the child's arm, hanging the saline drip on its rack and injecting a stream of solution into the port. She adjusted the input and turned to the vitals monitor, studying it for a time, watching the digital readout flutter chaotically. Once the numbers reflected something steady, her attention returned to her ministrations, the grim set of her features foretelling her prognosis.

The nurse backed away from the gurney and turned to Adam and Markey. "You should be out in the waiting room."

Adam looked away from his daughter to glare at the woman, not saying a word, his flinty stare as sharp as the knives he wielded. Markey held up a placating hand toward her, interceding where he thought best. "Will she be all right?"

"We're doing what we can."

"Are you her father?" Monica asked abruptly, appearing suddenly behind Adam. "You called her your daughter; are you her father?"

"Yes."

"She's very ill."

"Is she dying?"

Her lips formed a grim line. "We'll do what we can. That's all I can promise."

Adam solemnly nodded and made to turn away, but she caught his arm and held him in check. "She's going up to Pediatric ICU. There are some forms you'll need to sign."

Again, he nodded, his eyes cast to the floor. She let him go and returned her attention to the child. The nurse moved away to collect the necessary forms. Markey laid a hand on Adam's shoulder, offering what little comfort he could.

"She'll be all right. God wouldn't be such a bastard as to take her back now."

Adam met his eyes and studied them in earnest. There was a gleam of hope in the detective's face, more than Adam had himself. Something in Markey's words spoke of a faith the man had never ascribed to, yet now claimed. To Adam, it was mocking in the way someone who was once agnostic now proclaimed his belief in a benevolent God, and yet Adam couldn't believe Him to be anything more than a cruel prankster.

"I need to go back for Grace," he said, breaking away from Markey without comment about his hope that his daughter would make it through the night or why she was even alive.

Christopher had run up the stairs in his angst to reach the police and have his say before Drudge could get the upper hand, but by the time he reached the tenth floor, he was winded and weary. He wasn't overweight by a long shot and believed he kept himself in good shape, but the anxiety of the past few days, complicated by the poor nutrition he was sustaining himself on, exacerbated by his lack of sleep, was making this effort to climb the stairs even more strenuous than he'd hoped. He groped at the railing and heaved invigorating breaths of fresh air, hoping to fill his lungs with enough oxygen to keep him at such a necessary pace. There was no telling how long the police had been there or how much Drudge had told them already, so he had to keep moving.

After a short respite, Christopher gave a forsaking groan and pushed off the railing to continue his climb, craning his neck back to peer up at the height of the stairwell, wondering just how far he had to go before he reached the penthouse level. In his assessment, that was where he would find Drudge's living quarters, and therefore, the man himself and the police. At that point, he would have his say about what was really happening concerning this whole murder investigation/blackmail attempt.

Grace had reached a level of defeat so low that she could only curl into a tight ball and rock back and forth. In the back of her mind, she felt if she could only protect the child within her, she might still come out ahead. She knew Malachi Drudge wanted to destroy her baby—no matter what rose-colored, candy-coated spin he put on it—and she was determined to prevent that from happening. Such a determination was in spirit only, and the strain it put on her body made her feel like nothing more than a weak and sick kitten.

After she'd witnessed Drudge hang Adam from the rafter, she'd lost all hope for saving herself. Up until that point, Adam had been her hero. He'd understood in the most oblique way what was going on and seemed prepared for the situation they'd found themselves in. But in the end, he'd fallen victim to Drudge's inscrutable powers, and that had been the end of her strength and hope. She'd felt her energy drain out of her as if a cork had been removed and her body upended, and there was nothing left to subsist on.

Drudge had since disappeared for a time but then returned from another door across the room. Upon his return, he was dressed in an elegant Italian suit—gray in color—with a crimson tie and a monogrammed handkerchief folded primly in his pocket. His hair was slicked back, gelled with styling mousse, fragrant and shining. His eyes were riveted on her, and she shivered under his steely gaze. With an arrogant swagger, he strode toward her, and she shrank into the corner of the couch.

Standing before her, Drudge held out a hand for her to take. "I had a table set for us to have breakfast. Come."

She looked at his extended hand as if it was a poisonous snake, and shook her head, which was the extent of her ability to deny his invitation.

"Please, Grace, you haven't eaten properly in days. You need to keep your strength up."

He looked at her with sympathetic concern. When she didn't move, he gently reached down and took her hand, drawing her up with a steady tug. She wanted to defy him but couldn't, and she found herself powerless to do anything but comply with his direction. Reasoning with her debility, she thought if she didn't physically resist him, she would at least remain unharmed.

Grudgingly, she had to admit that once she was on her feet beside him, with his arm locked through her elbow, he had a very genteel way about him. He moved languidly, his stride held in check considering that he was a very tall man with long legs. Yet he showed deference to her shorter stride and weakened condition, and didn't hurry her as he moved her through the wooden doors that had once exposed a world beyond reality.

Behind those remarkable mahogany doors now was a dining room so exquisite and grand she had to catch her breath just to take in its expansiveness. A complex crystal chandelier hung over a tremendously long and polished table of cherry wood. Two settings had been laid out, one at the head of the table and the other at an angle to the first. Drudge moved her to the subservient position and pulled out a heavy chair with carved wooden arms and backrest, and an upholstered seat, motioning for her to make herself at home.

Weakly, she collapsed into the chair, finding it hard and uncomfortable on her weary body, part of the carvings protruding against several pressure points in her back. Drudge took his seat at the head of the table and removed a napkin from the side of his plate, which he shook out and laid on his lap. He poured each of them a glass of orange juice from a crystal carafe and set hers in front of her. Before retracting his hand completely, he lifted the silver lid off her plate and exposed a conservative collection of common breakfast fare, with steam rising as if to affect its hasty escape. Two eggs sunny side up, a slice of Canadian bacon, toast and preserves, all arranged in neat harmony with one another.

The savory aroma of the taunting meal made her mouth water and stomach kick. Drudge had been right; she hadn't eaten properly in days, not since the day she'd been with Christopher. The last thing she'd eaten had been stale cookies from the vending machine in the police lounge, and those had been pathetically unsatisfying. What Drudge was offering was a veritable feast, and she longed to indulge in it. But regardless of her tremendous desire to pick up a fork and start shoveling food into her mouth, if she accepted Drudge's hospitality, she'd only be committing the foulest betrayal to the one man who had helped her unselfishly. An inner part of her confirmed the belief that she would never be able to look at herself again if she so much as nibbled on a piece of dry toast.

"Please, Grace, for the baby," Drudge said, making a show of how good the meal was.

She shot him a malicious look, which he merely avoided by attending his own meal, handling his utensils around his plate with a delicateness that was very much out of character for the murderous villain he'd proven himself to be. She watched him consume his food with all the table manners of a connoisseur, and it infuriated her how he could remain so detached from what was at hand.

"You killed him," she finally said, feeling the tears building behind her eyes.

He looked up from his plate and met her accusatory stare. Slowly, he dabbed at his mouth with his napkin and set his fork aside. "We had issues that needed to be resolved."

"So you killed him," she accused bitterly.

"He would have killed me first, had he gotten the chance. You know why he came here." He gave her a look of earnest concern, his face placid, with no worry creasing his brow.

In contrast, Grace's face revealed the contention she felt. He was right; Adam had come to the Tower to kill him, and while she was dead-set against settling conflicts with violence, Drudge might have thought killing Adam was the only way to eliminate him as a threat. She shook her head, dismissing the argument defending Drudge's actions. "You killed his family. Why wouldn't he want to kill you?"

Drudge pointed his fork in her direction to emphasize a point. "I did not kill his baby. That child shouldn't have died; but she was sick."

"But you did kill his wife!"

Drudge dismissed her argument with a flick of his wrist and resumed eating, completely unfazed by her anger. She sat in front of her plate and stared at him, the intensity of her scowl doing him no harm. His lack of concern frustrated her, and she stamped her foot and pushed her plate across the table, where it sailed off the top with a surprisingly aerobatic grace, until it clattered to the floor. Drudge looked up and assessed her then, and the look of disappointment he gave her made her wish she hadn't acted so rashly.

"I'll have someone clean that up," he said mildly. "If you're not hungry, I'll just have someone take you to your room so you can rest."

"I want to go home."

"You need to be watched for a while, Grace. I'm concerned about your mental state. You shouldn't be left alone right now."

"You can't keep me a prisoner here," she wailed, tears of helplessness rolling down her cheeks. "Why are you doing this to me?"

"Why?" he asked softly, as if trying not to nudge her fully into hysterics. "Because it's important that you take care of yourself. You've been running around with a delusional maniac, putting your baby at risk, refusing to seek proper prenatal care, and—now—refusing to eat. Are those the actions of a rational woman?"

Grace suddenly exploded into a fit of weeping. She clutched at the table with her rigid fingers as her body stiffened with resistance. Drudge's words were patronizing and taunting. Her mind was swirling in a morass of confusing emotions. She wanted Adam now more than ever—now that he was dead and gone. His instability had been frightening, with its menacing focus and volatile conviction, but also comforting, mostly because it was directed at a vile source she understood to be evil, even if no one else saw it that way. Adam had been her champion—her hero—a true knight in shining armor. But no more. Now he was dead and she was sitting with his killer, trying to argue for her release.

"Grace, you need sleep. You probably haven't had a decent night's rest in days. An undisturbed rest will probably do you wonders. When you wake, I'm sure you'll have a clearer head and can think more rationally."

At the tone of his sympathetic words—so grossly outrageous—she covered her face and sobbed, recalling the last blissful sleep she'd had. That had been in Adam's bed, surrounded by sheer drapes filtering out the bright morning light and the soft lullaby of dozens of songbirds keeping her dreams untainted by nightmares. She clung to that memory and wrapped it around her to shelter her from the depressing gloom barreling in on her. A pain-wracking cycle of manic moods jerked her back and forth. The memories she had of certain touches Adam left her with brought about a glimpse of hope, only to be dashed apart by the image of his horrible end. Adam was gone and her future seemed bleaker than it had ever been. She was trapped in a bizarre world where reality converged with the fantastic and her prison guard was a man more powerful in wealth and wizardry than she could dare hope to contend with. His commands and wishes were absolute, and she was nothing but a pawn in his grand scheme.

A door opened and a well-dressed man with dreadlocks came in. He went to Grace and tugged on her arm. She looked up at him through tear-streaked eyes and then over to Drudge, who nodded at the man as he wiped his mouth with a napkin. Grace burst into another spew of tears as she was forced to her feet and guided toward the door.

Markey followed Adam through the lower levels of the hospital. They strode through the bowels of the building swiftly, negotiating the turns in levels no ordinary visitor should know. When he finally reached a hidden door concealed behind hissing pipes and a contraption of chugging machinery, Markey clutched his arm. "Is this how you got away from me yesterday?"

"I'm trusting you with this secret. Never tell anyone where you're about to go."

"Who the hell would believe anything I said about this night."

Adam wrestled the door open and led the way through the breach. Just inside, as Markey cautiously sidled his way through the rusted hatch, Adam lit one of the torches left in a carved-out niche, then tucked the rest of the matches into a pocket. Thrusting out the brand, he lighted the way ahead, which Markey was startled to see was a complex system of underground tunnels and caverns.

Markey followed with an unsteady hand trailing along the dirt wall, fascinated with the direction the adventure was taking him. He marveled at how the young man hurried through the tunnels, easily negotiating the uneven passageways while Markey tripped and stumbled in tow. Several times he called for Adam to slow down, but Adam either didn't hear him, or if he did, didn't heed his request. Instead, he twisted through the intersecting network of tunnels and caverns until he finally thrust the business end of the torch into the dirt, suffocating the fire and immersing them in total blackness. Markey caught a glimpse of a door amid rubble before the light went out and then his eyes registered nothing but a pitch blackness that was like an overpowering absence of all light—and shades of light. He felt the first twinge of stark terror, a fear of being left confined in this pit to grope blindly for hours, days, weeks, for a way out, until he finally lost all sanity and clawed madly through the rock and dirt until he withered away from hunger and thirst.

Then the insurgence of his fear was doused as quickly as the torch had been when the door grated open and a dim light intruded on the absolute blackness to create silhouettes of obstacles and obstructions. Once again, Adam took the lead, his footsteps hushed but still audible. Behind him, Markey felt for a way through the debris and then the doorway, tripping once and going down hard on his knees, eliciting a curse of pain that was in the course of creating a stream of consciousness when Adam's hand caught his arm and lifted him to his feet.

"We're here."

"Where's that?"

"Back in the Tower."

"No way."

"Just follow me."

Adam led the way with cautious but hurried steps. He kept one hand on Markey's arm, tugging him along, making sure the detective didn't trip over anything. When they finally broke out of the lower levels—mounting stairs from a sub-basement to the basement—they came out at the underground parking garage where Markey's sedan still sat. The lights of the garage were a soft fluorescent but their brightness surprisingly hurt his eyes, which had grown accustomed to the blackness of the tunnels under the city. He shaded them until they acclimated to the light and he was finally able to remove his hand. Even then, the buzzing of a defective bulb sputtered with the flickering of its light.

"What's that for?" Markey asked, pointing at the dead torch in Adam's hand, which he'd brought with him from the tunnels.

"I noticed something when I was upstairs with Drudge. There was the smell of smoke but no fire. That night, over a year ago, everything was burning. The barn, Odam McArthur's silo, the neighboring properties. There was an orange glow everywhere. But this morning, back at the ranch, there was nothing. Smoke but no fire. Drudge must be afraid of invoking the elements in the Tower. Maybe he can't control them."

"What are you talking about?" Markey asked, following Adam to the bank of elevators.

"Maybe nothing," he said, pressing the button for the elevator. "Or maybe the way to blow this building to kingdom come."

Markey opened his mouth to say something but the elevator made a soft ding as the doors parted languorously. They both looked in and saw two men laying in a pool of congealed blood from both their bodies, as thick as syrup and as deep in color as mahogany. Markey moaned when he recognized Peter Lumas from his rumpled and mismatched clothes, his faceless body slumped forward after he'd sat against the wall to die. Across from him, his assailant's eyes were vacant and glassy, but his mouth was set in a stupid grin.

Adam stepped aside as Markey knelt next to his dead partner and touched his arm, confirming only that the man was indeed cold and long gone. He closed his eyes to repress the anger surging through him and the tears that were common for fallen comrades. A prayer for slain officers went through his mind as he finally reached out and took the pistol from Lumas's clutching fingers. Before he retreated from the elevator, Markey relieved the cop killer of his gun as well. He stood up, checked the magazine of one and found it had eight rounds remaining. He handed that one to Adam, who hesitated taking it. After a moment of indecision, Adam took the gun and jammed it in the back of his waistband, while Markey counted the remaining rounds in Lumas's weapon.

"Let's get this motherfucker," Markey seethed.

The second elevator landed, revealing battered metal doors puckered at their juncture and the bullet holes Markey was already aware of. Adam showed no hesitation entering the elevator and glanced impatiently at Markey when he showed a reluctance to follow suit. After some mental quibbling, Markey finally sighed and joined him in what he equated was a transport vehicle to all kinds of hellish realms. Concluding that if he was going to ride in it again, this kid was the one person he wanted with him, and if he was there—which he was—then Markey could risk the ride as well.

Adam pushed the button for the top floor. Markey grabbed his hand, but it was too late. "Jesus, kid, I've already been up there. Believe me, you don't want to go there."

Adam's eyes glinted with a mischievousness that could only be interpreted as crazy. "Yes, I do."

The elevator doors closed on any further argument and the car started its ascent, along with a maudlin Patsy Cline tune. Markey looked at his watch as his stomach roiled and sweat dripped from every pore of his body. It was just after seven a.m. Employees were not scheduled to arrive for work for another hour yet. That left them precious little time to do whatever it was they were going to do to save Grace and find Drudge.

Nervously, Markey checked to make sure a round was in the chamber of his gun, although he already knew it was. Again, he checked the clip and counted the rounds. Ten remaining. That, with the five in his .380, made for only fifteen shots. He had better make every last one count.

To his side, Adam stood calmly watching the numbers light off, his face set grim and determined. When they were only five floors away from their destination, he hefted the torch in his hand.

"Maybe you should take out that piece I gave you," Markey suggested, feeling a feverish heat emanate from his body.

"They'll be asleep by now."

Markey made a silent vocalization of the word *oh*, finding himself somehow trusting the young man to know things he didn't, seeing as though he knew about the underground tunnels. He also seemed to be okay with the twist in reality that echoed the night of his family's death, while having some knowledge that the top floor of the Tower was given over to some extra-dimensional bat cave.

Despite Adam's infuriating calm, Markey again checked the status of his own weapon.

"If you fire off a round, you'll only wake them."

Markey shot his eyes over to Adam, whose fear, if there was any, didn't show on his face. He momentarily resented his unwitting accomplice for his quiet resolve, yet he remembered his last visit to the upper floor of the Spatial Tower and how a gunshot had stirred all the bats from their slumber. He quickly jabbed the automatic into his empty shoulder holster.

The elevator dinged once it reached its destination and the doors opened slowly, putting an end to the instrumental reaching its bittersweet crescendo. Markey took a wary step back, while Adam took one forward.

Adam peered out at the vast rookery and almost gagged. The horrible smell of sulfur and ammonia was overpowering. He wanted to cover his nose but held his breath instead, leaving his hands free to work. He took out a match from the box in his pocket and struck it. When the torch fumed into a blue-orange blaze, he stepped to the edge of the door and flung the burning brand as far into the cavern as possible. The light from the torch showed the bulbous mass of thousands of bats hanging upside down from the ceiling and outcroppings. There was movement coming from their ranks as they shifted in their sleep. On the floor, the bodies of the battle-slain, bats and birds alike—but more than he hoped of the latter—made a thick carpet of corpses.

When the torch fell to the floor, the guano of a thousand pissing bats ignited like a sea of gasoline. The blue-orange flame raged in a concentric tide from the center. A pillar of fiery combustion shot upward like a Roman candle, riding a stream of fumes up to the height of the ceiling more than sixty feet overhead. The stalagmites ignited and blew tendrils of fire like fireworks, creating an image of oil wells exploding. The gases were building and expanding, much too quickly for the narrow apertures in the walls to release the vapors, and the pressure was already increasing in the cavern.

At the same time, a gleam of light—unnatural and man-made—appeared off to the side of the cavern, its brilliance standing out as an alien phenomenon despite the fact that the cavern itself was as strange as anything could get in this place. Adam immediately noticed it and looked in its direction, concerned that it might be the introduction of another quirk in Drudge's realm of irreality. But the cause seemed innocent enough when it registered with him just what it was.

A door opening, exposing a lighted corridor—or really, a stairwell landing—beyond. Briefly silhouetting itself in the glow was a figure that lurched through the door as if making a charge onto a battlefield. The figure, which was indiscernible but human-like, staggered drunkenly as it crossed the threshold. Its momentum carried it well into the cavern before it suddenly stumbled to a halt. From that instant on, the figure seemed to be in an unhealthy catatonic state, which Adam puzzled over through narrowing, squinting eyes.

Markey lunged out of the confines of the elevator and laid a tenuous hand on Adam's shoulder, tugging him back only once he was sure Adam wasn't going to spin on him with a formidable clout to the head. But Adam simply resisted his tug, and Markey found any further effort would be like trying to move a well-rooted sequoia from its anchorage in the forest. When he opened his mouth to argue Adam back into the elevator, he suddenly saw what had the young man's attention so riveted. With his own disbelief, unable to trust what he was seeing, Markey dropped his hand from Adam's shoulder.

"I don't believe it," Markey muttered as he took a few quivering, unsuspecting steps forward. "This just keeps getting weirder and weirder."

"It's a man," Adam said intuitively, knowing the figure was not one of the minions, but someone human.

"It's more than that, I'll say," Markey said, taking more steps to bring him even with Adam. They both watched the newcomer collapse to his knees, whether in disbelief or in awe, it was uncertain, but definitely not retreating from the raging conflagration, which would have been the prudent thing to do at the time.

"If I'm not hallucinating, I'd say that's Christopher Purcell."

Adam shot him a look of puzzlement. "Who?"

Markey took a few steps toward the man, who was up to his thighs in powdery guano, his body shaking as pathetic strains of weeping made it back to Markey and Adam. "That looks like the District Attorney."

Clearly baffled, Adam glared at Markey with his own expression of dubiousness. "Who?"

As the two considered who the newcomer was, a wall of fire raced along the floor igniting another puddle of flammable detritus. The encroaching heat must have put up a formidable front as it approached the stranger, because he threw up his arms to shield his face and emitted a shriek so piercing it stunned Adam out of his reverie. At the same time, the bats roosting in the cavern shifted and sputtered awake, only to notice the condition of their homestead. Off to the side, where Christopher Purcell seemed to be the target of a rampaging locomotive of fire, a front guard of combustible air preceded the conflagration. The district attorney snapped out of his comatose state with an instinct for survival. He awkwardly and clumsily spun around in the drift and scrambled toward the open door. But before he got within reach of it, the concussive wave of heat swept the door and slammed it shut. The wall of raging flames pillaged the drift Christopher sloughed frantically through.

Without urging or solicitation, Adam bolted from his rooted spot and charged through the cavern to reach the engulfed man. He heard the roaring din of the fire and Markey screaming for him to do something—come back, maybe, or even an encouragement to help the burning man—but it was the cacophony of the awakening bats that caused him the most worry.

In his charge across the cavern, leaping rivers of fire and darting around rising walls of flame, Adam shucked out of his coat and unfurled it in his hands so when he reached the writhing, smoking, shrieking district attorney, he was able to fling it over him. At the same time, he tackled Christopher out of the pyre.

Adam's impetus sent them both rolling several yards across the rocky ground, until they came up hard and painfully against an outcropping of calcified rock. Adam lurched to his feet and tugged the man up, showing no sympathy for his injuries or third degree burns. For his help, he was rewarded with a slathering of ungrateful curses carried out on high-pitched shrieks.

The expletives rolled off Adam as if they weren't even directed at him, but which caused him greater concern for what they were doing to incite the bats into a frenzy. Not only were the minions aware that their rookery had been invaded, but that it had been set aflame, and they were in a maddened panic about it.

"Get up!" Adam cursed when Christopher's legs buckled out from under him. Adam pulled on his arm, but the man only wailed all the louder, setting even the small bones in Adam's ears into a painful quiver. Above them, the bats darted about the cavern in an ever-increasing frenzy, shrieking their own echo-location to orient themselves in the fire.

"Adam!"

The call came from Markey, who was standing between the doors of the elevator as they tried to close. When they hit his resistance, they rebounded back into their recesses. The detective was frantically motioning him back to the elevator, his face gleaming with heat and anxiety. Even the air around Adam was building with pressure, losing oxygen, swelling with carbon monoxide and poisonous burn-off. It would only be minutes, maybe even seconds, before the cavern either detonated, asphyxiated every living thing, or became a battlefield he couldn't hope to contend on.

"NOW!" Markey bellowed, his shout breaking the barrier created by the rampaging fire and shrieking bats, even the piercing wails and obscenities from the luckless stranger Adam had felt compelled to help.

Adam folded the man over his shoulder to cart him off in a fireman's carry, racing back the way he'd come across the cavern, making a few veers and detours to avoid growing pockets and curtains of flame. In remarkable time, he made it to the elevator and unceremoniously threw his burden into the car, chucking him off his shoulder easily.

Markey pulled Adam through the door and jabbed at the button to close the elevator, his hand pounding frantically at the panel. The fury of the fire raced toward them and the heat it caused was scalding even where they stood. Markey cursed and beat at the panel, alternately watching the curtain of flame barreling toward them and the panel to make sure he didn't hit any buttons other than the one to the basement level.

Finally, the doors began to close, slowly—infuriatingly slow—as the audible *whoosh* of fire sounded just prior to crashing into the closed doors. The temperature in the car rose several degrees as the elevator began to descend, toning a Janice Joplin dirge, mixed with the high-pitched strains of Christopher's wails, both of which went ignored.

Markey wedged himself into the far corner, praying the cables would hold out against the conflagration. He looked worrisomely at Adam and saw that he was finally showing some concern, which did nothing to soothe Markey's own anxiety now that it was there. It was clear to both that if they tried to stop and get off on another floor, they might become victims of yet another alternate reality, which wasn't something either of them wanted. Their only hope was making it to the parking garage before the fire breached the elevator shaft and consumed the cables.

Only that wasn't to be their only concern, and their luck didn't hold out before the burning heat of the cavern failed to vent off the flammable gases fast enough. The shrieking, immolated bats that had caught fire by their guano-coated fur darted back and forth in agonizing hysteria to escape the fire storm. Their bodies packed the narrow apertures in their frenzy to get out, corking up the gases behind them. The pall of the impending explosion was palpable in the pressure building in the cavern. Stalactites cracked at their bases, rocked, and finally separated from the ceiling, falling like flaming spears to the ground, becoming nothing but sparks and sulfuric shards. Finally, the heat and pressure reached a point where something had to give, and an explosion tore through the cavern with a force like that of a thousand sticks of dynamite detonating all at once. The bodies of the packing bats were the first to give way, hurtling thousands of feet from the rooftop, raining like thick oily auroras from the sky. Then the foundations of the narrow openings tore free from the building, sending chunks of granite and rebar like asteroids across the four streets around the Tower, pummeling nearby buildings, shattering windows, tearing off flagstaffs and awnings, and punching holes in rooftops. The Tower's own roof collapsed as the backlash sucked in surrounding air to equalize its pressure. Great creaks and groans could be heard from the street below as the internal girders buckled and foundered, taking out the support of the top five floors of the immense monolith.

CHAPTER THIRTY-NINE

Drudge remained seated at the head of the dining table even as Grace was removed from the room. He ignored the rest of his breakfast and stared instead at the slight quivering of the orange juice in its crystal glass. The tremor fascinated him, but his musing was soon interrupted by the tinkling of the crystal pendants of the chandelier over the table. His eyes shifted up to watch the immense fixture sway back and forth on its swag chain. Meditatively, he rose to his feet, his chair scratching across the marble. The floor beneath his feet gave the ever so slight impression of a quake. Then a rumble sounded deep within the bowels of the building's infrastructure and instilled a sense of uncertainty in him.

A moment of curious fascination kept him from moving. Then the roof blew off his building and shook it to the very core of its foundation. The floor trembled like a freight train speeding through an unstable tunnel, sending unsecured items—breakfast plates, the juice carafe, utensils, the center piece of calla lilies and birds of paradise, Wedgwood china in an antique hutch, bric-a-brac, and the like—spilling to the floor in a clattering din that sounded twice as loud on the hard marble. The walls shifted against the studs and tore loose from their bracings. Priceless paintings swung free from their mountings or hung askew, swinging dangerously close to dumping off once sturdy fastenings. Ancient sculptures of another era jostled precariously on their pedestals and fell one by one to the marble, shattering into dust and old plaster. The chandelier pulled free at the base of the ceiling and dropped a few feet before its wiring jerked it to a stop. Momentarily though, because the weight from the thousands of tiny crystals bore too much strain on its tenuous cord and the chandelier finally came crashing down on the massive dining table, spraying shards like shrapnel from a land mine and splinters from a redwood hacked at by a crazed lumberjack.

Drudge threw up his arms to protect his face as he turned away from the spearing projectiles. He staggered a few feet to a credenza and caught his balance on it. A horrendous creaking and groaning of massive metal girders gave way to the stress of the initial explosion. Plaster from the ceiling fell in chunks and showers of dust as the floor above suffered the same injury as the one he stood on.

He managed to make his way to the door and haul it open, his feet unsteady as his hand reached for the knob, missing his first try but snagging it on the second. When he staggered into the living room, he noticed the same damage had trashed it also.

Murdock ran into the room from the outside corridor, presumably to find Drudge and check on him. His expression was one of stricken tragedy and terror. When he saw Drudge, he skidded to a halt on the marble, catching his momentum against the back of a Queen Anne-style chaise lounge. "The top of the building just blew off, Mr. Drudge," he shrieked, his voice rising like a woman's.

"How did this happen?" Drudge roared, his voice not bellowing from fear but with fury. "Who's responsible?"

"Security thought they saw two intruders in the elevator, but there was no indication of a breach in the perimeter."

"Dozens of men and millions of dollars in security measures, and yet no way to keep out a couple of saboteurs! Two saboteurs who are capable of blowing off the top of my Tower! I'll have each and every one of you turned into one of a new rookery for this fiasco." The veins in his temple and neck stood out, and his face turned an ugly purple. His eyes scowled with hooded violence. "Unless you can remedy this."

Murdock dwindled in size under the wrath of his employer. "If they're still alive after the explosion, they'll show up on the security monitors. We'll get them."

"Don't get them," Drudge said viciously. "Kill them!"

"Consider it done."

"Have my car readied immediately."

"Yes, sir." He paused only long enough to ask next, "What about the girl?"

"Have her ready to travel also. I'm taking her with me."

Murdock gave a curt nod and sped off, his tremulous body lumbering out of the living room so expeditiously that he actually seemed competent to do what he was told.

Drudge felt the slight tremors of the weakening structural beams collapsing and folding in the floors above him. He scowled at the news of the two intruders, furious that his virtually impenetrable fortress had been breached by a pair of saboteurs. The fact that the top level was the target of destruction made him believe—with certainty—that the saboteurs were privy to his secrets. He wondered if he'd underestimated Sophocles. Had his old nemesis conscripted two heirs instead of one? Or a trio? It had seemed strange that the good of the city would lay in the hands of one ill-begotten hockey player, now that he thought about it. Especially a boy like Adam Mogilvy, who's faith bordered close to heresy. Perhaps Sophocles had been so clever as to create a Doppelganger of sorts in Adam Mogilvy, so the real champions could run amok without check.

The more Drudge thought about it the more he was sure there was another successor—apparently two, it seemed—who were the true defenders. Mogilvy must have been a decoy meant to divert his attention while the true warriors instituted an attack on the Tower.

Touché, Sophocles.

Drudge's fury with such treachery was more potent than his anger at the destruction of his rookery. Although he was mortified by the obliteration of his beloved creatures, he was more humiliated by the posthumous trickery Sophocles had managed. All around him was the evidence of his defeat, the collapse of his stronghold, the devastation of his treasures, the undermining of his penultimate glory. It infuriated him in a manner he wasn't accustomed to. His body shook and his blood heated to a boil. A film of perspiration coated his flesh under his clothes, slicking his skin. Mounting anger reached to a crescendo until he threw his head back to bellow a roar of outrage. He flew into a frenzy and launched himself about the room, tearing down anything that remained upright or firmly affixed, and smashed priceless artifacts and heirlooms to dust and splinters.

Several minutes passed before he was able to restrain himself with any amount of effort, which was even more exhausting than the expenditure of his fury. He relaxed to a weary slump against the wall, his breathing labored and his chest heaving as he gulped huge amounts of air. The smell of smoke in his nostrils was the final indication that he would have to abandon the building soon. The fire would descend quickly, with portions of the weakened levels collapsing onto each floor below. Rescue measures from the city's fire department would never reach the worst damage. The building was doomed.

* * * * * *

When the explosion blew the top off the Tower, Grace and her escort were walking toward a bank of elevators at the end of the hall. Devereaux's hand on her arm was pinching, creating an ugly bruise to the exact impression of his fingers. Regardless, she didn't recognize the pain of his grip. She followed him in body only; her spirit had been broken and left shattered on the floor in the dining room. Tears had finally dried from their seemingly endless supply, proving there was a limit to them after all, and her conscious mind floated on the motes of defeat, mere iotas of a faith rocked and splintered beyond repair.

Then the explosion rocked the building and the floor beneath her feet shifted despite the precise construction of the Tower. Devereaux kept one hand on her arm while his other shot out to maintain his balance against the wall, his mouth uttering unimpressive curses and expletives. Grace's balance was thrown off by the hand on her elbow, and she uncharacteristically ordered Devereaux to let her go. Surprisingly, he did, using both hands to anchor himself as he threw his back against the wall.

Grace fell to her knees and went down on all fours, looking around as the lights flickered and the bulbs popped. The walls seemed to shift against the floor, while the ceiling tiles disjointed and fell one by one, then in a pattering of several at once, leaving gaping holes where duct work, wires, and pipes were exposed. Above her, an aluminum duct for the air conditioning shimmied, bowed, and buckled. Sparks spurted from electrical wires. Again, the lights flickered, then went out, came on briefly, and finally winked out for good, immersing her in total darkness.

"Motherfucker!"

Grace zeroed in on Devereaux's voice and decided to make the best of the unexpected catastrophe. Next to the bank of elevators she'd seen a door to the stairs. The elevators wouldn't operate without power but the stairs should lead all the way down to the ground level. She thought such an explosion would surely bring rescue workers to the scene. They would be hounding the streets, breaking into the ground floor, swarming the building to check for survivors. She would take the stairs to the lobby and wait for them to come, then sneak out among their numbers and . . .

Then what?

She had no one to turn to. No champion to rally to her cause anymore. Adam was gone and the police had proven to be corruptible. Who else would protect her from the vast resources and malevolent power of Malachi Drudge? Surely not Christopher.

But then she thought of one person who could offer her a safe haven. Sanctuary, Adam had called it. He'd taken her there when they'd first fled from the minions.

Although Drudge's human henchmen had been able to enter the church, she was more frightened of the gargoyles that had come after her than the men. Adam had trusted Monsignor O'Dwyer unquestionably. Up to this point, she'd trusted Adam's instincts to keep her safe, despite questioning his sanity. She wouldn't so easily dismiss his allies now.

The massive quaking from the initial explosion dwindled to tremors, but the terrifying sounds of the aftershock causing the building to start crumbling down around them made her realize she was only safe for the moment. Awesome creaks of iron girders bending and buckling were enough to put the fear of God in her. Showers of sparks were bursting and raining down around her, momentarily lighting up the corridor with their fireworks. She caught sight of Devereaux staring fearfully at the ceiling, gauging the destruction around them, and took the opportunity to scramble on her hands and knees toward the end of the corridor.

The hall went dark again as the last of the sparking display was suddenly extinguished. Grace hoped her last view of the hall gave her an accurate estimate of how much farther she had to go. She sidled up along the wall and used that as a guide by brushing her shoulder along it as she went. It wasn't long before she hit the traversing wall and turned down it to find the door to the stairwell. A few yards beyond the corridor, she encountered the metal door. She walked herself up to it, feeling the tremors of the building in the quaking panel. Despite her fear of how extensive the destruction was, she grasped the handle and pushed.

"Hey!" Devereaux bellowed, hearing the door open. With distracted horror, he suddenly saw that she was no longer in his custody.

Grace panicked and stuck her hands out to find the railing. Frantically, she stepped onto the landing and let the door close behind her. Her toes nearly toppled off it, but she caught herself on the rail and saved herself from a fatal tumble down the stairs. With two hands on the banister, she took a few cautious steps, then hurried down until she stumbled when she found the next landing. Frantic to escape, she turned and jostled down to the next floor.

Adam and Markey were both unaware that the roof might literally blow off the building and were unprepared for the force by which their actions actually shook the Tower. The elevator jolted violently, grating against the shaft as it shimmied on its cable, jerking and grinding with a nerve-rending sound as irritating as—yet more terrifying than—nails raked across a blackboard. Both of them were thrown to the floor, despite their bodies being braced in the corners; and along with Christopher in all his glorious hooting and hollering, they tumbled about as the lights flickered on and off.

Markey cursed out loud, his heart hammering in his chest as he thought about being too young to have a coronary. His life flashed before his eyes, and he wondered if it was significant that he would die because the elevator crashed to the base of the shaft or that his heart simply gave out. Dead was dead, he figured, and it didn't matter what he died of, only how he accepted death. Wasn't that what all the philosophers and poets had ever touted? Right then he didn't think he was handling his pivotal moment for a noble end so heroically.

Adam, on the other hand, forced his body to lay flat on the floor and distributed his weight evenly. He had no idea how powerful the explosion would be or if the entire Tower would crumble down around them, but he knew it wouldn't make any difference as long as it took out Drudge in the meantime. His only wish was that he could have gotten Grace out first.

Initially going into the endeavor, Adam believed it was more important to destroy the rookery first, so Drudge couldn't pit them against him and Markey. Secondly, they had to do whatever it was they intended before the employees arrived for work. In retrospect, half of that plan had worked, since the obvious disaster of the Tower would preclude conducting any business for Spatial Industries that day. Instead, rescue workers would be rushing in to save whatever they could of the structure, which was pretty much what he and Markey would next be working against.

At the moment, though, they didn't present any more danger to the Tower itself. Rather, it was their lives that were hinged on the precarious strength of a cable that probably wouldn't last much longer.

Finally, the calamitous explosion—or rather, a series of explosions—dwindled to only the trembling of the building collapsing in stages around them. The car came to a bracing halt, throwing them both for a heart-stopping shock. The elevator hadn't struck the bottom of the shaft but the cable had drawn taut all of a sudden. A red glow replaced the white lights that had since gone out—emergency back-up lights probably, working off a generator—and provided some illumination.

Adam pushed himself up to his hands and knees as Markey worked himself up against the mirrored wall. Christopher remained where he was, whimpering and hiccupping in the corner. Cracks and fissures had splintered through each mirrored plate, making their reflections disjointed and incongruous—and ghastly with the hellish hue of the elevator's only illumination. For the first time, Adam and Markey could see what kind of damage had been done to the district attorney when the fire had enveloped him. Most of his hair had been seared from his head, and what was left was in straggly tufts that were still smoking. His face was charred and blistered and glistening with seepage. One eye seemed to have melted in its socket, along with its lid, while the other seemed to bug out at them in pop-up fashion. His clothes, once a business suit, now appeared to be the tattered rags of a vagabond, and smoke rose off his shoulders, sleeves, and back in a languid manner. In Markey's mind, getting the man to a burn center should be one of their first priorities.

"Pretty wild," Markey said, his voice shaky and uncertain. It was his own presumption that they were both doomed, but he was willing to make an effort at least to meet his end with a cocksure bravado, even if it didn't seem to come out that way.

Adam moved with the ease of a man retaining hope. He reached out for the edge of the carpet and pulled at it. The layer came up easily, held in place by tacks only. When he threw the length up and over, a hatch was revealed in the floor. He grabbed the recessed handle and yanked the panel up.

"How'd you know that was there?" Markey asked in astonishment.

Adam sat back on his heels. He glanced over at the city's district attorney, as if wondering how safe it would be to admit his confidences to Markey in front of him. The poor man didn't seem to be in any condition to worry about his minor criminal history, so Adam said, "The tunnels lead to the Building Department. On one of my trips there, I made myself a copy of the Tower's structural plans."

"You intended this break-in all along," Markey said with accusatory disapproval.

"Wh–what's going on?" Christopher uttered in the most pathetic voice that could croak out of a larynx seared by fire. "Wh–who are you people?"

Markey scrambled over to the man but didn't touch him. He was afraid to cause any more injury to his already severely damaged flesh. "Everything's going to be okay, Mr. Purcell. We're going to get you out of here. My name is Markey, Roy Markey, and I'm with the police department. I—"

"Markey!" Christopher gasped, lunging to grab at Markey's jacket lapels, hauling him forward with a strength that belied his injuries. "Detective, yes?"

"Yes, sir," Markey said, bracing himself against the floor when he was pulled off balance. There was a frightening look in the man's face that went farther than his hideous appearance. Markey saw madness in the man and wondered why it surprised him. By all his calculations, he should be crazy himself, but he was somehow holding steady on his own.

"I didn't do it!" Christopher said, throttling Markey, which caused the detective to push his hands off. Startled and repelled, Christopher flew back and fell against the wall. His impetus caused the whole car to rock, but Christopher didn't let it affect him. He scrambled to his haunches and babbled almost incoherently. "I didn't do it, I tell you. Wasn't me. Him. It was him. He did it. Framed me. Said he'd go to the police. Wanted me to be mayor. He was going to make it happen. I swear I didn't want to do it." He curled his hands together in a beseeching prayer, imploring Markey as his benevolent god. "I'm a pawn, I tell you. Bad form. Bad karma. All that. Didn't do it, I swear. It was him."

"Get a grip on yourself, Mr. Purcell," Markey said, shifting away as if Christopher was a leper. "Whatever it is, we'll talk about it later. Right now we have to get out of here." Markey directed his next question to Adam, grateful he wasn't alone with the madman. "We can get out of here, can't we?"

Adam ignored him and stuck his head through the opening in the floor. The elevator groaned with the shifting of his weight. He withdrew from the hole and looked up at the ceiling at the same time Markey did, mentally seeing beyond the roof of the car and visualizing the tenuous cables holding it aloft.

"This car isn't going to last much longer."

Adam didn't need Markey to state the obvious. Instead, he hoisted his body through the hole and swung his legs over to the recessed rungs of a ladder in the elevator shaft. Looking back at the police detective, whose head suddenly appeared in the floor's aperture, Adam said, "Help that guy through and I'll grab him, then you follow as quickly as you can."

Then he disappeared, leaving Markey kneeling alone in the suffused red light with the incoherently weeping district attorney, an eerie aura surrounding them with the distant groaning and creaking above. The floor shifted and rumbled, and Markey knew the time was getting close to when the cable would snap altogether. With a growing sense of abandon, Markey gripped the edge of the opening and thrust his head back through, looking down into the dark shaft that showed him nothing but blackness back.

A torturous groan and jostle from the car resolved his fear. He crawled across the floor and grabbed Christopher's elbow, which seemed to have been the least obliterated by fire. "Sir, we have to leave this elevator. It's not safe to stay. I'll help you."

Christopher suddenly snapped his one probing eye at him, fixating on the last sentence out of Markey's mouth. "You'll help me?" he sobbed, tears gleaming in his eye. "You'll help me?"

Markey recognized there was something significant in his offer. He clung to that idea as he softened his tone and said, "Yes, sir, I'll help you. Whatever you need, I'll be here to help you."

"Oh, thank God," Christopher wept, burying his face in his hands and sobbing. "Thank God, thank God, thank God."

"Time enough for that later. Let's get you out of here."

Using as much delicacy as he could, Markey guided Christopher to the hole in the floor and helped him put his legs through. He held tightly to the man's upper arm as he said, "I'm going to lower you through and someone on the other side is going to catch you."

"You won't drop me, will you?" Christopher asked uncertainly, as if it didn't matter if Markey did.

"No, sir, I won't," he replied as he lowered Christopher through the hatch. The going was slow and steady, but in short order, Christopher disappeared from Markey's hands. He could only hope that Adam had succeeded in getting the man through to whatever safety there was beyond the current death trap.

Wrestling with his own mounting fear, Markey mimicked what Adam had done, going through the hole feet first. His legs kicked out to find some purchase his predecessor had found but he couldn't reach anything. He began to panic until he felt a hand clasp around his ankle and guide his foot to a rung on the wall. His other foot found another rung, and with careful negotiation, he lowered himself into the shaft.

"Just a few feet," Adam said, moving down farther, himself burdened with Christopher clinging desperately to his back, warbling a fearful moan as he stared bleakly over his shoulder into the black abyss.

Above them, the elevator groaned and creaked. A whistle of air trilled through the shaft. Markey's chest tightened with the knowledge that sooner or later the elevator would break free of the cable and plummet down the shaft, sweeping them all along with it. Time was imperative, not only to find Grace and escape the Tower, but to escape the shaft itself.

As Adam descended, struggling to keep his balance despite the weighty burden on his back, he ran his fingers along the grimy wall, searching for the access panel that would take them out of the shaft. When his hand finally encountered it, he groped along its surface for the latch.

Abruptly, Markey's feet stomped on his fingers, crushing several.

"Hey!"

"Sorry."

"What's that! What's that?" Christopher shrieked, twisting and shifting to get a view of what was happening. He'd been staring downward, terrified and slightly enthralled by the idea of plummeting into the darkness when Adam stopped and cried out abruptly.

"Stop moving," Adam ordered, wrapping his arms around the bars of the ladder to reinforce his attachment to it.

"It's okay, Mr. Purcell," Markey said, hearing the desperation in both Adam's and Christopher's voices. "It's all right. I just stepped on his fingers. My mistake. We all make mistakes."

There was silence then, as the rustling of Christopher's shifting stopped. "Yes," he said understandingly. "Yes, we all make mistakes. Grievous mistakes."

A loud twang sounded. The elevator car lurched six feet down the shaft until it was caught by another cable taking up the slack. A painful groan echoed down the shaft when the cable felt the stress from the weight of the car pull heavily on it. A whistle trilled more loudly through the gaps between the car and walls.

Adam edged over to the end of the rung and kicked his foot at the panel, once, twice, three times; each successive time more and more potent, more damaging, until the panel buckled and finally snapped from its hinges. Two more kicks had the panel skittering across the floor of the corridor beyond, but not before Christopher grappled with him with hysteria and rearranged one of his arms around Adam's neck, clinging desperately.

Immediately and heedlessly, Adam threw himself and Christopher head first through the opening. He landed on his belly, where he felt the firm, if not quivering, floor of a corridor under him. He used both hands to wrench Christopher's choking hold from his throat and scurried back across the floor to the hatch. He stuck his head into the shaft and groped blindly to reach for the detective.

Markey was more than aware of the threat of the elevator detaching itself from the cable. He grabbed Adam's hand and struggled through the opening, the two of them scrambling over each other to get away from the shaft, thrilling with the fervor of surviving a remarkably close brush with death.

On the floor they currently found themselves there was still electricity, and the lights in the corridor burned brightly yet. They looked around where they lay and saw the number next to the closed elevator doors designating it as the tenth floor. Adam struggled to his feet, followed by Markey, leaving Christopher whining and curled up on the floor. Both listened to the far away noises of the destruction they'd caused.

"Now what?" Markey asked, deferring to his accomplice for direction. Since Adam seemed to have put a lot more thought into blowing up the Tower—and for some God awful reason Markey had joined his cause—it remained up to Adam to determine what to do next. In the meantime, Markey wondered what had possessed him to take up the mantle of a terrorist. He'd always sworn to uphold the law, so why had he dismissed his sacred oath for the insanity of one disillusioned young man?

Adam saw the controversy in Markey's mind as the detective quibbled with himself over questions of ethics and sensibility. In a moment of lucid silence, while they were both still, Adam tried to explain. "My father was a police officer in Alberta, so I was brought up to respect the law. This is as hard for me to do as it is for you."

"You certainly make it look easy," Markey said.

Adam was quiet and thoughtful, but then he admitted, "I never would have hit you the other day if there was any other way out of the alley."

"Is that an apology?"

"Yes."

Briefly Markey considered dismissing it, remembering how shattering it had been to his ego to lose a prisoner not once or twice, but three times.

"I remember going to a police funeral with my father once," Adam continued. "It was a remarkable thing—inspiring, really—how hundreds of police officers from every department around came to pay their respects to someone they considered a brother. I was just a kid then, barely six at the time, but I remember looking up at my father and seeing tears in his eyes." He grew silent at the memory of his taciturn father showing an uncharacteristic remorse during that solemn occasion. "My father is a big man—a private man who's not given to open displays of emotion—but I never thought him any less of a man for crying that day."

Markey was quiet, sharing in a memory similar to the one the young man recalled, having attended slain officers' funerals in his own dress uniform. Too many funerals. Now there would be one more he would have to attend.

If he himself didn't provide substance for a second.

"So what do we do now?" he asked, finally understanding what Adam meant, who was the son of a police officer himself and must have some idea what he was feeling. That there were lines drawn that shouldn't be crossed, oaths sworn that shouldn't be forsaken, and promises made that shouldn't be broken. But while those existed in a firmament of honor, there existed evils that required the compromise of those ethics for the good of everything else.

"I'll find Grace; you get this guy down to the garage level," Adam said, nodding to the district attorney, who was propping himself up on his hands and knees and rocking back and forth, still whimpering. "When I saw her the last time, she was on the fifty-fourth floor."

"Grace?"

Both Adam and Markey turned their attention to Christopher, who brought his head up and gawked at them with his one good eye, his disfigured lips curling down in a twisted version of a frown.

"Grace? Did you say Grace?"

"Get him down to the garage," Adam said with distaste.

Markey understood Adam's aversion to the district attorney. He didn't like the man either. There was something about him that rubbed him the wrong way, and it had nothing to do with the hideous appearance of his injuries. It was the way he said Grace's name. Markey got the impression there was a vileness in its rendering.

With some form of energized imperativeness, Christopher lurched to his feet. He stumbled for balance, then wobbled toward them, his arms outstretched in an imploring gesture meant to clutch onto either of them. Markey was intuitive enough to sense Adam's distaste and step between them to keep Christopher away.

"Grace, you say. She's here? Grace?"

"Do you know a woman named Grace?" Markey asked, connecting the district attorney's interest with the name to Grace's explanation for why she'd been in the suite at the Rialto. Robert Prescott had assured him that Christopher Purcell had denied having an affair with Grace Fitzpatrick, but here he was getting all bent out of shape at the mere mention of her name.

"I didn't do it, I swear," Christopher sobbed. "I did, maybe, but I didn't do that. Not *that*. And maybe not the other thing. She's lying, I think. Probably. I think that's more like it. She'd do that, you know. Lie."

A loud crash sounded deep within the building, sending a shock wave through the floor. Christopher completed the distance to Markey in a shambling gait and caught him in a bear hug. Markey staggered backward until he stabilized himself under the man's weight, although the trembling of the ground made it doubly difficult to correct his balance. In contrast, Adam kept a sturdy posture and looked upward with concern.

"We don't have time for this," Adam said.

"You want to go up?"

"Yes."

"That floor may have already been destroyed," Markey pointed out, holding Christopher at bay, disgusted by the stench of his burned flesh.

Adam knew it wasn't a total loss yet. The birds outside showed him that the destruction of the explosion encompassed only the top five floors, taking out floors fifty-six through sixty. Yet the conflagration swallowing up the carnage left by the explosion was on its way to the levels below in a manner that would have them consumed within minutes. The idea of reaching the fifty-fourth floor and searching through the rooms to find Grace was a notion of sheer folly, but he owed it to her to try after having blown up the Tower before coming back for her.

"Don't worry about me. Just get him down to the garage and out of the building," Adam said, bolting for the stairwell.

He heard Markey make some comment about having no other choice and then arguing with the district attorney before he heard nothing but his own tromping feet on the staircase.

Grace heard the door above her open and Devereaux take up pursuit. She sobbed to herself when she realized the brutish thug would overtake her in a matter of seconds. He could barrel down the steps two or three at a time, while she could only manage one. A dull pain was beginning to build inside her. The stress of the ordeal was causing muscle spasms in her midsection, making breathing difficult and her insides liquidy. At the front of her mind, she knew she had to protect her unborn child at all costs, which meant escaping Drudge. She couldn't let a little discomfort stop her.

As the pounding of the heavy footsteps reverberated in the hollow stairwell, Grace forced herself to descend more quickly, at whatever risk. She estimated that she had a head start by three levels at least, but her pursuer would still overtake her at such a rate. She briefly debated whether she should duck into the corridor of whatever floor she reached next but figured the man wasn't that dim-witted not to realize her diversion and take after her. Instead, she kept on her current course, crying all the while at the futility of her efforts—and at her uncontrollable compulsion to cry all the time.

"She's a liar, you know," Christopher said with desperation, clutching at Markey as if he was pleading for belief. "The tramp. She's just after my money, the whore."

"Mr. Purcell," Markey said with professional exhilaration, realizing in the back of his mind that this was an untimely confession. He should have interrupted the man with his Miranda rights but he could always argue that he didn't have time for such redundancy. Besides, what jury in America wouldn't believe that a district attorney didn't already know his legal rights? "Are you the father of Grace's baby?"

"Baby," Christopher snarled, his face contorting with even more twisted features as he glowered ruefully. "So she says. But me, I think it's just a scam."

Markey shivered at the thought of this warped man having anything to do with Grace. Even before he'd seen the hideous damage done to him, Markey couldn't imagine Grace having an affair with him. She seemed too innocent and naïve to be caught up in an adulterous relationship with someone who was so worldly and complex as Christopher Purcell, district attorney and mayoral candidate, and now, it seemed, murder suspect.

"But I didn't do it," Christopher wailed, once again throwing himself against Markey, nearly sending him reeling into the wall. Again, the building shook, and it was as if the impact from the attorney had caused it. Christopher's breath came out in wickedly vile pants as he pawed at Markey. "It was Drudge. At the hotel. The Rialto. He did it. Killed that sap, I mean. Not me. I didn't. Didn't have anything to do with it. Wasn't even there. A setup, that's what it was. Blackmail. Blackmail!"

"Get a grip, man," Markey said, wrestling Christopher off him. A frightening sound of the building collapsing upon itself brought his attention back to more imperative measures: that of escape. "Let's go. We can talk about this later, after we get out of this death trap."

He grabbed Christopher's elbow and pulled him toward the staircase.

Several floors below Grace and Devereaux, Adam mounted the stairs with the urgency of knowing time was running out. He took the steps two at a time, vaulting up them as if he was used to such prolonged strenuous activity, leaving Markey and Christopher below. At the thirtieth floor, the stairwell was dark, all power out from there on up. Adam paused when he thought he heard something echoing in the stairwell, something other than his own footsteps. When he filtered out their noise, he could still hear it. Steps coming from above, and something else. Weeping.

He put even more power behind his legs and drummed up the stairs with an exhilarating urgency. He knew the sound of that whimpering, had become accustomed to it in the course of the last few days. Hope swelled in him as he considered calling out to her, sending a message that she was going to be okay—they were all going to be okay—once he reached her.

But he heard other footsteps beyond hers and a man making threats of what he would do when he finally reached her. Adam decided that in this case discretion would definitely be the better part of valor.

Grace heard Devereaux threatening to thrash her to within an inch of her life when he finally caught up with her, and began to cry more in earnest, her hand slick with sweat and sliding along the cold metal railing. She tried to keep count of how many steps she descended so she didn't trip on the next landing, but it was hard to keep track. She misjudged her last step and nearly stumbled to her knees, but her hold on the railing kept her upright.

During that brief mishap, she heard the approach of someone else, other than Devereaux behind her, coming at full throttle from below.

In a panic, she froze, then abruptly threw herself against the wall to avoid the stranger's barreling upward charge. She hoped that whoever it was would collide with Devereaux instead, who was right then lumbering down on the last switchback. They could thrash each other for all she cared, but in the meantime, she'd be racing down the stairs.

Adam paused halfway up the stairs to listen, no longer hearing Grace's lighter footsteps from above. There was also no more whimpering. It was as if she'd stepped off into oblivion, leaving no indication that she was in this world anymore, which was entirely possible in Drudge's freakish Tower.

But there was still something intangible in the stairwell that gave him the impression that she was there yet, a presence of her, along with the pursuer who was now no more than two floors above. That was someone he would have to deal with first, and he was confident he could do so with minimal risk to either himself or Grace.

Treading softly, he continued his way up the stairs until he reached the top of the landing and paused, cocking his head to one side to listen. The threatening steps from above were now only one flight up. He tilted his head to the other side and heard it, a barely audible intake of breath to his right, in the corner of the landing.

* * * * * *

Grace knew someone was standing no more than four feet away. She shivered with fear and held her breath so that not even the air passing through her nostrils would make a sound. Yet she was very much aware of how heavy her heart was beating, so loudly she was sure the stranger would hear it. She bit her lip as her chest burned with the need for oxygen, and she mentally cursed the man for pausing so long on the landing—as well as her luck that it would be on this landing where he and her pursuer would meet.

Devereaux thundered down the stairs and bounded onto the landing, promising to do awful things to Grace for trying to escape him. They were empty threats but they made him feel more powerful and terrifying, and he got off on that. Drudge had given him no leeway for manhandling her, and Devereaux wouldn't be able to indulge his mean streak in anything more than a few rugged jerks and pushes once he got a hold of her again. If he made any move contrary to Drudge's orders, he would wake up to find himself nothing more than a spatter of ash on the floor.

But that didn't mean Devereaux couldn't use the opportunity to frighten her into a Godless fear in the meantime.

As he turned on the landing to start down the next flight, having heard the heavy tread of the woman making her way down, he was barely aware of an incredible sledge hammer smashing into his throat. But what felt like a sledge hammer was actually a forearm swinging at his neck, connecting mightily, knocking him off his feet, and landing him promptly on his ass. He thought his trachea must surely be crushed, and the rattle of his breath made him deathly afraid that it was. Because of that, he began to panic, and then more so when a heavy weight fell atop his chest and pressed out what little remaining breath he had in his lungs, while a sharp blade pricked his throat.

"Leave her alone," Adam whispered as he used two fingers to press into the arteries of Devereaux's throat. Blood ceased to pulse into his brain, and within seconds, the man was out.

Grace jerked spastically when she heard Devereaux and the stranger come together. They were only a few feet from her when it happened. Then a jolt of excitement went through her when she heard Adam's voice. She nearly cried out with joy at the sound of it but didn't; she knew she should let him finish whatever he was up to before celebrating.

When she finally heard Adam rise from the floor, Grace threw herself at him, her arms flinging around his shoulders. Tears of joy streamed down her cheeks, and she buried her face in the crook of his neck.

"Oh God, Adam, you're alive! You're alive!"

"Shhh," he hushed and stroked her hair to calm her. The man he'd rendered unconscious wouldn't remain that way for long. Adam had only gained them a few minutes before the man regained consciousness. After that, he'd come after them like an enraged bull prodded with a red hot poker.

"I thought you were dead," Grace cried. "I saw Drudge hang you."

"Detective Markey cut me down."

Grace peered through the dark to see who he meant but she couldn't see anyone. Confusion misted through her thoughts. "Detective Markey? He's here?"

"Down below, helping someone else out of the building," Adam explained, running his hands over her to make sure she was all right. "We've got to get out of here fast. This place is falling down around us."

CHAPTER FORTY

Markey was having trouble with Christopher in the stairwell. The man seemed to be single-mindedly geared to one purpose and that was following Adam up the stairs in his search for Grace. But Markey didn't think the district attorney was on any selfless mission to find the poor woman and bring her safely out of the building. Instead, if he had to guess, Markey thought it was for exactly the opposite reason that Christopher Purcell wanted to find her, and Markey was damn sure he wasn't going to let the man get anywhere near the poor girl.

All his hopes of getting the district attorney out of the building before Adam returned with Grace were dashed when he heard the two of them tromping down the stairs. Christopher heard them also and grew silent and passive in his grip, seemingly willing to be guided as Markey had been trying to do the whole time. But when Markey made just such a suggestion, intoning it with a respectful air that is afforded to lunatics on the fringe, Christopher suddenly attacked him and sent him reeling off the landing.

Markey toppled backward, his arms pinwheeling for balance but finding none. He fell head over heels down the staircase until he bounced off the next landing and struck the wall. He laid there for a minute, trying to take an assessment of his body's aches and pains before he sensed something more volatile was about to happen in his absence on the stairwell.

* * * * * *

Above Markey, Christopher stormed up the stairs, heaving laborious breaths and finding it difficult to draw in air through his scorched trachea. He was in excruciating pain and running on reserves, but he was more infuriated with the idea that Grace was in the building and this was all her fault. Everything that had happened to him in the past few days could be blamed on her.

I'm pregnant.

A lie maybe, but one that was a catalyst to start all the bad fortune in his life. Until she'd made that fateful statement—lie!—everything had been perfect. His life had been blessed. His future had been certain. His wagon had been hitched to a shining star. But now . . .

Bitch, he was going to kill her. He was going to wrap his hands around her throat and squeeze the life from her worthless Jezebel body. And if she was indeed carrying the spawn of some other man's seed—because it couldn't be his; he'd been far too careful to let that happen—then it could die, as well, as it should have.

In mere seconds, they came upon each other, Christopher coming up the flight of stairs as she and her companion—probably the real father of the imp she was carrying—came down. They spied each other as she and her lover turned the switchback. Everyone froze, surprised at the encounter, maybe even a little frightened by it, but it was enough for Christopher to see her and know she was indeed a tramp, a whore, because she looked trashy in her pullover shirt and sweat pants, with her hair hanging straggly and in disarray, and her face blotched with red patches, her eyes red and her cheeks glistening. She certainly looked like the two-bit whore he thought she was without all the primping and preening he was used to seeing.

And the man beside her, with his garish look of brooding contempt, that freakish tattoo on his forehead and cold eyes glinting dangerously back at him, looked every bit the rogue he imagined Grace to hook up with. The two of them had probably concocted this scheme to get him to pay them off, just so he wouldn't lose the election because of a scandal. They were probably in league with Drudge also, and he was just the patsy in their grand plan. Only that wasn't going to happen now, because he was on to them.

Above Christopher, on the next landing, Grace gasped and threw her hand over her mouth, while Adam gripped her arm to steady her.

Adam wasn't aware of the relationship between Grace and the man she now confronted but he sensed they knew each other. The reaction between the two was just too obvious for there not to be something significant in it. He imagined what Grace saw—what he saw himself in the same manner she must being seeing it for the first time—was a hideous parody of a man who might have been, at one time, extremely handsome and dignified. But the man looking up at them, staring with something akin to murderous hatred, looked grossly like what the Phantom of the Opera must look like without his ceramic mask. Something grotesque and nightmarish, and something that might have been pitied if it wasn't for the expression of fury contorting his features even further out of symmetry.

"Christopher?" Grace whispered behind her hand, her voice weak and tentative. She apparently didn't know what to think. "Is that . . . you?"

Christopher slowly pulled himself up the stairs, stalking up them with a hollow look on his face. His one eye never blinked as it remained riveted on her.

Grace stiffened at his approach but refused to back away. Perhaps she thought about how this was the father of her child and she couldn't turn her back on him. Not when he was going through something truly terrifying.

"Christopher, wh-what happened to you?" she croaked, pulling her hands away from her face. "You . . ."

"Grace," Adam whispered softly, warningly, noticing something palpable emanating off the man. He was already halfway up the stairs and close enough for Adam to sense it. Adam didn't need any special prescience to know when a man was besieged by hatred. It glinted in his one remaining eye. But Grace couldn't see it, and it was because they must have once shared a relationship that she didn't. She wasn't seeing the truth; she was seeing only what she wanted to see.

"Oh God, Christopher," Grace said, breaking out of her revulsion and apparently remembering him as the man she had once loved and would have agreed to share the rest of her life with.

Before Adam could stop her, Grace flew down the stairs in an effort to embrace Christopher and show him that she wasn't repulsed by the grotesquery of his injuries; that she would accept him no matter how hideous he looked. Even Adam knew that love was more than appearances and material things. It was self-sacrifice and generosity and sharing of oneself. It was enduring through all the trials and tribulations, and triumphing over the tragedies. You didn't do that alone; you had to do it with someone else. Grace obviously believed that, too.

But Christopher wasn't interested in any of that and only wanted to satisfy his need for revenge. He reached out for her as he took another step up and she ran down another, her arms reaching for him. He anchored himself in place as she neared him, so that when she was close—oh, so close—he lifted his aching arms and seemed to welcome her into his embrace, only to lift them higher, just a little higher, so his hands were even with her shoulders and his fingers clasped around her neck, slotting it into his crimped fingers so easily it felt just right. Christopher clamped it tight, so tight his fingers squeezed off her cry of alarm and wrenched out a squeaking noise that was so rewarding he gritted his teeth and squeezed even tighter still.

A second later, Adam flew down the stairs after Grace, barely in time to reach her before Christopher had a hold of her. But then Christopher had her and it was one of the most brutal choke holds Adam had ever seen on anyone, even worse than the rope that had been around his neck. He grabbed Christopher's hands and tried to pull them off her, but the fury in the man—the sheer determination to murder her—was livid in him. Grace's hands went up to his wrists, as well, trying in vain to pull them off, but her efforts were just as ineffectual. Teetering on the brink of the stairs, Adam was afraid they would all fall. Then he thought that that might not be such a bad idea, since it just might break Christopher's hold. But then he realized the futility of that option when he remembered Grace was pregnant and a fall like that could cause serious damage to the baby, if not Grace, and decided it was more important that she *not* fall. Only she was making this pathetic hacking noise as she tried to breathe and couldn't, and Christopher was grunting with exhilaration and, dear God, he was laughing, cackling like a lunatic as he rattled his hands and shook Grace like a rag doll.

Adam released Christopher's wrists and went for his neck, latching onto him like Christopher had Grace. Only Adam worked more dexterously with his hold and wrenched the man's body upward; up the stairs, lifting him off his feet, twisting him until he spun him around. Grace came with him, stumbling and struggling to keep her footing but tripping on the steps, kicking out with her feet. Adam hauled Christopher fully around, throttling him so he might choke the breath out of him, and if not just that, then the life, because one way or another, he was going to get the madman to let her go.

Which was what Christopher ended up doing. But when he did, Grace lost her footing and screamed, the shriek coming with the last of her breath and not lasting long. It was enough for Adam to realize she was falling, which was just what he didn't want her to do. He let go of Christopher and groped for her, hoping to snatch something of her, a limb, a piece of clothing, anything. He felt just a brush of fabric between his fingers before it pulled out of his grasp. There was another scream, this one higher, more desperate and more stricken with fear.

Adam reacted instinctively, launching himself off the step as well, thinking he could fly after her and save her from tumbling down the stairs. That was when Christopher attacked him and stopped his forward momentum, probably saving Adam from going headfirst into a deadly tumble down the stairs but not saving Grace from taking hers. Instead, Adam fell backward, which was actually *upward*, and he landed hard on his chest, feeling the corner of one step jab into his gut and send such a wave of pain through him he felt he was paralyzed. He got his hips and arms moving to twist himself over, just in time to see Christopher throwing himself down at him.

Instantly, Adam's feet connected with Christopher's midsection. He only meant to keep the lunatic from tackling him, but his legs recoiled from their contraction and pistoned, sending Christopher sailing through the air. The district attorney rode a crest of kinetic energy, arcing high enough to slam into the wall of the switchback, where he slid down and lay crumpled in a jumble of sprawled arms and legs.

Adam wasted no time in lurching up and running down the stairs, not really concerned with Christopher, but more with Grace, and he found her in a shell of her body on the landing.

"Grace," he exclaimed as he crouched next to her and gingerly touched her head, stroking her hair in fear that she might be dead, or if not that badly off, then paralyzed. "Grace."

His first indication that she was still alive was the crying. Adam discovered this not from her weeping but from the shaking of her body as she curled tighter into herself and sobbed.

"I'm an idiot," she mumbled into her arm, sniffling wetly. "Such an idiot."

"Are you all right?" Adam asked, more than ever aware of how dangerous it was to stay any longer in the building. He could feel the quaking of the structure more potently than the quivering of her shoulders.

"I'm such a pathetic fool," she babbled, ignoring him. She shifted just enough for him to see she wasn't paralyzed from the neck down, which was a good thing, if not for her crying. "I loved him. I thought . . . he'd love me back."

"We have to leave," Adam said, uncomfortable with her crying as much as he was about being trapped in a building that was falling down around them. "We can talk about this later."

She lifted her head, her eyes swollen and glistening, her face drawn with the saddest expression that could ever mar such a beautiful face. "I loved him, Adam."

Markey appeared on the next landing, pausing in his assessment of what had happened upward of him. When he saw Grace on the ground and Adam hovering over her, he darted up and joined them. At the same time, he spied Christopher in his unlikely alignment of body parts, and paused. He met Adam's eyes and decided not to ask, simply knelt beside the man and felt for a pulse at his neck.

"He's still alive," Markey said, breathing a sigh of relief. "But I don't think he can make it down on his own."

Adam straightened up. "You get Grace; I'll take him. Let's just get out of here."

CHAPTER FORTY-ONE

Drudge took his time descending from the upper residential floors. He looked around with sentimental longing as he said farewell to his priceless treasures and possessions, those pieces of art and sculpture that would ultimately succumb to the blazing inferno raging as close as the floor above him. Even now, the paint on the mural ceiling was cracking and bubbling, turning into liquid and dripping like sizzling oil onto the marble floor. The silk wallpaper near the ceiling was smoking and curling apart from the wall, the glue beading and releasing pungent odors of toxic gases.

He wasn't worried about asphyxiating on poisonous fumes but the fire frightened him a little. Hell was depicted as a burning inferno, and that was a good enough analogy, but only in the most metaphorical sense. Hell was so much more, a gloriously horrifying realm as unpleasant, frustrating, demoralizing and frightening as any bleak period in human history. The Black Plague had nothing on Hell, nor did the Spanish Inquisition or Nazi Germany, nor Somalia, for that matter. Hell was blistering, scorching, boiling, and raging, but only metaphorically so. Drudge could exist there in a thriving environment but not if it was the molten underworld it was believed to be. He had no control over fire, no power to bend it to his will or coax it into obeisance. His expertise involved manipulating time and space, twisting and folding them as if the two were pieces of paper he was working into an origami creation. The elements were out of his control; they were the furies of the cosmos and belonged to someone else, a collection of untamable forces that answered to no command of his.

A crash from a wall collapsing and the ceiling it upheld made Drudge abandon his maudlin musing for the loss of his palatial home. He'd left behind several lairs in the past, forsaking millions in material assets just to survive with his hide intact. He'd been forced to rebuild from nothing on other occasions, dragging himself up from the ashes and dredging up his fortune from the misery of others again and again. It hadn't been so hard; in fact, in retrospect, it had been enjoyable. And this time wouldn't be entirely too difficult. Although his most precious loss had been his rookery—setting his work back by decades—there were always seeds to plant and harvest into another roost. More people willing to sell their souls for riches, fame, glory, or depravation. It would take time; time for him to gather his lackeys, make good on his contracts, and slowly wean them into a colony, but it was possible. And his plans for this city were still reconcilable, so he wasn't so far from where his scheme originally planned him to be.

Drudge sauntered defiantly down the hall, toward the bank of elevators. He calmly pressed the call button and waited as one car rose from the ground level in good time, despite the main power being out and everything running on auxiliary sources. Showers of sparks burst around him from gaping holes in the ceiling. Aluminum ducts hung down like broken silver worms cut in half. Patches of fire already burned on the carpet. The electricity was out but the elevator still worked, still played Muzak—a Pat Boone song—still rose and descended as he stepped in and pressed the button for the parking garage. His car would be ready to drive Grace and him from the building. He would slip inside and ride next to her as they set out to rebuild in another part of town, leaving behind all this destruction.

It was just a minor setback, not insurmountable.

The building around him shifted and groaned in ever-increasing intensity, the imminence of its collapse evident in its agonized creaking and grumbling. The elevator protested against the quaking, making for an unsteady ride. But Drudge stood calmly and confidently, regardless of the tantrum the car was throwing, unconcerned that the cable still hung by a thread and that thread was slowly unraveling. The elevator would carry him surely—if a bit roughly—down to the garage, where he could make his exit. He was sure of it.

Regardless of the danger, it was imperative that he maintain a cavalier attitude for his public persona, to show his employees and the witnessing city that he was still all powerful and indefeasible, despite the attack on his Tower. Allowing them to see him overwhelmed and devastated would only reduce his image as a powerful financial mogul. The world loved a strong warlord, even if they only believed his interests lay in reaching superior status in business and not in conquering humanity. Pity never carried anyone to lofty heights—nor did he have it in him to evoke sympathy for himself.

The elevator finally reached the level of the parking garage, with the doors opening to disgorge him and the soft Muzak falling to silence. When Drudge stepped from the elevator, he was surprised and more than a bit irritated to see that his car was not waiting for him as he'd ordered. Nor was Grace ready to ride from the building with him. Instead, he heard a flurry of noise coming from the stairwell and spun on the door to acknowledge his employees' lack of efficiency in getting anything done right.

* * * * * *

THE UNFAITHFUL

Adam led the way down the stairs, carrying Christopher's limp body draped over his shoulder. Markey held onto Grace's hand as much to satisfy her need to feel his existence as to guide her down the stairs safely. She was no longer weeping, but she descended the stairs at a reserved pace. He tried not to pull too roughly on her in deference to her delicate condition and the trauma she'd already been through. His own exhaustion was mounting, but not as greatly as when he'd been racing up the stairs. So far, all the activity he'd been forced to endure had impressed on him just how much in need of exercise he was.

They reached the garage level almost on top of each other and burst through the door in a rush to make headway for the last leg of their escape, falling into the parking lot like laundry spilling from a chute. Adam was the first to see Drudge waiting for them only a dozen or so feet from the door, and he skidded to a bracing halt to maintain as much distance between his group and the minion lord as possible. Grace ran into him from behind and grabbed at his shoulder when she saw who was standing there. Markey came up more slowly when he registered that Adam and Grace had suddenly stopped. He looked past them to see Drudge standing alone and impertinently in front of them.

While Drudge's face showed that he was aware of someone coming down the stairs, by his expression, it was apparent he hadn't expected it to be them.

Drudge believed there was little that could surprise him in this mundane and trifling human world, but seeing a man he'd left for dead—not once, but twice—threw him for a loop. His mind flickered on the realization that this was the second time Adam Mogilvy had survived him, and that was unheard of. Fury was his first reaction after he swept aside his confusion, a rage that could wrench the monolithic tower he'd constructed from the very foundation it rested on—if it wasn't already falling down around him. His eyes blazed an inhuman red and his brow became a field of furrows as he scowled. The corners of his lips came up in anything less than a smile, and his teeth were sharp and deadly, unabashed in their daring display. Purple flushed his face to prove his blood was boiling in his veins, and the heat emanated off him like a burning pyre.

The three standing individuals at the entrance to the stairwell seemed just as surprised to see him as Drudge was to see them. Grace shrank behind Adam, while Markey boldly came around to the front, his gun pulled from his shoulder holster and aimed in Drudge's direction. As for Christopher, who remained unsuspecting of what was going on, he lay draped over Adam's shoulder as a severe disadvantage. Because of that, and because Adam had no respect for the man after what he'd done to Grace, he unceremoniously dumped him on the floor, freeing himself up to do whatever was necessary to get Grace out of the building.

Drudge narrowed his eyes as he spied the twisted and melted face of the man lying on the ground. Adam's gesture of dropping him seemed too much like a despoiler laying his booty before him for Drudge not to make such an assumption of superiority in the young man. He pointed at Christopher with an elongated finger and croaked out a disbelieving question. "Is that my district attorney?"

"That's Christopher Purcell, yes," Markey stated arrogantly, stepping forward so he could shield the unconscious D.A. with his own body. He defended himself with his gun. "And I've got some questions for you about his well-being."

Drudge ignored Markey's pompous authority. With fury, he screeched, "What did you do to my district attorney?"

"*Your* district attorney?" Markey challenged back.

"Markey," Adam cautioned, raising an arm.

"Adam," Grace whimpered against his back, using the man who'd once been her champion as her shield again.

"Mr. Drudge, you're under arrest for kidnapping and attempted murder."

Drudge shot his rabid eyes over to Markey, daring him with his violent but communicative stare not to make any move against him. Markey, having suspected an underlying malevolent power brewing within the businessman, hesitated approaching any farther.

"Are you responsible for blowing up my building, Detective?" Drudge demanded, his words a sibilant hiss of anger venting in measured stages. "Aside from making mince meat out of my district attorney."

"I am," Adam interjected, taking a step forward, leaving Grace behind but not far off.

"Then, my boy, *you've* wasted your time," he snarled. "Do you think you could set me back by such a dramatic gesture of destroying my Tower, attacking my material possessions like a petulant child who's not allowed to play with his brother's toys? You're a fool. Don't you know that I've kept up with the times. The building's insured. I'll recoup my losses faster than it takes this building to crumble to the ground." He looked with forlorn disturbance at Christopher. "But maybe not him, though."

"And not your rookery," Adam said and saw a flicker of volatile anger infuse Drudge's face. He turned quickly to Markey, speaking to him next, his voice low and determined, resolved to finish things that should have been finished the night it all began. He should have aimed for Drudge's head back then, which was what he was going to do this time. "Detective, get Grace out of here." He gestured to Christopher. "Then come back and get this creep."

Markey glared at Adam, his eyes narrowing with dispute. "This man is under arrest, Adam. I'm taking him in."

"He's not leaving here," Adam said in steadfast defiance. "Not alive, at least."

Drudge shot his blazing eyes over to Adam, a knowing challenge accepted. "So you want to wager again?"

"No," Adam said. "I want what you owe me."

"And what would that be, *Slash*?" he asked maliciously, his head inclining forward to show an interest in hearing what it was. By the tone of his voice it was apparent that he didn't believe Adam was entitled to anything. "The last thing I recall, you owed me obeisance."

"I owe you nothing," Adam shouted, anger brimming within him, infusing him with a fury difficult to contain. Off in the distance, he could hear—and see briefly through his remote avian eyesight—the arrival of emergency vehicles urging their way through spectators crowding the streets. Above them, the building was making angry sounds as the levels collapsed one on top of the other, rumbling the floor beneath their feet. The weight of each collapsed level made the next one doubly quicker to fall. Eventually, the tremendous weight would crumble down around them, ending their dispute without even the first punch thrown; which was fine with him, as long as it took Drudge with it. He would even hold the bastard in the parking garage as the building imploded if it meant the end of Malachi Drudge.

"I don't want to be here anymore, Adam," Grace moaned. Her legs were weak and about to buckle, and her stomach roiled with piercing pains.

Hearing Grace's tremulous voice was all it took to jerk Adam out of his infuriated daze and focus on his options. He'd accomplished two out of the three things he'd set out to do. Drudge's rookery was destroyed, scattered to the four corners of the city and not likely to be replenished any time soon. And he had Grace, as close to safe as being among a hundred police officers—if he could only get her out of the building. But he had yet to destroy Drudge. Without that, all he'd accomplished so far would only be a minor distraction for the lord of the minions. Drudge would simply rebuild his empire, his rookery, and his plans all over again, to reign supreme.

"Adam, it's over," Markey said, sensing the rage of vengeance growing too dangerous in the young man. "He knows it's over, too."

"Do I?" Drudge asked sardonically, his head cocked in a gesture of mocking inquiry. Then, with a tone of grating menace, he said, "It's never over. It's always and ever shall be an eternal struggle."

Markey chewed on something to say but forestalled it in favor of discretion. He sidled over to Grace, thinking she was the most vulnerable to an attack at the moment.

A distant noise of angry construction offered protest to the weight of the ever-persistent destruction above them. The catastrophic wreckage of the upper floors continued its rampage without mercy, while pieces of the burning conflagration fell to the streets below. Loud crashes and screams of bystanders were followed by the barking orders of people in charge commanding everyone to get back.

Adam took advantage of the clamor to act purely out of instinct. He launched himself at Drudge, barreling into him with a full-fledged body slam. He had checked the likes of the nastiest defensemen in the professional sport of hockey, and plowing into this impertinent warlord was comparably satisfying. His impetus drove the two of them into the police sedan, and Drudge's back connected with the hood with an impressive and resounding echo. Muscle memory took over as Adam pummeled Drudge's exquisitely crafted face with his bare fists. He lost all conscious thought of anything other than his stunned enemy at his mercy, his fists aching with each contact of bony tissue. But it also gave him an exhilaration he had never quite felt before, and the pain became nothing but a phantom ache in the back of his mind.

Drudge, on the other hand, felt the frailties of his human body suffer from the pounding, his legs becoming weak and unsupportive. He began to slide off the car but he was held up with a hand on his bunched clothing. His eyes puffed frightfully, although he could still see the pistoning fist slamming repeatedly into his face, and he thought he might be very close to suffering brain damage. When he tried to regain control of his body, his limbs were nothing more than slack extensions of himself. His astonishment at the sudden attack had prevented him from setting up an immediate defense, and now he was beginning to realize he had no control over his broken body anymore.

Markey held himself in check as Adam attacked Drudge, allowing the young man to take his pound of flesh. But when the expression on Drudge's face went past vacant and close to death, he forced himself to move forward and intercede. He hesitatingly laid a restraining hand on Adam's shoulder, a bit antsy about his own safety in case the ex-defenseman instinctively turned against him.

But Adam reverted back to memories conducive to times on the ice and remembered referees pulling him off a player when the fight became too violent, or after the issue had been resolved. A respect for the hand on his shoulder made him relinquish his hold on Drudge. He pulled away with a violent trembling surging through his entire body, his skin flushed and slick with perspiration. He watched breathlessly as Drudge slumped to the floor, his body crumpling like a bag of boneless limbs. A conflict of emotions assaulted him all at once, and Adam backed up even more from the body he would have easily killed if he was permitted to.

"Hey! You there! You have to get out of the building! Don't you people realize what's happening?"

Markey and Grace turned to the commanding voice echoing across the parking garage. Three fully geared firemen had entered through the same door Markey had come through at the beginning of the night. They carried axes but no fire hoses, and their mission was to make sure no one was still inside while the building burned. They jogged across the parking garage, their concern a race against time. But then they slowed when they saw that something significant had just taken place.

"Holy shit!"

Markey turned to see what one of the fireman meant, thinking he had an opinion about the brutality he'd just witnessed. But what Markey saw made him repeat the fireman's remark, only with his own twist of disbelief. Grace looked over his shoulder and screamed, while the other two firemen stared in wordless horror at the body by the car.

Adam had never taken his eyes off Drudge when the firemen made their appearance, but he took a few fearful steps back as Drudge sloughed off the clothing and human skin he'd used for his disguise as a millionaire businessman. His head and face fell away in several splitting pieces of bloody tissue, gory chunks of flesh and blood dripping from the true construction beneath. Bone shifted and reformed as the genetic makeup forsook its design and took on another more hideous convolution of cartilage and calcium. A feral face with red reptilian eyes and iridescent scales, sharp outstanding ears and a nose that lay flat against itself formed upon the shoulders of bulbous protrusions of bone. The thing's head reared up from the floor and twisted on a serpentine neck, coiling to look at the people who gawked in utter disbelief at its transformation. Its body shucked aside its human chrysalis, shedding its clothes and flesh like a dry husk peeling away. Beneath the human exterior was a humanoid body, with more prismatic scales covering its entire torso, transforming to stiff bristling limbs bending at awkward angles. Black claws and talons curled to raptor-like extensions, and massive leathery wings arched above its broad shoulders, the malformed evidence of a truly fallen angel. The demon rose to full height, towering over the car, nearly scraping its head against the ceiling.

"Oh. My. God," one fireman moaned as he dropped his ax from his shoulder and held it limply at his side.

Grace continued to scream as she clutched at Markey, who was the closest to her. He brought her into his body and aimed his gun at the hideous creature, firing several shots at the monster. The bullets hit in all the apparently vital spots but the creature showed no sign of faltering. Its head twisted and rose, howling at the audacity of the attack. It sprang forward with lightening speed, its long neck streaking out from its body like a jack-in-the-box, aiming directly for Markey.

Adam reacted instinctively, snatching a knife from his coat and stepping into the attack. He threw out his arm and jabbed the blade into the creature's throat, yanking it viciously to cut a length down its sinewy neck. The creature rose up high and pulled itself free of the blade, shrieking with pain and fury. Its arms clutched at its lacerated throat and closed over the wound, while its head swiveled around to take in where the attack had come from. It spied Adam turning to mount another strike, and roared, a resounding challenge causing Adam's bones to rattle. Adam danced backward several steps, putting distance between himself and the beast but not enough to indicate a retreat. In his hand he held a six-inch blade that evoked none of the confidence it had instilled in him when he'd confronted members of Drudge's minions. Regardless, it provided a measure of resolve that this battle would be to the death. One of theirs, at least. He'd see to it.

"Get her out of here!" Adam yelled at Markey, who was riveted to the spot where he'd stood when the demon first attacked.

Markey wrenched himself out of his paralysis and swept Grace along, the two of them running at full throttle away from the foray, toward the door in which Markey had made his illegal entry.

The demon howled with fury and launched itself at the two fleeing individuals, its clawed feet making terrifying scratches along the concrete floor. Adam ran after it, forcing all his available energy into his legs. At the same time, two of the firemen swung into action, their lives dedicated to service and rescue. Both hefted their axes and stood their ground, while the third beckoned Markey and Grace forward. Markey dragged Grace the final few feet as the demon hurled itself into the air, its wings unfolding and taking flight. One fireman swung his ax and caught the demon a glancing blow on the thigh, while the other missed his target entirely, the force of his tremendous swing turning him completely around.

The creature made a smooth turn in mid-flight and made another pass at Grace and Markey. Just before it reached them, Markey dragged Grace down behind a column so the creature would have to swerve to avoid colliding with another pillar. When it turned to make another pass, Adam stepped from behind a column of his own and reached out with both hands to grasp a dangling foot as it went by. He felt his arms nearly wrenched from their sockets by the velocity with which the demon flew. He dropped all his weight at that moment and managed to throw the creature off balance. Both of them tumbled across the floor with maddening speed, the velocity of their out of control skittering throwing them against the wall.

Adam was slow in getting up. His injuries from the past few hours protested against the exertion, and he was once again revisited with the thought that maybe a few of his ribs were broken instead of bruised. Yet the scrabbling sound a few yards away made him realize this was a race to see who could regain their feet first, and he was determined that it would be him.

He struggled up against the wall as something pressed painfully into the small of his back. With that, he suddenly remembered the gun Markey had given him. Despite the ineffectual consequences of Markey firing several shots from his own weapon, Adam pulled the gun and triggered off five rounds into the face of the leering creature, hoping the brain would suffer significantly and shut down. But even though the head rocked with each successive shot and pieces of its face blew away, the creature merely hauled its neck back and flexed its wings to take to the air again.

On the far side of the parking garage, near the exit, Markey glanced over his shoulder as Adam fired off the shots. He longed to help but knew his first concern should be Grace and then Christopher Purcell. He had to get them out of the building. The beast had been hell-bent on getting its hands on Grace; it was imperative that he keep her safe and worry about the district attorney later. In the meantime, the unwitting firemen would have to provide some distraction until he could return to do battle alongside Adam.

"Come on, you ugly old bat," Adam taunted, holding his hands—palms out—for show. "You kept saying you'd meet me on the other side. Well I ain't coming, so you'll just have to come and get me on your own."

The demon roared an ear-shattering ululation as it flung itself at Adam. Its wicked talons slashed at him as Adam armed himself with two knives, both blades scissoring in front of him. Claws raked across his chest, slicing through the sturdy material of his coat and the shirt beneath, then his very flesh, rivering lacerations across his chest, raking over the struts of his ribs, even as Adam made his own slices across the creature's torso, landing them deep, prying deeper, and then digging, digging, and digging even more. He grappled with the beast and spun it around into the wall, pinning it there with his weight while one of his blades ran down the beast's abdomen, severing skin, flesh, muscle and then guts, all in order to disembowel it. He felt his own body become drenched in a warm liquid as an inner heat radiated across his chest, and steam issued from between their faces.

The roguish gargoyle distended its jaws as it wailed in agony. A sickening stench of putrid rot fumed around Adam's head. Furiously, he pushed away from the demon and scrambled backward, looking down at his hands as they pulled away from his own body bathed in glistening blood.

The beast tossed its head back and forth in an agonizing thrashing, its claws clutching at its entrails straining to burst from its bowels. Its awkwardly bent legs thrummed.

One of the firemen raced forward and swung his ax, bellowing a primitive cry the likes of which Adam had never heard come out of a man before. The blade cleaved into the creature's thigh and toppled it like a felled giant. Its head came up and lunged at the fireman, its mouth opening to show razor-sharp teeth dripping venom. The fireman's cry became a screech as he swung his ax again, hitting the demon's jaw with the blunt end of the tool. A resounding clack impressed the other fireman and inspired him to join his partner, while the third of the rescuing trio helped Grace and Markey out of the parking garage, out of harm's way.

Adam's legs felt rubbery and distant, and became progressively weaker. He watched with blurry fascination as the two firemen repeatedly hacked with their axes at the demon pinned against the wall. He felt a surge of resentment. He was now just a spectator of what he should be a participant of. But his legs became even weaker still, until they eventually buckled out from under him, and his knees hit hard against the concrete of the garage floor. His hands barely caught him before he went face first into the pavement, and that was more a minor twist of luck than anything perpetuated by forethought. When he looked again at the firemen, his vision clouding around the edges, constricting to a very narrow focal point, he thought he saw a hazy nimbus around their heads, where once their helmets had been. And where they should have been hefting axes, he thought he saw burning swords, blazing with a fire of brimstone. A brilliant light flooded his vision and made it too painful for his eyes to bear further witness to. Yet he tried still and found that the vision was too incredible and wondrous to bear for long, and he became overwhelmed with the amazing phenomenon. When he finally succumbed to weakness and closed his eyes, his arms buckling out from under him, he fell into a blissful and deserving peace upon the floor.

CHAPTER FORTY-TWO

Sergeant Markey had a lot of explaining to do and pretty much no idea where to begin. The destruction of the Tower had continued until it suddenly stabilized near the eighth floor, where after that, the firemen were able to fight the raging blaze with dozens of pumper and ladder trucks, and then handheld hoses within the building. Debris from the devastated floors still dislodged from the damaged levels and fell to the streets below, causing a wide area to be cordoned off around the skyscraper. The mighty Tower stood bent and broken and silent like a slain giant otherwise.

Several hours passed before the rescue workers and investigators were finally able to emerge and pass judgment on what had happened. They made a preliminary guess that volatile chemicals stored in the uppermost floors had exploded from a mixture of combustible elements.

Markey thought that was a good enough conclusion and readily concurred. His knees felt weak and his legs were like molds of jelly. He was sick to his stomach and kept retching dry heaves into the gutter where he sat. Dry heaves were all he could produce because the more solid parts of his stomach had already spewed out their contents over the sidewalk close to where he'd exited the Tower.

The paramedics who'd met him and Grace—and the fireman who had assisted them out of the parking garage—had ushered them into a roped-off vicinity where on-site medical personnel were set up to treat the victims of the catastrophe. From there, Markey was given a cursory exam for injuries. Nothing out of the ordinary was found—other than a *rat-tat-tat-tat* of an elevated heartbeat and some shortness of breath attributed to his final sprint from the building—so he was released to go about his business, whatever that might have been. Grace, on the other hand, suffered more severely. She complained of insufferable cramping and made mention of the baby. Blood in worrisome amounts stained the sweat pants she wore, and all further inquiry ceased. Within minutes, an ambulance whisked her away, leaving Markey standing alone and cold and speechless. Too late he felt compelled to go with her, and it wasn't until members of his own department barraged him with questions he didn't feel up to answering that he truly wished he had. He suffered their incessant interrogation for as long as he could, with thoughts of Peter Lumas, Christopher Purcell, Adam Mogilvy, and Grace Fitzpatrick niggling his thoughts before he abruptly broke away and plopped down on the sidewalk, dropping his head in his hands and taking a moment to pray that everything would turn out all right, but knowing it wouldn't—couldn't—before he hurled himself forward and retched into the gutter again.

Only a few minutes passed before his prayer turned to self-effacement for leaving the building while the battle still raged. He should have stayed with Adam and fought alongside him. He shouldn't have worried that Grace couldn't have made it out of the building on her own—she hadn't been alone. The fireman had been there, assisting her as his duty demanded, thereby relieving him—Markey—to do his duty as a policeman.

Although the last time he checked, monsters didn't necessary fall into the stereotypical criminal category he was used to pursuing. It seemed to him there should be an entirely separate profession drummed up to combat them. But that was just a pathetic excuse for why he hadn't gone back in even after he'd seen Grace to safety, proving him powerfully unheroic and cowardly.

For the longest while, he sat in his place beside the gutter, grimacing at the sour stench of his vomit and the stink of his cowardice. Then he heard excitement and looked up. He struggled to his feet as a crew of paramedics carried Adam Mogilvy from the building, four of them arranged at each of his limbs and two between each arm and leg, like pall bearers carrying their burden of a dead friend. Markey tried to crowd between them to see how the kid fared, but the urgency of their hurrying jostled him out of the way, and he only caught a glimpse of what he would much rather not have seen—vivid, glistening red. The one thing that struck him about it was the amount of blood, which seemed to be as much as a gallon of paint thrown on a fur-wearing socialite, striking dead center in the poor kid's chest.

Markey stayed close to the temporary medical shelter after that. He suspected he should keep as close to Adam as possible in order to offer support and get their stories straight. As long as he deluded himself into thinking Adam would be able to give an account of the events that had happened, the kid just might make it through the morning, then maybe the afternoon. All that blood had to have come from somewhere, and even though it could have come from Drudge, it wasn't likely that all of it came from the businessman before he'd turned into . . .

No, he wouldn't think about it. He couldn't think about it. It was insanity. He was sure he'd seen something, but he wasn't sure it was what his memory was telling him it was. In fact, before he believed his own mind, he'd have to confer with Grace and Adam about what they'd seen themselves. And the firemen—couldn't forget them. They'd seen it, too. He'd have to hunt them down and ask them before trusting his own eyes. But later, because he couldn't leave Adam's side for his own sanity, not now, not after the danger was over and the kid needed support, even if Markey was only there in spirit.

Markey hadn't known a time when he'd hated himself any more than he did now. His self-loathing brought him close to tears and he knew there was more than a reason for them. He had no idea if the beast—no! Malachi Drudge, he reminded himself—still lived despite the thrashing Adam had given it, or if Grace was going to be all right—much less her baby—or if Adam had even made it out of the building alive.

All that blood.

As for Christopher Purcell, they brought him out as well, but on a stretcher, strapped tightly to it so he couldn't possibly move, his neck in a brace of hard plastic, anchoring his head in perfect alignment to his body. Markey only made a cursory acknowledgement of the district attorney's discovery and wasn't entirely concerned whether the effort on the paramedics' part was any indication that he was alive or not.

It wasn't just for showing moral support that Markey stayed close to the medical tent. He also used the quickly constructed facility to hide himself from his questioning command staff. Not long after Christopher Purcell had been brought out of the parking garage, a bustle of excitement rankled through the cluster of milling police officers and firefighters. This abrupt ripple caused enough curiosity in him to peer around the corner of the tent and watch as Peter Lumas's body was brought out of the Tower. He moaned to himself, both in grief and resentment. They'd be after him now, he thought miserably, and sure enough, betraying fingers pointed his way.

Wearily, Markey pulled himself together in order to meet them head on and give a sketchy account of what had happened. How he and Lumas had been on the trail of an unlikely killer and kidnapper, and how Grace had been brought to the Spatial Tower as his latest victim; how they'd pursued her and gotten separated, and Detective Lumas had lost his life in a tragic gunfight; how he, Markey, had encountered the district attorney at one point and still didn't understand what the man was doing in the building, but he assumed the poor wretch had been a luckless victim of circumstances and his own political ambition; how Malachi Drudge must have detonated triggers set in the building to avoid capture and how he'd tried to escape with Grace before Markey managed to rescue her; how he wasn't sure what had become of Drudge—perhaps he'd gotten away in the catastrophe, but if they were all lucky, he would have perished. No, he wasn't sure what Adam Mogilvy was doing in the Tower but it wasn't likely he was an accomplice in any crime as far as Markey and—God rest his soul—Lumas figured. Perhaps the young man had simply gone in as a Good Samaritan when he noticed some tragic disaster was afoot.

All this explaining went unquestioned initially. Later, when he was sitting in the office with members of the brass and a stenographer, perhaps with his own attorney, as well, they would pick him apart for exact details. He thought about complaining of an illness or debility, perhaps chest pains, in order to buy him more time, but he didn't think even an eternity reconciling what had happened would provide a response conducive to what his superiors would be willing to accept.

As Adam remained in a state of guarded critical condition, something unique and amazing happened, although it went unwitnessed by any of the hospital staff monitoring machines on the other side of the ICU doors. It began as a radiant light, a light that if anyone had been there to see would have been compelled to stand and watch—that is, if it wasn't so painful to keep watching. Because of the blankets covering him, no one would have seen how it began, but if they had, they would have dropped their jaws in open astonishment and nutty speechlessness. To anyone watching, the luminescence exuded from beneath the blankets themselves and surrounded Adam, forming an unnatural and disturbing cocoon about his entire body, swaddling him with a multitude of eerie tendrils that had the quality of being sentient. That sentience had a purpose, and intertwining their gossamer filaments into an all-enveloping sheath, they went to work.

When Adam awoke, he did so to another light, this one different than the one he hadn't seen earlier, but one that seemed just as radiant and painful to look at. Struggling to make out the source of the light, he thought for sure he must be in Heaven, although he doubted Heaven would make him suffer the aches of his corporeal body, which he brought with him. Slowly, with a dogged interest in identifying the light source, the outline of a window took shape.

He felt himself lying supine and warm, and he felt distinctly uncomfortable in such a defenseless posture. When he struggled to push himself up, he only felt the total exhaustion of his body weigh heavily against his chest. He collapsed, slipping back into sleep.

He awoke to a gentle palpating of his wrist, a flicker of a light in his eyes. He jerked his head away from the intrusive brightness and moaned, bringing his hand up to his forehead and rubbing away a slight headache. That surprised him; he hadn't imagined such a slight pain would make itself known among his other more severe aches, which, upon thinking about them, he wasn't really aware of them as anything more than a ghostly memory now.

"I thought you might be ready to wake up."

He recognized the voice, a gentle but stern one, and turned to look upon the implacable features of Monica Perez.

"What . . .?"

"You've caused quite a scene since the last time I saw you," she said cryptically. "The least you could have done during all this time was told me your name."

He opened his mouth but she waved aside whatever it was he had to say. "I've already found out. A lot of people have."

"What . . . happened?"

"You tell me," she said, though not unkindly. "You seem to have an uncanny way of finding yourself around trouble."

He remembered the last conscious act he'd been a part of and weakly brought his hand up to wipe away a dreary caul of weariness from his mind. "Grace . . .?"

Monica walked around the bed and poured a cup of water, which she handed to him in a gesture of distraction. "Drink something. You've been asleep for a while."

The evasiveness of her gesture was not lost on him. He pushed himself up, dismissing the water. "What happened to her?"

"You know, Adam, I'd hit you if you weren't so badly beat up already." She set the glass on the bedside table, giving up the effort to avoid the issue. "Grace miscarried the baby. I told you she needed to be in a hospital. I don't understand what you and Detective Markey had going on, but you overstepped your bounds putting her at risk."

Adam closed his eyes and stanched the tears he felt rising. He wanted to ask Monica to leave him be but he was afraid his voice would quaver too much. Instead, he tried to keep his breath from hitching on sobs.

Monica demurred her attention when it became apparent that her words had too much of an ill-effect on him. His face had gone a deathly pale, and tears would certainly have been in his eyes if he opened them. Despite what dangers Grace had been subjected to, it was clear that this man had suffered through them also.

"By the way," she said abruptly, remembering something important, "Detective Markey came by to ask about you and your daughter. I remember he came with you the other day when you brought her in. She was very sick, I'm sorry to say, and she had to go into ICU."

Adam's eyes shot open to focus on her. Indeed, they were glistening, but now their main focus seemed to be on the issue Monica brought up

"I went to check on her for him, but she wasn't there."

Adam pressed his eyes closed, his arm coming up to bury his head under it, unable to keep the tears from coming then. The taunting game with his daughter had been the last laugh Drudge had had with him. He didn't think he could bear losing Marie again, not when she was all he had from his past life.

"She'd been transferred to the pediatrics unit on the fourth floor," Monica said. "She pulled through quite nicely. She's going to be just fine."

The words didn't immediately register with Adam, but then they slowly filtered through his misery. He pulled his arm away from his face, blinking back tears, looking at the face of the doctor who'd shown him nothing but conviction and competence before. Now her features were less scornful and more sympathetic.

"I'm sorry if I was a little abrupt a minute ago," she said, moving about the bed with something akin to repentance. "I don't understand what went on, but I suppose it wasn't your intention for Grace to lose the baby."

Adam looked sharply at her. "I did everything I could to see that she didn't lose it."

Monica swallowed thickly, justifiably chastised. "I suppose you did. Maybe it was just that the baby was never meant to live."

He didn't say anything after that, smitten by the fact that God—or fate—must have had a grander plan. No doubt God—or fate—would have sent His avengers much sooner if the baby was to have a place in it at all.

But he still had no right to rationalize away the pain of someone else's loss just because it was a part of a divine design. Grace would have to deal with the miscarriage according to her own convictions. He just hoped she was resilient enough to muddle through the terrible confusion death left one in, and she wouldn't dissolve entirely into despair. Perhaps she hadn't seen the end of what he'd witnessed, which might have made her more receptive to recovering from the ordeal; but each person had to make their own decisions of what to accept for fact. He believed now more than ever that he'd only been an instrument by which Malachi Drudge would be defeated. Whether each act or step had been orchestrated to the letter that it had happened, he didn't know, but he'd been played according to a plan that had been laid out. He only wondered if Grace had been similarly used.

"A word of advice, Adam," Monica said. "You may want to take up hockey again. It's less violent."

About the Author: Alex Bloodworth has a particular interest in politics and what the ramifications of diffidence in voters can entail. While he writes purely for pleasure, his day job is much more fascinating. He currently holds many certificates, clearances, and credentials to take fact and turn it into believable fiction, without compromising the status quo. Among some of his many facets are being a Water Response-Trained Vessel Operator, for response to waterborne terrorist actions or major incident on the open seas; and a certified Police Diver. He has worked a number of aircraft crashes and cruise ship disasters.

Visit Alex Bloodworth at his author's page at the website www.wolf-pirate.com.

ALSO AVAILABLE FROM WOLF PIRATE PUBLISHING

THE SERPENT AND THE SAUL

by Alex Bloodworth

When what appears to be a robbery gone bad suddenly turns out to be something much more complex and appalling, Sergeant Stephen Shendly and his team of homicide detectives are faced with the biggest case the country has yet to see. Their investigation leads them to a suspect more cunning and evil than any they've ever encountered before. And with good reason. Their suspect isn't a man at all, but a devil of sorts—or maybe the one and only himself. Given this overwhelming obstacle, Shendly and his team must not only figure out a way of taking him into custody, but how to prosecute him for the crimes he's committed.

Price
$16.00
ISBN: 978-0-9798372-1-0
LCCN: 2007939337

Pick up this book at all fine bookstores or at our website at www.wolfpiratebooks.com. Or send payment, plus $2.00 shipping, to:
Wolf Pirate Publishing Inc.
4801 SW 164 Terrace
Fort Lauderdale, FL 33331

ALSO AVAILABLE FROM WOLF PIRATE PUBLISHING

LADY OF THE LAKE

by Mary Glynne

When the crew of a commercial fishing trawler discovers a body in a fifty-five-gallon drum in Lake Michigan, FBI Special Agent Daniel Kleison is called in to determine the jurisdiction of the crime. Evidence leads Agent Kleison to suspect an unlikely and disturbing connection to an even bigger conspiracy. He is joined by outside consultant, Elizabeth Brumer, in his efforts to track down the suspects before any more murders can occur. In the meantime, strange phenomena take place that have everyone wondering if the victim might not be the cause of miracles.

Price
$15.00
ISBN: 978-0-9798372-0-3
LCCN: 2007939229

Pick up this book at all fine bookstores or at our website at www.wolfpiratebooks.com. Or send payment, plus $2.00 shipping, to:
Wolf Pirate Publishing Inc.
4801 SW 164 Terrace
Fort Lauderdale, FL 33331

ALSO AVAILABLE FROM WOLF PIRATE PUBLISHING

UNFORGIVEN

by Casey Mason

Fed up with the failure of the criminal justice system, Americans want to put a crimp on the rising rate of recidivism. They demand a solution to the problem of violent criminals on the lam, and have called for the Constitution to be rewritten. The answer is the radical and controversial formation of WANT bureaus in police departments around the country. These highly trained and clandestine officers are federally sanctioned to bring in or put down the most vile, psychotic, and irredeemable criminals ever to avoid imprisonment. But one WANT officer in particular discovers that nothing comes without a price.

Price
$15.00
ISBN: 978-0-979872-2-7
LCCN: 2007939338

Scurvy Dog

Pick up this book at all fine bookstores or at our website at www.wolfpiratebooks.com. Or send payment, plus $2.00 shipping, to:
Wolf Pirate Publishing Inc.
4801 SW 164 Terrace
Fort Lauderdale, FL 33331

ALSO AVAILABLE FROM WOLF PIRATE PUBLISHING

ENTANGLED

by David Wren

Eric Roman is a healthy twenty-one-year-old American boy living the idyllic life. Having learned that a congenital heart defect, which kept him from enjoying the rigors of childhood, was misdiagnosed, he intends to pack as much extreme living he can into life before deciding what to do with his future. His parents aren't happy with this decision and want him to settle down with school and an internship at his father's company. When Eric resists, he finds the repercussions are deadly. As his life spins wildly out of control, he learns things about his parents no child should ever discover. And worse than that, about himself.

Price
$15.00
ISBN: 978-0-979872-4-1
LCCN: 2007941748

Pick up this book at all fine bookstores or at our website at www.wolfpiratebooks.com. Or send payment, plus $2.00 shipping, to:
Wolf Pirate Publishing Inc.
4801 SW 164 Terrace
Fort Lauderdale, FL 33331